SHADOWS
OF KARAKAN

SHADOWS OF KARAKAN

DRAKA BOOK TWO

AvaritiaBona

Podium

Podium

SHADOWS
OF KARAKAN

CHAPTER ONE

Headmates

On the steep side of a mile-high mountain, a thousand feet above the trees below, I sat on the ledge in front of my cave. It was a mountain and a cave I had known for years, and yet not; the mountain I'd known had not been in sight of the sea. Its peak had not been quite so sharp. And the cave had opened onto a small, wooded parking lot, not into open air. In the moment, though, I was glad that it did, because the view was breathtaking.

I was watching the shadows swallow the vast, rolling forest that stretched from the mountains to the distant sea as the sun set on the day that, by my count and by what my human friends had told me, should mark the beginning of my fourth month on the island of Mallin. From here I had watched dozens of sunrises, slowly getting used to my new home—and to the fact that the sun rose and traveled to the south here, rather than the north where it belonged.

I'd been resting and psyching myself up for a few days now. I felt strong, both physically and mentally. I felt ready. That night, I decided, I would return to the pit where I had first woken up as a dragon.

Deep in my gut I carried an unexplained anxiety about going down there, and the dragon I shared my head with wanted nothing to do with it. But the time was right. I could no longer ignore that pit. In every way that mattered, it was the place of my death and my rebirth. And beyond the symbolic value, there was an opening down there, a tunnel which led deeper into the mountain. I had to know what lay beyond that tunnel, or I would never feel that my hoard was truly safe.

I had spent the last few days preparing myself mentally, but more than that I had tried to get the dragon to warm up to the idea. She was still firmly against it. She wouldn't even discuss it, refusing to reply when I tried to speak with her. All I got from her were feelings of anxiety and antipathy, no matter what I tried. But they weren't as strong as they had been. There was none of the paralyzing fear that I had once felt. Destroying one of the valkin's dragon-bone staffs seemed to have instilled in her some courage. So, even if she could, I had a feeling she wouldn't try to stop me if I attempted to descend into the pit. Even if she really didn't like the idea, at the very least, I had to try.

Once the sun had vanished behind the mountains, I made my way down the winding cave to a crack in the wall, one I'd once entered in my own world, and in my human body. The thin layer of glowing slime on the walls cast a weak light, but I didn't need it. My shadowsight enabled me to see darkness as light and vice versa. At the crack I shifted, melting into the darkness. As a malleable shadow I drifted through the narrow opening in the stone, becoming solid again on the other side of the long gap. I found myself standing on the narrow ledge above the pit, which had until recently held my hoard, before I moved it. I looked down and felt anxious to the point of some slight nausea, but I didn't let it overwhelm me. I could fight it. I steeled myself to jump down.

"Please do not make me do this," said the voice of the dragon in my mind, speaking up for the first time in days. *"Please."*

I sympathized with her. A dragon does not beg, but she did now. She wasn't just reluctant, she was afraid. There was real fear and pain connected to this pit, just like there had been in the large chamber we'd found inside this mountain. By doing this I was hurting her, even if I knew that it was for our own good.

"I'm sorry," I whispered into the darkness, "but we have to. We have to face this fear, and find where the passage goes." I had some suspicions about that, but I needed to be sure. I had to secure my home.

I wish I could say that I bravely leaped down, but it took a few false starts before I managed. I could fight the dragon's fear, but I couldn't ignore it. I stood for a while with my wings spread, but in the end it was a little like jumping off a cliff into deep water. The anticipation was far worse than the reality. I leaped and landed on the floor of the pit, and as I looked around, I began to wonder why I'd let it turn into such a big deal.

I'd looked down often enough, so I knew there was no point in looking for any of my things from when I was human. The only thing I'd taken with me to this place were my memories. Instead, the first thing I wanted to do was to get a look at the cut stones placed regularly around the walls of the pit. I got close to one, but other than some vague scratches, I couldn't see anything out of the ordinary with my shadowsight. It was just a carefully shaped block of smooth stone. However, I had planned for that.

I had learned from the books Herald had given me that reading in the dark didn't work. Quite simply, with my shadowsight I only saw the book's pages, and not what was on them. I suspected that it had to do with depth, or physical edges, or something like that, and ink on paper just didn't have enough of whatever I needed. Since the pit was obviously made by people—my bet being on the Old

Mallineans or their near descendants—I had guessed that there might be something to see, and I'd come prepared.

Before I leaped down I had put on my harnessed leather satchel. I couldn't carry anything when I shifted, so I'd gotten it past the gap the hard way—with a long pole. From it, I took out my light-ball, a smooth sphere of stone that fit comfortably in the palm of my hand. I hadn't charged it for a while, and it shone weakly until I pushed some magic into it, causing it to flare up with a bright yellow light. I was so glad I'd figured out that I could change the color of the light; the pale blue that the valkin had used annoyed me.

As the light brightened, I held the ball closer to one of the stones. At first I wondered if the surface of the stone had cracked into a fine network of lines, but as I looked closer, I saw that there was a pattern to it, regularities and angles that couldn't be from anything natural. Soon I realized what it reminded me of: Boot's heating disc! The lines were not at all the same, but I thought I saw some similarities. That, I assumed, meant that there was some kind of enchantment in play, but I couldn't see any obvious way to activate the thing. With Boot's disc you twisted an outer ring so that the pattern lined up with the inner one, but I didn't see any moving parts on the stones.

I knew another way to activate enchanted objects, though. It probably wasn't a good idea since I had no idea what might happen if it worked, but I could always just try to push a little magic into the stone and see what happened. It might not do anything. It might do something awesome. Just a trickle of magic couldn't hurt.

It turned out to do something awful. I gave the rock just a hint of magic, and a wave of nausea slammed into me. Fortunately, the shock made me lose my focus, and the effect immediately stopped, though my stomach took a moment to recover. So, I knew what that did. Or at least what it did when I tried to activate it.

I wished I could bring Herald to have a look at it, but that would have to wait until she had the time, and I worked up the nerve to bring anyone—even her—so close to my hoard.

Having messed with—and recovered from messing with—the stones, I turned to the opening of the passage. It was lined with a masoned arch. At first I wondered if it was just decorative, since there was no way it helped to hold anything up, but when I looked closer at it in the glow of my light-ball, I could see that each stone brick was covered with the same spidery lines as the stones circling the pit. I assumed that they did something, and I was not going to mess with them. Not right now, at least. I'd have to figure them out some day, but at the moment, I'd had more than enough. Besides, the passage waited.

The passage leading from the pit was not quite like the tunnels I'd gotten used to, which waited behind hidden magical gates in the mountainside. The surface of this tunnel had the same finish as those others, but this one was cut on a larger scale, both wider and higher. It descended in a long, wide curve, but instead of a smooth descent, it had steps of flat sections that were several feet long and connected by gentle inclines.

The dragon begged me to stop, but I pressed on. The fear in her voice, and which I felt from her, grew with every step. As I walked farther, she went from begging to incoherent whining. It was emotional torture, and I couldn't imagine what it was like for her. My steps faltered. I felt like a monster for continuing as far as I had.

I stopped, turning my head to look the way I'd come, and despite all of my earlier determination, I considered going back.

The dragon became silent, but the fear grew stronger.

"*No,*" she said. "*Not up. I cannot go up there.*" Suddenly, going on felt infinitely easier than going back, and I found my feet moving again, determined to put more distance between myself and the pit.

The tunnel went on forever, until it ended.

I came to a room. It was big, but not huge. Maybe fifty feet on a side with a ceiling thirty feet high. In the middle of the floor was a square hole, several feet on a side and surrounded by the withered remains of some kind of mechanism. Considering the hole, I guessed that it had been a lift of some kind.

I walked up to the hole and looked down. I wasn't entirely surprised by what I saw. I'd had a feeling.

There was a shaft with nothing on the sides that would help me climb down. The shaft wasn't that deep before it opened up, though. I could possibly have flown if I was careful, but there was no need to risk it. I was sure of what I was looking at. I remembered what I'd seen before I fled from the tunnels here, in my mountain.

The main chamber that I'd found weeks earlier, when I'd entered a tunnel at the base of this mountain, had a large, square hole in the ceiling. The dragon feared that chamber, just as she feared the pit above me. And here I was, looking down through a big square hole onto a smooth floor, far below. This was all connected, clear as day—clear as night, in my case. And there was history here, terrible enough to make a dragon beg.

But the place was dead. No one had been there for years and years. There was, as far as I could tell, nothing to fear, not anymore, and it raised a lot of questions. What was this place? What had happened here, and how long ago? How long had the dragon waited in that pit?

How could I use this?

I could worry about that later. First, I needed to get out. *Dragon?* I thought, feeling a little silly. I really needed something to call her.

She didn't answer.

We need to leave. I need you to tell me which way is easiest for you.

More silence. I had shamed her into answering once, but after what I had just done to her I couldn't bring myself to treat her harshly. She was *my* dragon, a part of me. In a way it felt like I'd hurt a twin sister.

The danger is gone. You can see that, right? Whatever happened to you here, it was long ago. There's no one here now. No one is going to hurt you.

"*You did.*" It was almost a whisper. I could feel her shame at admitting that. I knew how hard it must have been, and I forced myself to ignore the guilt I felt, so that it wouldn't color my thoughts.

I did, I admitted. *And I wish that it hadn't been necessary. But now that I know what's at the end of the passage, we need to get out. I need to know what will be easiest for you. Back up? Or down into the chamber?*

She was silent for a long time, before she said "*Down.*"

Back up would have been easier for me. I might have been able to press on upward despite her, but I owed her for what I'd just put her through. Unfortunately, I only knew one sure way out from the chamber, and it was a risk. I knew that there were other exits as well, of course. I'd found my way out through one of them before. But I'd rather risk going out the front door, so to speak, than days of boredom and hunger.

One day you'll have to face your fear. You know that, I told her as I prepared to drop through the shaft.

She didn't even deny that she was afraid. I considered that progress and hoped that I was right. "*One day*," she said. "*Not tonight.*"

I dropped.

The ceiling of the large chamber, which I'd started thinking of as the throne room, due to its general vibe and the faint scents of gold and silver in the air, was high enough that I had time to spread my wings and land softly. Looking up, I felt sure that no one was getting into my cave from here without wings, which was a big relief. I was also pretty sure that I could gather enough speed to get myself back up through the shaft with my wings folded, so I didn't need to risk banging my wings on the walls. That would have to wait, though. My dragon was in no state to go back up there, not after what I had just put her through. But something about the experience had her talking, and I was not going to waste the opportunity.

What happened here? I asked her as I walked toward the exit. *Will you ever tell me what you remember?*

"*You should know*," she said. "*But it is not clear. Fear and pain. That is most of it. That and being unable to flee.*"

And the big one? I asked, referring to the dragon whose bones had, according to my mental companion, been used for the staffs that the valkin leaders had carried. *He was here?*

"*Yes.*"

Who was he?

"I do not remember clearly. But . . . our father, I think. Why do you not know these things?"

I considered that statement for a moment. *What am I to you?* I finally asked.

"A voice in my head."

I am a voice in your head, I repeated. *And you are in control?*

"Obviously," she said.

Then what just happened up there? In the pit, and the tunnel?

"I . . ." she hesitated. *"I did not want to go. But you were right. It was necessary to secure the lair, so I fought my fear, and triumphed."*

And when you begged me to stop, and we went on anyway? I asked, trying to load that thought with as much kindness and sympathy as I possibly could.

"That . . ." She faltered.

You believe that you're in control?

"It is my body."

I think that it's mine, I told her honestly. *Or at least, that I'm in control of it. To me,* you *are a voice in* my *head.*

"That is ridiculous. We are constantly doing things you do not want."

Like what? I asked, loading the thought with a challenge.

"You think I do not feel your disgust at matured meat? Your pity and horror when I tear our enemies apart? Your constant pining for companionship? Your horrid desire to . . . to share the hoard with those humans? If you had your way we would be destitute, starved, and slain!"

What are you talking about? I asked, genuinely confused. *I feel none of those things.* At least I didn't think I did.

"Of course you do not. Because I will not have it. Some of the things that come from you are bizarre, like your lust for some of the humans, but they are of no consequence. And the intolerable feelings, those I discard. We do not need them."

I stopped.

"You are thinking," she said. There was spite in her words, and triumph. *"You are wondering if I am lying to you. As though I would lie to a voice in my head."*

Was she?

"Here," she purred. *"I will show you."*

I wondered what she meant, and—

I was in the cold and dark, crawling along on all fours, on hands and feet tipped with vicious claws. It was pitch black, yet I could see. But my field of vision was too big, the area with real depth perception too narrow, and I knew why. My face was too long. My eyes sat in the wrong places, too far on each side of my head instead of the front. I felt my teeth with my tongue, and they were all sharp fangs, curving inward to make it impossible for prey to get free. My skin, all over my body, felt strangely dry, and my scales rattled across each other as I moved.

I turned my long neck back to look as I lashed my *tail* in agitation and flexed my *wings*, and this was all wrong! God, I just wanted my body back. I wanted to run and swim and screw and *climb*! And I wanted to listen to old music and sing with my dad, and talk about pointless shit with my brothers and watch movies with Andrea. It had been months, and I missed them all so much, and I'd never see them again, would I?

I had killed people. I'd ripped a man's throat out with my teeth, and I could remember the taste of his blood, sweet and coppery and so, so delicious. I tore another man's head from his body and threw it at his friend.

I fought the urge to vomit, and then it was over. Everything felt normal again. "*See?*" my dragon said. There was no malice now, no spite. "*Useless. It took some time to learn what to discard, but we are better off without such feelings. Do you not agree?*"

Yes, I agreed, slightly stunned at the confusion and building horror I had just felt, and then their sudden absence. I had to start walking again just to convince myself that I could.

"*Just as we are better off with you pushing me to do things I need, but do not want. Like controlling my hunger and rage, and facing my fear.*" She paused. "*And letting the Herald acquire soft or interesting things for us. We work well together, do we not?*"

Yeah, I thought. *Sure.*

This was becoming more and more uncomfortable, but I couldn't stop. Like scratching a bad itch, I kept going past the point that I was hurting myself.

If I am a voice in your head, where did I come from? I asked. *How do you explain all this?*

It took her some time to answer. "*You are just there,*" she said. "*My first clear memory, more than just a mess of images and feelings, is in that pit. Us clawing our way up, and out into the light. You were a confused, broken thing, but I could see your value. My mind was still hazy, so I let you guide me. The gold helped to make things clearer.*"

She paused as we shared a moment of contentment, thinking about the first small handful of dragons we had claimed from a dead man. "*I know where you think that you came from,*" she continued. "*Perhaps you are right. But what harm does it do to me if I have a human ghost riding along in my head?*" Some affection entered the voice. "*I like you. Perhaps that is unnatural, something you have given me, but I am glad for it. You are useful, and amusing. And you are good with the humans. That will serve us well.*"

I wasn't sure what to think at that point. My dragon was utterly convinced that she was in control. Anything I made her do against her will was just her acting on my suggestions. The whining, the begging, the abject terror as I dragged her down that tunnel . . . I could only assume that she chose not to acknowledge that it had even happened. She was back to the proud and arrogant creature I'd gotten used to.

I was in control of this body. I went where and when I wanted. But inside, she clearly had more influence than I had thought. I couldn't tell where the line was drawn between us, and I had no idea how thin that line was. But I knew that I didn't just feel her emotions; she chose which of my own I was allowed to feel. That should have terrified me. It didn't.

I could only assume that such fear was another useless emotion to be discarded.

CHAPTER TWO

The Problem With Scholars

I would be exiting through the gate at the base of the mountain. I hadn't wanted to go out that way for one simple reason: A pair of archaeologists and their guards had set up camp there. They were the ones who had dug out the gate in the first place, freeing it from the several feet of soil that had hidden it for God knew how long. On the bright side, deciding what to do about them was on my list of things to deal with, so being forced to make progress on that might not be a bad thing.

They weren't always there. The last time I checked, they'd been gone, but that had been a few days ago. Nor was their camp right outside the gate, so unless they had someone watching it, they were unlikely to notice me. Whether there was anyone outside the gate when I reached it, I was going out. That was happening. Even the thought of going back into the mountain was met with unhappy resistance by the dragon, and after what she'd just done—letting my emotions run wild—I didn't want to push her too much.

That whole revelation was confusing more than anything else, though. Sure, maybe she was filtering any outrage or horror I should be feeling, but how would I know? Clearly she could get rid of emotions before I even became aware of them. But, she was also being pretty restrictive with what she stopped. Anything that didn't hinder our survival or enrichment seemed to be fine. I had no reason to suspect that she'd messed with things like affection, embarrassment, guilt, fear, joy, or a host of other emotions. Considering she could pretty much cripple me with emotional overload anytime she wanted, why hadn't she just stopped me when I pushed on, despite her fear?

The only satisfying explanation I could think of was that she truly didn't see our relationship as adversarial. She hadn't stopped suppressing my feelings to show what she could do *to* me, but to show what she was already doing *for* me, all the time. And if she saw me as part of herself, why would she try to hurt me?

Again, I wondered where the line between dragon and Draka was. Part of me wondered if there even was one, because that was another possible reason. If she felt everything I did, perhaps she was only suppressing what she disliked, emotions that came from me that she didn't want to deal with. I had no problem with the idea that she could simply ignore whatever fear or embarrassment bled through from me. Perhaps embarrassment and guilt were simply emotions that she didn't feel, or even understand. It would fit pretty well with what I knew of her.

That had nothing to do with the problem in front of me, though. I didn't *expect* anyone outside the gate. There hadn't been anyone there when last I checked, though there were signs of them coming and going. They hadn't dismantled the campsite, and I'd seen a bunch of stakes in the ground around the gate last time I was there, like markers. There should be an hour or two left until dawn, at least, so even if they were there, they should be asleep. But I still didn't want to risk being seen. If they saw the gate itself open, that was one thing. So be it. Let them try to explain it best they could. If they saw me, I'd have to do something about it, and I didn't have many options.

Are you sure that you won't at least try to go back? I asked my dragon. *This seems like an unnecessary risk.*

At first all I got was an annoyed grumble, but then she said, "*I cannot be bothered to turn back when we have gone this far. If there is anyone out there, we will deal with them. Either you take the lead and we do it your way, or I can happily do it my way. I leave the choice to you.*"

Right. She wasn't scared; she just couldn't be bothered. And she probably believed that.

At least I tried.

As I got closer to the end of the tunnel, I began to move more and more carefully, listening for any sound, but all I heard were my own steps. The scholars didn't seem to have gotten the gate open, but they might have figured out the trick and would be returning. I wasn't going to chance it. When I reached the gate, it was still closed, though, with no sign on the tunnel floor that anyone had entered but me. So far, so good. Now, to try something new.

I shifted, becoming one with the darkness, and continued forward until I was touching the gate as much as I could in that form. Then I tried to channel my magic into it, willing it to open. It was a strange feeling. Usually I would just put a hand on the stone and make a connection that way, but as a shadow it felt slippery, for lack of a better word. Like my magic slipped and skidded off the stone, until I found just the right angle where I could push, and the "force" went straight into the target. It was exhausting in a way that I had never experienced before, but after several tries, I felt the familiar pulse of magic from within me moving to the stone, and the gate slowly opened with a hiss of loose, disturbed soil.

With every inch that the doors moved, I expected torchlight to fall through the crack, and I was prepared to push the shadows before me so I could slip out, but I never needed to. There was no one outside. The dig site was empty. I still remained in shadow form as I moved out and looked around, but there was no one around. I was a little disappointed, but consoled myself with a reminder that the point of caution was so that you don't get screwed the one time out of a thousand that it's warranted. With a mental shrug I shifted back and turned to close the gate. All that caution for nothing.

As I prepared to close the gate, I heard excited voices coming from up top, just outside the large hole that had been dug against the mountainside. I shifted again, and not a moment too soon, as the voices were quickly followed by lights. Two blurry blobs marked the two people who approached. "See?" said a female voice, quick and full of enthusiasm. "I told you I heard something, and look! It's open! It opens, just like I said!"

I quickly moved along the stone and up the slope of the dig, keeping away from the light. I would prefer not to draw any attention, and a shadow moving where there should be none would probably stand out.

"Right up to the markers too," she continued. "I knew it! What else could have disturbed the dirt that way?"

"Well, I . . . yes," a male voice said as they moved down the slope well away from me, sounding very put-upon. "It's not like I can deny it. Well spotted. You were right, I was wrong."

"Ah!" the female voice groaned. "That's not important! Well, it is," she said, giggling with excitement, "but it's not the *point*. The point is those old texts you found were right! There's a passage into the mountain here, look! And it's ours to explore. Ours!"

I got out of the hole and shifted back, crouching flat with just my head peeking over the edge so I could see them. As I'd thought, two people—a round, lively young woman and a lanky older-looking man—were approaching the open gate. The woman was dressed in fine but practical clothes, while the man was wearing what I could only describe as a night shirt, who had clearly been dragged out of his bedroll moments ago.

She thrust her lantern into the opening, lighting up the featureless tunnel. For reasons beyond me, that excited her even more.

"Who knows what could be inside?" she said with wonder, as her bemused companion looked on. "Do you think this is it? The Dark One's lair?"

"Tavia, again, the Dark One is not a confirmed historical—" the man began, but he was cut off by a third voice.

"Sir? Madam?" a man called, and I retreated toward the trees as I saw him approach. He was a rough-looking guy, lean and muscular with long, messy hair, and he was carrying a sheathed sword in one hand. "Please!" he said. "I have asked you before, let me or one of my men know if you want to leave the camp!" His tone made it clear that, yes, he had asked them before, and he was fed up with it.

"But, Mister Barro, the gate—" the woman began. The rough man, Barro, cut her off.

"Madam, I understand that something exciting happened," he said, "but there are wolves and bears in these woods, and worse. That wyvern has been spotted in this area. For all you know it's waiting around our camp, just hoping for one of us, a distracted young lady perhaps, to wander off on their own. Vulnerable. Exposed. Please," he said emphatically. "I do not want you to go missing only for someone to find your stripped, bloody bones."

Even though I couldn't see her, I could almost hear her rolling her eyes. "Fine," she said. "I apologize for frightening you. Now would you please rouse the others? We're getting an early start today."

The whole situation was annoying. Half an hour ago, I'd thought that I wouldn't mind much, but now that I was faced with the reality of people, *strangers*, going into *my mountain*, I didn't like it at all. I didn't want people inside the mountain, at least not people I didn't know, and I needed to figure out what to do about it. The fact that it was my own fault didn't help. I could have tried to find another way out, but I'd been too impatient.

I considered just killing them. It wouldn't be a problem. I'd just pick the guards off one by one, and then the two scholars would be easy. I could even wait until they went inside, then follow them and shut the gate behind us. No one would ever find them.

I stopped that train of thought as soon as I became aware of what I was thinking. *Dragon*, I said to my constant companion, *are you preventing me from feeling anything for these people?*

"*They are obstacles, are they not?*" came the reply after a few seconds, along with a sensation of not understanding my concern. "*We should consider our options. You know what my solution is.*"

They are, and I do, I replied. *But would you please not block my pity and empathy for innocent people? They haven't done us any harm. When I . . . advise you, I would like to feel all the consequences of . . . solutions like that. Please.*

I felt something akin to a mental shrug. "*I suppose. But if it makes you unreliable, I will remove it again.*"

It wasn't sudden this time, perhaps because the dragon wasn't trying to make a point. The idea of eliminating this little expedition, piece by piece, gradually became unacceptable. I didn't hate myself for thinking of it—maybe the dragon was blocking that—but it became obvious that I couldn't kill them just because they did something I didn't like. They hadn't hurt me. They didn't even know that I existed! And really, what was the worst-case scenario? They got in there and started exploring the place? So what? Unless they built a huge scaffold and tried to climb up the hole in the ceiling, they'd never threaten me. Hell, I wouldn't even *hear* them . . .

But they would be there. And I would know. And there would always be the risk of them actually building that scaffold, or someone with abilities I'd never even considered might have another way of getting up. Maybe I shouldn't take their quiet disappearance off the table just yet. It would be so easy.

I really needed to talk to someone about this.

I spent most of the next few days hanging out by the dig site. Switching back to being awake during the day was always annoying, but with my exceptional ability to nap, it wasn't as bad as it might have been.

The two scholars, the woman named Tavia and the older man, whose name was Ramban, spent the better part of two days preparing to enter. Most of those days were spent arguing over a collection of books, scrolls, and loose leaves of paper, trying to figure out exactly what they should expect. I couldn't understand what the point was, because in the end they did what they should have done from the start: They packed some basic gear, took the man called Barro, and entered the tunnel. Unfortunately, they had a guard by the door, and he took his job seriously. Otherwise I would have followed them in.

They returned maybe three hours later, talking excitedly. From what they were saying, they had only reached the initial chamber, the "hub," as they called it. Listening to them, I might have thought it was the most amazing find in the history of archaeology.

To be fair, maybe here, and to them, it was.

CHAPTER THREE

What Do You Want?

Though I was both curious and a bit worried about what the scholars might do now that I'd opened the gate for them, I still had to leave for a while every day. I had to eat, drink, and take care of the natural consequences of both of those. I also wanted to check on the lake once a day, in case my friends came looking for me. On the second day I found a message. I was a little disappointed that there was no one waiting, but it was nice to hear from them at least.

When I first looked at the paper, I was confused. I couldn't understand a single word. I began reading the first line over and over, sounding it out, until I realized that the language was not Karakani, but Tekereteki, spelled out phonetically in the script I'd learned. It made reading slow, but it left me no doubt about who'd sent the message.

My dear friend,

I hope that you are well. I am sorry that I have not been to see you, but there is much to take care of, and we have not been able to spare a day. Soon, I promise. My brother and his love are traveling to Tavvanar, to meet a possible buyer for the item. They left yesterday, and will be away for some time.

That sounded promising. I wondered how much we'd get for the book we'd found in the north. From what the others had said, it was an amazing find, worth enough that they may be set for life, or at least rich enough to make adventuring something they did for its own sake, and not a necessity to meet basic needs.

My sister and I have spent some time dealing with the temple, and are now looking for investment opportunities in the city. We hope to purchase a profitable business or something in that vein, though opportunities are limited as not everyone is willing to sell to us due to our background. Their loss. If the item brings in enough money, we should be able to afford enough property to establish us as a real family. It is a strange thing to think about, but exciting.

Again, I promise that I will see you as soon as I can. Another two days, at most. I cannot stand to be apart for so long, and I have not forgotten my promise to go hunting with you. I look forward to it.

Yours forever,

Herald

She'd signed it with the feminine form of the Tekereteki word for "herald." Clever. That "Yours forever" worried me a little, but I had no idea how people usually ended letters here, and it wasn't any worse than "I am, of course, eternally your humble servant" and whatever else people used to sign off with.

I also couldn't deny that on a purely selfish level I liked it. Herald was my best friend. She was mine, and every confirmation that she felt the same way made me feel all warm and fuzzy inside.

With her brother Tamor and his lover Valmik away, that left Herald and her older sister Makanna for me to talk to, and I couldn't blame them for not coming around if they were busy. I had no doubt that when they were done for the day, they wanted to relax and spend some of their hard-earned silver, and the twenty or so miles from the city to the lake wasn't exactly a distance you'd travel casually. Unless you had wings, of course.

But getting this letter drove home something I'd been thinking about: I had no way of getting in touch with them. Right then I really wanted to talk to someone about these scholars and how to handle them. The fact that I couldn't contact anyone, and that every meeting happened on a minimum of a one-day delay, was beginning to bother me. I mentally added an item to my to-do list: Figure out a way to contact people when I wanted to. I didn't know where to start, but it was something I needed.

It struck me that I had lumped Mak in as someone I might be able to talk to, like Herald. As I thought more about it, I realized that, yes, I probably could. We'd talked more on our adventure in the north than ever before, and on the way back home, it had changed from her scolding me for my recklessness to friendly, if short, conversations. I still didn't feel like she trusted me fully, though. There was always something between us, and it was safe to assume that the something was a certain young, six-foot-something woman. On something like this, though, how to handle the scholars camped on my doorstep, I thought that she might give me good advice.

In total, I spent four days and nights watching the scholars waste time. It got to the point where I fantasized about the monster bear I'd once fought wandering up from the south and solving my problem for me, but I hadn't seen the beast since my trip with Lalia. For something so large, it sure was good at hiding, and I wondered if it had left for good. Maybe it had gone into the mountains to terrorize the local goat population?

Or perhaps someone had already killed it. One thing that I learned during those four days was that the situation around my mountain had changed in the last month or so. I had heard the guard, Barro, tell the scholars that a "wyvern," i.e., me, had been spotted in the area, and clearly he was not the only one who knew. Three separate groups of would-be monster hunters approached the camp during those days, being sent off politely each time with the news that no, no one had seen the creature as long as they'd been camping there. Neither did any of them show a hint of seeing me as I watched them from the trees, so I wasn't too worried.

I had a moment of recognition when one of the groups turned out to be Big Beardy, Short-and-Wide, Awesome Curls, and Baran, a group of adventurers I'd seen a few times but never contacted. I followed them for a while after they were sent off. Curls and Baran had been fighting the last time I saw them, but now seemed to have made up and were being cloyingly sweet with each other, to the constant discomfort and eye-rolling of their two companions. It was all very cute, and I hoped that I wouldn't have to kill them at some point.

After the first group, the scholars had the guards rig up a large sheet over the open gate. They were guarding their discovery jealously, and I approved. Both because the fewer people who knew about it, the better, and because it meant that they were unlikely to tell anyone else.

On the morning of the fifth day after I opened the gate, things were different at the camp. The packs that the scholars and their usual companion had prepared were bigger, and Tavia, whose excitement had been falling the last few days, was back to her same exuberant self, the one I'd first seen when she found the gate open.

They were going in, and they were staying. At least one night, maybe more. And I badly wanted to follow them. I checked in with my dragon headmate, and she agreed. As uncomfortable as she was with going back inside, she wanted to know what the humans were up to. And what they might find.

Unfortunately, the two remaining guards seemed to take their duty seriously. One of them was always present at the gate, changing every few hours, and the whole day, I never had a chance to slip in. Of course, once the light began to fail, it was they who didn't stand a chance of keeping me out.

The sun set behind the mountains, and as night set in fully, I shifted into the shadows. I slid down the side of the dig, and the guard didn't even glance my way. He didn't have any light—a good idea, I'd learned—since it would make him stand out but wouldn't help him see anything more than a few feet off, anyway. The guy was taking his job seriously, but against me, a being who was functionally invisible, it didn't matter how good or dedicated he was.

Silently, I slid in past him. I went three hundred feet or so up the tunnel before I shifted back, just to be sure, and then I set off at a trot, only slowing down and focusing on stealth once I felt that I should be getting close to the first, central chamber. I expected the scholars to be asleep, but who could know with those two? Or with Tavia, at least. She definitely seemed like the kind of person to pull an all-nighter if she got into something. But, even if they were settled in for the night, they'd probably have one person sitting guard, and I didn't want to spook them just yet.

They had set up near the entrance of the "hub," as they called it. They had a fire burning. It must have been for light and peace of mind rather than heat, since the inside of the mountain was perfectly comfortable no matter how warm or cold it was outside. Not that I was a good judge of that; I walked around naked, which didn't mean much anymore, and neither temperature nor weather made me particularly uncomfortable. I'd have to see when winter came, or if there was a real scorcher one day. I imagined that my black scales might make that uncomfortable.

Either way, they did have a fire. It didn't seem like a great idea to me, since they couldn't know for sure if there was any way for smoke to get out or fresh air to get in, but I couldn't blame them. The hub was big, empty, and silent, and even with the fire, the far walls were lost in the dark.

The older scholar, Ramban, was sitting guard when I found them. Because of how close the fire was to the entrance I couldn't get past them without pushing shadows ahead of me, and I decided not to risk it. I could have gotten away with it, though. Ramban was very much a scholar and not a guard. He spent his shift reading in the firelight, instead of being alert to possible dangers. And even if they thought that the place was safe and empty, I knew that there was a cave full of gremlins connected to it. A good way off, but still. If any of them got in here, Ramban would likely be dead before he even knew he was in danger. That would be a good start to solving my most immediate issue, but the idea was to *avoid* that "solution".

After a few hours of nothing, Ramban woke Barro, who took over the watch. A few hours later, Barro did the same with Tavia, and when her watch was over, she woke both of the others. As they ate a simple breakfast, the two scholars talked about which tunnel they'd explore. They were clearly in new territory here—*my* territory, a central part of me insisted—and none of their texts were any real help when it came to what they might find and where. All they had, as far as I could tell, were second- or third-hand accounts of people who had been here, either when the "Dark One" still lived, or afterward, when humans had taken over his lair. Ramban repeated the same objection as the first time I'd heard them talk about the subject, and many times thereafter: They didn't know whether the Dark One was real.

To be fair to Ramban, his insistence that the Dark One had never been proven to be a historical figure was apparently pretty well supported by a lot of texts. He could quote plenty of authors who doubted whether it was an actual person, or creature, or a myth.

But, to be fair to Tavia, it was impossible not to connect this Dark One to my dragon's "big one". Her, or our, father. Maybe.

Considering that the authors the scholars were quoting had lived hundreds of years ago, and that was apparently after the Dark One's time, I wondered again just what had happened to my dragon, and how long she'd been—what, exactly? Sleeping? Frozen in time? All she remembered was being trapped in what I called the "throne room" and unable to escape. Maybe chained up or caged by whatever group had killed her father. And then, nothing. Hundreds of years of nothing, until I lost my grip on a slick rock wall and came crashing into her head.

I wonder what these two would give to talk to my dragon.

There was an idea. I'd been hiding myself—mostly—because the humans might try to hunt me down if they found out about me. Like, as a matter of public policy. But two scholars, who were obviously excited about this place . . .

Of course, they'd never mentioned the word *dragon*. I didn't know if they had any idea what the Dark One was supposed to be, assuming that my hunch was correct. Maybe they thought it was some warlord, or another powerful monster. The tunnels certainly didn't look big enough for a giant, terrifying reptile. Unless that reptile could do what I could, of course, becoming shapeless, which would make sense if they called it the "Dark One."

But Herald had never heard of a black dragon, so maybe I was wrong, or maybe whoever had killed it had kept the details secret. Maybe, maybe, maybe. More reasons to talk to the scholars!

I needed a list. Two columns: Kill and Talk. Live or Die, and reasons for either. That would make everything clearer, right? Live: They may know useful things, and maybe I could get some silver out of them. Die: They had found a place that had a direct connection to my hoard.

My dragon's opinion on the matter was clear, but she was willing to defer to me when it came to dealing with humans. Lucky them.

Something else struck me. Something that I had known for a while, sure, but whose implications I hadn't understood. My dragon had been here. As far as I could tell, she had grown up here. And her last memories of this place were of fear and pain. She had suffered for an unknown time, and then she had awoken with me in her head. I'd thought that must have been strange for her, but I'd never really thought *about* it, so to speak.

And there was something else. From what my dragon had told me, it sounded like she was barely self-aware when all of that happened. She'd slunk around, hiding from her father when he was there and stealing food from him when he wasn't. But that wasn't right, was it? Herald had told me, way back when we barely knew each other, that I was too small. That I should still be in a nest, being fed by my mother. The throne room could be a nest, couldn't it? And our father kept bringing food, which he left conveniently lying around for us to "steal."

We were pretty much an infant, weren't we? A toddler, at best. No wonder we were growing so fast. And maybe it was objectively true that whatever happened to her was hundreds of years ago, but from her perspective it had been months.

That . . . no wonder she was such an emotional mess. Her old life ended horribly, and then she had to deal with me, both muscling in and sharing space in her head *and* possibly, I suspected, forcing her suddenly into full sapience.

"I do not need your pity," she grumbled.

. . . and *of course* she'd heard that.

So what do you think about it? I asked, since I had her attention.

"I have told you before. I do not remember those times well. I was too young. If you are right, perhaps I still am. Perhaps your presence made me more." There came a mental scoff. *"Or more likely, the time between has rotted my mind. It matters little."*

Still, I'm sorry for being dismissive before. I put all my sincerity into the statement. *I thought that whatever happened was long ago, but to you it wasn't, was it?*

After a pause, the dragon replied, *"No. It was not."*

But whoever killed the big one, your father, they are long gone. They can't hurt us.

"Perhaps you are right. But know that I feel your intent, and that my . . . aversions will not be dismissed so easily."

I know. Take your time. I waited, but didn't get a response. *You're talking more now,* I tried.

"You are becoming more worth talking to," she answered, *"now that you are more focused on worthwhile things."*

Like what?

"Properly securing the hoard. Establishing our dominance over our territory. Finding hidden ways to relay commands to our servants. All fine goals," she said, her approval clear in her voice.

Friends, I corrected. *And associates, I suppose. Not servants.*

"*If they serve our purposes and further our goals, the distinction is meaningless. We can coddle them, if you wish.*"

I shouldn't be surprised, I suppose, I thought with some annoyance. *Of course you'd think that.*

"*We can only have servants and enemies. You know this as well as I do. Or maybe you learned nothing from the sell-swords?*"

My thoughts immediately went back to the fear and awe that I'd seen on the faces of the mercenaries I'd briefly worked with. People who'd been becoming downright friendly, until the moment I tore a man's head off.

"*You think we can trust them?*" she continued. "*An ally who fears us is only an enemy who has not realized their position yet. They must adore us, or be so terrified that they would never act against us, or die. Nothing else will do. Nothing else will keep us and what is ours safe. The same is true of your current dilemma.*"

The scholars.

"*They know too much. Subjugate them, or kill them. Only stop dithering.*"

And just like that, I knew what to do.

CHAPTER FOUR

Bump in the Night

I would have liked to close the gate behind us. Doing so would have made it all but impossible for the humans to escape, but it would also alert the guard outside who might send for help. Whether they could go out that way was unlikely to make a difference. They couldn't escape me, not in the darkness.

Hopefully it wouldn't come to that.

After they had finished their breakfast and their preparations, both scholars and their guard took their packs and headed out. They left much of their gear in the camp, bringing mostly writing materials, light sources, fuel, food, and things like that. Instead of letting the fire burn itself out they smothered it using some kind of blanket. That was clever, and very convenient for me. The less light, the better.

I followed them into the darkness.

They had come well prepared. Perhaps they were experienced, well read, or simply clever, but every so often they would drop a small stone that glinted in the light of their lanterns. Quartz, perhaps. If they returned, the stones would be easy to see in the darkness, leading them back to the camp. Of course, if they ran for it, the stones would help them as well, so I considered collecting the pebbles as I followed them. I'd left my bag at home since I wanted to be able to shift, and anything I wore or carried just fell off when I did, but I could have put them in my mouth or something. I wasn't squeamish. But, even though I wanted to stack the deck as much as possible, I wanted to get lost down here again even less. Besides, I preferred the outcome where the humans agreed to leave and never return. Them getting lost down here and dying of thirst would rather defeat the point of letting them live in the first place.

But if they weren't reasonable . . .

If this doesn't work, I thought, not bothering to catch my dragon's attention first. She knew when I was talking to her. *If I can't let them leave, can you make it easy for me?*

"*We will not hesitate. I will make certain of that,*" she reassured me.

That was a relief. I honestly wasn't sure that I could do it. These people had done nothing to me, and planning to kill someone who was innocent, even when I knew I wouldn't feel any regret afterward, was difficult.

I felt a brief flash of disgust at my own selfishness, and then it was gone.

I had expected the humans to go straight for the largest tunnel, the one that led to the throne room, but instead they chose the one closest to their camp. Much like the tunnel I had fled through the first time I was here, this one turned, split, and merged often, and the pebbles proved their worth. I had no more idea where I was than the scholars—perhaps less, since they rarely hesitated to choose a direction. But with the pebbles on the floor, they would always know which way to turn on the way back, as long as they had light.

I wondered how the ones who had made these tunnels had found their way around. I hadn't seen any markings anywhere indicating any kind of direction. I was fairly sure that there should be little groups of rooms here and there, because there had been in the other tunnels I'd explored, but I had no clue how to find them. Maybe that was the point? If the tunnels were confusing enough, and the people who lived there just knew how to find their way around, attacking them would be hell. That would kind of make sense. Considering how easy it had been for the gremlins to surround and ambush Herald and the others in the mine, this place would be a slaughterhouse.

We hadn't been going for long, only half an hour perhaps, when the tunnel ahead of me filled with excited chatter. As I got closer I understood why: They had found a room. And when they moved on and I followed them in, the layout looked eerily familiar. There were no doors here that I could see, but the tunnel opened into a small, empty room. In each side wall, toward the back, empty doorways gaped. If I took the left door, where the humans had gone, I suspected that I would find a dormitory. Through the right, a larger hall with an exit.

My curiosity overwhelmed me, so I moved quickly through the right door. Sure enough, there was a hall. On the shorter side opposite me was a doorway into another room, and on the long side to the right, the empty door gaped into a long, smooth tunnel.

I hoped I could find this place again. I'd love to know where that tunnel went, and if the first complex I'd entered, where I'd first seen the slavers, had the same layout. Perhaps it was all standardized in some way? But exploration was not why I was here.

I could hear the scholars' voices echoing through the empty rooms. They were talking with great enthusiasm about the stonework, which was a perfectly fine thing for archaeologists to be excited by, I supposed. Unfortunately for them, this was where their expedition would end, one way or another.

I'd ruled out trying to make friends with them. I wanted to, for sure, but it was just too risky. When I'd tried it with Herald and the others, I had been alone and barely surviving, and the risk had been acceptable. Now, only two months later, I had so much more to lose. Negotiating didn't seem like an option either. We each knew things the other wanted. I'm sure they would have given almost anything to speak to a living dragon with memories—or access to memories—of the one who had once lived in this place. And they obviously had some kind of knowledge about what this place had been, though it was patchy at best. The problem there was that I had no real way to hold them to any agreement. Once I'd given them what I wanted, they would know about me, and then there was no way for me to know that their greed, for gold or for knowledge, wouldn't make them move against me.

That left two options. Death, or terror. I desperately wanted not to kill them. Once you kill someone for your own convenience—which is what it would be, really—you've crossed too many lines. If I did that, I had no idea where I might end up, considering how many inconvenient people there were in the world. So instead, I thought I might try scaring the shit out of them, and work from there. I wished I'd watched more horror movies back when I could, but I'd never found them interesting, Andrea had been way too easy to scare and hated them, and Alex, my ex, had thought they were downright offensive. My brothers had roped me into watching one or two, but when it came to scary movies and terrifying monster strategies, I was woefully ignorant.

At least I'd watched the *Alien* movies. Not that I had any good ceiling vents to run around in, but the vertical ventilation shafts might do in a pinch.

As I watched and waited, I formed the barest beginning of a plan. First, I needed to get them in the dark. That seemed like common sense to me. For one, darkness was my element. For another, if you want to scare the shit out of someone, everything is scarier in the dark. Besides, if they saw me, I'd probably have to kill them, and the whole point was to avoid that.

For light, they had two directional lanterns and Barro's weak torch, which had been burning down during their trek. I figured that if I could get rid of the lanterns I would be all right, but since I didn't have a plan for how to do that, I just had to be patient and wait for an opportunity to present itself. Fortunately, I didn't have to wait long.

Barro, for all the fine qualities that he surely had, was far less patient than I. After five minutes of listening to the two scholars talk about how the stone walls had been shaped, he excused himself to make sure that the nearby rooms were safe, telling the two scholars to stay put and then leaving through the door in the farthest wall from me.

It only took seconds after he left for Tavia to start chafing at his order.

"Do you think . . ." she said, turning her lantern to light up the door on the right-hand wall and parts of the room beyond.

"The man is overly cautious," Ramban said, full of cheer at their discovery. "Go ahead. We'll get so much more done if we split up!"

"My thoughts exactly!" Tavia said excitedly, taking her lantern and practically running out of the room, while Ramban took out a writing board and some paper.

In the near absolute silence, even my soft steps should have been audible, but the man was so focused on his notes that he didn't realize anything was wrong until I'd already grabbed his lantern and flung it into the room's ventilation hole. It fell in a flare of spilled, burning oil, the loud banging and clanging of the brass housing receding into the distance, bouncing off the sides.

With a loud, startled noise, he stood and whirled around, but it was far too late. In the pitch black I had already shifted and moved away, taking up a position by the doorway the woman had left through. "Tavia?" Ramban exclaimed. "Was that you, girl? This is no time for jokes! Tavia?"

"What?" came Tavia's distracted voice from the next room, and I heard footsteps. "What happened?" she said as she came into the room. I could hear Barro's voice from beyond the far door as well, so as quickly as I could, as soon as Tavia had passed me, I shifted back, reached out, and ripped the lantern from Tavia's hand. She stumbled from the force of it and shrieked with fright as I scuttled through the door she'd come through, the light dancing ahead of me until her lantern met the same fate as the first.

"What's happening?" Barro called as he stormed into the room behind me. "Are you hurt?"

"Something—" Tavia said, her hand on her chest, trying to get her breath under control. "Something—"

"There is something here with us," Ramban said, his voice shaking. "It stole our lanterns!"

"Oh hells," Barro muttered. "All right, stay close to me. I'll get some more torches out. What was it? Did you see? Gremlin? A ghoul? Any idea at all?"

"Ghouls aren't real!" Tavia said. "But it moved in the dark. I never saw it."

"Nor I," Ramban said.

I could hear Barro opening his pack, and I didn't want him lighting any more torches. It was time for part two—theatrics. I'd never been a drama kid, but I was sure that I could overact with the best of them. They'd probably not notice if my performance was less than perfect.

"You . . . you . . . you . . ." I said quietly to myself, testing my voice until I found a low, menacing tone that should work.

"You brought light into this place, where no light is welcome!" My declaration echoed through the stone rooms. Watching through the doorway, I was quite satisfied to see them all startle at the sound. "By what right do you invade this place?"

Then, just to fuck with them, I shifted. Pushing the shadows ahead of me, I drifted right past them, through the room and the doorway of the room Barro had come from.

"Who are you?" Barro called through the doorway as I passed. "Show yourself!"

"Show myself?" I said from behind them. Tavia squeaked, and Barro whirled around, drawing his sword. "You already see me. I am the darkness, and these halls are mine!"

I repeated my trick, slinking past them to the door we had all originally entered through. Ramban must have seen the shadows move as I passed, because he suddenly pointed and exclaimed, "There! I saw something!"

Barro waved his torch around, but I was already gone.

"We're sorry!" Tavia said. Her breathing was quick and shallow, and she sounded on the verge of tears.

"You are not welcome here," I hissed from my new location, and now they were turning in confusion, not sure which way to look. "But I am feeling merciful. I do not want to foul this place with human blood. So, I might be persuaded to let you go." I extended my claws, raking them slowly down the stone and making an awful scratching sound before I moved again.

"What do you want?" Barro said, and even his voice was a little unsteady now.

"Is it not obvious? I want you to leave." I said, and moved.

"I want you to return to your camp, and take everything there." I moved.

"Leave nothing! I want no reminders of your intrusion." I moved.

"Forget this place!" I moved.

"Never return!" I moved.

"Do not speak of this to anyone!" I moved.

"Do not even think of it!" I moved.

"I will know. The darkness is mine." I moved.

"And if you fail to do as I command, the shadows will take you."

I approached them, not bothering to shift and instead pushing the shadows before me and around them until they nearly enveloped even Barro's torch, throwing the three into near total darkness. As one, their breaths caught. Then, only a few feet away from Tavia's back, I roared, "Now *go!*"

They fled, Barro shoving the two scholars ahead of him. He stared into the darkness, backing up rapidly and didn't turn back around until he was through the door. Then he turned forward and hurried after the others.

I followed the three as they rushed back through the tunnels the way they'd come. Credit where credit is due, once they'd left the rooms, they didn't run.

Barro kept a short leash on the two scholars, and they walked quickly, making sure to identify every turn until they reached the camp, barely speaking except to point out the direction they needed to go. Once there, they risked my wrath by lighting more torches as they began to pack the camp.

I couldn't help myself. From the darkness I hissed, "Leave *nothing*!" and almost laughed as they desperately searched the ground to make sure they hadn't missed anything. They even collected the ashes of their fire, shoveling it into the bag in which they'd carried their firewood. When they left, I followed them down the tunnel. I could hear them speaking in low, fearful voices, but couldn't make out what they were saying, which was unfortunate. It would have been good to know if they meant to disobey me the first chance they got. I followed them out in shadow form, closing the gate behind me, which elicited another fearful reaction from them as the gate hissed shut. Even then, I stuck around until I was sure that they were leaving, watching them break camp and get on the road back to the city.

"If nothing else, that was certainly amusing," my dragon said.

It was, wasn't it? I answered. *I just hope it worked.*

I meant what I'd said. If they came back, I *would* kill them. And I didn't feel bad about that decision. I'd given them a choice. I'd given them the option of not doing anything to force my hand. I'd given them a chance.

If they decided to throw that chance away, it was their funeral.

CHAPTER FIVE

Mistakes

It had only been a few days since Herald's message, but it had been more than a week since I last met my friends. In the letter Herald had said "two days at most." I was getting antsy. And since Herald had promised to come hunt with me, I didn't really feel like doing it on my own. And so, after the sun set on the day that I drove away the scholars, I headed for the lake.

To my disappointment there was still nothing waiting for me at the old, lone tree. I hadn't expected anything so soon, but I had hoped, and after our trip north, I had gotten used to having my friends around. I was getting lonely, plain and simple, and it affected my mood more than I'd expected. Not enough for my dragon to do anything about it, but enough that I didn't have it in me to go back home or do anything else. Instead, I curled up in a familiar tree, waiting and hoping that the morning would bring me something.

I woke to the sound of hooves. Judging by the sun it was mid-morning, so I had slept for several hours. When I looked down through the leaves I saw a familiar, if not entirely welcome, figure. Lalia, of all people, was surreptitiously pinning something to the tree.

Sure, we'd done well together against that bear, but I hadn't forgotten how generally shitty she'd been to me before that. Her chopping me in the neck with a sword hadn't endeared her to me, so I didn't exactly want to talk to her. At the same time I couldn't just let her leave. Maybe she was carrying another message from the sisters, or maybe Commander Rallon wanted something? No matter how strangely his scouts had looked at me after last time, I'd still made bank, and so had they, and I'd definitely want to listen if the Wolves had a proposal. Sure, I could just wait until she cleared out and read the message, but what if she knew more and I had questions?

And I was lonely, dammit.

Making sure that Lalia was alone, I slunk down from the tree and snuck through the undergrowth until I was close enough. "Psst!" I tried to say, but it came out as more of a hiss. It startled Lalia, though, which would never cease to be funny. She even jumped a little! "Lalia!" I said as she turned toward the sound. "Here, in the ferns."

I stuck my head up to let her see me.

Lalia looked around, then approached, leaving her gelding, Windfall, by the tree.

"Mercies," she said in a low voice, seeing that I had to look down on her now. "Were you always this big?"

"I'm a growing girl," I told her. It was no surprise to me, considering I'd just realized that I had the body of the dragon equivalent of a toddler. It was quite enjoyable to see how she fidgeted under my gaze, but I was the one who wanted something from her. I lay down, putting myself lower than her as a gesture of peace.

A significant tension left Lalia. "Make it quick," she said. "My squad is waiting for me."

"What, no small talk? It's been weeks since we last saw each other. Don't you want to catch up? What happened up on the mountain?"

She shrugged. "It was nice and quiet. We spent the night playing cards and telling stories, mostly. Oh, and I think two of my soldiers snuck off to screw behind a rock. That's about it. I heard you all had a hell of a time of it down in the forest."

"That's one way to put it. But, we're all alive, and the slavers are mostly not, and we got the prisoners out, so . . . yeah."

Lalia looked toward the campsite. "Are we caught up enough? I really do have to get back to my squad."

"I guess. What's the message?" I asked. "From Rallon?"

She shook her head with a frown. "From Mak. I got it by messenger this morning, with a note asking me to leave it here as soon as I could. Which is fine, since I come this way every few days, but I wish she'd come to me herself. I haven't seen either of the girls for a few days now, which is unusual. Getting a little worried, to be honest. Tell Mak to get in touch with me when you see her, will you?"

Lalia must have been beyond worried to ask me for anything. "Sure," I told her. "I'll let her know. Did you read the note?"

"Yeah, and I don't like it. She says she'll be here every night after sundown until she's seen you. Sounds important."

"And I'm mad that she didn't come to me first" went unsaid, but I agreed with Lalia. I didn't like it either.

"I'm going back to my squad," she said, then hesitated. "I'm on this patrol for a few days. If you see Mak tonight . . . any chance you could meet me here, same time tomorrow morning?"

Forget "worried". She must have been desperate if she was asking me to meet her. "I'll be here if I can," I told her.

"Thanks." She mounted Windfall. Then, as she was about to leave, she turned and said, "Lahnie's been talking about you. Not anything incriminating—" She gestured to me and my general dragon-ness. "But I guess you made a real impression. I, uh . . . I told her that I met you. That you told me about her. She liked that."

I smiled at her. One of my friendly, practiced smiles, without so many teeth. "In that case, tell her I said hi."

"I will," she said, with the barest hint of a smile, and rode off.

Lalia was one of the people I absolutely did not want to show weakness in front of, and so I had forbidden myself from freaking the fuck out until she left. But this was definitely a freak-out-worthy situation.

I read and reread the note. It was short and to the point, just as Lalia had described it. Mak wanted to meet me. No mention of Herald, but Mak would be here after sundown every day, starting the day the note was posted. That probably meant traveling here and back every day and every night, or even morning, which would take up most of her waking time. It also meant that she wasn't spending time with or looking after Herald. And Lalia hadn't met with either Herald or Mak for a few days.

This was clearly important. Something was wrong. Something that Mak couldn't go to Lalia about. That should have made me suspicious, but I'd been getting along with Mak last time we parted, so I decided to trust her.

Part of me wanted to go to Karakan immediately to find her, but common sense prevailed. No, I would have to make sure that I was here and ready when Mak arrived. That meant making sure my mind was sharp and my body rested, and the best place for that was my nest.

I sped back to the cave, keeping low over the densest parts of the forest to minimize the risk of being seen in the daylight. The bestiary that Herald had given me said that wyverns were most active during the day, and daytime was when the various groups of hunters had approached the scholars' camp. Flying during the day was a risk, albeit a small one, but one I took gladly.

"You worry about the humans," my dragon said as I reached the cave and began the descent to my nest. *"This Makanna, the sister of the Herald, she is an annoyance. Why do you concern yourself so much with her?"*

Can't you see that in my thoughts? She is important to Herald, I said. *If something happens to her, it would hurt Herald. And I think Mak is beginning to trust me, at least a little. But that is not the issue here.*

"Then what is?"

I don't think she would come to me if she herself had a problem. You heard Lalia. She hasn't heard from either of them for days. Herald loves Lalia. And now Mak has sent a message instead of meeting Lalia herself. Something is wrong. I think they may all be in trouble.

"You think the Herald is at risk?"

I hope not. But, yes.

Despite my worries, I still slept soundly, lulled to sleep by my hoard. My dragon woke me, saying that it was time to leave, and before my mind started churning again I wondered idly how she knew. She was right, of course. Her sense of time was excellent. When I reached the mouth of the cave, the shadows of the mountains were just beginning to stretch across the forest. It was not long until sunset.

I didn't have any food lying around, but there was no time to hunt. I had a quick drink, but that delayed me by five minutes at most. Hydration is important, no matter your species. When I arrived at the lake, I landed as close as I dared without exposing myself to anyone who might be using the campsite. Night had fallen, and I made my way through the woods straight to the lone tree.

Mak was waiting for me, holding a lantern.

That definitely should have made me suspicious. Mak had no need for a light source, not underground and certainly not outside, under a clear sky with the moon and stars to give her all the light her magically enhanced eyes could possibly want. But I was too worried to consider that. When I saw Mak's harrowed face I couldn't think straight. I barely looked to see that we were alone before bursting out of the trees.

"Mak!" I said. She jumped and turned as I broke out of the undergrowth, and barely calmed when she saw me. "I met Lalia. She gave me your message. What's happening? What's the problem? Lalia is so worried about you, she says she hasn't seen you for ages. Where's Herald? Is she all right?"

"Oh, Mercies be blessed." Mak's voice sounded . . . broken, somehow. It was rough and almost hopeless, and I could smell the fear coming off her. I'd never seen her like this, not when Herald stood with a sword to her throat, not when Val lay dying with his shoulder smashed into his chest. Dread gnawed at my guts as she continued, "I was afraid you wouldn't see the message today. That I wouldn't see you tonight. That I'd have to—" She swallowed. "I'm glad you're here now." She fidgeted with the lantern, and I noticed that she wasn't holding it very firmly. Like her fingers couldn't close properly.

"Mak, what's going on? Tell me. Please."

"It—it's Herald!" Her voice broke, tears spilling down her face. "I need your help. Please."

The dread in my stomach crystalized into a jagged lump.

"What's wrong with Herald?" I asked, feeling faint for a second. "Is she hurt?"

Mak bit back a sob. "Come. Please. I'll show you. Over here, come!" She turned and began to walk back toward the campground, twisting to make sure I was following. I did, of course. With zero hesitation, running on pure fear for my friend, I followed Mak. She skirted the campground, keeping close to the trees until we reached a narrow path, barely more than an animal trail.

"Here," Mak said urgently. "In here. Follow me."

I did.

Only a few dozen yards into the trees Mak stopped, and so did I. She turned to me, tears streaming from her eyes, and sobbed, "I'm sorry."

I understood that something was wrong when there was a rustle of leaves above me, and then the world went white. My ears rang, and my mind was a void of pain and confusion. I dimly felt the ground beneath my chin. I must have fallen. Odd. I never tripped anymore. I tried to stand, but my legs didn't move like they were supposed to, like they were stuck in something, or stuck together. Pushing with my arms worked better, and I looked around, trying to make sense of what was happening.

"It's awake," someone murmured, and I felt a sharp sting under my right wing.

This time I had a chance to see the man in front of me, as he wound up and smashed his hammer into my head. The world went white again.

". . . hope you didn't kill it," a voice said sometime later, when my hearing came back. "Boss'll be real pissed if you killed it."

The world was bouncing. I forced one eye open, and the ground was passing beneath me. I was being carried. Mak walked next to me, her face blank, her eyes empty.

The world faded out again.

I awoke to cold water splashing my face. I reflexively tried to gasp, but I couldn't open my mouth, something pressing into my scales all around my face when I tried. My head was a mass of pain, and I only reluctantly opened my eyes. As they slowly focused, I saw a cage of iron around my mouth, keeping it tightly shut.

Even moving my head made me want to hurl. Confusion sloshed around my brain for a little while before I understood. I'd been muzzled.

Sheer outrage woke me up another fraction before a woman's voice said "Again," and another load of cold water splashed over me, salty when it seeped in at the corners of my mouth. I struggled to rise, but all my limbs were tightly pinned to my body. I turned my head and saw a mass of chains binding me tightly.

I had a moment of near panic. I was chained. Trapped. I couldn't escape. It was happening again!

But that wasn't right. I wasn't so limited anymore. I could escape. Easily. The chains were nothing, and the fear faded.

"Hello, Draka," the voice from before said. It was warm and smooth and full of promises. "I'm so glad that you've joined us."

I slowly turned my head toward the voice, fighting the nausea, and saw a small group of people in front of me. Metal bars separated us. A woman crouched in front of me, her hands resting lightly on the bars. Warm light flickered across her smiling face from a lantern in the hand of the man next to her. Long, black hair spilled over her shoulders. She was the only one of the group that didn't smell like prey. She smelled of musk and jasmine, and even as her prisoner there was something about her that made a part of me grateful she'd noticed me.

The part of me that wasn't grateful hated her instantly.

"I would love to talk to you, you know?" she said. "Our mutual friend in the other cell has told me so much about you." She sighed. "But I can't have you killing any more of my men, so until I'm sure that you can be trusted, this stays on." She punctuated each of the last three words with a tap on my muzzle.

I drew my head back indignantly, straining futilely against the chains. She laughed with delight, a wonderfully musical sound, before rising smoothly. "I have to go now, unfortunately. I'm a busy woman. But don't worry. I'll be back soon. One of my men will explain the situation to you later, so that you understand why you being a nice, friendly little lizard is best for everyone involved."

I practically shook with scarcely contained rage. My mouth was filled with the bitter taste of venom. This woman was going to die. Once I could focus properly, she was going to die.

She looked down at me. "Oh, don't be like that," she said dismissively. "It'll all be fine. You'll see. Now, Vic," she said, turning to one of the men, "you keep an eye on our guests. I'll be gone for a few hours, and I don't expect any trouble from anyone. That includes you." She poked the man in the chest. "No more kicking the woman! I don't care if she annoys you. Some crying is normal, and you'll just have to bear it. Understood?"

The hulking man hung his head like a scolded schoolboy. "Sorry, boss," he mumbled. "I won't."

"Throw some water on her if you absolutely must do something, or bring down the other one and break one of her fingers or something. That usually shuts this one up. But if you damage her, I'll be taking the cost of the potion out of you."

"I know, boss. I won't."

"See that you don't. The rest of you, with me."

The woman swept out of the room with the men, except for Vic, following her. A lantern in the ceiling cast a weak light through the prison, but not nearly enough. They left me in the dark.

I was equally impressed and offended at how adoringly the men looked at her, and how meekly they followed her. I wondered idly if she was sleeping with any or all of them, or if it was just the implied possibility that had them acting the way they did. Not that there had been anything overtly sexual about anything she'd done, or said . . . or how she dressed . . . Honestly she was just an elegant, charismatic woman, who had a bunch of men wrapped around her fingers, but I wasn't exactly feeling charitable.

In the shadows, my draconic side wondered just how stupid she was, leaving us here, and how much of her entrails I could eat before she died.

Makanna

A few days earlier

How am I going to get her out of this?

The thought had hounded Makanna for days, and had finally driven her here, to the tavern that was her secret watering hole when she absolutely did not want to be found. She had hoped to quiet her thoughts with strong drink, to finally be able to relax for an evening, but it was not to be. With every cup, she drank herself deeper and deeper into her worries, but she was far past the point of no return. She didn't know how the night would end, but she was sure that she wouldn't remember it. Maybe she'd stumble home and embarrass herself. Maybe Herald would have finally sussed this place out, and would find her and drag her home, which was worse. Or maybe she'd wake up in an unfamiliar bed again. That might be nice. Any way it went, she was past the point of caring. She just wanted to stop thinking for a few hours. Was that so much to ask?

The object of her worries was, of course, Herald. It usually was. Makanna was often confused about whether she saw the girl more as a sister or a daughter. She'd certainly done everything expected of a mother for most of Herald's life— raising her, teaching her, and protecting her. Either way, Makanna was the head of the family. Herald was her responsibility, and she seemed determined to get into trouble.

The boy, Maglan, had been bad enough. They'd been sneaking off together for months that she knew of, and probably longer. Makanna didn't know for sure everything that had happened between those two, but she could guess.

Makanna didn't have anything against Maglan. She'd met him a couple of times, and he seemed sincere and responsible. But now Maglan was gone, for Mercies only knew how long, and Herald might get her heart broken.

She really should talk to her about that.

It didn't matter, though, not really. Herald was young, and heartbreak was part of growing up. That was not what worried Makanna. No, what worried Makanna was the dragon, Draka, and Herald's relationship with her.

The dragon. Even after months, the very idea was ridiculous to her. There was a dragon. Here, on Mallin! She knew its—her—name! And her little sister was *friends* with her! Hells below, Makanna suspected that she herself was becoming friends with Draka. At the very least she respected her. Of course, Makanna knew that she was a piss-poor judge of character, as evidenced by the many ways in which she'd been fucked over before Lalia and Valmik got her back on her feet. But she had tried not to get taken in. From the first few days, when Draka had conveniently walked into their lives and suggested that they form a partnership, and Makanna had seen Herald's excitement, she had been suspicious. She had tried to fear and hate the dragon. Back then, she had even been tempted to report the encounter, the promises she'd made be damned. But she couldn't. Honor, the risk of hurting Herald, and the danger of throwing suspicion on herself and her family, all of these held her back, weighing heavier than her fear, and those factors had only grown over the months since.

What would she be if she sold Draka out now? After the blood they'd shed together and the trust they'd built? The riches they'd found together? After Draka had likely saved their very lives?

Even if she'd be lauded as a hero and showered with praise, and if she thought that Herald might one day forgive her, how could Makanna live with herself?

Besides, judging by her actions, Draka was a better, well, person than some people Makanna considered friends. Sure, the dragon could be reckless and brutally violent, but so could Lalia who, by the way, had actually expressed some grudging respect for Draka lately. Draka was greedy, but that was hardly a damning character flaw. Makanna wasn't averse to grabbing some silver herself. Her greed, her literal nose for silver, was honestly a point in the dragon's favor, considering how much money they'd all made thanks to her. And while Makanna knew that the dragon kept secrets from them, her intentions toward them were always . . . well, not pure, perhaps, but benign at least. As far as Makanna could tell. Reading Draka could be hard sometimes, like the dragon didn't know herself what she felt. She certainly felt protective of Herald. That, at least, was always clear.

So, for all of Makanna's caution and suspicion, she couldn't actually find anything truly objectionable about Draka. Other than the fact that she was a *dragon*, and thus a danger to them all. Probably. It didn't seem reasonable for every culture to have the same stories about dragons without there being some truth to them, no matter what Tam said.

And yet, even *that* wasn't really the problem. Maybe Draka was different. In many ways she acted more like a human than what Makanna would expect from a dragon. If she closed her eyes she could almost pretend that Draka was just some odd foreign woman with a lisp. And so long as they were careful they should be able to work together, with no one the wiser.

The problem was, Makanna realized, since meeting Draka, she couldn't trust Herald's judgment. And because of *that*, Makanna was afraid that something bad was going to happen. Herald hadn't bothered to hide her outrage when the alchemists posted their bounty. The first night after that, her sister drank a little too much wine and spoke darkly about setting their guild house on fire, and Makanna could tell that those hadn't just been empty words. Ever since the incident with the Barlean fishermen—which even Lalia had admitted she couldn't blame Draka for—the bounty was up to a dragon and twenty eagles, and Makanna wouldn't be surprised if it hit two full dragons soon. People were talking openly about hunting the supposed wyvern. Adventurers between jobs were organizing parties to go out and try their luck. Rumors were flying about where it was last spotted, and which areas it frequented.

The forest was big. Draka was clever when she had to be, and she was stealthy. The business with the trolls had proven that beyond all doubt. But no matter how well Draka hid herself and their meetings, how long would it be until Herald said or did something unwise? How long until someone turned up some good intelligence on where to find Draka, and Herald decided to do something about it to protect her friend? Or, even worse, what if they got careless, and someone found the easily recognizable Tekereteki girl spending time with a godsdamn *dragon*?

Because that was the crux of it, wasn't it? Anyone being friendly with a dragon would be suspicious, but a Tekereteki? They were already suspect by their very nature. Some people saw a Tekereteki and assumed that they were spies, as though their very presence meant that a slaving fleet might descend on the city any minute. Anyone else would probably be taken into custody, but a Tekereteki? They would lynch her on the spot. That was no exaggeration. If anyone saw Herald talking to Draka, they would try to kill or drive the dragon off, and then they would string Herald up from the nearest tree, or just beat her to death where she stood. And, once someone remembered that the tall, dark girl had family, they would come and do the same to them.

And Makanna was too damned weak to even try to stop Herald. Because, despite her fears, and the weight of her responsibility to keep them all safe, she couldn't bear the thought of Herald hating her. She'd already been relegated to third place at best in Herald's heart, after Maglan and now Draka. To lose her entirely . . .

She'd tried to explain. What she felt from Herald when the girl talked about Draka, it was . . . wrong. It was almost closer to religious fervor than friendship. But even hinting at that just made Herald angry. After their trip to the north, Makanna had tried again, and for the first time that she could remember, Herald had responded with outright hostility. Not just anger, but suspicion.

That was the last straw. Makanna just couldn't do it anymore. She'd given up. It was unforgivably selfish, but at this point Makanna would rather die protecting Herald while she still loved her, than have her sister be truly safe but hate her.

It was all so damned *stupid*. Half the people in this city would want Draka killed for merely existing, based on half remembered myths and legends. They wouldn't bother learning anything about her. The good she had done, and could do. They wouldn't see how selfless she could be, or what a strong sense of fairness and justice she had, or . . .

She wasn't sure where that came from. She must be drunker than she thought if she was openly admitting things like that to herself.

She swirled the dregs in her cup around. She'd gotten through quite a few over the long evening, but wine had been a mistake. She was melancholy, and too drunk to think straight. The right thing would have been to go for something stronger from the start, so she'd be passed out by now. She had the money for it, thanks to Draka. More money than she'd ever had at once in her life. But it was too late to switch drinks now. She may as well go home.

It took a false start or two, but Makanna got up, if a bit unsteadily. The barman offered to send his boy with her, but she declined his repeated offer and made her way out the door. A couple of street dogs looked at her curiously, but she gently shooed them off. They didn't mean any harm. She could tell.

It would be a bit of a walk, but she was drunk enough that she'd probably hardly notice. She had to stop and steady herself every so often, but that was fine. She leaned her forehead against a wall for a moment. A few deep breaths and she could keep going.

"Mercies and Sorrows, miss, are you all right?" said a warm female voice.

Makanna looked up. The street was empty besides the woman next to her, elegantly dressed in a finely patterned two-part body wrap, and she was looking at Makanna with concern in her eyes. Gods above, but she was pretty. Long, silky hair. Didn't see hair so well cared for often. But her intentions? Pfft. She didn't want to help. Makanna was drunk, but she could tell that much.

"'m fine," Makanna lied. "Just need . . . y'know."

"Now, now, Makanna," the woman said. "There's no need to pretend. But don't worry. We'll take you somewhere you can sober up."

The words registered slowly in Makanna's mind. "What—" she began, but a strong arm wrapped around her from behind, while a hand pressed something thick over her mouth. As she jerked in surprise she felt a quick, stabbing pain in her thigh, and she looked down to see the woman removing a thin, inch-long needle dagger from her leg. Makanna screamed and kicked, but the cloth muffled her cries. Blood welled from her leg, and she almost immediately began to feel dizzy. Dizzier.

"There we are," the woman said, wiping the short dagger on a handkerchief. "Hold her down until it takes full effect, would you, Hardal? I don't want any fuss on the way."

"Yes, ma'am," said a voice behind Makanna, and she was forced down and pinned on her back, the cloth still pressed to her mouth. The man was strong, and he was heavy. In her state, there was little she could do.

Makanna's leg had gone numb, and the woman's words finally made sense. Right. Poison. Some kind of numbing or paralyzing poison. Her healing magic couldn't do much about those. Couldn't even fix the wound in her thigh. Too hard to focus.

As the poison spread through her, she stopped struggling. When she couldn't move her body anymore the man released her. She looked at his face. There was something . . . Had she seen him before? He looked so ordinary. His lips had been split at some point, but that was his only distinguishing feature.

Oh, yes, she thought before everything went dark. She did recognize him. The dead man.

How strange.

Makanna came to slowly.

A bone-deep pain in her thigh beat in time with her heart. She was still drunk. She noticed that much immediately, but the logical part of her mind took stock of her situation. She was in a small room, seemingly cut out of solid stone, lit by a single lantern hanging from the ceiling. She was in a chair, with a table in front of her, her wrists manacled to its surface.

She looked at the iron bands holding her fast, then tested them. They were tight enough to hurt when she strained, and the table was too heavy for her to move. Her breathing quickened, fear welling inside her, and it only grew when she heard soft footsteps behind her. She craned her neck to look, and a short man walked past her, rounding the table. He didn't even look at her until he'd sat down in the chair opposite her.

"Where am I?" she croaked, unable to keep her voice steady. "What do you want?"

The man observed her, his eyes hard and piercing. "So predictable," he said finally, his voice a squeaky tenor. "Do you know how many of the people I've had in that chair said the exact same thing?"

Makanna didn't answer. Danger oozed from this man, and a feeling that the wrong word might set him off. Better to stay silent unless an answer was necessary.

"To answer your question," he said, "I want your cooperation. That's all. My boss wants something, and you can help us get it."

"What?" she asked, before she could stop her mouth. Damn wine.

The man frowned. "I was getting to that. I don't know if you recognized my associate who brought you in, but let me be clear. Makanna, we know who you are. We know that you helped the Gray Wolves disrupt one of our operations recently, one where several of our people died. And we think that you know more than perhaps anyone about the . . . creature that was present. You will help us capture it."

Makanna blanched. "I don't know what you're talking about."

The man frowned again. Another, much larger, man handed him a bundle of rolled up leather, which the small man placed on the table. He unrolled it slowly, and Makanna felt a cold sweat break out at what she saw. Needles. A long, thin knife. A small hammer. Pliers. A cleaver.

"All we want is your cooperation." The man's voice was calm, but Makanna could feel the cold fury behind his words. And he was lying. Her advancement told her that he didn't care what she told him. This man, more than anything, wanted to hurt her.

What followed was a waking nightmare, and when they left her, Makanna was half delirious with pain. They put the chair back under her—she'd kicked it away at some point—but they left her manacled to the table so that she couldn't even cradle her ruined hands.

"This is where I would normally start on your face," the short man said into her ear, breathing hard from his efforts. "Luckily for you, the boss thinks that you could fetch a good price, so she's forbidden me from removing anything. I'll just have to think of something else. See you tomorrow."

A door slammed heavily behind her. She heard the clinking of a chain, and she was alone.

She didn't think that she had told them anything. It hadn't taken her long to lose her dignity, but she had her pride and her honor. She didn't think that she had told them anything they could use, at least. It was hard to remember what she might have said as they . . .

She'd stopped crying at some point, but now she looked at the bloody, twisted ruins of her hands, and a low, keening wail escaped her before she bit it off. She had to focus. The pain was so bad. But healing herself was an order of magnitude easier than healing someone else, and now that she was alone and no one was hurting her, she should be able to . . .

The soothing warmth of her magic flowed into her hands and the other parts of her they had abused, taking the pain away and starting the healing. Perhaps she was only prolonging her torture. But all her fingers were still there, and if she didn't begin healing now, the damage might become permanent. If she was careful, they wouldn't be able to tell what she'd done.

Once the pain finally subsided, she looked around as much as she could, trying to find anything that might help her escape, but it was useless. The room was bare, the door was heavy and chained shut, and the table was too heavy for her to move. And she was weak, both from the agony and the healing. She didn't give up, but she didn't see any point in using more of her energy than necessary. She would need it.

She laid her head down between her arms, and fell into a restless sleep.

She woke alone to silent darkness. The lantern had burned out, and she didn't bother with her darksight spell. It would be a waste of energy. No one came to give her food or water, and so she just waited and rested the best she could, trying to keep her fear in check. Trying not to imagine what they might have planned for her.

She might have been awake the whole time, or she might have slept again. It was hard to tell. But she sat bolt upright, her entire body tense as the chain on the door rattled. The door creaked open. Light spilled in, and she felt a pat on her cheek.

"Good day to you, Makanna," said the short man. "Did you sleep well? You looked tired."

He replaced the dark lantern in the ceiling with the one he was carrying, and then stepped out of the room briefly. Makanna blinked against the light, and looked up at the man as he came back in and stood at the table. He was . . . amused, she decided. The anger was still there, but controlled.

The man reached down and squeezed her partially healed hand, and she whimpered pitifully, the manacles cutting into her wrist as she tried to pull away.

"I might have overdone it last night," the man said. "So sorry for that. Let me make it up to you!"

He reached his hand out behind Makanna. She tensed, but nothing happened. She only heard movement, and when the man brought his hand back he held a familiar looking bottle, which he placed on the table in front of her, among the dried blood and the fingernails.

It was a healing potion. A good one, judging by the style and markings.

"I would like to offer you a deal," the man said. "Your cooperation, in exchange for that potion. Help us capture the creature, and you can have your hands back."

Dragon. Just say it, Makanna thought. *You know what she is. Just say it!*

She took a long, shuddering breath. "No," she croaked, her throat still raw from screaming. But, despite her refusal, she couldn't tear her eyes from the potion. She wasn't sure that she had enough healing in her to fully restore her hands, not without food and proper rest. That potion would—

"You know," the man said brightly, "I thought you'd say that!"

He stepped outside the room and called something in . . . *Barlean*, Makanna thought. After a moment she heard yelling. It got closer, and louder, and when she recognized the voice, her heart froze.

"No," she whispered, as a large man carried a larger, furiously struggling and screaming bundle into the room. It was Herald. She had a split lip and a swollen eye, was gagged and had bound hands and feet, and gods bless her, she was still fighting like she'd take on the whole Tavvanarian navy.

The large man dumped Herald into the chair opposite Makanna, and they looked at each other. "Oh, baby," Makanna croaked. "I'm so sorry." So much for her pride and honor.

Herald looked at Makanna's face, then down at her hands, and redoubled her struggles. When she looked back at Makanna, her eyes brimmed with tears, and she screamed something through her gag.

There was a loud *crack* as the small man casually backhanded Herald across the face. Her head snapped around and she sat still in the chair, dazed. Makanna flinched, but didn't say anything. The fury was back in the man.

"I rarely make an offer twice," he told her, "but for you, I'll make an exception. Your cooperation, in exchange for that potion."

Makanna looked at the man and said, "I'll do anything you ask."

"Yes. You will," he said.

Then he drew a long dagger and stabbed Herald in the gut.

Breaking

had awoken on a stone floor to cold water thrown on me and some woman gloating over me, telling me to be a "good little lizard." To say that I was furious couldn't even begin to describe what I felt.

I looked around. The small jail I was in looked to be carved out of solid stone and was dimly lit by a lantern hanging from the ceiling. A weak draft chilled my side, and in the silence I could hear water dripping and sloshing in the distance. There was a wooden door to the left of my cell, and the open doorway through which the woman had left with her men was to my right. The man who'd been left to guard us, Vic, sat on a stool next to it, a heavy-looking axe leaning against the wall beside him. Despite all their precautions, he was watching me warily, so he wasn't entirely stupid.

I was chained, muzzled, and behind bars. I couldn't move or speak. I couldn't even open my mouth enough to breathe.

They thought that they could keep me here. They were wrong. I just needed to be patient, and await the right opportunity.

Across the floor was another cell. In that cell was the woman, perhaps friend, who had betrayed me. If I had been more myself—in less pain, less blindingly furious, and not slightly concussed—I might have considered her vacant stare and the way her wrists were connected to the wall by a short chain. As it was, all I saw was betrayal. The shattered faith I had placed in her. All the progress we'd made, the long nights by the campfire, the times we'd fought beside each other, wasted and worthless.

Right from the beginning, all the time we'd known each other, from the mines to the trolls, she had never trusted me. I'd thought that she'd warmed up to me. That we'd been getting close. Clearly, I had been mistaken.

A hundred different scenarios for what I'd do when I got to her fought for my attention, but one thing was clear. I wasn't leaving her there. Not alive.

My opportunity to act came when Makanna flipped her shit. It started small. She turned her head to our jailor and said, in a dead voice, "Where is she?" Vic didn't answer, but switched his attention to her, looking at her with annoyance. "Where is she?" Makanna repeated. She began to sniffle, tears leaking from her eyes. "Where is she?" She got to her feet and started yanking on her chains, throwing herself toward the bars and repeating herself between heaving sobs, her voice rising in pitch and volume until she was screaming, "Where is she? I did it! I gave you the dragon! I did what you said! I gave you what you wanted, now let me see her! Where is she, you fucking animals? Where is she?!"

She kept going, screaming, almost raving. I could see blood running down her arms from beneath the manacles around her wrists, and I didn't care. I wasn't really hearing her. I certainly didn't listen to what she was saying. All I cared about was that the man guarding us had finally had enough. He walked over to Makanna's cage, banging on the bars, screaming nearly as loudly as she did for her to shut up, how he was fed up with her screaming and crying and whining.

I made my move.

The room was dimly lit. It was too bright to simply shift, but shadows were everywhere. I pushed, and the shadows behind me enveloped me, flowing out past the bars.

If Vic had a better hold on his temper, he might have heard the chains and the muzzle clinking to the ground as they fell. As it was, he only turned when Makanna backed up against the wall, her face turning from despairing rage to astonished horror, looking past him at me as I merged with the darkness and flowed out into the room.

Vic faced me just as I came back together, standing on my back legs before him. He opened his mouth to scream, and I simply reached up and shoved four talons in his mouth. I took a firm grip, and whatever he'd been about to yell turned into a muted scream of pain as I yanked his head down, my claws digging in around his jawbone, then used my grip for leverage as I tore the front of his throat out with my free hand. He punched me a few times. He was strong, and it hurt, but by the time he thought to defend himself, it was already over.

As Vic slumped to the ground I turned my eyes on Makanna. She was sitting limp against the wall, staring at me with wild eyes, breathing quickly, her mouth open.

My head hurt. Manipulating the shadows around me had made it worse, and I didn't want to do it again. I looked at the lantern. I wanted to smash it down, but, no. Oil. Fire. Bad idea. It took three tries, but I managed to leap up and grab it off its hook instead. With a furious calm I used a claw to open the little hatch on its side, and sprayed some venom inside it, extinguishing the wick. Blessed darkness swallowed us.

Makanna still hadn't spoken to me.

I stalked up to her cell, claws out, clicking and scratching on the stone floor as I went. I could hear her breathing, quick and shallow. Between the screaming and the shock, she was hyperventilating. I thought she might pass out. I couldn't have that.

I flowed past her bars. I didn't think that she could see me—she hadn't glowed, and her eyes didn't track me—but she took a sharp breath, feeling my presence in the small space when I shifted back in front of her.

"Dra—" she tried to say, finally, before my talons closed around her throat. They weren't large—I was still young, after all—but her neck was thin. I was careful not to break her skin too much, but I made sure that she felt my claws as I squeezed.

"Hello, *Mak*," I whispered, arcing my head down toward her, my teeth inches from her face. She choked and gripped my wrist with both hands, her chains rattling, but my grip was as sure as death. "This has not turned out well for you at all, has it? First the bastards you sell me to stab you in the back, and then it turns out that they cannot even keep me locked up. All those chains, two sets of bars, yet here I am. With you."

She started kicking at me and trying to pry my fingers open, but that wasn't happening. She had some muscle on her, I knew that, but she couldn't have broken the grip of the human body I remembered. Against the body of a creature built to kill, with magically enhanced strength, she may as well have not even tried. Still, her survival instinct was strong.

"I have been feeling a little bad, did you know that, *Mak*?" I spat the name she'd asked me to call her. "Asking myself why I did not tell you all that I can do. I know how important it is to you, keeping your advancements secret. Surely that would make you trust me, if I revealed something like that? But I figured that after our talks and after finding the treasure and all, it would not be necessary. So I held back. Was that wrong of me, *Mak*?"

I waited for an answer until I remembered that I was choking her. Oh, well. "Did you ever think of me as a person, *Mak*?" I asked her. "As someone who could doubt? Who might just want her friend's sister to like her? Were you just stringing me along? Was I just a tool to you, that you could get rid of once you got a good enough offer?"

Her struggles began to weaken, and I relaxed my grip just enough to let her take one coughing breath, then tightened it again.

"I guess I must just be fucking prescient or something. If I had told you everything, they would never have left me here with so little light. They might have just killed me when they had the chance. So maybe I should thank you for being such a suspicious bitch, *Mak*."

I gave her another breath, and she managed a croaking "Pleash!" as I did. It only infuriated me further. After all I'd given, she had the fucking *gall* to ask for *more*?

"Did you think you could betray a *dragon* and not face any consequences, *Mak*?" I growled, close enough that my snout nearly touched her face.

I tightened my grip further and felt my claws dig into her flesh. The feeling was intoxicating. I literally held her life in my hand. I could choke the life out of her, tear her throat out, gut her. Fast, slow, now or later, I could kill her however I wanted, and there was nothing at all she could do. Her useless struggles intensified, and in her terrified eyes I could practically *see* the line I was about to cross. All I needed was the tiniest push. The wrong word, the wrong look . . .

Then something changed in her. I saw, and felt, the fight go out of her. I could almost smell it. The acceptance that she couldn't resist me. She stopped struggling. Her hands still gripped my wrists but otherwise she went limp, staring toward me but not at me in the dark.

It brought me back from the brink. Her struggles had been feeding my rage, pushing me forward, and her complete surrender created space for me to think. I'd been dead set on killing her, but perhaps I shouldn't be so hasty. If she wasn't fighting me, she might be useful, at least in the short term. Waste not, want not and all that.

"I am going to relax my grip now," I told her, "but I want you to understand that I do not want to hear a word out of your treacherous mouth unless I ask for it. If I do, I will kill you. If I think that you are lying to me, or holding anything back, I will kill you. If you do not do as I say, I will kill you. I have made it a point of honor to never eat human flesh, but today has made me want to make two exceptions. Do you understand?"

She tried to nod. I relaxed my grip enough to free up her throat.

"I understand," she croaked.

"Good," I said. "Can you see me?"

"No."

"Fix that."

It took her some time to collect herself and focus, but I saw her cast the spell. She gave off a very satisfying little whine as her eyes focused on me. I could only imagine what she saw in my eyes.

"Now," I told her, "do something about the pain that is pounding in my skull."

She hesitated, then released her grip on me and placed her hands on the sides of my head. Soon I felt the same soothing warmth as the last time she had healed me, and the pain receded.

I sighed with relief. "Good," I said. "Well done. Now convince me not to kill you."

"Herald!" she said immediately, and my grip tightened a fraction. This again? That was the lie she had used to bring me into that cell. She must have seen the renewed fury in my eyes, because her words became desperate.

"Please!" she said, her voice quavering. "Kill me if you want, but I'm not lying! They have Herald! They've been hurting her. They wouldn't let me help her if I didn't do what they wanted!" Tears were flowing freely down her face again, but she kept her breathing under control. "I don't care what you do to me," she said, "but, please, save my sister."

I considered her. Ever since the first time I'd met her, there had always been a strength in her eyes, a fierceness. It was gone now. I saw fear, regret, and a grim acceptance. She looked ready, almost willing, to die.

I released her. She slumped back against the wall, alternately gasping and coughing. There was a nasty bruise already forming around her neck, blood trickling from where my claws had dug in.

"We are going to find the Herald," I told her. "If you are lying, and she is safe somewhere, I will rip your tongue out and eat it in front of you. As long as you do as I say, and as long as your usefulness as a healer, or as a go-between, or just as a comfort to her is greater than your usefulness as meat, you get to live. Otherwise, you are expendable. Is that clear?"

"Yes," she said, her voice rough.

"Does the jailor have the keys for your chains and your cell?"

"Usually."

I looked at Vic's exsanguinating corpse. Flowing back outside, I found a key-ring on his belt, along with a small pouch of coin and a dagger. I removed them and tossed them to Makanna, who did nothing.

"Free yourself," I ordered, and she did.

"And heal that," I said when I saw the raw flesh under her manacles, and she did.

"Get out here," I told her, and though she hesitated to come closer to me, she did, unlocking the cage and stepping out.

"What are you good for, besides your magic? What advancements do you have?"

She only hesitated for a breath. "I have excellent control of my movements, and I can both move and react faster than most. And I can feel strong emotion from others, and their intent toward me to some degree."

"Does that last one work on me?"

"Yes," she said and swallowed, "though it's much less clear. Usually. Your emotions can be confusing. Messy."

I snorted. "Fair enough," I muttered, then switched languages. "*How well do you speak Tekereteki?*"

Mak looked at me, afraid and confused, so I repeated myself.

"*I . . . not good, now,*" she said, slowly and carefully.

"Get better," I told her, switching back. "Practice with your sister. It would be good if Tamor got better at it too. Do you know how to get around here? Where the Herald is?"

She didn't stumble at the change of topics. "No. They blindfolded me when they moved me. There is a short tunnel, and a long staircase. Farther to walk between the street and the stairs than you'd think. The entrance is in a house in the northeast part of the city."

"We will just have to improvise. Anything else I should know?"

Mak hesitated. "I don't know who the woman is, but this is the same gang as the slavers we stopped. I'm sure of it. The man we captured and gave to the Wolves, who's supposed to be dead, he was there when they took me."

I sighed. "At least there is only one bunch of bastards to deal with. How are your hands?"

"Better than they look, but not fully healed yet. I haven't eaten for a few days."

"All right. Stay behind me. Leave the axe, but use that dagger if necessary. No one kills you tonight but me."

Love or fear. I needed at least one from anyone close to me. If Mak couldn't be a trusted friend, then she would be a tool. A servant. I tried not to think too much about the fact that this was Herald's sister, and Tam's. Val and Garal's friend. Hell, even Lalia's opinion of her mattered a little. They all loved and respected her. But she had betrayed me. It didn't matter if her reasons were good. For her sins, she would serve me loyally, or she would die. I couldn't afford to treat her any other way. I'd deal with the consequences of that as they caught up to me.

Leaving through the open doorway, we went to rescue the one person who would never betray me.

CHAPTER SEVEN

Extreme Prejudice

had wanted my first visit to the city to be fun. Perhaps not a big, happy celebration out in the open—that probably wasn't ever going to happen—but I'd had this hope, this vague dream of a night in the future when I could sneak into the city to meet up with a few friends, and they'd bring me somewhere we could all relax and have a good time. Maybe we could find a secluded rooftop in the higher part of the city and look out across it. Something like that.

Instead I was stalking through a stone tunnel, a broken Mak following meekly behind me. I was going to find the Herald, and I was going to kill anyone who got in my way. And when the Herald was safe, I was going to find the captivating woman who smelled of jasmine.

I was showing admirable self-control. I knew myself well enough to realize that. I should have been tearing down the tunnel, mindless with fury and fear for my friend. And by rights, Mak should not be alive. When I'd seen her in that cell across from me, all I had felt was rage. An all-consuming hate like nothing I'd ever felt for anyone before.

I could only assume that my dragon wasn't done with Mak yet, and despite everything, I found the idea of her being the conservative one darkly amusing. Her, the dragon who defaulted to killing anything inconvenient, who'd wanted to kill and eat both Mak and Lalia not that long ago. And it was nice to know that most of the time at least one of the spirits sharing my head could be responsible.

The tunnel was not long, a hundred and fifty feet at most, and unlit. At the end was a wide, spiraling stairway, neatly cut from the stone, descending from above and continuing down past us. The exit would probably be up, but for all I knew this was only one level of cells, and so I went down first.

There were no cells downstairs. Instead, a short passage of perhaps thirty feet connected the stairway to a long, natural cavern, mostly filled with water that sloshed calmly against the stone. There was a small wooden dock there, with a boat tied to it, but I couldn't see any way out.

"What do you think about this?" I asked Mak, who had followed me silently.

"I don't see anything across the cavern," she said, "but if there's nothing there, the boat should mean that there's a connection to the sea. Maybe it's high tide, and the opening's hidden?"

"Eh, maybe," I said noncommittally. I hadn't seen any sea caves except the one with the sewers when I flew by, but I had no idea what the tides had been then. Either way, we'd seen everything we had time for, and I led the way back up, past the level we'd come from. Like Mak had said, the staircase carried on for a while, and I felt a petty satisfaction that a couple of the bastards would have had to carry my limp ass down all those stairs. When I saw a trickle of light from above, I slowed, stepping more carefully.

I looked at Mak and hissed, "Wait here," and she nodded, stopping where she was. Her eyes grew wide, and she backed down a step when I shifted. She'd have to get used to that if she wanted to remain useful to me.

I continued up the stairs until the light became too bright for me to continue, and then I brought the darkness with me, preparing the way for me to ascend to an open doorway at the end of the stairs. Someone stood there, a blur facing the brightly lit space beyond, their shadow creating a space behind them where my vision was clear and sharp.

I got as close as I could before the brighter light made maintaining my shadows too strenuous, then shifted back. I threw myself at the figure—a man, now that I could see clearly—before he had a chance to notice me. I managed to get my feet on his hips and a hand clenching down on his throat before he could make a sound, but I hit him harder than I'd expected and he fell forward, quite loudly, into the hallway beyond. The hallway was only a few yards long, with a door at the far end and in each of the walls, and while I raked out his throat, I heard footsteps, and the door began to open.

I didn't waste any more time. The man would bleed out in seconds, so I moved toward the door.

"Hey, Rosh, what was—" said a voice, and the face that stuck in through the half-open door fell back with a face full of venom, whining and coughing.

There goes the element of surprise, I thought with a touch of regret.

"Mak!" I called back down the stairs before hurtling forward. "Get up here!"

I crashed through the door before me, shouldering it the rest of the way open. The young man I'd sprayed was crawling blindly on the floor, but he wasn't alone in the small room. Two others, a man and a woman, had stood from the table where they'd been playing some kind of game with a board and lots of wooden markers. The room erupted into shouting as I came in. Probably something like, "Alarm! Alarm!" or "Gods help us, it's loose!" but I wasn't really listening.

I ignored the man wheezing on the floor. He wouldn't be a problem. The other man had the bad luck to be the closer of the two still on their feet, standing between me, the table, and the woman. It meant that, instead of taking the time to make sure that I killed him, I just disabled him quickly. I aimed past him, raking his knee with my claws as I passed, tearing muscle and ligaments. He went down with a scream as his leg folded, while I hit the table hard with my shoulder, sending game pieces flying and knocking the table itself into the woman, who bent forward as it caught her in the gut, the sword she'd drawn clattering to the floor.

I heaved, and the table pushed the woman along until it smashed her against the wall and stunned her. Then I leaped on top of the table and tore her throat out. *The human neck is ridiculously vulnerable*, I thought with disgust. *At least the chest has a bunch of bones to protect the really vital parts.*

The man, not much more than a boy, had fallen on his back and was facing me. Come to think of it, the woman I'd just killed had been pretty young too. I probably should have been disgusted, but I suspected that my dragon was keeping a lid on everything except cold, calculating rage. The man was screaming something, one word, over and over, while crawling backward on his hands and his good leg, trying to get through a doorway leading to another hallway. He had a sword on his belt, but he hadn't even tried to draw it. I took that as a surrender. That was good. I had questions. The man I'd sprayed venom at was still on his hands and knees, but all he could produce were small, whistling sounds, so he didn't have long. Maintaining eye contact with the young man I'd crippled, I grabbed the other one by the back of the head and smashed his face into the stone floor, hard, then again for good measure. He became still and quiet.

"Be silent," I growled at the man as I advanced on him, but he kept screaming. "I said, be silent," I repeated, close enough for him to feel my breath on his face, and his screams stopped with a strangled squeak, replaced with rapid, pained breathing. I heard footsteps from the way I'd come, and Mak came through the door, looking sick as she looked around. I turned back to the man on the floor.

"Where is the Herald?"

"I don't—I don't know—" he panted.

I wrapped my claws around his knee. "If you scream, you die," I told him and squeezed. To his credit, he didn't scream, though I could hear his teeth creak as his jaw clenched and his other leg kicked convulsively.

"Where is the Herald?" I asked again. "The tall Tekereteki girl. Her sister." I gestured toward Mak with my head.

"I don't know," the man sobbed through his teeth, and then he really looked like a boy. "I've seen them take her toward the boss's office. Maybe there. Please, my leg . . ."

"Do you understand what I am?"

"You're . . . you're the dragon," he said. "The others were talking, but I didn't know! I swear, I didn't know you were here! We were just supposed to keep anyone from going down without the boss! Oh, Mercies and Sorrows. Berek. Ava—"

I ignored his babbling. "Mak," I said, turning to her. "Take his sword, then get him up." I turned back to the man on the floor. "Mak is going to help you show me to your boss's office. I want you to know that Mak means nothing to me. Trying to take her hostage is useless. Obey, and you may live. Do you understand?"

"Yes!" the man said, hissing as I released his knee.

Mak came forward carefully, but did as I said, taking the man's sword from its scabbard and then helping him up and supporting him, resting the point of the sword under his chin. "I don't recognize you," she said. I got the feeling that it was a good thing she didn't.

"How many more humans are in this place?" I asked him.

"I don't know," he said quickly, adding, "I really don't!" when Mak pushed the point of the sword into his skin. "Could be two, could be ten or more. It depends on if the boss or Tark are here or not."

I looked down the hallway that he'd been crawling toward. It looked cut from the stone, like everything else I'd seen so far, and ended in a closed wooden door.

"The office is that way?" I asked, and the man quickly nodded.

"There's a shelf behind the door that slides away," he said, "and then you're in a storage room in the house. It's a normal house but, like, big. Fancy."

"All right. Mak, bring him. If he tries anything stupid, kill him."

"Yeah," Mak said uncertainly. "Okay."

I walked quickly through the short hall our prisoner had indicated. The door opened smoothly inward, and then there was a wooden wall in front of me with a recessed handle. With some effort, it slid to the side, making a grinding noise and revealing a dark space beyond full of boxes, barrels, and amphorae, with shelves of jars and baskets along the walls. I passed them all, going straight for the door set in the left side of the opposite wall. I did, however, notice that the far wall was made of stone brick, where the near one was cut from the bedrock.

Beyond the door was a kitchen, warm and brightly lit. It was occupied by a middle-aged woman who screamed and cowered when she saw me. "The office?" I growled at her, but she either didn't understand me or was too frightened to function, and only pressed herself harder into the corner where she'd sought refuge.

There were two doors other than the one I'd come from, but my choice was made simple when a young man came through one of them, probably drawn by the cook's scream. *Another damned kid*, I thought. He wisely turned and ran the moment he saw me, wide-eyed and shouting in alarm as he went. I pursued.

The door opened into a large, open room with a small pool in the center, and the space was brightly lit through an opening in the ceiling above the pool. Beyond that I didn't take much in. I was focused on my prey. Humans were faster than valkin, and I couldn't run him down, which was frustrating, but in the open space of the atrium we'd just entered, I could use my wings for a boost to close in on him. The large double doors he was headed toward opened partially, showing another man looking in with surprise and annoyance. He'd had the presence of mind to grab one of the short swords I kept seeing, wide and tapering smoothly to a point.

"Go back! Go back! Run!" the young man I was hunting shouted, but the man in the door hesitated and raised his weapon, which cost them both.

As the running man slowed down to squeeze by his companion, I caught up, barreling into them both and smashing both doors open the rest of the way as I did. I felt the blade punch into my wing's shoulder joint. Clever bastard. Or maybe he was just lucky. The way my scales lay, I was almost impossible to hurt from the front, but they were smaller and lay differently around the joints.

One day I would have to learn to fight, to really think about what I was doing, but shock, fear, and overwhelming, unthinking violence had served me well so far. In this case, he still went down, but he had a good grip on his weapon, and I pushed him with that as much as with my body.

Unfortunately for him, I didn't need my wings to fight. The room was open enough that I might have been able to use them to batter my opponents, but they'd always been an afterthought as weapons. Instead, I whipped my head down and tore my teeth through the guy's forearm. He screamed, and his hand went limp as my teeth scraped bone. His other hand punched uselessly at my jaw a few times, but he jerked and went limp after my foot raked him deeply from sternum to groin.

My mouth was still clamped down, but from the corner of my eye I saw my prey trying to escape. We were in some kind of entrance hall, and he was half crawling toward the doors that no doubt led outside. His hand closed on the latch just as mine closed around his ankle.

I met Mak and the captive as I dragged the two torn bodies back into the atrium, the floor dark and slick behind me. I threw both corpses in the central pool. I didn't have a reason, at least not a conscious one. Maybe I was making a statement. The sword had wrenched itself out from under my wing at some point, and the pain was catching up to me even through the adrenaline. I was sure that I was bleeding pretty badly. *I must have some large veins and arteries running there,* I thought distantly.

As the bodies splashed into the water, I locked eyes with Mak and she didn't hesitate. She left the injured man she'd been supporting to balance as best he could and approached me, sword carefully pointed down.

"*Hurt,*" she said softly in her halting Tekereteki. "*Make better?*"

I looked at her. She was half starved, and physically and mentally exhausted. Healing me was difficult for her, much more so than healing a human. As much as I wanted her to take the pain away, I couldn't risk it. I'd trust in whatever magic made me what I was.

"*Wait*," I said, speaking simply. "*The Herald*."

She nodded and returned to our captive. "The office," she said coldly as she put the tip of his own sword under his chin, then slid in under his shoulder. The man had been shaking with pain and fear before my little display with the pool. Afterward he became still, complying with Mak's instructions with a detached calm. My guess was that he'd completely given up hope, and only wanted to prolong his life for however long I allowed it.

The man led us to a door at the back of the atrium. I opened it and went through, making sure that no one was waiting on the other side. "Second door on the left," he said, softly and very carefully. "That's the office. But I only saw them take the girl through this door."

"Stay here," I told the humans, then continued inside silently. When I listened carefully, I could hear panting and ragged breathing. The second door on the left was closed. The one on the right was open.

I had thought that the blood I smelled was the stuff coating me, but as I approached the open door the smell grew stronger. I began to feel a fear that grew stronger the closer I got, and when I saw the red pool on the floor of the room, I rushed the last few yards to get inside.

I didn't know what to expect. I didn't want to imagine. But whatever I'd thought I might see, a body on the floor and Herald holding a knife was not it.

CHAPTER EIGHT

Busting Out

The man I found on the floor of the small room, which looked like it might have once been a spare bedroom, was practically dead. He was lying unconscious in a pool of blood, his breathing sharp but shallow. He'd been trying to crawl away from a wooden cage, about four feet wide, which was set against the wall. He'd been prevented from doing so, however, by the dagger that was sunk through his lower leg, held firmly in place by a long, brown arm coming out from the cage.

"Herald!" I exclaimed. Seeing her alive and mostly unharmed quelled my rage and gave way to relief, for a moment at least.

"Draga?" the girl slurred, peering out between the thick wooden bars. "S'at you?"

Herald was curled up on the bottom of the cage, other than the arm that held the dagger. She was thin, pale, and her clothes were in tatters. She was also utterly pissed.

"You're alive," I said, more to myself than to Herald. "Thank the stars! I am going to get you out of here!"

"This fugger," she said, raising the dagger and stabbing it down again. The dying man didn't even react. "This piece-a-shit. He told me they had you. Fuggin' . . . *Fucking* gloated aboudit. Stood right there," she said and pointed with her free hand in front of the cage, "an' said they had you inna basement with Mak. Got so angry when I told him he was gonna die if you're here. Tried to stab me when the noise started an' I told'm the guards with you were dead already." She grinned and turned to the man on the floor. "Didn't expect me to get the knife off ya, huh? Stab you inna gut? Jus' some dumb drunk girl inna cage for you paw at, right? Arrogant shit! Don't know what I can do! Bitch doesn't even hire real fighters to guard her—" Then her face suddenly became concerned. "Where's Mak?"

"She is with me," I said. "It is all right. Mak!" I shouted. "Get in here! Now!"

Mak came through the door almost immediately, having left the prisoner behind somewhere. It wasn't like he'd get far, not with one knee ruined.

"Herald! Mercies be blessed!" Mak rushed to kneel by the cage, reaching in to cup Herald's cheek. "Are you hurt?"

"Hey, Mak!" Herald pointed at me. "You really did it, huh?"

Mak slumped. "I did," she said, barely above a whisper.

"You let 'em use me to get her."

"I couldn't lose you," Mak said, looking down, her voice heavy with shame.

"I know," Herald said, letting go of the dagger to take Mak's hand in both of her own. "Jus' . . . damn it, Mak. I came lookin' for you, you know?"

"I'm sorry," Mak whispered, tears running down her face.

"Mak," I said coldly, interrupting their reunion. "Get this cage open."

Mak wiped her face but didn't hesitate to obey. The cage was held shut by a thick chain secured by a robust-looking padlock. Mak studied it for a second. "Do you know where the key is?" she asked Herald.

"Uh . . ." Herald said, blinking between me and Mak. "Hook behind th' door. What's goin' on?"

"Later," I said. "Let us get you out first."

"Nah-ah," Herald said, as Mak found the key and went for the lock. "Mak, whass with you?" Her voice became low and sad. "I know they hurt you, but . . ."

"Tell her," I told Mak. "I do not have any patience for dancing around this."

Mak looked at me, her eyes pleading, but when I didn't say anything else, she took a deep breath and swallowed. "Draka and me," she said to Herald, "we had a talk after she broke us out. About how I've treated her. And how I will treat her in the future."

I snorted. "Good enough," I said. "Will that do for now, Herald?"

She looked like she wanted to push it, then relented. "Yeah, okay. For now," she said.

Mak finally got the cage open and helped Herald to crawl out. "Dammit, Mak," Herald whispered again, then grabbed her sister and pulled her in for a long, tight hug. "Thank you," she said into Mak's shoulder, then went silent as Mak hugged her back. They stayed like that for a while, silent. I wouldn't even have known that Herald was crying except for the way her body would sometimes give a small shake in Mak's arms.

"It's all right." Mak's own voice quavered as she spoke. "It's all over now."

It took a little while before Herald got herself under control, wiping her eyes and standing with some difficulty. I got my first good look at her, and was horrified. Herald had always been an athletic girl, but now she was almost skeletal, her limbs looking thin and her cheeks sunken. Between her drunkenness and her general weakness, she could barely stand. Besides that, her clothes were stained with blood and full of slashes.

"What did they do to you," I asked, my words clipped with barely restrained rage.

"Can't you see that?" she asked and giggled unnervingly. "They healed me. Over and over. And between that . . ."

She didn't finish the sentence. She didn't need to. And while I didn't forgive Mak, I understood why she broke.

I was starting to feel a little unsteady, so I let Mak heal me enough to at least stop the bleeding. It took a lot out of her, and I didn't dare use her more than that. Someone needed to help Herald walk, leaving me free to fight if needed.

When we left the room our captive was nowhere to be seen. He'd gotten a respectable distance, almost halfway across the atrium, when I grabbed him by the ankle.

Dragging him back toward the sisters, I told him, "If you make yourself useful we may find a potion to fix your knee. Or I might at least leave you alive. But try to escape again, and I will kill you, and it will be bad. Do you understand me?"

"Yeah," he said hoarsely, "I understand."

I left him on the floor with Mak and Herald, neither of whom looked like they would hesitate to finish him off if I let them.

The boss's "office" was finely decorated, though it didn't look so much like a place to work as it did a lounge. Four low couches sat on a rich carpet, surrounding an equally low table of lacquered wood. While there was a shelf with a multitude of scrolls and books on it, none of them seemed to be ledgers or anything like that. Instead, from what I could tell with my quick flipping, they were a mixture of informational texts on various subjects and fiction, ranging from epic poems to outright smut. But I didn't care about those. My nose had caught a wonderful scent the moment I opened the door. There was gold hidden here, and I wasn't going to give up until I found it.

My first thought was that there must be a secret drawer or something in the table. The scent was stronger there, but after flipping the damn thing over, it became clear that there was no room for a drawer anywhere. The legs were pretty thick and with some effort I broke them off, but no dice there either. No hollows full of coins, just solid wood. I tore the couches open, too, but all I got for my effort was the satisfaction of destroying that woman's stuff.

"Havin' fun?" Herald asked, leaning heavily against the doorframe.

"There is gold here," I told her, tearing the stuffing out of the last couch. "I am going to rob that bitch blind."

"Prolly . . . *probably* ain't 'er real house," Herald pointed out.

She was probably right, and that just made me angrier. "Whatever she has got stashed here, I am taking it!" I snarled, heaving the remains of the couch into a wall with a loud crash.

"Okay, okay." I could tell that Herald was trying to calm me down, but it wasn't working. I wanted to *hurt* that woman. I wanted to feed her her own fingers. But that would come later. Right now I'd have to be satisfied with taking what was hers.

Just like she did to me, a voice whispered in the back of my head. I couldn't even tell if it was me or my dragon. It didn't matter. I'd stopped pretending. The Herald was *mine*. Mak was *mine*. The rest of them were *mine*! And that arrogant piece of shit had stolen from me! Taking me prisoner was secondary at this point. They never had a hope of holding me. They should have killed me when they had the chance, or at least kept me sedated. Instead, all they had done was bring me into their midst, and then they had set a handful of weaklings and goddamn *children* to guard me, instead of their finest warriors. The gall of it! The fucking *disrespect*!

I was going to make that woman suffer.

"Draka. Draka!"

The Herald's shout brought me out of my own head.

"You get it all out yet?" she asked, and it took me a moment to understand what she meant.

The room was trashed. I'd smashed the couches to pieces, the surface of the table was cracked, and I had torn down half of the shelves. Books and scrolls lay strewn across the floor, some of them smeared with blood from where they must have hit me as they fell.

"Oughta check behind the books," she said. "You got a good start."

I wanted to snap something at her, but it was a solid suggestion. Behind the bookcase was pretty much the only place left.

I emptied the shelves quickly, but there was nothing obvious there. Fine. I leaped up and grabbed the edge of the whole damn piece, and swung myself back so that it toppled, crashing down on top of the scattered debris and exposing the wall. Something *thunked* as it fell.

Jackpot.

About waist high on a human, there was a cubby in the wall. I looked at the back of the bookshelf, and there was an obvious panel that could be slid up to expose the cubby. At the bottom corner of the cubby was a metal tube, and a small bolt was embedded deep into the back of the bookshelf. A trap! Cute. I wondered if it would have gone through my scales if I'd opened the panel. The thing had gone through some pretty thick wood.

I looked into the cubby, and smiled.

"Mak," I called over my back. "Go to the kitchen. Bring me a bag."

Twenty minutes later we walked out the front door into a courtyard. Mak had proven herself useful by finding not only a decent-sized bag but some food for Herald and herself, and they both looked a little better for it.

Herald, apparently feeling merciful in her drunkenness, had convinced me not to kill our captive by pointing out that he could carry the bag with our loot while Mak supported them both. She'd even talked me into letting Mak pour some healing potion we'd found on his knee, to start the healing, before using the rest on my wounded wing joint. And so, three humans instead of two, all look-ing the worse for wear, two of them supported by the smallest by far in the group, stepped out into the wide, cobbled street in front of the property. The sword was back in the captive's scabbard, but with a complex knot around the hilt, which Mak called a "peace-tie." This made the weapon impossible to draw quickly and legal to carry in the city. Other than that, they were unarmed, with my presence being enough for the captive to promise to behave. They moved slowly, since one of them still had a ruined knee and another was staggering, barely staying on her feet. With no obvious observers, nor any hidden ones likely to be focused on the three humans, I snuck out and disappeared into the nearest shadow.

What I *wanted* to do was wait in the shadows of the house until the woman showed up, and make her watch as I tore out her entrails. The smart thing might have been to go back down into the depths and make my escape through the water, or try to float myself out on the boat. But in their states, Herald and Mak couldn't go out that way. I was not going to let them out of my sight, and secrecy was sec-ondary to getting them to safety. I'd prefer not to be seen, but anyone who tried to get in the sisters' way as they headed to the Gray Wolves' quarters would regret it.

So, there I was, finally in Karakan. I wasn't exactly strolling down the streets, but I was there. It was something. We were in the eastern part of the city, on the hill. The cobbled street we were on wound its way down, with steep, narrow stairs giving more direct routes downhill. And while we weren't anywhere near the top of the hill, whenever I shifted back, the view from up there was still great, with the harbor and the western city beyond visible between the buildings or across one of the several tiny plazas that dotted this part of the city. Most of the city was a mix of sandstone and wood, but almost all of the roofs were red tile, so I looked out across a sea of tans and grays, browns and reds. Trees poked up here and there, and laundry and colorful awnings hung in the still air. I would have loved to take a minute to just get up higher, where my view would be unobstructed, to take it all in. Instead, I was scurrying from shadow to shadow, moving deep into alleys, shifting back and forth and pushing whenever I could to merge two shadows and let me pass without showing myself.

While there weren't many people on the street, there were some. I had to move in bursts, letting the others go ahead while I waited for an opportunity and then catch up. It wasn't perfect by any means, doing this in the middle of the day. I was sure that I'd been spotted. I didn't think anyone got a good look at me, but I expected there would be people who weren't sure what they'd seen, and soon rumors would spread of a monster living in the shadows of the upper city. The idea didn't bother me. The slavers had known about me, and they had vastly underestimated me. Maybe this would make them, and others like them, think hard about trying something that stupid again. Hell, maybe I should have piled the corpses I'd made by the gate and declared myself openly, showing what happened to those who challenged me and mine.

But, no. My rage was still there, but it was a cold thing. I would stay in the shadows, where I belonged, and while the average citizens of Karakan would hopefully never notice, I would go to war. I would bring down such pain and terror on the organization that had imprisoned and tortured *my* people that any survivors would never sleep in the dark again. I was going to find out who the woman that smelled of jasmine was. I was going to find what she loved and take it from her. I was going to find what she feared, and give it to her. And when she was alone and broken . . .

Well, idle musings aside, I hadn't gotten that far yet.

Down the street, ahead of my humans, a group moved. They were jogging up the nearly empty street, and as they got closer their uniform appearance became clear. They were city guards, armed and lightly armored. There were a dozen of them. Mak stopped and searched for me anxiously in the shadows until I showed myself briefly and she relaxed, turning back to the approaching guards.

Their leader, a man distinguished by a red sash worn diagonally across his chest, stopped his group thirty feet in front of the trio. "Halt, citizens," he said, raising his hand palm up. "In the name of the city, I require your cooperation."

CHAPTER NINE

Streets of Karakan

I am Captain Vakkal of the city guard," said the leader of the group, blocking my humans' way. "There have been reports of a severe disturbance at an estate higher on Cloud Street. Answer my questions quickly and to my satisfaction, and you can be on your way."

Mak glanced my way. "Of course, captain. But please, be quick. This man is injured."

"So he is," the captain said, his suspicion clear. "What happened?"

To my surprise, the captive spoke up. "A vicious animal, captain," he said. "A night black nightmare of claws and teeth! I was running an errand for my mistress when it attacked me. I barely fended it off, and then these women found me and offered to help. We were just on our way to report the attack."

"I see," the captain said thoughtfully. "And the two of you? What are you doing here?"

"What?" Herald slurred. "Can't walk inna streets anymore?"

"Quiet!" Mak hissed at her, then said tiredly, "Captain, as you can see, my sister is drunk, and I was just bringing her home when we found this man bleeding in the street. Her sweetheart is with the army in the south, and the worry got too much for her. She used to come up here with him. Please don't judge a lovesick girl too harshly."

The captain's expression softened. "I understand. My own daughter's betrothed is with the army as well. But, one more question. What is in the bag?"

Mak and the captive both froze. Herald barely seemed to have heard.

"My errand—" our captive said.

"Go on, just show me and we can be off," the captain said, gesturing for them to approach.

The captive hesitated. "Ah . . . can we . . . can we do this away from the ladies? It's sensitive."

"Fine," the captain said. "Lorra, help the man."

I watched the captive carefully as a guardsman helped him limp away from Herald and Mak together with the captain. When he spoke he lowered his voice so that I couldn't hear, making me even more suspicious. I prepared, if necessary, to shift back and turn this into a bloodbath. But the captive surprised me again. After a short exchange, he was led back and handed over for Mak to support again. The bag remained unopened.

"Well, everything seems to be in order," the captain said. "Apologies for delaying you. There is no need to report the animal attack, just get yourself to a healer quickly. Good day, citizens!"

With that, the captain led his troop up the street and away from the trio, some of the guards casting curious and suspicious looks back.

"Come here," I ordered from the shadows when the street was clear. They obediently limped over. "What did you say?" I asked the captive.

The captive saw the displeasure on my face and swallowed. "I told him who my boss was, and that she would not like her delivery being delayed."

"That boss being the same woman who so stupidly took me and my *friends*"—I looked at Mak pointedly—"prisoner? Who is she?" I asked.

"She's called the Night Blossom. I don't know her real name, but some of the guards are in her purse." He swallowed again. "I gambled."

I slowly showed him my teeth, and he and Mak both flinched away slightly. "Congratulations," I told him. "Your gamble paid off, and you get to live another couple of hours. Maybe longer, if you remain useful and do not tell anybody anything about me." I turned to Mak. "Now, get everybody to Rallon and the Wolves."

Herald, who was only half conscious at the time, lifted her head and gave me an unreadable look when I commanded Mak. I ignored the pang of regret that I felt and melted back into the shadows. We needed to have a proper conversation about what had happened, the three of us, and I wasn't looking forward to it.

The presence of the guards had cleared the street very effectively, and I could keep up with the others more easily for a while. But soon the number of people increased again, until it started to turn into a crowd, with people throwing curious or concerned looks at the small group—a short woman supporting a drunk girl and an injured man. The cobbles changed to a smooth, unadorned style, rather than the patterned ones we'd seen so far. We'd moved into a lower, denser and, no doubt, less wealthy part of the city, where the buildings were taller and more tightly packed, and private residences gave way to combined workshop-homes and what looked like some ancient style of apartment building. With the number of people in the streets, there was no way that I would be able to move quickly without giving myself away.

Mak seemed to realize the same thing, stopping and moving the group into the mouth of a deeply shaded archway that opened to a courtyard. "We will keep moving," she said into the shadows. She looked in my general direction, so she must have figured out how to distinguish me from the natural shade of the buildings. "This street leads to a small square. Turning left on that square onto a similar sized street takes you past many warehouses. The Gray Wolves have converted one into their lodgings. They have a sign up, so you cannot miss it."

I shifted back for just long enough to tell her, "Go. Keep the prisoner alive. I will come when I can."

Mak nodded, and then left with the others.

I found my way up onto a nearby roof, taking the risk of shifting out of the shadows to heave myself over the edge and into the light. A tan cat had been sunning itself there, and sprang three feet in the air before tearing off, leaping from roof to roof as it got as far from me as it could. The roof had a fairly high edge and no nearby buildings that overlooked it, so I thought I might be able to remain unseen there until nightfall. There was a raised hatch that allowed access, but I dealt with it by curling up on it. If anyone was determined enough to open the hatch that they pushed me off . . . I'd deal with it.

By nightfall the crowds in the street had thinned out considerably, though there were still people outside. There were oil lamps burning every couple of dozen yards along the main street, but they seemed to be more to show where the street ran than for any real illumination. I glided along the street, not bothering to hide or keep away from passersby; I was exhausted, though I'd mostly slept away the hours since I'd separated from the three humans. It was an emotional exhaustion, as much as a physical or mental one. I had been in a constant state of anger ever since I woke in that cell, and it had worn me down.

Can you do anything? I asked into the silence of my own head, but all I received in return was incredulous confusion. I was sure that my dragon must have been doing something with my emotions, but she'd been absent since before Mak lured me into the ambush that led to all of this.

That thought made me wonder if I should have just killed Mak in her cell, but when I remembered how Herald had cried into her shoulder, I was glad that I hadn't. I couldn't see how I could ever truly trust her again, but . . . it was Mak. Mak, who had never truly trusted me, but also Mak, whose first instinct every time she saw me hurt was to ask if I needed help. Mak, who just wanted Herald to be safe and happy.

I hoped to whatever gods might be listening that she wouldn't make me kill her.

The square at the end of the street wasn't all that small. There were some slightly fancier buildings facing it, probably higher-end shops or inns or whatever. A larger street left the square on each side, and they weren't symmetrically placed, nor were any of them centered, which bothered me more than could possibly be reasonable. I took the left-hand street, and a couple hundred yards down, just like Mak had said, was a warehouse among other warehouses, which was unmistakably the Gray Wolves' base of operations. Not only was it the only one with armed guards and two large flaming pots outside, but a sign had been erected above the door featuring a gray wolf, midstride.

The problem here was that I didn't know how many or which of the Wolves actually knew about me. It might be all of them at this point. I hadn't exactly been inconspicuous the first time I "supported" them, way back when they raided that bandit camp. But, there was no point in just showing myself and demanding to be let in, in case word hadn't spread and someone decided to be an idiot and try something violent.

I was already exhausted from staying in shadow form for so long. At best, I could manage another few minutes. I swept into the alley flanking the place. The second floor had a row of windows, about four yards up from the ground. Most of them were lit, but at the far end I could see one that was dark and open, which I took as an invitation. There was a guard in the alley, but that wasn't a problem. I passed him with no reaction. Below the window I stretched myself up the wall, elongating until I just barely managed to reach the windowsill, and that was all I needed to pull myself up. I entered a small, darkened room with the feel of an office, and shifted back with a sigh.

I was not alone, but with an invitation like that, I hadn't expected to be. Still, Garal clearly hadn't expected me to just appear out of the darkness like that, and nearly fell off the chair he was sitting on.

"Mercies, Draka!" he hissed once he recovered himself. "I damn near pissed myself! Where did you come from?"

"I got in through the window, of course," I told him. And it was absolutely true. "Did no one tell you how good I am at sneaking?"

"There's sneaking," he said, "and then there's whatever that was. I don't think even Rib could have done better." He paused, then said, "Do you mind if I light a candle? You're barely a silhouette."

"Go ahead," I told him, blinking over to regular vision as he struck some light. "Where are the Herald and Mak?"

"Gods, you've grown," he said as he looked at me, and then answered my question. "Sleeping. What happened to them? Herald passed out drunk as soon as we got some food into her. Mak won't talk about it, and she made us promise not to interrogate the prisoner until you got here. All she'd say was that we have a traitor among us and that she and Herald were kept prisoner somewhere. Then she ate enough for two men twice her size and passed out in the middle of the day."

"It can wait until they are awake," I told him. "Where are they? I want to see them."

"In the infirmary," he said. "But there are people—"

I locked eyes with him. "Then clear them out," I said, interrupting him and biting out each word. "I want to see them. Anyone who has already seen me is fine."

He raised his hands, speaking gently. "All right. You just relax and wait here. I'll see what I can do."

He opened the door onto the second floor of the warehouse, where cloth partitions had been set up to section off beds with some sort of privacy. I heard him issuing orders, telling people to clear out into the street until he told them that they could come in again. There was some grumbling, but when he sharpened his tone he was obeyed, judging by the sound of hurried dressing and boots crossing the floor to scurry down a set of wooden stairs. Soon I heard him give the same orders downstairs, his voice loud and surprisingly clear even through the floorboards.

"Come on," he called up the stairs after a while. "It's clear all the way to the infirmary."

Walking on the wooden floor felt strange. I was used to my claws digging into soil or clicking on stone, but here there was a little bit of resistance with each step as the tips of my claws sunk in, and then they stuck just slightly when I lifted my feet. I ended up having to pull my claws in as much as I could and then lift the tips of my toes as I walked. It was less uncomfortable than having my claws pulled on every step.

The stairs presented another problem. In my limited experience with stairs, I'd usually been able to just jump down, but these were too narrow and too long. I suddenly understood why dogs had such trouble with the damn things. I very much wanted to shift and flow down the stairs, but Garal wasn't supposed to know what I could do, and I wanted to keep it that way. Mak's betrayal had made me reevaluate how much I could trust the people I thought were my friends, and as amiable as Garal was, I didn't actually know the man.

I ended up carefully sidling down the steps like a nervous animal. It was not my most dignified moment, but Garal wisely kept a straight face.

It seemed that everyone slept on the second floor, because the first was sectioned into an armory, a training area, a mess, and various other smaller areas that I couldn't identify. I could see Boot and Arlal, two of the mercenaries that I'd worked with, in the armory. They were tending to equipment and waved uncertainly as I came down the stairs. I acknowledged them with a dip of my head before Garal led on.

The infirmary was one of the few areas that was in a fully separate room, behind a sturdy wooden door. Inside were several beds, though only two were occupied. Herald and Mak slept next to each other, Lalia sitting next to Mak, watching her sadly with her hands clasped in her lap. She looked up as we entered. She must have been prepared when Garal cleared the place out, but her face still turned stormy when she saw me.

"What happened?" she hissed at me quietly, rising from her chair to approach me. "You weren't there at the lake in the morning, and then I come back in to find my friends in our infirmary!"

"*Fuck you*," I hissed right back at her, throwing all of my simmering anger and frustration into it. God, it felt good, and the tone was enough to make both Lalia and Garal take a step back, with Lalia visibly reconsidering her attitude, perhaps realizing that she was unarmed in a small room with me between her and the only door. "Last night I got smashed in the head with a sledgehammer, and then I had to break *your friends* out of a slaver prison. That is what happened. That is where I was this morning."

I realized that I'd been stalking toward Lalia, driving her back, when her boot bumped against an empty bed. "All right, all right," she said quickly, her attitude melting in the face of my anger, palms out toward me as she tried to make some distance between us. "Sorry. I do that. I get angry when I'm worried, yeah? Lots of that going around, all right?"

"Yeah," I said noncommittally. With the pecking order firmly established, I stopped advancing on her. "How are they?"

"Starved and exhausted," Lalia said. "Herald shows signs of overhealing, having been healed over and over again. Her clothes are bloody and full of cuts, from a knife or dagger, probably . . ." Her voice caught in her throat, and I saw her eyes shimmer with tears before they turned hard and angry instead. "Mak's hands are a mess. She must have been healing them as much as she could, but we can only hope that it's enough. Her nails are mostly gone. She whimpered when I tried to touch her. I don't want to imagine what they've gone through."

Garal picked up when Lalia stopped. "I was here when they came in," he said. "I couldn't speak to Herald—she was so drunk and exhausted that we could barely feed her—but Mak was . . . She's different. Twitchy. Broken, almost." He looked at Lalia. "It's worse than when we met her."

"That bad?" Lalia asked, and when she turned to look at Mak this time, a few silent tears ran down her cheek. Garal put his arm around Lalia and drew her to him.

I watched them and looked at the women on their beds, and all I felt was the anger boiling in my gut.

CHAPTER TEN

Coming To Terms

I lay curled at the foot of Herald's bed until she woke up. I was awoken by a pitiful groan, which made me look up just in time to see and hear a wide-eyed scream, the screech of wood on stone, and the flapping of sheets as Herald threw herself out of her bed, eyes wild and arms flailing. She scrambled across the floor until she hit the wall and ended up huddled in the corner in only a night shirt, breathing heavily and staring blindly around the room while she slowly took in where she was.

I approached her carefully, and while she looked in my direction, she didn't really see me. "Just a dream," she whispered, closing her eyes and pressing herself into the corner. "They got me out. Just a dream."

"*It is all right, Herald,*" I told her in Tekereteki, but she just sat there, taking deep, slow breaths as Mak sat up in bed and Lalia came rushing in through the door. She continued repeating the phrase until we were all huddled a short distance from her, giving her some room. She started breathing more normally as her eyes opened and slowly focused on each of us. She sat silent as Mak crept forward carefully and put her arms around her, pulling her in and stroking her hair.

"My head hurts," Herald groaned weakly into Mak's shoulder.

"Yeah, I know," Mak said.

"And I feel sick."

"You've been very drunk for a few days," Mak told her, ignoring the other things that had happened during that time. "That's what happens when you sober up."

"We'll get some nice, fatty food in you, all right?" Lalia said, inching closer. "Some oily fish and some sausages. And some tea for the pain. How's that sound?"

"Okay," Herald said, pulling Mak closer, then looked at me as Lalia rose and left the room. "Draka. You came."

"Of course I did," I told her.

"How did you find us?"

I saw Mak stiffen a little. I'd seen how ashamed she was of what she'd done, willingly or not. It was hard not to pity her. "They captured me," I told Herald. "Then I got loose and killed every bastard in that house, except the cook and the man we captured."

"We captured someone?" Herald asked weakly. "Oh. Right. I do not remember much. Just . . . pain." She closed her eyes and swallowed hard, her hand going to her belly.

Mak hugged her tighter. "It's all right now. We don't need to talk about it now. You don't even need to think about it. Plenty of time later."

"Yeah, okay," Herald said. "Later sounds good. Thank you, Draka. For getting us out. Thank you."

"They would not have taken you if they did not want me," I told her flatly. "And I am sorry for that. All I can do is to promise that this Night Blossom woman, and everyone around her, will regret it."

Lalia came back in, carrying two bundles of clothes, which she handed over, and announced that she'd told the cook to prepare his best hangover breakfast. "You too," she told Mak as the sisters dressed. "Mercies, you're both rail thin. Let's get some meat back on your bones."

"We're coming," Mak said, helping Herald to her feet and handing her over to Lalia. "Get my sister fed, would you, Lalia? I want to talk to Draka first." She looked at me, and I nodded.

Lalia looked between the two of us and put her hand gently on Herald's arm. "C'mon, Herald," she said. "Food's waiting."

"Great," Herald said, without conviction, then looked at Mak and me. "Go easy on her," she said, not bothering to specify whom she was talking to. As they left she pulled at the bag of a shirt she was wearing, looking down to ask Lalia, "These are men's clothes, are they not?" and getting an apologetic noise back.

Once the door closed behind the two, a change came over Mak. She didn't relax, exactly, now that she was alone with me rather than comforting her traumatized younger sister. But she didn't have to put on a brave face anymore. She didn't have to pretend to be whole. While her expression, the whole way that she held herself, was full of shame and no small amount of fear, some kind of tension had been released.

I waited for her to speak. After a few attempts to start, she sat down on the edge of the bed behind her. Even with me sitting on the floor, I had already been looking down at her, and now when she looked up at me, she looked so very small. Her face was a mask of pain.

"I won't ask for your forgiveness," she said thickly, "but I want you to understand what happened, and why."

I waited impassively for her to go on. I was trying to keep an open mind, but I didn't see what she could say to change anything.

"Everything that happened was my fault," she began, her eyes roaming around the room as though searching for the right words. "I recognize that. The Night Blossom was the one who gave the orders, but I gave her the means and the opportunity. I went out and got drunk, because I didn't trust Herald, or you, to keep her safe, and rather than talk or do anything about it, I tried to kill my worries with wine. I used to do that a lot. I've been better recently, but . . ."

She looked at me. I looked back, still waiting for her to say something that would make me care, make me feel a shred of regret for the way I treated her.

"You don't care about that," she said. "And why should you? Those are my own failings. I just want you to know that I never told them anything that they could use, never agreed to do anything to help them. No matter how they abused me, not even when they broke my fingers and tore out my nails."

I could see her hands twitch with remembered pain.

"Not until they brought in Herald. Do you know what they did, Draka? They sat her across the table from me. Let her get a good look at what they'd done. They put a healing potion on the table, and then they stabbed her in the gut. And while she screamed and bled on the floor, they told me that if I told them how to find you, they'd let me give her that potion." She looked up at me, her eyes as empty as the night she'd betrayed me. "I still held out. I held out until she stopped screaming, and just cried. I think I did pretty well, don't you?"

She gave me a hollow smile, and a little voice inside me actually agreed with her. Yeah. That was pretty impressive.

"Then I talked, and they unshackled me so I could give her the potion. And they didn't touch me after that. They just put me in that cell where you found me." She was speaking more easily now, like she was retelling a story she'd heard, not something that happened to her and her sister. "But the next day they manacled me to that table again, and they brought her back in. She was drunk, and pale. They must have kept feeding her more potion. Hard to say, but the torturer really made a mess of her with his dagger, so she would have needed a lot of healing. She said something nasty, I don't remember what, and he broke her nose, then kicked her around a little. It was almost comical. He's such an angry little guy, with a squeaky voice. You remember, from the forest? Anyway, then he put a healing potion on the table. And he took out his dagger. And when she was screaming and bleeding again, he told me that they wanted me to write a message. So I did."

Her eyes had become unfocused at that point, her voice slipping into a droning monotone.

"They'd grabbed her off the street when she went looking for me. They wanted me to know that. That she was only there because of me. Then, the next day, or at least I think it was the next day, it was hard to tell down there, they locked me to that table. And they put a potion in front of me. I promised them that I would do anything, if only they didn't hurt Herald. It didn't matter what they asked. I'd do anything they wanted. And then while Herald was screaming on the floor, the little man said that they needed my help to bring you in. I agreed. I tried to be helpful. I made suggestions. And it worked pretty well, I think, until you just walked out of your chains and turned the place into a slaughterhouse. I didn't expect that. If I'd known, I would have warned them. Because the little man told me that from then until we returned, he would make sure that Herald kept screaming. And if we didn't bring you with us, we'd just have to try again the next night, and the next."

She turned her eyes toward me, but stared right through me.

"I can't tell you how grateful I am that you showed up that first night."

Then she blinked, and a shiver ran through her before she said, "That's why I betrayed you. And if they had me back at that table, with a potion in front of me, I would do everything in my power to help them again."

"*Jesus Fucking Christ*, Mak," I said, though it didn't feel like it was me saying it but some distant, buried part that still felt useless things like pity and sympathy. I believed every word she'd said. I'd expected tears, begging, and excuses. Not this. I knew that the bastards had tortured them, but what the hell did I know about torture? Intellectually I understood the idea. You do cruel things to someone to make them tell you what you want to hear, or make them do what you want them to do. It sounded pretty straightforward. But sitting there with Mak, seeing how she just went somewhere else as she talked about it . . .

"I understand," I told her. "I might even be able to forgive you, someday. But you understand that I can never trust you completely again? If you have to choose between me and Herald?"

"I do," she said, and slid down from the bed so that she was on her knees in front of me. "And you shouldn't. But I'll do whatever I can to earn back whatever trust you can spare for me. I swear on my life. But . . . you understand?"

"Yeah," I said.

"And as long as Herald is safe, we shouldn't have a problem, right?" she said, with a glint of hope in her eyes.

"Probably," I said, though if it were Tam instead, or someone else she loved, who knew?

She inched forward until we were barely a foot apart. She had to lean her head all the way back to look me in the eyes. "And you think it's possible that, one day, you might forgive me?"

"Yeah. Maybe. One day."

She reached out tentatively with one hand. I noticed that her fingers, for all the healing, were still nailless, the joints swollen. When I didn't pull back or reprimand her, she put her hand on my chest, then silently stood and put her arms around me, pressing her face into the scales of my shoulder.

"Thank you," she whispered. "Please don't kill me. Not until you've forgiven me."

I didn't know what to say to that. I just defaulted to what I felt. "Please do not give me a reason to," I told her, and I felt her nod into my shoulder.

I curled my neck around her. It felt natural. For all the anger that I was still holding onto, I needed that hug almost as much as she did.

After I let Mak go and eat, I expected to be alone for a while, but it didn't take long for Garal to slip through the door, closing it behind him.

"Would you like to get out of here?" he asked, jerking his head toward the exit. "I could tell the soldiers to clear out again."

I could hear people outside bustling, talking, laughing . . . pretty much the sounds of several dozen men and women having breakfast and getting ready for the day.

"No," I told him. "I can wait until they have eaten at least."

"As you wish," he said, sitting down on one of the beds. "I was hoping that we might talk," he continued after a short silence.

"About what?" I said, with more snap than he deserved. I didn't mind talking to Garal. Other than his inexplicable love for Lalia, he seemed like a decent guy, and besides that, I just liked looking at him.

"Tam told me about your adventure in the north," he said with an easy grin, deflecting my irritation. "That sounded like a decent experience. Lucrative."

I snorted. "True enough."

"And there was something about you killing five trolls and eating their hearts?" he went on.

"One troll. I killed the one troll and ate her heart," I protested. "I was just part of the team for the other four. If you want to be really picky, I think Tam got the killing blow on two, Val on one, and Mak on the last one."

"Congratulations all the same," he said. "Five of you going up against five trolls and all coming out alive is a real accomplishment. And as much as I love those four, I doubt they could have done it without you."

"Flatterer," I told him, my anger cooling somewhat. "Go on. Keep telling me how great I am."

"Lalia told me that you wrestled a monstrous bear."

"I did! It probably would have eaten me if your girl had not come back to help me, though."

"She made sure to tell me that too," he said, still smiling.

"I am sure she did." I said, then, "Garal, you know her better than anyone else, right?"

"Better than anyone you know, for sure. Yes."

"What the fuck is wrong with her?"

Garal's smile faltered and he looked vaguely uncomfortable. "Would you like to elaborate on that?" he asked.

"She has been an utter bitch to me since the first time I met her," I told him, and he turned his face slightly with a pained look. "We have had moments where we kind of got along, sure, but last night the first thing I got from her was a thinly veiled accusation. Does she just not have a survival instinct, or what?"

"She's very protective. But you wouldn't have hurt her," Garal said, though he didn't sound entirely sure of himself.

"Garal," I told him flatly. "I was literally seconds from killing Mak yesterday, and I have spent weeks learning to like Mak." That made him slowly lift his head and look at me. "If I had not had hours to cool off before I came here, I might have killed Lalia just for talking to me the way she did. I am not telling you this as a threat, though you really should let her know. I'm telling you this because I honestly want to know: What *the fuck* is wrong with her? She knows what I am. She must have heard from Rib and Pot and the others what I did to the slavers and the valkin, and the troll for that matter. What does she think will happen if she actually tries me again, or if she pushes me too far at the wrong time?"

"You wouldn't kill anyone over some insulting words," he said confidently.

"Are you sure? You may be the first person I met here, but you do not really know me."

"No. Sadly, I don't. And I'd like to change that. But I know Tam, and Val, and Herald, and they all vouch for your character. Even Mak, who has always been very careful in how she speaks about you, doesn't think you're a monster, or some thin-skinned thug. When I say that I don't think that you'd kill or even harm someone without good reason, I rely on their judgment. As for offering you violence . . . well. She did it before, and you restrained yourself. I can only hope that she never does it again, or that you are as strong then as you've been before. I truly do love her, Draka, and I would hate for you and I to become enemies."

"Me too," I told him honestly. "So please talk to Lalia before she does something we will both regret."

He nodded, then said, "Did you mean what you said? About almost killing Mak? Were you serious?"

"Completely."

"Mercies, Draka. Why?"

"You said you do not think that I would kill anyone without good reason."

"I did."

"I had a good reason. If you need details you can ask her, and she will tell you if she wants to. Her shame is her own."

Garal shook his head. "I'm not sure that I want to know. Can I ask why you didn't?"

Because I made her so terrified that something in her broke, I thought. But I wasn't going to tell him that. "For the Herald," I said instead. "And for Tam and Val and you, and for the good times we shared. And because I could use her."

"I never expected this side of you," Garal said, but the look on his face wasn't fear or disappointment. It was a kind of dispassionate appraisal, like he was seeing me for the first time and sizing me up.

"Me neither," I told him. "But I guess crucibles form character, or however that goes." I wasn't sure where I'd heard that, but it came to me like it should have been familiar. "Or maybe that sledgehammer to my head shook something loose."

Whatever it was, I hadn't been myself ever since I was captured. Or maybe I was more myself than I'd been for months. I wasn't sure which possibility worried me more.

CHAPTER ELEVEN

Ardek

I waited in the infirmary until all the Wolves who were going out on patrol had left, and there was a window of opportunity before another patrol was expected to return. I amused myself by messing with my magic. Manipulating shadows had become so second nature over the last several weeks that I barely thought about it anymore, but that also meant that I hadn't actively worked on figuring out my limits. I knew that I could nearly cover a weak light source if I started from darkness, but the infirmary was bright. The two windows weren't glass, instead covered with some kind of organic membrane that I couldn't see through, but they let in plenty of light.

There were still shadows, though. Even if I had been in a bare room with a dozen one hundred-watt lights surrounding me, all I would need to do was get close enough to the floor and I'd have something to work with, if I could just handle the pain and exhaustion of pushing as hard as necessary. Here, every bed had darkness beneath it. So did the cabinets. The solid frame of the bookcase, which sat against one wall with various scrolls and bottles in it, cast part of every shelf in shadow. And then there were the unlit lanterns in the ceiling, the chest against the wall opposite the windows, even the corners. I had plenty to work with.

On a whim I looked down and focused on my own shadow. It wasn't particularly sharp or dark, but I could fix that. Looking down at myself, I could see a glow gathering in my chest. It was an odd thing to see. Depth perception told me that I was seeing something inside of myself, past skin and bone and muscle, yet I saw it as clearly as if I were made of glass. Then it released, flowing out of me in a tide of darkness, not in a specific direction or through a particular limb, but from every part of me, as though I had a gold-limned shadow coming from every pore. If I had pores. I wasn't sure that I did. I didn't have any hair, obviously, and I hadn't noticed myself sweating, so maybe not.

I wonder where all the heat went when I ran or flew.

Even with my thoughts running away from me, I still maintained enough focus to deepen my shadow and make it stretch and merge with the darkness under the nearest bed. I grunted with satisfaction. Two months ago, allowing my focus to slip at all would have messed everything up. Now, I could both watch how the magic flowed and swirled as it made the shadow do my bidding, and wonder if lizards or other reptiles could sweat.

With the shadows connected, I focused on myself and tried to shift. There was still too much resistance. The room was too bright, my shadow not dark enough. I dug deeper, drawing in more power and letting it flow out of me in the form of an ever-deeper darkness, forcing the light away until I, in the middle of the room, was covered in shadow. My head began to pound, and I was beginning to grow faint, but I kept pushing until the resistance finally gave, and I shifted. My world immediately shrunk into the short stretch of darkness between me and the bed, everything outside being too drenched in light for me to see. I quickly slipped under the bed, which I hadn't fully expected to work. The beds only had a couple of inches of clearance from the floor and were a little over six feet long and less than three feet wide. It didn't seem like there would be enough space underneath to fit all of me, but as far as I could tell, no part of me was sticking out.

Then I shifted back, causing my front to smash into the floor and my back to smash into the bed, lifting it and nearly flipping it over as all of my very real, very solid volume had to go somewhere. There was a clatter as I scrambled out and the bed fell back to the floor, but no harm had come to either me or the furniture, as far as I could tell.

All right. Good to know. I could fit in spaces that were too small, then shift back. I should just make sure that I was in a place with some give, because when there's no space for me, my body would damn well *make* space. Or it would try to. I was sure that I wouldn't like the effect if I tried to shift back in a space with less give than my body.

I also noticed that there was a fine scattering of dirt and scale-flakes on the floor where I'd first shifted. I'd never shifted on a clean surface and hung around to see the aftereffects before, but it made sense. If the dirt and the dead bits weren't part of my body, they didn't shift with me. Everything inside me did, though, or there'd be a far more unpleasant mess on the floor.

My train of thought was interrupted when Garal came through the door, probably wondering what the hell all the noise was about. "Is everything all right?" he asked, looking around and finally resting his eyes on the one bed that stood askew.

"I bumped into the bed," I lied.

"Okay," he said, while his tone said, "Yeah, right." "Everybody has finished eating, and the patrol has left. Do you want to see the prisoner?"

"Yeah, that is what I should be doing, is it not?" I said, and he went to clear out the rest of the Wolves remaining on the bottom floor.

Once he'd done so, I met Herald and Mak in the mess. Lalia had left with the soldiers. Garal and Lalia had apparently obtained permission from Rallon to stay as long as I was there, and Garal told me that he'd be coming down himself as soon as he could. Despite having permission to stay, Lalia went out on patrol, both to keep up something of a facade of normalcy and to keep her away from me. The Wolves were obviously going to know that something was going on, considering Garal's odd orders, but hopefully they would just think that there was a normal, *human* visitor who, for whatever reason, needed to be kept secret.

I told Mak to come with me, and asked Herald, who agreed after a thoughtful look that shifted between me and Mak a couple of times. She was going to need a proper explanation, but until she asked for it, I wasn't going to volunteer any information. It was a conversation I wanted to put off as long as I could.

"The warehouse had a strongroom when we took it over," Garal told me as he led the way to the back of the building, somewhere beneath where I'd entered. "We converted it into a lockup for soldiers who show up to duty drunk, get into fights, or other disciplinary problems like that."

It wasn't like a vault or anything, but the door to the lockup was thick and banded with metal. Pot and Med, two of Rallon's scouts, sat just inside the door and greeted us as we entered, Herald and Mak with friendliness, Garal with the respect due someone who outranked them, and me with the respect due someone you desperately don't want on your bad side. Although, to be fair, Pot at least looked excited to see me again.

"We've had two of the command squad scouts on guard since you brought the prisoner in," Garal explained. "The interrogator who accidentally 'killed' the previous one vanished yesterday, soon after Mak and Herald came in together. He took one of the new guys with him. Damn traitors, and we don't know if there's anyone else who's been bought or planted. As much as I hate the idea, there are few we can trust with secrets right now."

"But us, we're special," Pot added happily. "The commander trusts us implicitly, don't he, Med?"

"Wouldn't be on the command squad if he didn't," Med agreed, still looking at me warily.

"Did you talk to the guy?" I asked the room in general.

"Nah," Pot said. "Got him breakfast, but that's it. Hasn't volunteered anything either."

"I asked them to wait until you got here," Mak said. *Great,* I thought. *Very proactive of her.*

"Thanks," I told her, then looked at the Wolves in the room. "Shall we?"

At the other end of the room were two cells facing each other with a narrow aisle separating them. By the bars of the left-hand one sat our prisoner, who'd been watching us silently since we'd come in. He didn't look defiant or angry or anything like that, just thoughtful and apprehensive. But he couldn't hide his fear. The room stank of it.

His knee looked better, but that's magical potions for you.

The lockup was not large. The walk between the two cells was maybe two feet wide, and with five humans and a dragon in there, it got crowded. I took the lead, walking over to the prisoner. He moved back from the bars, his eyes wary.

"Hello," I told him. "I have some questions for you."

"I can hardly believe that you're real," he said, then shook his head. "I can't talk. I never should have helped you at all in the first place. I don't know what came over me."

His refusal was almost amusing, but this was no time for humor or softness. He smelled like prey, and he would obey or face the consequences. "What is your name?" I asked him through the bars.

He hesitated, then said, "Ardek."

"Ardek, you know that it is far too late to change your mind, right?" I asked him.

"You don't understand," he said, "If I tell you anything and she finds out, she—"

"Garal," I said loudly. "Open the cell."

Garal hesitated, and I looked at him with annoyance. "If I wanted to kill him, I could do that from here," I told him. He nodded, then looked to Med, who tossed him a set of keys. Garal opened the lock of the wrapped chains that kept the cell door closed.

I pulled the door open and stepped inside. I knew just how to deal with this.

"Ardek," I said, stopping two feet in front of him, "have you decided to stop being useful to me?"

The temperature in the room seemed to drop in response to the tone of my voice, and the humans behind me fell still and silent.

"I—I'm sorry," Ardek stuttered. "I can't. I can't!"

"Mak," I said. "Come in here."

She did so, slowly, and stood next to me. "*Mak, tear his throat out,*" I said in Tekereteki.

I heard the Herald take a sharp breath outside the cell. "*I have no knife,*" Mak protested haltingly in the same language.

"*You have teeth,*" I told her, and sat down to wait. "*Go on.*"

"Draka, what are you saying?" the Herald said urgently. "This is not funny!"

Mak looked at me, swallowed hard, then looked at Ardek and took one heavy, hesitant step toward him.

"Mak!" the Herald called to her sister. "What are you doing? You cannot . . . Mak, stop!"

Ardek, confused and frightened, looked from me, to Mak, to the Herald. He didn't even try to fight, he just scrambled backward into the corner of the cell, putting another two feet of distance between himself and Mak. "What's going on?" he demanded. "What are they saying?"

Somewhere in the back of my mind a little voice was screaming that I couldn't do this. It was sick. Mak had made a mistake, but she was still my friend, and the Herald's sister. Ardek was just some kid who'd ended up with the wrong crowd. They were both people. They didn't deserve this, either of them. I couldn't do this to them.

The voice got so loud and insistent that it actually began to make me feel a little bad, so I silenced it and said, *"Mak. I'm waiting."*

Mak took another slow step toward Ardek. "I'm sorry," she whispered to him, low enough that only he and I could hear her.

"Mak, please!" the Herald said again, even more urgently, though she didn't come inside the cell. "What is this? Stop!"

The other humans just stood, watching, not understanding any more than Ardek did, though I'm sure they could read the situation. But, he was my prisoner, and the Herald, Mak, and I were victims of the group he belonged to. They clearly weren't going to get involved.

Mak took another heavy step toward Ardek, and he caved. "All right!" he nearly shrieked. "I'll talk! I'll tell you anything! Just get her away from me!"

"Stop!" I commanded, and Mak froze, standing rigid in front of Ardek. I could see her trembling faintly.

Mercies be kind, she would have done it. I told her to tear a man's throat out with her teeth, and she really would have done it.

"Well done, Mak," I told her. "You can go."

Mak fled the cell like a coil unwinding, pushing past the others out of the room. The Herald shot me an agonized look, then followed her sister.

"Now, Ardek," I said, leaning in close, "tell me about the Night Blossom."

Ardek, it turned out, didn't know a whole lot. The Night Blossom recruited mostly from gangs of kids who'd survived to adulthood on the streets. Ardek himself was only nineteen and had only been brought in a month ago, together with three of the guards I'd killed. The younger members were backed up by more experienced heavies, many of whom had two or three fighting-related minor advancements and a few, as I'd seen first-hand, with combat majors as well. Her people, mostly men but a few women as well, were fiercely loyal. He described her as pulling people in. Just being near her was enough to want to make her happy, and I'd felt some of that myself. Other than that, he didn't know much about her. Not her real name, nor her age or background. When pressed, he guessed that she was about thirty, and that she probably didn't grow up rich.

He did know where she made her money. Ardek didn't know anything about trading in slaves, and seemed honestly horrified when I told him what we'd found. The Night Blossom's usual business was vice of all kinds—running brothels, gambling houses, and drinking holes, usually all in one building. Ardek had spent his time working for the Night Blossom doing security at a few such places and, through some utterly shit luck, had been assigned, along with his friends, to the house where I'd found him only days before I happened to them.

I wondered if those friends would be a problem. From what he said, he'd known them for years. They'd been like family to him. I considered killing him right then and there just to nip any potentially annoying attempt at revenge in the bud, but something stopped me. Something about him. Maybe it was the way he smelled, or the way he held himself. It made me certain that he'd told me the truth, and that he'd never dare do anything against me. That made him useful. This feeling had been getting stronger over the hour or so that I spent with him, and was similar to how I felt about Mak, though in her case I had other reasons to spare her.

I left him sitting in his cell. Garal locked the door behind me, then went to clear the way for me. The Herald had come back in at some point, and had been standing silently in the aisle as I spoke to Ardek. Now, as we were leaving, she spoke up.

"*Draka,*" she said in Tekereteki, "*I deserve some answers.*"

"*You do,*" I said with a sigh. We hadn't spoken properly this whole time, and this was how we'd begin. "Unfortunate" didn't begin to cover how I felt about it.

"*My sister cried herself to sleep in the middle of the morning, Draka,*" she said accusingly. "*I tried to ask her about what happened with that prisoner and she just kept saying that she deserved it! What happened? Why is Mak suddenly obeying you, like a . . . a slave or a servant? What happened to my sister? What did you do?*"

Garal returned and led us out. We quickly decided that the cellar would be a better place for me than the infirmary, so he led us there. Once we were alone in the dark, with only a lantern for the Herald to see by, I swallowed my fear and answered her.

"*Mak does deserve what I did, and worse,*" I told her. "*Yesterday I almost killed her.*"

The Herald just stared at me in mute horror, and distantly I felt my heart break.

CHAPTER TWELVE

What Have You Done?

*P**lease tell me that I heard you wrong.*" The Herald's face twisted, not with anger, but with sorrow. "*Please, tell me that you did not just say that you nearly killed my sister.*"

"*I did,*" I told her. "*I had my hand around her throat, and if not for her terror, I would have done it. I will not apologize for that. I do not regret it. But I regret the necessity of what I did.*"

"*By all the gods, Draka,*" the Herald breathed, "*what could possibly justify that?*"

She was so much calmer than I'd expected. Sad and horrified, sure, but I could feel, or perhaps a better word was *smell*, what was bubbling under the surface. She wanted to scream. She wanted to hit me. She wanted to hate me. But she didn't. Perhaps she couldn't. Instead she said, "*Please, tell me why! Do I not deserve to know?*"

"*Of course you do,*" I told her. "*And your love for her and my love for you is one of the reasons Mak is still alive. But it is like I told Garal, her shame is her own. She can give you the details when she is ready, though I think you have an idea already. I can tell you that in the moment I truly believed that she deserved to die for what she had done. I am not sure that I do not still believe it. Mak does. She is ashamed, and she wants to earn my trust back. That is why she does as I tell her.*"

The anger coming off the Herald was sharp and acrid. She wanted to . . . I wasn't even sure. Fight me for dominance? For ownership of Mak? As insane as that notion was. But she didn't show it, not at all. We were friends. We loved each other like sisters. So instead of raging at me, cursing me, challenging me, instead of anything like that she asked, with love and humility, "*Please, Draka. Do not hurt her. Do not mistreat my sister.*"

She stood up from the box she'd been sitting on. Alone together like this I could tell that I'd grown. We were nearly face to face now when I sat with my head held high, with her just taller than me. Rather than look down on me, however slightly, she knelt in front of me. She reached up and took my face in both of her hands, and looked up at me. *"Please. I love her."*

"I know," I said softly. *"Please, Herald. Help her. She will resent me. And I do not want to be angry with her, but I am. I do not want to hurt her, not any more than I have, but I will if I must. Do not let her do anything foolish."*

"I will not," the Herald said with conviction. *"Whatever she did, I will make sure that she does not do it again."*

And just like that, it was clear where her loyalty lay. The little voice at the back of my mind screamed that this wasn't right. She shouldn't be choosing us over the woman who'd loved her and raised her for nearly her whole life. We were doing something to her mind. We must be, whether we knew it, or wanted to, or not. There was no pretending anymore that there was anything normal about this friendship.

I heard the voice, and this time I couldn't silence it. *"Thank you,* Herald," I said, and I meant it in more ways than I could possibly tell her.

We waited in thoughtful silence for a long time, until I broke it. *"The boy, Ardek,"* I said. *"I may have to kill him."*

"What boy? He is older than I am," Herald said reproachfully. We were lying on the floor. She had found an old bolt of cloth and had unrolled it on the floor, using it as a mat as she rested her head on my side.

"That is what you take issue with?" I asked. *"The young man then. I may have to kill him. He knows too much about me."*

"He could be useful, could he not?" Herald asked. *"If you can force him to submit and offer his loyalty."*

"Perhaps," I said. *"But if he betrays one mistress to swear loyalty to another, can he be trusted?"*

"He had not been with the Night Blossom for long," Herald pointed out. *"And I believe that you can offer him more than she did, both in threats and in rewards."*

"Rewards?" I asked.

I felt Herald shrug against me. *"We have the bag of loot,"* she said. *"Think of it as an investment. A dragon should seal his loyalty nicely. It has a nice symmetry to it. A golden dragon if he accepts, a black dragon if he refuses."*

"And if he lies to me?" I asked.

"Then we kill him and take the dragon back. Mak and I can keep an eye on him," she said, a little too casually. It was a transparent attempt to show me how Mak could be useful to me, but it wasn't like I could blame Herald for that. Nor was it a bad idea. A team is almost always stronger than an individual, and I didn't doubt Mak and Herald's ability to keep Ardek in line.

"We will need to explain it to Tam and Val, though, when they get back," Herald continued.

"*We will need to explain more than that,*" I said. Another conversation I wasn't looking forward to. They would find out sooner or later about Mak, and while I didn't know how they might react, I didn't expect it to go well. I didn't have the close relationship with either of them that I did with Herald.

"*It might help if I am the one to speak with them,*" she suggested. "*But on that subject, I should speak to Mak. And not only to see if she is ready to tell me. She will need support.*"

"*You are probably right. Have you spoken to her properly since . . . you know? Garal said that you both just ate and then slept when you came in.*"

"*I have not,*" Herald said, and deflated against me. "*Mak has been evasive, and I have not truly wanted to push the issue. I still . . . Thinking about what happened is painful.*"

I curled my head back and rested it on her chest. "*You are strong. And talking is a step toward healing. You both need this, and I do not think Makanna can take that step without help. She needs you.*"

I felt Herald's sigh more than I heard it. It rolled all the way from her belly. It was the acceptance of someone who truly did not want to do something but would do it anyway. "*I should go, then,*" she said and stroked my neck.

"*Will you ask Garal to clear the way to the cells?*" I asked. "*I should talk to Ardek before Rallon gets here.*"

Five minutes later I was back in the cell with my prisoner.

"Ardek," I told the young man cowering before me. "I am going to offer you a chance. I will ask the Wolves to release you"—I looked at Garal, who gave me a very eloquent shrug—"and in exchange for your life and your freedom, you will swear to serve me. When I need you to do something, you will do it. You will not question it, unless you need to know more to do a better job. Other than that, I will ask Mak to keep an eye on you. You know what will happen if you refuse or if you betray me."

Ardek looked at me with a glimmer of hope. I could only assume that he'd been hoping for nothing more than a clean death instead of whatever he'd imagined that I'd told Mak to do to him.

I moved in to seal the deal. "You should know that I am your only real chance of survival," I told him. "Since you are involved with the slavers, the council and the Wolves will probably—Actually, I am not sure how criminals are executed here. Hang you, maybe? It is unlikely that you could escape, but if you do, the Night Blossom will probably kill you in some horrible way for helping us. As my servant you might still get killed, either while doing something for me or because the wrong person spotted you in the wrong place at the wrong time. But you will have a chance, and you will have allies."

Ardek barely waited for me to finish speaking before giving his answer. "I'll do it," he said eagerly. "I'll serve you. I swear that I'll be loyal to you!"

I'd expected a little more reticence, and it made me suspicious. "As loyal as you were to the Night Blossom?" I asked.

"She left me and my friends to guard a *dragon*," he answered angrily, then seemed to realize how he'd spoken to me, and his face filled with apprehension.

"She did," I mused. "What exactly did you think you were guarding?"

"A new, valuable prisoner," he said. "That's all we were told. There'd been rumors that Tark and some of the heavies had fought a dragon, and lived. You, I guess. Nobody really believed it, I mean, a dragon, here? We figured they were talking about that wyvern. And for sure, none of us ever thought they'd try to capture it. You. But yeah, we weren't told who we were guarding, just that we weren't to let anyone down there except with the Night Blossom or Tark."

Tark was the little man who'd escaped us in the forest, and who had tortured my friends. Learning that he was alive and well, back working for the boss he'd failed, had surprised me. Either he was extremely valuable to the Night Blossom, or she was far more forgiving than I'd expected. On the bright side, this meant that I could kill him myself, or let the girls do it.

"You knew that they were holding the Tekereteki sisters?"

"Only the younger one. The tall one. I'd seen them take her up from below and toward the office."

"And you knew what they were doing to her?"

He looked away from me. "I had a pretty good idea. But we were new, and asking questions is a good way to get hurt."

"Well, here is my first order for you. When I am not around, you will be in the hands of those two women. The older one is Makanna, the younger one is the Herald. You will obey them as you would me. If they contradict each other, you will listen to the Herald. Is that clear and understood?"

"Yes, boss," he said earnestly.

"You understand that I am taking a risk in letting you live, and that they will not hesitate to kill you if you betray me?"

"Yes, boss."

"Good. Here is my second order: When the Wolves question you, and they *will* question you before they release you, you will answer them truthfully and as helpfully as you can. Understood?"

"Yes, boss."

"That said, you understand that you are not to tell *anyone anything* about me, no matter how close you might think that they are to me, unless I have *explicitly* told you that they are allowed full knowledge?"

"Yes, boss."

Either he was an excellent liar, I was a complete dope, or he was being fully honest with me. I decided to go with the latter, or I'd have to kill him. "Good.

The Herald is allowed to know anything and everything about me. She is the only one," I said, turning to give Garal an apologetic look.

"That's all right," he said, though he gave me an odd look. "If *Herald* is the only one with full clearance, I'm not too offended."

"I am glad to hear it. Bleed and cry with me, and we can talk."

"Right. Already did the bleeding, but I know what you mean."

Afterward, Garal brought me back to the cellar. These secret moves must have looked shady as all hell to the mercs who kept getting ordered out or upstairs, and I hoped that it would be the last time before I could leave. I was hiding. Even here, the only safe place for me in the city, I was hiding. I didn't like it. It chafed my pride horribly.

This time I was alone. Herald was probably with Mak, talking, comforting her, or just being there. Being alone was fine with me, though. I needed to think. I poked around in the bags, barrels, and boxes that filled the small space, but they weren't all that interesting. It was mostly oil, dry foods, spare clothes, and other things a large company of people might need. I'd been hoping for dried meat or something like that, but no luck.

I needed to decide how to handle Tam and Val, as well as the Wolves. I also needed a plan for dealing with the Night Blossom. Tam and Val should be easy. If they opposed my dominance over Mak, I would have to either dominate them as well, drive them off so thoroughly that they wouldn't oppose me, or destroy them. At least that was what my gut told me. But the little voice in my head insisted that this was wrong. That they were our friends, and we needed to treat them with respect and make them understand, so that they wouldn't abandon us.

Respect. Was it not respectful to recognize that they couldn't just be ignored? Had the voice always been this annoying?

But that didn't feel right either. I didn't listen to "the voice." I listened to my dragon, didn't I? And this wasn't my dragon.

The voice rarely steered us wrong. I knew that much, so I should listen to it, annoying as it was. The voice was good with humans.

No, *I* was good with humans. Because I was human. Mostly.

Garal and Lalia were problematic too. Garal was respectful, but he was more careful than I was used to. That was reasonable, but annoying. Lalia was being more fearful than aggressive, which I approved of. But the voice—no, my reason, or perhaps my conscience—told me that these were bad signs. From my impressions, Garal was carefree and irreverent, and Lalia was naturally domineering. Any change from that was a cause for concern. And I couldn't just dominate them or kill them, because we liked Garal, and Lalia had been slowly warming up to us. Kind of. A little. Besides, Lahnie would miss her. We wanted them to like us, so that would help us because they wanted to, not because they were afraid not to.

I wasn't sure why I needed to be reminded of that. The situation had been so clear when I woke up in the prison. Punish Mak. Show her where she belonged in the hierarchy. Rescue the Herald and kill everyone in my way who would not submit. Simple. Clear. Everything had been getting steadily less clear ever since. The voice had been getting louder, more insistent, almost indignant. Silencing it had been getting harder.

It was my own voice, wasn't it? My own reason. This wasn't me. I wasn't this cold, calculating, and spiteful, especially not against people I liked or who I wanted to like me. Mak had been cagey and suspicious, and then she had done something stupid, but she'd had good reasons for it. Lalia had been a pain in the ass, but I had never actually wanted to kill her. That was the dragon. My dragon.

I was right on the edge of something when Garal called down the stairs.

"Hey, Draka? You hungry? I sent some of the, uh . . . support staff out earlier. They brought back a bunch of fresh fish."

"You're a legend!" I called back. I wasn't sure why. I was hungry. I'd been ignoring it, but I'd been hungry since the day before. But it was only right that he should tend to my needs, wasn't it? I was stronger than him. He should seek my favor, so why should I thank him? But the voice disagreed. It insisted that he probably knew that we'd be hungry, and he had considered our needs not because he feared that we might eat him, but because that was what friends did. And when I hadn't intended to dignify him with an answer, it was the voice who had spoken for us.

Garal came down the stairs carrying an open-topped box full of long, slender fish. He stopped at the foot of the stairs, and I realized that he could barely see. Of course he couldn't. There was no light down here, except what spilled down from the open door.

"Sit down on the stairs for a while," I told him. He put the box on the floor and took a few steps back up before sitting.

"Are you all right down here?" he asked.

"Sure. Better now that you brought me some food." I walked up to the box. The fish smelled as fresh as if they'd just come from the sea, making my mouth water. I snatched one up and swallowed it whole. You'd think that I wouldn't be able to taste much that way, but I did, and it was delicious. I quickly wolfed down another one, and another after that.

"So . . . you like the fish?" he asked after the fourth one had gone down my gullet.

I paused before going for another one. "Yeah, they're good. I always liked fish. Don't have a good way of getting them now, so this is kind of a treat. Thanks."

"That's good to hear. I think the kids I sent out got fish because it's easy to get fresh here, and cheaper than meat. They probably pocketed half of what I gave them, honestly."

"Appreciate it either way. These are great." I sucked down numbers five and six.

"So, uh . . . do you want to talk about what's going on with you?"

I stopped. "What do you mean?"

"Well . . . Mak, mostly. I've never seen her act so deferential to anyone. And the prisoner. I know that I don't know you very well, but the way you spoke to him . . . it doesn't sound like the Draka that my friends have told me about."

"You disagree with how I treat a member of the group that tortured our friends?"

"No, not as such, but . . . he's barely a man. His friends are dead. He wasn't even involved, if he can be believed. Hasn't he been punished enough?"

"The punishment is not the point. The point is to let him make himself useful, and make up for his mistake."

"And Mak?"

"Exactly the same. Does it make you feel better to know that she agrees with me?"

"No, not really. And I find it hard to believe that she could have done anything to deserve the way you treated her today."

"Perhaps you don't know how far she'd go for her sister."

He sighed. "Draka. Come on, please. What did she do? Help me. I want to believe that you're justified in treating her the way you did, but I've known Mak for years. Honesty and honor are so important to her that I just can't make it fit. What could she have done? Why is it so important to you that she tell me herself?"

"Because I want her to remind herself of what she did," I said. I didn't even think about my answer, but I knew that it was right. I wanted her to humiliate herself. I knew that she wouldn't be able to hide something like that from the people she loved, and I wanted her to be reminded, every time, of the shame she deserved.

The voice said nothing, but I could feel its quiet condemnation.

"She betrayed me," I said after a long silence. "That is what she did, if you have to know so badly. She told the slavers how to get in touch with me and how to draw me in, and then she went with them to lure me into an ambush. She didn't want to. I know that now. They used the Herald to make her do what they wanted. But she was my friend, and she helped them chain me in a cell, like a goddamn animal. How do I forgive that? How do I trust her after that?"

"I'm so sorry that that happened. For you, and for her," he said, his voice heavy with sympathy. "Do you want to forgive her? To trust her?"

"More than anything."

"Then please, give her a real chance. I understand that you're angry. I can't tell you how I'd feel in the same situation. But the way it is now . . . I don't know what you asked her to do with the prisoner, but I think it broke her just a little bit more when she was already broken. Let her heal. Let her show you that she regrets what she did, and that you can trust her, but let her do it her own way. Please.

She was so skittish when Lalia first met her, and she had come so far. Now she's . . . Please, Draka."

"Sometimes when I look at her," I whispered, "I just want her to hurt."

"She is hurting. There's no need to hurt yourself to make it worse."

I snorted with frustration. I was getting annoyed with him, the way he questioned me. I wanted to dismiss him, or tell him what a weak fool he was, but the voice told him, "I can try to be less harsh."

"Thank you. And Herald?"

"What about Herald?"

He smiled. "Nothing. Forget it."

I shook my head and went back to eating.

CHAPTER THIRTEEN

Never Overstay Your Welcome

These things are *really* good," I told Garal between sucking down my ninth and tenth fish. "Those kids deserve a bonus. Or at least a pat on the head."

"I'll pass that along," he said. "Can you wait here for a minute?"

I took an exaggerated look around the small cellar, gave him a pointed look, and went back to finishing off the fish.

"Right," he said, and disappeared up the stairs. I heard some muffled voices from the main floor of the warehouse-cum-mercenary headquarters, and Garal called back down, "When you're done, would you come up here? The commander wants to see you."

"Be right up!"

It probably wasn't polite to make them wait while I ate the last two fish in the crate, but in my defense, I was still hungry, the fish were good, and they were going to start stinking up the place if nobody ate them.

The cellar stairs were behind a door, and the moment I looked out into the main space of the building, I sensed trouble. Or, if not trouble, drama.

"What's this?" I asked, looking at the small group of assembled humans as I stalked into the open. "An intervention?"

On one side of the room stood half the humans I knew in this world. Rallon stood flanked by his cousins Pot and Rib on one side and Lalia and Garal on the other, with Herald and Mak looking awkward a few feet off. On the other side of the room was me, facing them all alone.

The atmosphere was softened somewhat by Rib and Pot looking at me with much less wariness and much more friendly interest than the last time we had been together; though, I couldn't help but note that everything which might have been between me and the door had been moved.

"Madam Draka, thank you for joining us," Rallon said. "I understand that this may appear unnecessarily confrontational, but I have been presented with some concerns about your recent behavior."

Wow. It was like a fucking intervention. They'd been careful, though. They got me fat and happy on fish, and they made it clear that I could leave if I wanted to. No cornering the murder-lizard. Very smart of them. Unfortunately for them, I felt backed into a corner all the same.

"I do not like being ambushed," I told Rallon, pacing back and forth in front of them, my tail lashing with a mind of its own. "I had a bad experience with it recently."

I looked at Mak, but she wouldn't meet my eyes.

"I'm sorry to hear that," Rallon answered evenly. "And I understand that you have recently had some unfortunate grievances with Miss Makanna, which I am sure has done nothing to improve your mood. Disputes between friends rarely do."

"We are working that out," I said, staring at Mak until she lifted her eyes from the floor and looked back at me. *Mak. Come over here.*

She hesitated for only a moment, then crossed the floor to stand beside me where I'd stopped. Herald came with her a heartbeat later.

"There," I said, sitting down. "See? Working it out."

"I'm glad," Rallon said, his voice dry and devoid of humor. "Now, as I understand it, Miss Makanna and her sister sought shelter here yesterday, bringing a prisoner with them. As young Miss Herald tells it, they were held captive for some days by a criminal organization, most likely the same one that we rescued several innocent citizens from several weeks ago. They only escaped when you, also having been taken, arrived and subsequently broke all of you out. Does that sound correct?"

"It does."

"This appears to have happened in retribution for an action which was ultimately my responsibility. A person I trusted, my interrogator, was also quite clearly involved in the escape of our previous prisoner. This prisoner was one of the men who took Miss Makanna off the street, as her sister tells it. Therefore, I clearly owe you all some help. However, let me be blunt. I cannot help you directly against these criminals unless they attack my people. Nor can I allow my people to help you, since there is no way for me to maintain deniability. Mercenaries are forbidden by law to act in a law-enforcement capacity inside the city, citizens or no. However, I can, and do, offer Makanna and Herald shelter here for as long as they need it. And yourself, of course."

The request that I not accept their hospitality for too long was clear from his tone.

"That is generous of you," I told him honestly. It wasn't like Herald and Mak could stay at their inn anymore, not until Tam and Val came back at least.

"However, I was hoping that they would come with me, if they feel up to it. I know a place where no one will be able to harm them."

Herald and Mak looked at each other, then Herald looked at me and nodded. "As Draka says," Herald told Rallon, "your offer is truly generous. We know that we have been disruptive to your company and that we may cause further problems. While we appreciate your kindness, we will go with Draka when it becomes possible."

"I would be happy to show Garal or Lalia where I am taking them," I added. "I trust them not to do anything to endanger Herald or Mak."

"In that case, I expect you will wish to take the prisoner with you as well. For the same reason that I cannot help you in the city, I cannot keep him here, or even turn him over to the guard. However, Garal has told me that you wish to give miss Makanna and miss Herald custody of him. I have no objection to handing him back to you, though, since he seems cooperative now, I would like my people to question him before his release."

"Please do. I have told him to cooperate, and Mak can make sure that he remains helpful. Right, Mak? You know what to do if he doesn't behave?"

Mak went a little pale, looked at me, and licked her lips nervously. "Sure, Draka. I know."

"Great!" I flexed my wings and stretched to my full height where I sat. "Then I think that we are done for now. Commander Rallon, I want to be entirely clear about just how much I appreciate your help, and that of your people, in keeping Herald and Mak safe since yesterday. I have no doubt that the Night Blossom will be furious about our escape, not to mention the half-dozen of her people I killed on the way out. Considering she did something as monumentally stupid as attacking me, I would not be surprised if she tries to come after your people if she learns that you helped us."

"That would be foolish of her indeed, as that would allow me to act against her even inside the city. And I do not take violence against my people lightly."

"Neither do I." I looked fondly at the two women at my side. Let the others interpret that as they wished. It's not like there was any point in pretending that the relationship between myself and the two sisters was in any way equal. Then I turned back to Rallon.

"I owe you a favor, and I do not say that lightly. Call on me for anything, and I will do what I can. But I need to ask for just a little more. Herald and Mak will need to get their things from their inn, and they will need preserved food and other supplies for a long stay in the wild. Can I count on your people to help them prepare? Mak can take care of any costs."

Rallon gave me a rare smile. "A favor from a dragon, hmm? A precious thing, I would think. Lalia, take Rib and go with the young ladies to their inn. Garal, prepare whatever you think they may need for several weeks from our stores, and send out for anything we may lack. Including the prisoner, I suppose," he added after a moment.

His meaning was clear—*I will be glad to have you out of my hair at your earliest convenience, and I will dangle this favor over your head if I think it will get me anything.* I couldn't blame him. They were clearly worried about me, in the sense that having me lurking around was scaring the piss out of them. I'd already bent Herald and Mak to my will, clearly, with Ardek the prisoner being number three. How long until I started picking off Wolves, or challenged Rallon and took over the company?

Not that I had any intention to. No, I was going to be a good ally, and get out of their hair. I was going to put some distance between us, let them cool down a little, and make good on my promised favor if it was asked of me. After all, I knew nothing about running a mercenary company, and I knew nothing about city politics. I was much better off with everything as it was, as long as the Wolves didn't turn on me, which I didn't see happening.

Of course, I never saw Mak turning on me either, which was one of my reasons for getting some distance between myself and the Wolves. I needed some room to breathe until I figured out what to do, and I wouldn't have that if I was constantly worrying about my humans in the city. No, it would be much better to have them safe and secure underneath my mountain, where I could keep an eye on them.

Rallon didn't have anything else for me after that. The relief in the room was palpable, and my guess was that he was happy that everything had ended amicably and didn't want to upset what must have looked like a pretty fragile balance. God only knows what Lalia had told him before we met, but he'd clearly been worried.

After a few words, Herald and Mak went with the others. They had things to fetch, after all, supplies to prepare, and prisoners to interrogate. And the faster they were done, the faster night fell, the better. I was going to be glad to be out of there. The confrontation, careful as it was, had made me conscious of the constant cloud of unease that had hung over me ever since the prison. When I returned to the cellar, I was very much aware that there was only one way out. On the bright side—or 'the dark side' might be more appropriate in my case—there was only one way in, and the small room was nice and dark, with plenty of nooks and crannies in which to hide if necessary.

I could hear people moving around and talking upstairs, and the mood was heavy. Everybody clearly knew that something was up, but since nobody bothered me, I didn't care much. Someone must have been on guard at the cellar door, because no one even tried to come down except Garal, who was putting together supplies for my people. Food, mostly. Dried meat and fish, some cheese, plenty of flour and hard tack, stuff like that, but also some lamp oil, hard soap, and other useful things. The man was thorough. We made some small talk, but that was it. Other than that, I half-napped, with one eye on the stairs. I didn't think that anyone there was a real threat to me, and my sleep had been all messed up lately, anyway, but it couldn't hurt to be careful.

"Draka?"

It felt strange to be awoken by someone else. It had happened once or twice when I was out with the others, but usually I would wake up on my own whenever someone approached me, when the sun rose, or some other event would alert me. The other one, my dragon, was always watching, somehow, but this was twice in a row now that hadn't happened.

Still, I felt good. The best I had in a few days. Happily, it was Herald who woke me, and carefully at that. She squatted on her heels a couple of feet away, wearing her own clothes—they must have been hers since they fit—and a set of leather armor that I hadn't seen before.

"Good evening, great sleepy one." She smiled and waited for me to stretch and sit up. *"We are packed and ready, and the sun has been down for some time. Whenever you wish, we can go."*

"Thank you, Herald. No time like the present. Is the way clear upstairs?"

"Not at the moment, but I will ask Lalia and Garal to take care of it. They will be coming with us."

"Lalia. Fantastic."

"She insisted. I think she is worried about Garal." Herald smiled, reaching out to scratch the snarled patch of scales where my left horn should be. *"She will come around. She just does not know you."*

Dear, sweet Herald. It was like her anger from that morning had never happened. She loved me, and in her mind, I thought, so would anyone else if they just got to know me. How much of our friendship was real? I desperately hoped that the answer was "more than none," and that it wasn't all some kind of dragon magic getting into her head.

Herald disappeared upstairs and soon shouted down that the coast was clear. When I came up the stairs, my traveling companions—the sisters, Ardek, Garal, and Lalia—were waiting for me, along with Pot and Rib, who were there to see them off, or something.

"I hope that you've got a plan," Lalia said. "We need to get through quite a bit of the city before you're in the clear. Are you sneaky enough to get through the streets and out the gate?"

"With you looking after Herald, Mak, and the boy?" I spread my wings demonstratively, then flapped them hard enough to lift myself off the floor for a second, nearly bumping into the ceiling. "Yeah. As long as I have a hidden place to take off, I'll be fine."

Most of the humans flinched. The rush of air, the loud *snap*, the terrifying vision of teeth and claws suddenly moving . . . that was natural. Ardek was the only one to actually jump. It gratified me to see that the others all accepted what I was, wary though they'd been. Ardek, though . . . It would be interesting to see him come to terms with just who he'd promised to serve. And it was just plain funny to see him squirm.

Ardek was completely out of place in the group. He had no weapons and no armor. The pack in front of him was obviously smaller and lighter as well. At least he wasn't in the clothes I'd found him in. Someone had outfitted him simply and had even given him a pair of decent boots, but I noticed him favoring his injured leg.

"How's your knee, kid?" I asked him. "You've got a good eight or ten hours of walking ahead of you."

"I'll be fine. It's healing well, thank you. And, uh . . . Miss Makanna massaged it a little, which made it feel much better."

She probably healed it, I thought with some surprise. "You should be grateful," I told him. "She was probably worried that I'd eat you if you couldn't keep up."

I turned to the others without expanding on that. Seeing him trying to figure out if I was serious was rather amusing. "Shall we? Like I told Ardek, there's a lot of walking ahead of us."

"We'll get Melon and Windfall from the stables," Garal said. "Along with the mule."

"Stalwart," Herald supplied.

"Right, Stalwart. We'll get them from the stables. That side of the building is clear, so you can come out with us as long as you get into cover immediately. Just, please don't scare the horses."

"I'll see what I can do," I said. "Let's go."

CHAPTER FOURTEEN

Leaving Karakan

The large side doors of the warehouse opened onto a yard. The stables looked pretty new and solid, so I guessed the Wolves must have had them built after they took over. I doubted that the warehouse had needed any—there wasn't much need for draft animals when they could hire magically strong workers with high endurance from a labor pool the size of a city.

The yard was clear, just like Garal had said. "I'll meet you outside the north gate," I told them, then leaped into the air with a few beats of my wings. It was a nice, cloudy night, dark as hell and perfect for flying unseen.

But I didn't head for the gates. I didn't want to let them out of my sight and, besides, my wing-shoulder still ached a little. Instead, I climbed high enough that there was no way they'd be able to track me and then came back down, landing on the roof of the warehouse, on the side opposite the yard, and shifted. Then I crossed the ridge of the roof. The yard had some light, but was dark enough that I could see a little. Sure, I'd told Lalia that I'd be fine with them looking after my humans, but I wasn't going to risk the Night Blossom sending a bunch of her goons after them on their way out, while I sat there by the road like an asshole wondering why they never showed up. In the dark I could follow them without being seen just fine. The buildings were generally close enough that I could cross between them, and when they were not, I'd either fly or figure it out.

I was not letting anyone take Herald and Mak from me again, that was for sure.

They got the animals prepared and ready to head out, saddling and bridling and packing and loading, and whatever else needed to be done for horses and pack animals. I was never a horse girl. Garal and Lalia chose to walk, out of consideration for the horses or the others. I guessed that it was probably for the horses, though. From what little I'd seen, they really liked those horses.

Each of them threw at least one surreptitious look at the sky at some point. If it made them feel better, more power to them, but it was pointless. They wouldn't have spotted me even if I'd been there. The city wasn't bright enough to light up the clouds, and I would have been swallowed by the darkness, black on black.

After checking all their gear, they wasted no time getting their move on. They trooped out the gate and into the street, a few stray dogs looking at them curiously. I followed them, moving to the street-side edge of the roof. There were quite a few mercs milling about in the street, and the half-hearted cheers and mutters told me everything I needed to know about how popular it was to be kicked out this late. Most of those poor bastards would probably have been sound asleep if not for me. Luckily for them, it was unlikely to happen again.

The travelers moved down the street, away from the small square I'd seen the day before. There were still some people in the streets despite the hour, but anyone who acknowledged the group quickly moved on, not wanting to draw the attention of four visibly armed people, two of them in the blues and grays of the Wolves. I'd been able to tell from my initial flight that we were close to the harbor, which made a lot of sense since we'd been in a warehouse. It also meant that there was indeed a lot of city between us and the northern gate. By some kind of silent agreement, they moved along small streets instead of heading for any of the wider, more brightly lit thoroughfares I'd seen. I moved, silent and invisible, from rooftop to rooftop, keeping ahead whenever I could and shifting back to rest while I waited. I scared the crap out of more than one cat as I did this; even while I was moving in the shadows, they seemed to sense me and fled as I approached.

Every so often, I would move farther down a street to find a place narrow enough that I could stretch my shadow form across. Failing that, I simply leaped, helped along by my wings. If anyone was sleeping under those roofs, they might wonder what was going on, but I was confident that I wouldn't be spotted, and on some level I simply didn't care. *Let them see*, I thought. Let them wonder, and let them fear. They'd know soon enough.

But, no, the little voice reminded me, that was not a good idea. And the voice was right. But I was so tired of hiding. I was being hunted, and I was not retaliating. It galled me. The most annoying thing was that if I just kept out of sight for a few months, it would probably just . . . go away. The humans would think that I'd moved on, and they'd stop hunting me. And if I didn't want it all to start up again, I could just stay in the shadows, hiding like a frightened animal. Like prey.

And that was the smart thing to do. Because if I started killing the people hunting me, they would just keep coming, because that's what humans did. Hell, the bounty would probably just keep going up until adventurers and hunters seeking their fortune would come from across the sea just to take a shot at me. Which would be flattering, but annoying and ultimately dangerous. Especially if I had my humans with me.

Right. The humans. I'd been drifting, moving along without really paying attention where I should. I was maybe fifty yards behind them and started moving to catch up, but then something caught my eye. Across the street, two figures moved in the shadows of an alley, looking out at the party and then quickly sprinting up to the next alley where they did the same thing. They were clearly following my humans.

My anger flared, but with it came a cruel anticipation. My thoughts had driven me to an impotent frustration and here, conveniently, was something to vent that frustration on. Fighting was good. I didn't need to think and worry while I was fighting.

The two figures were trying to stay in cover, which forced them to move in short sprints. I had no such issue. I shifted out of the dark and took a flying leap to a rooftop across the street, then pursued the pursuers and overtook them, dropping into a dimly lit alley seconds before they themselves reached it.

As they joined me, they almost missed me entirely. They were so focused on their quarry that one didn't see me. The other caught me in his peripheral vision, then turned and looked at me, a choked, squeaking "Run!" escaping his throat.

As I pounced, I got a good look at his face and realized that, God fucking dammit, it was another kid. An actual child, thirteen years old, fifteen at most if he hadn't eaten properly for most of his life. And while I wanted so very much to kill something, I couldn't do it. The voice of my conscience screamed at me, and I retracted my claws and snapped my jaws shut on empty air just before I slammed the boy to the ground. As this was happening, his partner turned, and it was another child, a girl no older than him. She looked at me, then at him, with shock that turned into impotent terror.

"Rel!" she whispered.

"Run!" he choked out again, and she did. With an anguished sob, she turned and fled, her steps echoing down the empty street.

I let her go. What the hell was I supposed to do? Cripple or kill this boy so I could go after her without letting him get away? I growled, more out of frustration than anything else, and the boy on the ground went limp. I could see him trying to be brave, but he soon began sobbing silently.

"Are you one of the Night Blossom's people?" I asked, my face less than a foot from his. I didn't know what I could do even if he said yes.

He squeezed his eyes shut and just lay there, crying, while my humans got further away.

"I'm talking to you, boy. I'll give you one more chance to answer me, before I get rid of you and go after the girl. Are you, or are you not, one of the Night Blossom's people?"

He shook his head violently. It made me think of a baby who didn't want to eat his mush.

"No? No, what? 'No, don't kill me?' or 'No, I'm not?' Answer me, boy!"

"No!" he sobbed. "I'm not! We're not! Some guy paid us to watch the Wolves, and if two dark-skinned women came out, we were supposed to follow them and tell him where they went! He may be one of hers, I don't know!"

"Yeah? Well, here's a new job for you. I want you to take a message. I want you to tell whoever was paying you that the Night Blossom's special guest says that if she's so eager to see me again, all she has to do is wait. Can you do that?"

The boy sobbed silently.

"Words, boy."

"Yes!"

I patted him on the cheek, careful not to scratch him. "Good. Run along now. And if I wasn't clear, I plan to do some terrible things to the Night Blossom's people. You'll probably want to stay away from them for a couple of months." I got off him and used my wings to leap onto a building across the street without waiting. Maybe he'd do what I told him. Maybe not. I didn't expect a child to try to deliver a threat to a crime lord.

If I wanted to keep my head down, I should have killed both him and the girl, but the voice hated that plan, so I didn't. Now they were probably going to start spreading all kinds of stories, and I wondered how long it would take before a description of me found the wrong ear. Days? A week? A month at most?

Still. Terrorizing children was not my proudest moment. Having a conscience was awful sometimes.

As far as my little group of humans knew, their whole trip out of the city was uneventful. Nobody challenged them, and the guards at the gates didn't question why two squad leaders from the Wolves would want to leave the city at night together with two easily recognizable adventurers. Especially not when everyone was in full gear. Ardek drew some questioning looks, but the guards clearly didn't think it was worth an argument.

I crossed the wall on the wing a few hundred yards away, then flew a few miles ahead of the party and settled down by the road to wait. I greeted them with a cheerful "What took you so long?" when they got close enough to hear; though, by their jumpy reactions, most of them hadn't seen me yet.

"*Have you been waiting long?*" Herald asked when she got closer. I matched steps with them, falling in next to her.

"Not really," I answered in Karakani, for the others' benefit. "I was keeping an eye on you for a while to make sure you made it out okay, but all that happened was that some kids were following you. I got rid of them."

I heard a sharp intake of breath from somewhere behind Herald, but when I looked, it surprisingly wasn't Lalia. Ardek was looking kind of sick.

"I scared them off," I huffed at him. "I didn't hurt them. They were children. Harmless. They may have trouble sleeping for a while, though."

"But they saw you. And you spoke to them," Herald stated.

I sighed. "Yeah. Would you have preferred if I killed them?"

"No," she said sourly. "I suppose not."

"There you go. Hopefully no one will listen to a pair of hysterical kids, and if they do, I guess I'll just have to lay low for a while. That, or just give up on being unknown and kill a lot of people."

"Could you not just have left them alone?"

"They were following you!"

"And what harm did that do?"

"Maybe none, maybe they were directing an ambush. I didn't know. That's the point. I had no idea what harm they might do, so I dealt with them. And . . . I needed to vent a little," I admitted after a short silence.

Herald seemed about to say something acidic, but closed her mouth, puffed some air out her nose, and instead said, "That, I can understand. We are not just going to let this stand, are we? I think both Mak and I need some . . . I do not even know for sure. Vengeance, I guess, but that seems like too limited a word."

Vengeance? That was a good start. I let all my grievances with the humans of this world rise freely to the surface. They had convinced me to endure a litany of indignities and annoyances, whether they knew it or not. The loneliness, the discomfort, the constant knowledge that there were people out there who would kill me for clout or for gold, just because of what I was. And now, recently, the very real pain and fear and loss that had been inflicted on me. I took all of that and focused it into one form, an avatar of all my frustration and suffering. A woman who smelled like jasmine.

I couldn't do anything about every human, but I could do something about some of them. And I could do some very specific things to her.

"No," I said. "We are not going to let this stand."

We were silent for a while, then changed the topic to happier things, things that had happened before the Night Blossom ruined everything. Herald talked a little about businesses she and Mak were considering making offers on once Tam and Val came back with the money. An inn was still an option. Since we didn't know if the men would sell the book we'd found or not, and if so, for how much, the sisters hadn't been able to go very far. Even showing too much interest at this point could work against them, possibly driving up prices. But when they hadn't been working or planning, they'd had pleasant evenings, going to the theater or listening to music or, in Herald's case, spending long, relaxing hours in the academy's library—which you could apparently get into by being respectful and dressed nicely enough—and Herald could now accomplish that easily. Not needing to worry about money was, we agreed, a wonderful thing.

I told Herald about how I'd scared off the scholars, and while she didn't quite laugh, at least I got some weak smiles out of her. "*I cannot believe you did that!*"

she said, slowly shaking her head. "*Though I suppose I should not be surprised. You can be so dramatic sometimes!*"

"*It worked, did it not?*"

"*It sounds like it did, but . . . I am glad that no blood was shed. Are you certain that it was wise to let them leave?*"

"*Wise? No, I am not at all sure that it was wise. But it was important to me to give them a chance, for one reason or another. I cannot quite remember why, now. Either way, it is done, and if they return at some point, I will deal with it then.*"

"*Well, at least it was funny,*" she said, putting her hand on my neck for a moment before lapsing back into a comfortable silence.

About an hour after we entered the forest we took a break, and when we were getting ready to move again, Garal and Lalia insisted that the others get on the horses. Ardek was noticeably limping on his healing leg, and both Herald and Mak looked wiped. I should have expected that. They'd had just over a day to recover from several days of horrible abuse, and the fact that they were willing and able to come this far was impressive enough.

Garal and Lalia had made repeated, valiant attempts to engage the rest of us, even Ardek, in something that resembled normal conversation. They'd warmed to Ardek somewhat after it became clear that his only involvement in the sisters' ordeal was a short stint as a guard, before I came along and shattered his life. He'd been a petty criminal before joining the Night Blossom, sure, but from what any of us could tell, he wasn't *bad*, just unfortunate and with limited options. Sadly for our two mercenary friends, he was as taciturn as Herald and Mak. They all had things to deal with.

"What about you, Draka?" Garal asked, lengthening his step to catch up with me. Herald and I were at the front, her riding Melon and me just off the side of the road, eyes open for anyone I needed to hide from. "Are you feeling any better now that we're out of the city?"

I was. The deeper we got into the forest, the more I felt like myself. "I guess, yeah. Fewer people to hide from. Probably won't run into anything we can't easily handle. Still pissed, though. I'd looked forward to it, you know?"

"To what?"

"Visiting the city. I'd wanted to go there ever since I first saw it, but thanks to the goddamn Night Blossom, my whole experience there has been killing and hiding. So. Kind of pissed about that."

"You'll be back, in better times," Garal said with a confidence I wished I could match. "You may not be able to move around openly, but I'm sure we can figure out a way for you to relax with the people you trust at least. It's a big city. Lots of safe, hidden places." He grinned at me. "Think about it. We could get you those fish whenever you wanted. They grill up really nice, too."

"Really nicely," Herald said softly from beside him.

He turned to her. "Hmm?"

"They grill up really nicely."

"Oh. Thanks," he said, with far more grace than I'd expect from a grown man being corrected by a teenage girl. "So, what do you think, Draka?"

"Figure out a place for me to stay, and I'll put you on the full disclosure list."

"There's an incentive if I ever heard one."

"Garal," I said after another mile of silence. "Do you ever feel left out?"

"How do you mean?"

"Maybe that's the wrong question. Do other people ever make you feel left out? Do they exclude you?"

"Because I'm a mercenary? Or because I'm so devilishly handsome?"

He followed that up with a rakish smile, and I snorted. "No. So . . . Herald, Mak, and Tam are Tekereteki, right? And I understand that's giving them some trouble."

"Right," he said, and the way his tone and the set of his face and shoulders changed told me that he knew where I was going.

"Well, you look different from the average Karakani person, if you forgive me for saying so. And you've got a bit of an accent. You're Barlean, right? I've seen a few other Barleans, but not many."

He sighed. "I was. I don't really consider myself Barlean anymore, nor do they. But I'm not alone. There's a small community of us former Barleans here. Besides, I have the Wolves. And our common friends," he said, smiling back at the others. "Do I feel like an outsider? Sometimes. Rarely. When I see a Barlean crew in a harbor tavern, laughing and singing in my mother tongue, it can be hard."

"What happened?"

He smiled sadly. "Nothing. I committed no crime. No one exiled me. I was born without a love for the sea, that is all. If I went to sign up with a crew, they would welcome me with open arms. But I won't, so I'm lost to them. They're not angry. They don't even look down on me, most of them. To them, I'm sick. They're just sad, because they don't understand. But I will never live on a ship again, and so I am no longer Barlean." He looked past me into the darkness of the forest for a while. "I'm sorry. I'd rather not talk about this anymore. Not now."

CHAPTER FIFTEEN

Full Disclosure

When we figured that sunrise was not far off—me by my internal clock, and the others by how the moon stood in the sky, somehow—we stopped for another rest and a short nap. We'd been going for a good seven or eight hours at that point. Everyone was pretty beat, and we still had another two hours to go by my estimate.

Ardek was having the worst of it. He was a life-long city boy. Not only was this his first time in this or any forest, with every sound making him jump, but he had also never ridden a horse before, and from the noises he made, the saddle soreness was getting to him. Add to that the fact that he'd been sitting behind Mak and doing his best not to touch her, likely fearing she would shank him, and the kid was a mess.

When I informed him that it was time to saddle up and move on, he faced it with grim determination. The second time he almost fell out of the saddle, Mak told him to "Just fucking hold on to me," and I'd never seen a man so frightened of putting his arms around a woman's waist. A few restrained titters from Herald soon turned into a wave of laughter that crashed through the rest of us, ebbing and then picking up again whenever anyone looked at the two, leaving Ardek bright red and Mak giving death glares to anyone who wasn't me. For all the weirdness of the situation, it felt almost normal. A little mean, maybe, but that's been half of humor since the beginning of time. Besides, it was good to hear Herald laugh properly.

It was a few hours into the morning when we arrived at the scholars' abandoned campsite, and the relief that washed through the group when I informed them all that we'd arrived was a thing of beauty. Ardek fell out of the saddle with a look on his face like he'd been pardoned on the steps to the gallows, while the others dropped their packs and started pampering the animals before sitting down on the logs that still ringed the firepit.

"Hey, Herald," I said as I stretched out on the ground, sticking to the common language for the sake of the others. "Remember the scholars I told you about? This was their camp."

"The scholars?" she said, sitting down near me. It had been a while since we talked about them, so she didn't show any immediate signs of remembering. Then her eyes lit up with understanding. "Oh! So that is where you are planning to hide us!"

"Can you think of anywhere safer?"

"If you give me time, perhaps. But I doubt I will think of anywhere you could come with us, so practically, no."

The others looked at us quizzically until Mak decided to be the one to ask. "What exactly are you talking about?"

I pointed lazily toward the excavation. "Walk for about a minute in that direction and you'll understand."

She looked like she was about to argue, but got heavily to her feet.

Herald spoke up quickly. "There is a gate here. We are going inside."

Mak's face went carefully neutral. "I see," she said, and looked at me. I shrugged, and she sat back down with a grateful nod. If anyone noticed the exchange, they didn't comment.

"Is that safe?" Lalia asked.

"I've checked it out. If you roam for a long, long time in the wrong direction you might come across some gremlins, but otherwise it's all clear."

"Excuse me," Ardek piped in, "what's this gate you're talking about?"

"Don't worry about it," Mak said flatly. "You'll see soon enough."

"And you're both all right with this?" Lalia asked, looking between Herald and Mak.

"If Draka says that it is safe, then I believe her," Herald said. Mak just shrugged glumly.

Right. Mak's last time in one of these places had ended with her being a few days from starvation before Herald and I rescued her. I hadn't exactly considered that when coming up with the idea. Part of me felt like I should have, but I stood by my decision.

"Look, Lalia. This is *my* mountain. I have my home, or nest, or lair, or whatever you want to call it literally minutes from here by flight. If you want to come check on Herald and Mak, just come here and set up camp. I'll check regularly and let you in if I see you. All right?"

"Yeah," Lalia said doubtfully, then more confidently, "Yeah. All right."

We ended up spending the rest of the day and that night there. The animals needed to be properly rested for the return trip to Karakan, Garal and Lalia didn't want to ride at night if they could avoid it, and everybody wanted to spend some more time together before parting anyway. I could have easily returned to my nest, but as much as I wanted to sleep and recover properly on my hoard, I also didn't want to leave my humans until I was sure that they were safely tucked away in the mountain. I slept with the others and took a watch like everyone else. The nights were getting cooler, but we had a fire going and the weather was fine. Despite all the awful shit that had led to us being out here together, it was quite nice, really.

"Will Rallon not be upset that you were away a whole extra day?" Herald asked as they were saddling up, with Stalwart's lead tied to Melon's saddle. He'd be returning with them. It wasn't like we could bring the poor thing into the tunnels with us.

"We'll have to explain ourselves, for sure," Garal said. "But the commander can be most understanding. We'll be fine."

"Well, if he kicks you out of the company, I am sure that we will have more than enough room here. Right, Draka?"

I snorted. "Sure. The more, the merrier."

"I'm sure it won't come to that, but I'll keep it in mind," Garal said and leaped into the saddle.

With a few goodbyes and well wishes, they were gone. We'd already moved everything down to the gate, so there was no point in delaying. I brought the three remaining humans with me down the slope, shooed them back a bit, then put my hand on the stone and willed it open. I heard a muttered "Mercies and Sorrows . . ." from Ardek, who was suitably impressed by the display.

"Come on, get in," I told them. "If you can't carry everything, just leave the least important stuff inside the door. I can guarantee that nothing will touch it."

"So it just . . . goes into the mountain?" Ardek said, stopping at the entrance to the tunnel. "What's in there?"

"Miles and miles of empty tunnels, lots of empty chambers, and nothing else. That's the whole point. Now get in there!" I said, a little more harshly than necessary perhaps, and lashed my tail at him. I couldn't do any real damage with it, but a swat on the back of his legs got him moving.

They left most of the dry goods at the entrance, taking two- or three-days' worth with them and prioritizing waterskins and other necessities.

I guessed Mak didn't want to reveal too much to Ardek, because I hadn't seen her cast a spell. I approved. I didn't trust him either. Instead, Herald had taken out a light-ball and they all walked in a tight group, with Ardek nervously asking questions, seemingly about anything and everything that came to mind, from how the sisters knew me to what kind of food they liked. He clearly did not like going into the mountain.

When she reached the remains of the scholar's camp in the hub, Mak knelt down and curiously touched the remains of the campfire, rubbing the ashes between her fingers.

"I had some unwanted guests," I said, coming up behind her, and she froze, then turned to look at me.

"Herald told me. Something about scholars digging out the gate. I'm guessing it was them?"

"Right."

"So, here?" Herald asked.

"Here," I agreed. "There's plenty of tunnels leading away from here, but it will be long before you reach another chamber."

"Good to be somewhat close to the exit too," Ardek said. I hadn't expected him to give his opinion, but nerves made him brave, I supposed. For a city boy, even the forest must have been preferable to these dark tunnels.

As they all began to unpack and set up a simple camp, Herald approached me. "Can we talk, once we have set up here?" she asked in a low voice.

"Sure," I said. "I think that would be good."

When they'd finished making some kind of order, Mak discreetly cast her darksight spell on Herald, which suited me fine. It just meant that I didn't need to tell her to do it. I still approached them.

"Let's take a walk," I told Herald, then looked to Mak and switched to Tekereteki. *"Kill the boy if you have to. I leave it to your judgment. We cannot afford to keep someone untrustworthy here."*

I didn't feel great about it, but I meant it. The look Herald gave me didn't make things any better.

"I understand," Mak answered, but no matter how annoyed she had been at him, she looked so miserable that I wasn't sure if she'd manage it. But, she was good with people, or had been, at least, and if he acted up, she wouldn't let it go that far. I was sure of it.

Just to be on the safe side, I turned to Ardek. "Herald and I are going for a walk," I told him. "Make yourself useful to Mak, and be smart."

"I will, boss," he said earnestly.

I took Herald with me away from the camp. I followed my feet toward the throne room, a little surprised with myself that I hardly felt any anxiety about it. Perhaps my apprehension over the talk I needed to have with Herald drowned it out. The whole way there Herald didn't say a word. The air was thick with the tension between us, until I brought her into the middle of the throne room, sat down, and said, *"Well?"*

"I am angry with you, Draka."

Right. We were having that conversation, for real this time.

Her eyes bored into me, but there was only pain there, and it hit me so hard, all of me, that if I had not been sitting, I might have stumbled. *"Or rather, I am not,"* she continued, her voice tinged with frustration. *"And I am furious with myself because I am not angry with you. I have tried. I have tried so hard. And nothing."*

"I know," I told her. *"In the cellar, back with the Wolves, I could smell the anger coming off you. I thought that you would actually hit me."*

"What would you have done?"

"I do not know. With anyone else I think I might have killed them. With you . . . I do not think I could hurt you."

"You know what this is about?"

"Mak. And you."

She broke the stare, then nodded and turned away from me. *"I have trusted you, Draka. I have defended you, and helped you. And now this. Whatever this is. What do you have to say for yourself?"*

"Did you talk to Mak?"

"I tried. She still will not tell me what is wrong. All she will say is that she betrayed you, and that she deserves it, but she will not tell me what it is. She will not tell me what she did to you, or what you did to her, or why. I am left to guess, and imagine, and every possibility I think of is worse than the last. Please, if my own sister will not tell me, will my friend? Will you?"

I sighed, and laid down. *"Come here, would you? Sit down?"*

She was slouched on her feet and looked close to tears, but after a while she slowly came and sat down. Even though she looked down at me as she sat there, hugging her knees, she looked so small.

"What I told you was true," I said. The voice, my conscience, the human in me, whatever it was . . . it wanted me to shut up. It was afraid of how she might react. But Herald should know. She had done nothing to deserve being lied to, even through silence. *"I was going to kill her. I was looking forward to it. I wanted her to tell you why, but if she will not, well . . . like you said in the cellar, you deserve to know.*

"Mak betrayed me. She lured me to the tree. Our tree. Then she used you to draw me into an ambush, where I was beaten, poisoned, and chained. She walked with my attackers as they brought me back to the city and locked me in a cell. I know why, of course. Now I know, and I admit that I have some regrets. But at the time . . . Once we were alone, I killed the guard, and I went into her cell, and I was going to kill her."

"But you did not," Herald said.

"No. But not out of mercy, or even out of love for you. It was because at some point, something in her broke, and I knew that there was no point in killing her. You know. Do you think she could betray me again?"

"No," she said sadly. *"She is different. But it is more than fear or repentance. I have watched her, when you speak to her. It is not just that she does not dare to disobey you. I do not think that she can, even when she wants to."* She swallowed. *"Draka, you told her to tear a man's throat out with her teeth, and it was killing her, but she was going to do it. That is far beyond normal, and it is not her. You must have done*

something to her. And to me, for that matter. Because no matter how justified you might have felt in the moment, I know that I should hate you for what you have done to Mak. I have tried to hate you. Do you know what that is like, to try to hate your friend? Yet while I pity my sister, with you, all I can do is sympathize with you for having to make the choice._

"We talked about this before. You were worried that I was too focused, even obsessed with you. I brushed it off. But I think that you were right. I know that I love you. I have no doubt about that. But there is more to it, and it is not natural. I deserve to know what you are doing to us, do I not?"

"You do," I said. My throat was tight, but I forced the words out. "_You deserve to know everything. The truth is that I do not know. I am not doing anything knowingly. But I do not know if my dragon is._"

Herald's face scrunched slightly with confusion, as though she wondered if she'd misheard. "_I do not understand. Your dragon?_"

I paused to think, looking around the room and gathering my thoughts. "_This chamber is impressive, is it not? I often wonder who made it, and the tunnels and all._"

"_What does that have to do with anything?_" she asked softly.

"_There is a lingering scent of gold and silver here. I think of it as the throne room, but I think it was a lair. The lair of my father._"

Herald's face scrunched in confusion. "_You have told me about your father. He is human._"

"_One of my fathers is, as is my mother. My human side's parents. But my dragon had a father, and a mother, presumably, unless I have misunderstood gender in dragons._" I caught her gaze. "_Herald, there is something I have not told you, out of fear for how you might react. But it is too late for that now, and you deserve to know everything. Telling you is the least I can do after what I have done to you._

"_This was my father's lair. At least I think so. The memories are not clear, because they only belong to part of me. They belong to my other half, and are very new to me._

"_Herald, what I told you about how I came here is true. I had an accident, and I woke up in this body. But I didn't tell you everything. I am not alone in here. I share this body with its original owner. Or maybe that is not right either. Perhaps it is more correct to say that I am joined with her. And she . . . I believe that you were right. Remember how you said that I was too small? That I should be in a nest somewhere being fed by my mother? Well, I remember my father bringing food into the lair. I am quite sure that it was there for me to steal. Then it is all a blur. I believe that I was caged, then brought up there,_" I pointed to the hole in the ceiling, "_for some purpose that I do not know. And then my dragon lay there, asleep and untouched by time, for centuries. Until I came along and woke her._"

As I spoke, and in the silence that followed, Herald's face went from surprise and confusion to skepticism, until it became carefully neutral, and she stated flatly, "_You are telling me that you are two people._"

"Well, yes and no. The last few days have been confusing. The way I see myself, and think of myself, the way I hear the other part of me, it has been a mess. I will think something that is perfectly reasonable at the moment, and then be horrified a moment later. I used to think of my dragon as just a voice in my head that gave me its opinions and sometimes told me something useful. A remnant of what this body had been. But she is more than that. She can affect my emotions, I know that for sure. And now I believe that she is not so much a separate entity as a part of me, which becomes stronger in times of stress. Like when I'm fighting. Or most of these last few days. And I do not know if there are things she can do that I cannot, or that I can do unconsciously when she is stronger."

"Well," Herald said slowly. *"That explains things. The problem is not that you are slipping into arrogance and cruelty after your success."*

"Is that what you thought?"

"It is what I feared. But if what you say is true, then I see that the problem is that there is a part of you that is human, and it is so worried and ashamed of what she is doing that she can barely speak of it, while the rest of you is a tyrannical toddler throwing a tantrum because her world was turned upside down and someone took away her favorite toy."

"What?" I said, not sure what I was hearing.

"You say your dragon is basically a baby. And I have spoken to the others. Are you aware that when you speak to them of me, half the time you call me 'the Herald', rather than Herald? And it is no wonder if it is as you say. Dragons do not forge relationships with humans the way humans do with each other, I am sure. To the human part of you, I am a friend, but to the dragon part of you, I am a possession." She smiled wryly. *"I cannot say that I am pleased about that, and it makes me worry about why you brought us here, specifically. But I also cannot blame you, either part of you. It sounds as though the human Draka has not been making the decisions lately, and the dragon, well . . . she is just a baby. She does not know better. You cannot blame a baby for its actions, can you?"*

Perhaps I should have just taken the win. Herald was taking all of this too calmly, though already knowing that I was a human shoved into a dragon's body must have helped. She was giving me what was pretty much a free pass, but I felt . . . unsatisfied. Defensive, almost. I had done her wrong. I had been cruel to Mak, much harsher than she deserved, even once I knew her motivations. Her acceptance was almost worse than any condemnation I'd expected.

Maybe I felt guilt. Maybe I wanted her to blame me. To hate me for what I had done.

"You cannot be serious!" I told her. *"My dragon may be young, but she is rational. She is more eloquent than I am. You cannot just say, 'Oh, that is children for you, what can you do?' She is responsible! I am responsible!"*

"Perhaps you are. But if you are two halves of one mind, as you seem to think, could she not simply be using your adult faculties, while her own emotions and motivations control what she does with that? Those of a selfish child?"

All the dragon wanted was to fulfill its base desires. Food, gold, comfort, and to punish those who frustrated that fulfillment. She didn't really make long-term plans. Our shared desire for revenge on the Night Blossom was the closest she came, and her—My? Our?—plan had been to find her immediately, and tear her apart as publicly as possible.

"There may, perhaps, be something to that," I said hesitantly. Herald smiled, sighed, and laid down against me.

I was not satisfied, but she was, and that would have to do.

CHAPTER SIXTEEN

Rationalizations

I need to tell you one more thing, and then I think that you will know all my secrets," I told Herald. It felt good. I hadn't liked keeping anything secret from her, not with how kind, trusting and, above all, trustworthy she had proven. "You see the hole in the ceiling, there? The square one? Up there is a room that is connected by one of those long tunnels to a pit, where I woke up. And beyond that is a cave where I have my nest, and my hoard. It's connected to an opening in the mountain, so that is how I usually go in and out." I paused and thought for a moment. "I think that is everything."

"Thank you for trusting me with this, Draka," Herald said, reaching out to stroke my neck. I loved it when she did that. It was relaxing. Calming. Especially with her resting against me the way she was. It reminded me of rainy afternoons cuddled up under a blanket with Andrea, drinking chai and binging Netflix. Physical contact for the sake of comfort and companionship is a rare thing when you're a big ol' murder-lizard, and I missed it often.

I still had to push a little before I could let our conversation . . . perhaps not go, but rest. "The fact that you are refusing to hold me responsible for whatever is affecting you and Mak, does it not bother you? It seems like you are rationalizing it away, or ignoring it."

"Perhaps I am. But now that you have told me everything you know, it is easier to accept. I believe you when you say that you are not doing anything intentionally, and I hope that you believe me when I tell you that I can still tell when you are hiding something from me. Whatever this is, it is not making me believe you blindly. But sure, this unknown power of yours may be making it so that I do not worry about it. I worry about that, and I hope it is not so. But what am I to do then? Not trust my own mind? Believe that my own thoughts are lying to me, as well as my emotions? Until . . . what happened, you have only ever made me happier, richer, and more fulfilled. You have never taken advantage of me, as far as I know. So, I will not blame you for things you have no control over."

She reached up and put her hand on my chin, guiding my head so that we looked directly at each other, and solemnly said, "*But if you want to keep my friendship, I ask . . . no, I demand, that you be kind to Mak. That you try, at least. Perhaps she deserved some reprimand, even punishment, but what you did was disproportionate and unjust. You know that. I know you do, and if I cannot be angry with you, I can at least shame you. She had no control over the situation. She was a victim, no less than you. She did what she had to do to protect me, and she could do nothing else. If she could have died instead, she would have. We both know that. She has been punished, and she continues to punish herself. Enough. I understand if you cannot undo what has been done to her, but do not abuse her. Promise me that.*"

She didn't rage, or lash out, but I still cringed. She was implacable. There was nothing yielding or compromising in her voice. She meant every word.

"*I promise,*" I said, knowing that she would hold me to that promise, and that there was no way I could break it. I could not risk the consequences. "*But I will need you to remind me of that promise. If the dragon part of me comes to the forefront, I may use her however it feels most beneficial in the moment. I need you to keep me honest.*"

"*I will,*" she said, and that too was a promise. I had her sister's life and happiness in my hands, and Herald was not going to let me handle them roughly.

It was hard to know exactly how I was affecting her, but no part of me was willing to risk Herald's friendship and goodwill. I didn't know what I would do if I lost her, whether someone took her from me or I drove her away. She was my lifeline. She made me feel connected to my own humanity in a way that no one and nothing else did, and the dragon part of me treasured her over everything else.

"*I wish I could take you up there,*" I told her. "*To show you my hoard, and what I've done with the things you brought me.*"

"*Is that the human or the dragon talking?*" she asked, one side of her mouth quirking up. "*I am not sure I would want to go if it is the dragon. I wish to see the sun again someday, you know.*"

I played along, grateful for the change of mood. "*Do not worry. There is a ledge you can watch the sunrise from. It is a thousand feet or so above the forest, with a lovely view all the way to the sea.*"

"*Do you have a bath?*"

"*Not as such, but perhaps I could arrange something?*"

"*In that case, I think we will have to keep it to a short visit. I would prefer not to become a permanent fixture unless I can have a bath every so often.*"

I snorted. "*Jokes aside, I do want to show you my home. Perhaps we could set up a rope ladder. Or I could teach you to climb, if we can get the right equipment.*"

"*What about . . .*" she said, reaching out and touching my wing.

"*No. I do not dare. Not yet,*" I said, and she nodded, taking my word for it. "*But Herald. Thank you. For understanding.*"

"Is that not what friends do? Try to understand?"

"Maybe. But thank you anyway." I stood. *"Now we should return to the camp and see if Ardek has managed to keep himself alive."*

"Stop projecting," Herald scolded me, though her tone was light. She got up with me, and even though it was my suggestion, I felt a gut-wrenching absence at the loss of contact. *"Mak is not violent by nature. If anything she will have scolded him into submission."*

"Kinky," I muttered, but the word didn't translate.

"More of your draconic? What does it mean?"

"I will tell you when you are older," I answered, and she rolled her eyes at me.

"What is your plan now?" she asked me as we walked back.

"Plan? I am flattered that you think I have one. Three days ago, I was expecting you to be happily wasting your silver in the city until you felt the itch to come hunt with me. Now all I can think about is how to keep you and your sister—and the boy you wanted me to keep—safe until we know how to handle the situation."

"But you want revenge, do you not?"

"Yes. But saying 'Let us go kill the bitch who wronged us!' is very different from actually doing it. Believe me, I wish I could just fly into the city and start tearing through anything that looks criminal until I find a lead, but I also know that will only get me killed in the long run. We need to know how to find her, and how to get to her. And before that, we need to know how to get that information."

"And that," Herald said in a lecturing tone, *"is why I wanted you to keep Ardek alive. He was part of the Night Blossom's organization. He must know something!"*

"He did say that he worked as security at some of her businesses . . ." I mused.

The conversation didn't go much further, but we agreed that we had somewhere to start.

As we neared the hub and the camp, we began to hear voices echoing in the distance. As we got closer, I heard clear sounds of pain and got a little worried, since my conversation with Herald had made Ardek's importance rise in my mind. But when I heard Mak's voice, steady but annoyed, I calmed again.

"—wouldn't hurt so much if you didn't try to play tough all the time!" she was saying as we approached.

"Stay silent," I whispered to Herald, and we carefully stalked closer.

Ardek's voice carried through the darkness, strained with pain. "The dragon barely tolerates me as it is. How do you know she wouldn't have just killed me if I slowed you down?"

Mak sighed audibly. "Probably because my sister asked her not to. Besides, she doesn't kill needlessly. I've never seen her hurt anyone who didn't deserve it. If you asked for a rest she would have been annoyed and said something threatening and snarky, but she wouldn't have hurt you."

We got closer. Mak had set up another light-ball to support the first, and in the overlap of the two, Ardek lay on his back on some furs, his injured leg propped up on a bag. His trouser leg was pulled up to mid-thigh, and Mak had her hands on either side of his knee with a focused look on her face, gently massaging as her magic flowed from her into the joint. I stopped to listen, and Herald stopped with me, her hand on my back.

"You really don't think she'll kill me as long as I try to do what she wants?"

As though it was the hundredth time she'd been asked this question, Mak answered, "No. I don't think she would. I don't think she'd kill you even if you refused to do something, as long as it didn't hurt anyone else. I don't know what she'd do, but I don't think she'd kill you. Now hold still. You keep making this more difficult than it needs to be."

I could see that Mak's healing was only trickling in, and I guessed that she was trying to hide the fact that she was using magic. I remembered the soothing warmth when she'd healed me; it would be hard to miss. She was clearly hiding her abilities from Ardek, but she must have formed some kind of attachment to him. Why else would she be healing him? Perhaps it was just her role as team mom shining through, but I hoped that there was some kind of bond forming between them. Everything would go smoother if my minions got along with each other.

Minions. That was what they were. A day ago I had been quite smug and satisfied about that, but now I wasn't sure how I felt about it. Herald was right. I could see that now. Mak had been punished enough. But as much as I might want to—and I didn't even know if I did—I had no idea how to reverse something I had done when I'd never known how to do it in the first place.

Ardek was another story. I still had no good reason to believe that he didn't harbor some hidden loyalty to the Night Blossom, and I wasn't letting him back in the city alive until I was sure. Keeping him under my clawed, scaly thumb was just common sense. Besides, Mak seemed to have adopted him now, or something, so I couldn't in good conscience get rid of him without good reason.

And honestly, now that I was calm and safe again, I could admit that Mak was right in what she'd told him. I wouldn't kill him for no reason. I couldn't let myself. I could very easily see myself becoming the kind of person, or creature, that would kill out of spite or annoyance—when you don't feel horror or guilt at taking a life, it's easy. And because I could see myself becoming that, because it was so easy, I couldn't allow myself to cross that line even once. I didn't know where my line for an acceptable murder was, but I wouldn't kill anyone out of convenience; I knew that now. If he was the one to cross the line in my direction, though . . . Well, then all bets were off.

"How are you holding up, really?" Mak asked Ardek as she released him and picked up a long strip of cloth from somewhere on the ground, which she began to wrap around his knee. "I get that you're scared. Anyone would be. Want to talk about it?"

Ardek lay silent on the ground for a long time as Mak tended to him, and I almost started walking again. "It's a mess, isn't it?" he said suddenly. "I didn't even know that there were any dragons anymore. Then *she* comes tearing out from below with you in tow. I don't know what she did to Berek when he went to check on that other guy, Ras or Rosh or whatever his name was, but she just smashed through the door. By the time I understood what was happening, I was on the floor, Ava was dying on the table, and there was this . . . creature in the room with us, smashing Berek's face into the floor until his head cracked."

He propped himself up on his elbows and looked at Mak. "You have no reason to feel bad for them, or for me. I get that. We all had a good idea about what they were doing to you two down there. I mean, we didn't feel good about it, and Ava couldn't even look at your sister when they brought her through, but we didn't do anything about it. Ava and Berek . . . they weren't nice people. They weren't good either, I guess. But I ran with them for years, and they were my mates, you know? And the dragon—Draka, I mean—she killed them easier than I'd swat a mosquito. But she left me. I guess . . . I keep expecting her to change her mind."

"I can't say I regret your friends' deaths. I might have done it if Draka hadn't. For that matter, I might have killed you if she hadn't wanted you alive." She paused and tied the wrapping. "But I sympathize with your loss, for what it's worth."

I looked at Herald, who shrugged and gestured questioningly away from the camp. We took a walk with me leading her in the direction the scholars had gone. We talked about inconsequential things, until Herald asked, "*Was your father like you?*"

"*How do you mean?*"

"*Could he turn into shadow and everything?*"

"*I am not sure, but I do not see how else he could get in and out of the lair. Judging by the size of his teeth, he must have been five or six times the size I am now.*"

That gave her pause, and for good reason. The old lizard was terrifying to think of, even to me.

"*So how did he bring you food?*" she continued after a while. "*You cannot carry anything when you turn into shadow, can you?*"

"*Perhaps he was more powerful than I am? Able to do more things? Or . . .*" Something struck me. "*Well, when I eat something, it stays with me when I shift.*"

"*I should hope so. It would get horribly messy otherwise.*"

"*Funny. So, where is the limit? I feel rather foolish right now, but what if I just keep something inside my mouth and shift?*"

"You could not carry anything large that way." She considered me for a while. *"Not yet, at least. But it is worth a try."*

With that in mind we continued talking, returning to the camp maybe half an hour later. Mak was showing Ardek how to properly sharpen a sword. If I'd been her, I wouldn't have wanted a weapon anywhere near his hands, but she was the one who could supposedly read people, and I had to trust her judgment.

"I can't believe that you know this little about caring for your equipment!" Mak's annoyance carried loud and clear across the cavern. "You *had* a sword when we met you. I took it from you. It was a decent blade. Did no one show you how to maintain it?"

"Not really," Ardek replied. "I bought it because it looked good. I don't know how to use a damned sword! I'm a knife fighter. Barely."

Mak scoffed. "Considering you're alive and don't have many scars, you must either be a really good one, or you've never been in a knife fight in your life. You don't have the money for the potions if you lost, and if you were any good, you'd know how to care for a blade."

"I mean—"

"We're back," I interrupted. "Did he give you any trouble?"

"None at all," Mak replied. "Happy to help and eager to learn. Not so quick on the uptake, but we'll get there."

"Glad to hear it. How about you, Ardek? You doing all right?"

"Yeah, boss," he said, carefully pointing the sword in his hand away from me. "Miss Makanna's been showing me how to care for some of the gear properly."

"Making yourself useful, huh?"

The nervous look he gave me made the most vicious parts of me very happy.

"Yeah," he answered quickly. "I figured if I'm going to be part of this group I should pull my weight."

I'd been about to say something like, "Great, there won't be any room for freeloaders here," or something similarly ominous, but Mak cut in. "Draka, what's the plan?" she said. "What are we doing now?"

Right. Plan. I couldn't exactly tell them that I was winging it.

"First," I told them. "We're going to get you set up here so you can stay a few weeks at least. That means securing the place, including the forest and hills surrounding the entrance. We might as well take the opportunity to get rid of the wolves and bears that have been sniffing around my territory."

"So how long do you expect us to stay?" Mak pressed me.

"As long as it takes. Short term, I need you to be safe. That means you'll stay here until Tam and Val get back, unless the guard or the Wolves do something about the Night Blossom before then."

"Not fucking likely," Ardek muttered.

"What's that?"

With my attention on him, Ardek shrank in on himself. "Oh. Sorry, boss. I didn't mean—"

"No, go on. Why isn't it likely?"

"Uh, well . . ." When I just waited patiently he rallied, and said, "That guard captain we met. He's not the only one the Night Blossom is paying off, and not the highest ranking either. They say she likes to throw her silver around, and, uh, some of the people on the council are in business with her. Supposedly. So don't expect any help from the city. And they'll probably block the mercs from doing anything either."

"All right." I nodded to him. *I really shouldn't ever doubt Herald*, I thought. This guy is useful already. "In that case, we'll have to be even more careful not to be discovered, so we don't make any inconvenient enemies. But speaking of money—Mak, do you have the bag of loot?"

"Yeah, Draka. In my pack."

"Get it out, would you?"

"Sure." She lifted out some clothes and a book from her large rucksack, before removing the large pouch with the valuables we'd taken from the Night Blossom's estate.

"I've been meaning to split that with you," I said, looking at Herald and Mak. "I'll be taking my half with me when I leave. But first, Mak, would you get a dragon out?"

She shrugged and put her hand in, digging out a gold coin by feel. She held it up, and to my disappointment, it glinted a dark blue under the light of the stones. I really needed to teach Mak how to change the color they gave off.

"Take it, Ardek," I said. He hesitated as if fearing a trap, and I snorted. "Come on, man. I don't need an excuse if I want to kill you. Are you going to insult me by refusing?"

That got him moving. He took a few slow steps over to where Mak was standing and took the coin when she offered it to him, then stood watching it as he spun it in his fingers.

"That's yours," I told him. "Consider it a signing bonus. The ladies here can both tell you that it's been very lucrative for them, being my allies, and I intend for that to continue. If you stay loyal and survive, I can guarantee that you'll make a lot more money than you'd ever make working for the Night Blossom. And once we get back in the city, if you have any trustworthy friends, you can introduce them to Mak, and maybe we can extend the same offer to them."

He stood, mesmerized by the piece of gold in his hands. "Never had a whole dragon before," he whispered, then snapped himself out of it and pocketed the coin. "Strangest two days of my life. Thanks, boss. I know some people."

"So," Herald said, "once Tam and Val are back, what then?"

"Then we get you back into the city. You should be safe enough, all four of you together."

"Right. And then what?"

I felt my dragon rise inside me, demanding and proud. Whether she was her own person or we were just two sides of the same coin, she was willing and eager. Eager to begin, to act, to shed blood, and sow fear. But for once we agreed that we needed to wait. We needed to gather information and allies, and so she could be patient. She was very good at being patient when necessary.

"Then?" I said. "Then we go to war."

CHAPTER SEVENTEEN

One Hundred Days

It had only been days since I was last in my nest, but it felt like much, much longer. I still didn't feel up to going back up the tunnel from the throne room to the pit—just the thought made me feel sick—so I'd gone the long way around, heading out the gate and flying up to the cave's mouth. I walked the familiar path down into the mountain, enjoying the feeling of normalcy that it awoke in me. It was the only thing that I had left of my old life. There were some small differences from what I'd known—a rock missing here, a new stalactite there—but the twists and turns were all the same as they had been on Earth. That normalcy, though, now blended seamlessly into my new memories of this place, and the emotions they brought with them.

It had been a hundred days since I first woke in the pit, by my own count and what the others had told me, and my life on Mallin had become my new normal. It had become comfortable and familiar, somehow, and when I reached my nest and ignited the light-ball—I badly needed a better name for the things—it really felt like returning home. I was comfortable there, safe and happy, and it smelled so good! The only thing I lacked was my friends but, as sad as it might sound, my hoard more than made up for that. Its draw only became strong when I was away for a long time, like when we'd gone north, but every time I returned after being absent for more than a day it was a joy and a major relief to see everything unspoiled and in its place.

I would have loved to actually stay and rest on my hoard, but I was not comfortable leaving the humans alone. Not that I thought Ardek would try to murder Herald or Mak in their sleep, but I wasn't going to take any chances. I didn't know him well enough to trust him not to be stupid. So, a quick visit to drop off my loot and make sure that everything was right with the hoard would have to be enough.

The loot, though. It was a good haul. Back on Earth, criminals were usually depicted as keeping a stash of wads of hundreds. The Night Blossom's stash had been in gold coins, which I had decided that I liked much, much better than some sad slips of paper. Sure, there was silver, too, and some jewelry, but most of the value was in good old dragons. I'd let the girls take their pick of the accessories, and even after splitting whatever was left fifty-fifty, it was a lot. I hadn't counted it. Exact numbers meant little when it came to my hoard. All that mattered was that I knew I was bringing home a fortune.

I curled up on my blankets and dropped the pouch from my mouth, letting it clink onto the colorful fabric. I took it and upended it, letting the contents pour out in an all-too brief jingle of metal on metal, and looked at the pile with great pleasure. My haul from the journey north had been in the hundreds of coins, but they had all been silver. Here I had only a few dozen, but half of them were golden dragons, and the rest silver eagles. I had no way to judge the value of the small amount of jewelry, but they were set with small gems and smelled as delicious to me as the coins did. With no one around, I allowed myself a long, luxuriating rumble.

I was surprised when the familiar pressure of a threshold reached began to build. I'd expected it, considering the size of the haul, especially when I hadn't gotten anything after adding the Old Mallinean coins. I'd even tried to remember what my previous options had been and tried to guess what might be available this time. I hadn't heard a voice, yet there was the unmistakable pressure. My dragon didn't speak to me, and I felt an emptiness at her absence. Yet, I knew my available choices, like they'd been dropped straight into my memory, and when I became aware of the new option, I knew that I'd take it.

I'd already decided to pass on "greatness" indefinitely, but without a second mind to filter it for me, I understood more about it now. Physical greatness, at a cost. I'd guessed that the cost was that I'd need more space, obviously, as well as more food, but now I understood that it would have been a cost to the human in me. It would make me more *dragon* in a sense, with all that meant. More arrogant, more aggressive, less caring about the consequences my actions would have on others. Maybe not less human—those were all very human things—but less *me*. I couldn't accept that.

The promise of near invincibility with greater fortitude was, of course, very tempting. But I only saw it really helping in a fight. It felt like I was already getting into fair fights far too often. I was a shadow dragon, a creature of stealth, and I needed to be better at acting like it. I shouldn't be giving myself excuses to throw myself bluntly at every problem, no matter how satisfying it was.

Charisma would become more and more useful the more people I interacted with, and cunning would likely be a strong option no matter what. They were both good choices, but it was the new option that made me grin. It was just what I needed, which supported the idea that advancements weren't offered in a vacuum. I could have been offered even greater strength, or perhaps better stealth.

Maybe something to make me more terrifying, or to make my venom more powerful. But I had gathered a small following now, and we were going to war.

I was offered command, to better guide my subjects. And with that came a feeling for what that meant, a little like the way Herald and Mak had described it being for humans, though without the visions they had mentioned. It wasn't about telling people what to do in a fight, though I felt that it would make them more likely to listen to me. No, at its core it was about loyalty, to me and to each other, about making them stronger and making them work together. Sure, it would mess with their heads a little, and that was a concern, but we'd all just have to live with that. My small group of humans needed a leader, not a tyrant, and that was what the command advancement promised me.

Choosing it was a no-brainer.

I couldn't make myself return to the humans immediately. Lying in my nest, surrounded by my treasures, I was simply too comfortable, too relaxed and satisfied. The smell of precious metals was heavy in the air, and I felt calm and completely safe. After the previous few days I sorely needed that, and it gave me room to think about uncomfortable things.

I was glad for my conversation with Herald. Both of us acknowledging our less-than-healthy relationship had been a relief, and hopefully a first step in doing something about it, if that was possible. There was no way to know if her acceptance was part of whatever effect I had on her or if that was truly her own unaltered opinion, but it was out in the open now.

What concerned me more was my dragon. Or the part of myself that was draconic, as the case might be. The last time she had spoken to me had been days ago, when she woke me for our ill-fated meeting with Mak. Since then we had been more like a single entity, shifting between acting more like what I thought of as her and me. But whatever *she*—or that part of myself—had been doing to regulate my emotions, it was clearly still happening. All the existential terror that had been so demonstratively released in the tunnels was still safely locked away, and I felt nothing about the poor bastards I'd killed on my way out of the prison. Nor did I feel any guilt about Ardek, and I knew myself well enough to be sure that I couldn't have crippled and subjugated another person and not felt terrible about it when I was fully human.

There might also be the possibility that I *was* the dragon, thinking that I was human, and I wasn't ready to deal with that, hoard or no hoard.

Either way, I felt a little bad about Mak. Not a whole lot, but a little, which was better than nothing. I doubted that the dragon would feel bad about anything. And while I couldn't tell if it was the effect of my new advancement or just common sense, I found myself thinking about how my small group of humans must be feeling. That didn't seem like a very draconic concern either.

It was clear to me that keeping three humans cooped up in the dark was not going to endear me to them even if they understood why, nor would it make them any more useful to me. Herald would probably handle it just fine, though she might not be happy about it. But Mak and Ardek? They'd hate it, and it would give them one more reason to resent me. I couldn't afford that. I needed to lift their spirits somehow.

I decided to surprise them.

The next time I returned to the camp it was late. The sun had just set behind the mountains when I entered the gate, not that they'd know. My increased strength and fortitude helped significantly, because I was carrying a fair load up the tunnel.

I knew that I was making some noise, and I was happy not to see anything when I reached the hub. There were no lights, and no sign of anyone until Herald and Mak stepped out from behind the rock pillar where they'd taken cover, weapons at their sides.

"You can come out, Ardek," Mak called. "It's Draka."

"And what is she carrying?" Herald asked from the darkness as they approached.

What I was carrying was the hindquarters of a mountain goat, as well as my sack full of firewood. It had been a pain to drag in. Flying with the sack on my front was perfectly fine, but to walk anywhere with it, full as it was, I had to move it to my back, which was awkward. And I'd had to carry the meat in my teeth with my head held high, since I didn't want to drag it, so now my neck was sore. Still, I hoped it'd be worth it.

"I brought dinner," I told them after putting the meat on the ground. I'd done my best to bleed it while I gathered the firewood, so it didn't make too much of a mess. "I thought you might want something fresh."

"Did you just hunt this?" Mak asked.

"It is not *aged*, is it?" Herald added, reminding me that I'd told her about my habit of keeping carcasses around for a few days.

"Is that half a goat?" Ardek asked at the same time. He'd just joined the group, and was eyeing the meat hungrily.

"It was bleating no more than two hours ago," I confirmed. I'd had to go old school and pretty much drop on the thing from the air, which was not nearly as easy as sneaking up on one in the night, but much easier than the first embarrassing attempts back when I was starving. It only took three tries!

"I left the skin on, thought that might keep it fresher," I continued. "And the sack is full of firewood. I wasn't sure if you had enough."

"What about the smoke?" Mak asked.

"This chamber is huge, and there's little air shafts here and there. Don't worry about it," I told her. "Now come on, you guys must be starving. Did you eat anything?"

"A light snack after you left," Herald said, emptying the sack and beginning to sort the twigs and branches I'd collected, then getting out a small axe to break the bigger pieces into more manageable logs. "We wanted to wait for you—" she said, grunting, as she chopped into a particularly thick piece of wood "—before we settled in for the night."

"Well, here I am. Mak, Ardek, one of you skin this. I could do it, but it'll get messy."

Soon there was a fire going, and chunks of meat were roasting, filling the air with a wonderful aroma. We all sat around, watching the flames and the food, listening to the wood crackle and echo oddly off the stone as it burned.

"Draka," Mak said after a while, staring into the fire. "Not that I'm not grateful, but what is this?"

"Goat," I said, knowing exactly what she was talking about.

"All right." She stirred the coals a bit. "Why did you bring us half a goat? Why go through all the trouble with fresh meat and firewood when we have provisions for at least two weeks? We all appreciate it, but . . . why?"

"Mak . . . Herald, Ardek. I dragged you all out here. I could have asked, but we all know you wouldn't have said no. I could have left you with the Wolves, where you would *probably* have been safe, but I couldn't stay there, and I need you all somewhere I can keep an eye on you. I know that being kept in this darkness is not comfortable for any of you, especially you, Mak. Isn't this the least I could do?"

"No," Mak said softly. "It's far more."

"Nice to be appreciated. So, the reason is that I don't want this to be a terrible experience for you all. I want it to be as comfortable and rewarding as it can, under the circumstances." I switched to Tekereteki, making Ardek flinch—he probably remembered the last time I'd used the language in front of him—and said, "*You are the one who can feel people's intentions, Mak. Are mine anything other than what I say?*"

"No," she said. "But I still don't understand what's changed. I don't understand why you *want* to do this. But I won't force the issue. Thank you, Draka."

"Just enjoy the meal. Believe me, this damned goat did *not* want to get caught."

My idea to have a morale-boosting barbecue had been a spur-of-the-moment thing. I'd expected it to go over about as well as an office pizza party, but it was surprisingly effective. Most people in Karakan, including my friends, until very recently, simply couldn't afford to gorge themselves on meat whenever they wanted, so "all the goat you can eat" had been a nice surprise for my three humans. Once everybody started eating, the mood had turned much more cheerful, and I was on the verge of convincing myself that I wouldn't need to terrorize or harm either Ardek or Mak any more than I already had. That was a relief. I could, if I had to, but I'd prefer not to. Especially with me having promised Herald that I wouldn't.

I honestly couldn't see Mak pushing me to do anything unpleasant unless it involved Herald. The only thing I could see putting her against me would be if she got it into her head that she needed to 'rescue' Herald from me, in which case nothing would stop her. But even if the worst happened, if I was fully justified and forced to hurt Mak, I was terrified of how that would affect Herald and my relationship with her.

Herald and I both knew that her relationship with me was not rational. We'd talked about it. She had openly acknowledged that she was simply unable to feel anger or outrage toward me, even when she knew that she should. Yet, she still tried to slap a veneer of rationality on it, to frame it as not such a big deal so that she could happily accept it, as though a single argument for her to not be mad at me outweighed every single reason for why she should.

My biggest concern was that if I did something to Mak, Herald would break off our friendship. But a close second was that she might simply accept it outwardly, justifying it while it broke her on the inside. The emotions were there. I could literally smell her rage when I had first told her what I'd done to Mak, and yet she'd never been conscious of it. She knew, rationally, that I had wronged her and her sister, intentionally or not, and she had threatened to withdraw her friendship if I didn't try to do better, but I didn't know if she'd be able to follow through. I had no desire to test her. I had no way of knowing what the breaking point for our relationship might be, and I hoped to never find out.

CHAPTER EIGHTEEN

Cracks

I didn't sleep much that night. After the meal, we let the fire slowly burn itself out; it wasn't needed for warmth this deep in the mountain anyway. The humans talked a little, mostly Herald and Mak telling Ardek about their adventures with and without me, and then they stripped down as much as they were comfortable with and got into their bedrolls. With the lights covered, the darkness swallowed them completely, which would have been a pretty effective defense against any possible treachery on Ardek's part, but it didn't seem likely that he even wanted to try anything. Mak trusted him enough that she didn't suggest a watch rotation, which I took as a good sign.

Herald snuggled up against me and was asleep almost immediately, but it took a while for Mak and Ardek. They both had a lot on their minds, and Ardek was a city boy through and through. The fact that he managed to sleep at all, in this place and under his circumstances, was a small miracle. But eventually they each fell asleep, and I lay there, listening to them all breathing.

I couldn't relax completely for a very long time. I couldn't keep them here, not this deep in the mountain. They needed to be closer to the outside. That should have been obvious from the beginning, but I'd been thinking like a dragon. I hadn't considered how their needs differed from mine. I'd been so focused on their safety that I hadn't even considered their sanity. Or sanitation, for that matter. Maybe they could camp just inside the gate? That way they could be outside most of the time, and still be able to retreat to safety at a moment's notice. Getting as much sunlight as they could would become more important once I started turning their days around, so they'd be awake at night instead, the way I preferred.

We'll figure it out, I thought as I finally, slowly, drifted off to sleep.

That first morning, I showed them around the area, and they were all clearly relieved to go outside. There was a stream nearby where they could wash and get fresh water. Herald noted some signs of game by the water and suggested they could go hunting once they'd finished off the goat, which I thought sounded like a great team-building exercise. That was, as long as Ardek didn't screw everything up and get throttled by the two sisters. He'd been a street kid and insisted that he was stealth itself in the city, but in the forest he made more noise than a whole family of wild pigs.

In the worst case, I supposed, Ardek would learn a lesson about woodcraft and they would go home empty handed. I could always bring them something, but they had plenty of dry food, and I liked the idea of them providing for themselves, together.

Ardek. I wasn't sure what the sisters saw in him. Maybe it was just sympathy and pity, but Herald had done her best to convince me to spare him, twice, when I was not at all inclined to do so. And now Mak had apparently adopted him, or at least taken responsibility for him. Maybe it was just her role as team mom kicking in. Maybe she felt guilty for the way I'd used her to scare the crap out of him. Or maybe she just felt bad for him. Whatever the case might be, she was making sure that his knee healed properly, had been teaching him how to take care of the various gear they'd brought with them, and once they got outside, it didn't take long before she'd cut two straight sticks, each a little less than a yard long, and was starting him on sword drills. She'd apparently taken it personally when he told her that despite being nineteen years old and having bought a sword when he joined the Night Blossom's organization, he did not actually know how to use one.

Herald mostly tolerated him. She wasn't openly unfriendly, and they made small talk occasionally, but she'd seen him in the Night Blossom's estate, guarding the prison when she was brought in and out, her agony used to force Mak to cooperate. She'd been constantly drunk on healing potions at the time, but maybe she still recognized him and resented him on some level. Or maybe she was just wary and uncomfortable around a man two years older than her, a confessed life-long criminal whom she didn't know and whom she was now forced to share a camp with.

She'd still convinced me to spare his life. Once while drunk, and once while sober. My best friend wanted him alive. That had to count for something.

Come to think of it, why hadn't I just killed him the first time I saw him? I went past him to kill the woman he was with, but I only injured him. Sure, shredding someone's knee isn't nothing, but it would have been so easy to just tear his belly open instead, or to finish him off once he was down. But instead, I decided that he'd surrendered and kept him around. I'd folded pretty much instantly when Herald argued for keeping him around. That could be because I wanted to make her happy. It could also be because this was a world where magic was very real, and Herald and I were living proof that it could mess with your head.

It was afternoon. The kid was just sitting down, totally wrung out and trying to catch his breath during a break in Mak's "lessons."

"Ardek," I said, walking up to him, and he twitched and half turned, raising his stick until he saw that it was me. I stared him down until he put the stick away.

"I need to know what advancements you have," I told him once he'd calmed down a little. He hesitated, which actually impressed me. I'd have thought that he'd just tell me anything without hesitation.

"You don't keep secrets from me, Ardek. I'll give you privacy, but if I ask you for something, you tell me. And I won't ask unless I need to know. If I don't know what you can do, I can't use you."

I could see the gears turning in his head as he hesitated again, and the result he came up with under my stare was 'Be useful. Don't be useless.'

"And don't bother trying to lie," I added. Mak was sitting by a tree about twenty yards away. I looked at her and she nodded to me.

"All right," Ardek said finally. "I'm really healthy. I don't get sick, ever."

"Anything else? You're about nineteen, right? You must have at least another one."

"Ah . . ."

"You don't want to tell me. You think it will piss me off."

"Well . . ."

"Ardek. If you won't tell me this, I can't trust you, and if I can't trust you, I can't keep you around. And I can't let you go either. That leaves me with no options. Do you understand?"

I could almost see his mouth go dry. "Yeah," he said hoarsely.

"So?"

"People just . . . like me, right?" he blurted out. "It's not anything I do, just, people who I talk to and spend time with start to like me."

"And?"

"And, nothing. I've got three, and I took the second one twice. It seemed to be keeping me alive after the first time, so doubling down felt right, right?"

That might explain why Herald wanted him alive at least, no matter what she'd told herself. I couldn't say that I liked him much, but I had spared him, so perhaps I was being affected. Not that it mattered that much. I still felt fully capable of getting rid of him if it came to that.

I nodded. The trick to nodding with a long neck, I'd found, was to make sure to only bend the last bit, otherwise you looked weird. "That's about what I thought," I said, turning to walk away. "Thanks for telling me."

"That's it?" he asked. "You're not pissed?"

I stopped and turned my head back toward him. "Nah. Now that I know for sure, I can keep it in mind. And having someone on hand that just naturally gets along with people sounds *useful*." Then I jerked my head toward Mak, who was getting up. "Looks like the break's over. Your taskmaster is getting ready."

I spent most of the rest of the afternoon lying just inside the gate, while Herald sat in the sun outside. She was treating it like just any day off. She'd done her sword forms and some sparring in the morning and some archery practice in the afternoon, and then she spent the rest of the day reading, napping—she and Mak both did a lot of napping, with how poorly they were sleeping—and talking to me or Mak during her breaks. Mak was taking Ardek's training surprisingly seriously. The sounds of sticks clacking together, Ardek's yelps and groans, and Mak's instructions were a constant in the background.

"*Did you ever hear back from Maglan?*" I asked after Herald had closed her book and put it aside, closing her eyes and relaxing in the sun. Her mouth flattened a bit from the relaxed smile she'd been wearing so far.

"*No, I have not. But it is too early to be disappointed, I think. I sent my letter before we went north. If he has even had an opportunity to send a reply, it may not have had time to arrive yet.*" She sighed. "*And there is this whole mess. It might have arrived since we were . . . you know.*"

"*Would it not be delivered to your inn or something?*"

"*Most mail would, but this I would need to get directly from my contact. I have no doubt that he would hold on to it. I just need to have the time and occasion to meet him.*"

"*Then we will arrange something as soon as we can.*"

"*Thank you.*" She opened her eyes and looked at the patch of sky visible between the mountainside and the tree. "*At least there has been no news of fighting, which is the most important thing. As long as there are no skirmishes, Mag should be safe.*"

"*I am sure that he is fine,*" I said. "*Do you think that I can meet him once he is back?*"

"*If I am to keep seeing him, that will be unavoidable, I think. You are too large a part of my life to hide you from him. Only . . .*"

"*Hmm?*"

"*There is the issue of secrecy.*"

"*Right,*" I said and paused. "*Is it him or me that you are not sure about?*"

She turned her face to me, meeting my eyes sadly. "*Him, for keeping the secret. And you, if he does not.*"

"*I see.*" I looked away, suppressing a flash of annoyance and anger. It was a fair thing for her to say, I reminded myself. This was Herald. I relied on her to be honest with me, and I'd been particularly aggressive and threatening lately.

It still hurt to hear any distrust from her.

When I turned back, I could see in her eyes that she knew what was going through my head. She waited with a patient smile.

"*And if I promise not to hurt him?*" I asked.

"I would love to hear such a promise, but if he tells his friends or his fellow soldiers about you, the damage will already be done. No, I will have to talk to him before introducing you, and then I will have to make a choice."

The choice she meant was obvious. *"Herald, I do not want to get between you and your . . ."* I searched for a word. Tekereteki was surprisingly limited here, and I settled on *"consort."*

She snorted. *"Consort. That is a massive overstatement of what we have so far. But believe me, Draka, I will not do anything lightly. The truth now is the same as when you asked me before, when we were traveling to rescue the others from the valkin tunnels. I love him, certainly, but I do not know if I am in love with him. I love you, as well, and I will not risk your safety. If I do not think I can trust him to meet you, then . . . I do not know. Perhaps I can try to keep you secret from him. Or perhaps not."* She closed her eyes and leaned back against the stone. *"I just do not know, right now."*

No one complained when I brought them back inside while the sun was setting, and the next morning I woke them even earlier. Mak had slept especially poorly, even waking Herald with her thrashing at one point, but I thought nothing of it at the time. The day went much like the previous one, with Mak continuing her efforts to teach Ardek the sword, while I mostly lounged with Herald. I'd brought my bestiary down, and we leafed through it together, with me reading the descriptions out loud. We'd have to start doing something more useful soon, but I was too content to interrupt the moment.

Herald had been silent for a while when she said, *"Do they sound more heated to you?"*

I listened, and it was like I could hear a crack forming in our little group.

Thwap!

"Faster! I told you to parry, didn't I?" Mak shouted. She sounded truly angry at this point. "I showed you exactly how I'd attack, and how to defend against it! Again!"

Thwap! The sound of a stick hitting flesh was loud enough that I could hear it even by the gate.

"Ow! I'm sorry!" Ardek called out.

"You're sorry?" *Thwap!* "What are you sorry for?" *Thwap!* "What—" *Thwap!* "Have—" *Thwap!* "You—" *Crack!*

At the sound of what must have been Mak's stick snapping, Herald sat up straight, her face drawn with concern.

"Done—" *Thud.* "To—" *Thud.*

Herald rose and got moving in one motion. I followed.

"Be—" *Thud.* "SORRY—" *Thud.* "FOR?"

Mak was screaming as we crested the ramp up from the gate. Ardek was lying on the ground, his hands over his head, while Mak had discarded her broken stick and was kicking the ever-living shit out of him.

"You didn't do anything!" Mak screamed as she let loose on the kid. "What do you have to be sorry for?"

Herald didn't bother with words. She ran in, wrapped her arms around her sister, and broke the situation up by quite easily lifting Mak off the ground.

Mak barely noticed. "All *you* did was sit there!" she howled as she kicked and struggled in Herald's arms. "You didn't do anything!"

"Mak, stop!" I roared, and it was like I'd thrown a switch. She went silent and almost limp, breathing hard, and there were tears of rage streaming down her face.

"Herald, put her down," I said, and she did.

"Heal him," I told Mak, and her face fell in a look of utter dismay as I revealed one of her most tightly held secrets. "He was going to find out sooner or later. Now heal him!"

"Fine," Mak whispered. She turned her eyes from me, and walked up to Ardek. "Get your shirt off," she told him. He looked at her warily, then at me, and then gingerly sat up and pulled his long tunic over his head. He was covered in welts and fresh, angry bruises, and Mak looked over them systematically. As she channeled magic into them, Ardek's eyes slowly went wide with understanding.

"That's what you did to my knee," he said, almost accusingly.

"The massage and the wrapping helped," Mak said brusquely as she worked, not looking him in the face. "But I did this too." She stood and backed away. "There. Done."

"Herald, can you look after Ardek for a bit?" I asked, and she nodded. "Good. Mak, come with me. Let's take a walk."

CHAPTER NINETEEN

Recover What You Can

Mak followed me obediently as I led her toward a stream that ran through a shallow gully, not far from the campsite. She looked both unhappy and unsure of herself. I wasn't particularly happy myself. I'd thought I knew where I had her, that I could predict what she'd do. Clearly, I'd been mistaken.

"I won't ask you why," I told her. My voice was sharper than intended. This was partly my fault, and I was annoyed with myself. I should have seen it coming somehow. "I know why, and I understand. But why now? You've been . . . nice. Taking care of him. What changed?"

"Nothing." From the slight tremble in her voice, I knew that she was fighting to keep her anger and shame under control. "I didn't sleep well, and I lost my temper, that's all."

"How far would you have gone if we hadn't stopped you?"

"I don't know. I'd like to think that I would have stopped before I killed him, but . . . I don't know." She clenched her hands into fists and unclenched them again, over and over, as though she wished that she had Ardek in front of her so that she could keep beating him. At least her hands looked better now. They should be good as new in a few days at this rate. *That's what plenty of food, plenty of rest, and constant magical healing does for you*, I thought.

"So, again," I said. "You've treated him kindly so far. What changed?"

"Nothing. Really. The only reason I've been soft on him is that if I don't force myself to be nice, I might kill him." She laughed bitterly. "Perhaps an activity where I have to hit him wasn't the greatest idea."

That was news to me. Maybe I should have seen it, but I just figured that it was Mak having a naturally caring personality or, after what Ardek had told me, that she was being affected by his "Love me!" advancement. Excessive kindness to avoid committing murder had never occurred to me. "I didn't realize that you hated him that much," I said softly.

When Mak replied, her voice carried more venom than I'd ever heard from her. "He worked for that *putrid bitch*! He sat in that guard room and watched them take Herald down and carry her back up again because she was too broken to walk on her own! I don't know if I hate him personally. Maybe he couldn't have done anything even if he tried. But he's the only one in that whole rotten gang that I can touch, so he's a good start." She paused, then said, "I've never felt like this before. This . . . bone deep desire to hurt someone. Not even with the bastards who thought they could abuse me because I was the *entertainment*." She spat the last word. "In his cell, when you told me to tear his throat out, I . . . if I'd had a knife, he'd be dead now. But I didn't. And when you told me to use my teeth, it scared me. I was going to do it, but I was fighting myself every step of the way."

"Because you didn't want to be a monster?"

Mak laughed darkly. "No! Because I was afraid I might *enjoy* it. Not the act itself, but doing it to *him*, to what he represents. I had the perfect excuse. You'd ordered me to, and I couldn't refuse, right? We both know what the situation is. I don't know what you've done to me, but we both know that this isn't just fear or respect or remorse. You say go, I go; you say stop, I stop. You say kill . . . I've never killed a person before, but I will if you tell me to. I don't know if I'm physically strong enough to tear a man's throat out with my teeth, but I would have tried. What held me back was that, when I imagined the satisfaction of doing that, of destroying something belonging to the Night Blossom in such a primal way, I couldn't help but imagine Herald seeing me covered in gore and *grinning*. That terrified me. The idea of her seeing me do something like that and enjoying it. Of her thinking less of me." She ran out of steam there and walked in silence for a while, before managing to say, "It would destroy me, I think."

Her voice was hollow at the end, and the way she looked at me . . . There was such pain there, from just the thought, that I never wanted to see what she'd look like if she actually lost her sister's love. I knew that same fear all too well.

As much to reassure myself as Mak I said, "I tore a man's head from his shoulders, and she didn't judge me for that."

Mak shook her head slowly. "He was not a defenseless prisoner like Ardek. And you, with all due respect, are a terrifying creature straight out of our legends, not an older sister who's coddled and cared for and consoled her for her whole life. I think she expects some extreme violence from you."

"Maybe. But we have that in common at least, you and me. We both want Herald to love us. We worry about what she thinks of us."

"Yeah." She sighed. "So what now? What about me? What about Ardek?"

"I can't let you kill him, obviously. I don't want you hurting him at all, unless he gives you a good reason. At this point, as long as he cooperates, it would be really messed up to kill him. And he's our best source of information on the Night Blossom, for now."

"You won't punish me?" She sounded incredulous. Relieved, sure, but more surprised than anything. "I hurt your . . . I don't even know what to call him. Your property?"

I flinched internally at her choice of words, in part because I didn't like how appropriate they felt. Property. "Please don't use that word. Minion, maybe? And no, I don't see the point. You know what you did wrong and look like you regret it already. Besides, I can't say that I wouldn't have done the same or worse if I were you. Just don't do it again, yeah?"

She relaxed a little, walking beside me. "Yeah, all right. Thank you. And I do regret it. I don't know if I'm sorry for beating him, but I'm disappointed in myself for losing control. It won't happen again. I've just been so *angry* these last few days. With the Night Blossom, with myself—"

"What about me?"

She stopped and looked at me in silence for a while, as though she was searching my face for something. "No," she said. "Whatever you've done to me, it's less than I deserve. I made my choice. I betrayed you. For Herald's sake, sure, and I would probably do it again, but I know what I did. And I can't blame you for retaliating. I would say that I forgive you, but I am the one who needs forgiveness."

"Herald can't bring herself to be angry with me either," I said suddenly. The words just came, and I wasn't sure why. The idea of a Mak who couldn't be angry with me should have been a comfort, but instead it disturbed me.

Maybe I was goading her, trying to force some kind of negative reaction out of her, but all she said was, "Yeah, that figures. That girl has worshiped the sky you fly through since the first time we met. She talked about you all the way back from the mines, and then again until we fell asleep, once we were back in our room at the inn. She was always a romantic, fanciful girl. The idea that a dragon might want to be her friend? I can't remember the last time I saw her so happy and excited."

"I think it's more than that. I think that I'm in her head somehow. Maybe not the same as with you, but I've done something to her. Some kind of magic that I can't control."

"Maybe. But in that case, it works fast. Like I said, from day one, she never stood a chance."

There was no point in arguing. She was doing the same thing as Herald, rationalizing away what I was doing to them and framing it in a way that she could handle. It was uncanny. No one wants the people close to them to be mad at them, but when you know that they literally can't be angry with you, it's not the same thing. But I would just have to learn to live with it until I could hopefully get whatever this was under conscious control. If that was even possible.

At least there was comfort in knowing that neither of them would turn on me. Betrayal hadn't been a big concern a week ago; I'd thought that I knew who I could trust. Knowing that I could trust both Herald and Mak completely, knowing that I could control them to a lesser or greater degree . . . as distasteful as it was, was a great relief. It calmed the dragon in me. But there was still the issue of whether I could trust them with others, which currently meant Ardek. He was mine, and I didn't want to turn up one morning to find him dead and Mak looking embarrassed.

"Anyway," I said casually, turning us back toward the gate. "Do you think that you can keep yourself from hurting Ardek anymore?"

"Yes. But I should let Herald take over his training, if she's willing. Remove the temptation, you know?"

"That's probably best, yeah," I said, then brightened as an idea popped into my head, something that I should have been doing for months and just never got around to. Now there was no excuse. "You know what, though? I could use some training, if you're up for it."

"You?" Mak said, surprise saturating her entire demeanor. "I saw you tear through a whole house less than a week ago!"

"And I was wounded badly enough that I might have bled out doing it," I pointed out. "You saw the wound. Hell, you healed it. And, as you pointed out, you've seen me fight. I do well in fights, but I am not good at fighting. I charge in, fight by instinct, and hope that I'm hard enough to come out the other side mostly unscathed. Ideally, I should strike from the shadows, and there shouldn't be a fight at all, but that won't always be possible. I need to learn to fight properly. One day I'm going to come up against someone who's quick and prepared and really good at fighting big, dangerous creatures like me, and I have no idea how that'll end. What do you think?"

"I . . . If you want to spar with me, of course I'll accept. I'm sure it would do me good as well, in case I have to fight a bear or something."

"Heh, yeah. Did Lalia tell you about the bear we fought?"

"Loudly, and with gestures. She was pretty drunk at the time. Did you really wrestle the thing?"

"That . . . is a very generous description of what I did. The thing had me pinned, literally trying to eat my damn head! Then Lalia comes charging in on that horse of hers, screaming like a *banshee* or a *Valkyrie* or something—"

"I have no idea what those things are."

"Whatever, she was impressive, all right? Don't tell her I said that. So, Lalia comes charging in . . ."

When we got back to the gate, Herald and Ardek were nowhere to be seen. I almost got a little worried when we walked over to the campsite and they weren't there either, but then I heard a *thunk*, closely followed by Herald's voice, calm and measured. "Better. But you are moving your left shoulder when you release. You are trying to throw the arrow. Release it! Again!"

We followed the sound toward Herald's improvised archery range. A dead tree had snapped in half at some point, and the remaining half still stood, dry and crumbling. The previous day, Herald had marked a simple target on the trunk for use as archery practice. Now we found her standing behind and to the side of Ardek, who was holding her bow. She was watching intently as he nocked one of the simple practice arrows she'd brought. He fumbled a bit but got it lined up after a few seconds. With a look of complete concentration, he drew back the string, trembling under the unfamiliar strain, then released. The arrow sailed toward the trunk, barely nicking it before continuing toward the bushes and the hillside.

"Well, you hit the target that time! Not bad for a beginner! Once you get it inside the lines a few times, we can start to work on distance. Again."

I knew nothing of archery, so I couldn't comment, but I didn't think that hitting a tree from thirty feet looked that impressive. We watched Ardek shoot a couple of arrows, missing some, hitting some, with Herald giving him feedback between each shot. She spotted us two shots in and gave us a silent nod before going back to instructing Ardek.

"Good," she said after he'd used all the practice arrows. "Now comes the fun part. Those things cost a couple of bits each if you get the cheap ones, the ones that are not quite straight and have fletchings that fall off after a shot or two. Mine are a peacock each. So now you go and find them."

"Shit. Really?"

"Think of it this way. You can only bring so many arrows with you. Learning to keep track of them is an essential skill for an archer. But you can always go back to sword drills with Mak, if you prefer." She jerked her head toward Mak and me.

Ardek looked our way, locking eyes with Mak for a second. "I'll go look for those arrows," he said, handing the bow to Herald before jogging off past the dead tree.

"*So, you found something to keep him busy,*" I said, the Tekereteki coming naturally with her. "*How is he?*"

"*Shaken, but bodily he is fine now. I think he will be completely recovered by morning. He was hurt, not injured.*" She turned to Mak. "*How are you?*" she asked, slowing her speech a little and making her enunciation just a little more careful, her voice a little softer, more caring.

"*I am . . . not satisfied. With myself,*" Mak replied, speaking slowly and thoughtfully, her face reflecting her words. "*Lost control. Should not have happened.*"

"*I spoke with Ardek. He understands. He had hoped that he was forgiven, because you were nice. But he understands that he was not. If he is angry, he hides it well. I think that he is scared, and sad.*"

Mak shrugged, her expression showing just how little she cared about how Ardek felt about her. "*If he wants forgiveness, he should help us . . . hurt? Night Flower. I know that's not the right word but you know what I mean,*" she added in Karakani.

"*He should help us defeat the Night Blossom,*" Herald corrected with a nod.

"*Defeat the Night Blossom. Thank you.*" She gestured toward the bow in Herald's hand. "*You teach him bow?*"

"*I am teaching him archery, yes. I think it would be good.*"

"*Agree. Will you teach him sword as well?*"

I cut in. "*Mak and I thought it would be better if she does not have any more sword practice with Ardek for a while. But it would be good if he keeps learning. Would you take over until Tam and Val are back?*"

"*I am far from an expert, and I have never taught anyone the sword. But I can try,*" she said, with only the slightest bit of doubt. "*Do you think that he will listen to me?*"

"*He did just now, when you taught him archery.*"

"*Fighting with swords is more personal, more dependent on individual strength. He may not like being taught by a girl younger than him.*"

"*A young woman,*" I corrected her. "*And I commanded him to listen to you and Mak. If he is difficult, remind him of that.*"

"*It will not be a problem. I think.*" Mak said. "*I am a small woman. He did not question me. Wants to please, I think. And Herald is bigger than him.*"

I chuckled. Yeah, she sure was. Taller than most men and with a strong build from years of archery, even starved as she was, Herald was quite simply bigger than Ardek. He wasn't short, being around Val's height, but he was also no bruiser.

"*Your Tekereteki is coming back quite well,*" I told Mak. "*Have you been practicing with Herald?*"

"*No. But try to think in this language sometimes. To remember. Helps, I think. I speak it once. Seven years in Tekeretek, then with father.*" She shrugged. "*Most of it in memory, somewhere.*"

I knew nothing about language learning, but it sounded reasonable to me. Surely forcing yourself to keep a language in mind must help? And I hadn't even considered that she'd spent half of her childhood in Tekeretek, before they fled. Of course, she would have spoken it fluently once.

"Miss Herald?" Ardek's voice cut clearly through the trees. The kid could call, that was for sure. "How many arrows did I shoot?"

"Twelve!" Herald called back. To us she said, "*He shot ten. But I think this will help him keep track of his shots better in the future. I was not exaggerating about how important that is. Remember with the trolls? I almost ran out of arrows on that trip.*"

"*Some were broken,*" Mak objected.

Herald only nodded. Then she looked between Mak and me. "*Sometimes things break. That only makes it more important to recover what you can.*"

She was right. It *is* important to recover what you can. And I got a strong feeling that she was talking about more than just arrows.

CHAPTER TWENTY

Beating Around The Bush

The next several days passed rather peacefully. The sisters' nightmares grew a little less frequent and a little less intense, and a week after their rescue they could both usually go back to sleep after waking from one, which did wonders for their general moods. They were also filling out a little. I made sure they had plenty of meat, and the frequent meals I forced on them slowly began to undo the damage of a week of healing-induced starvation.

There was no repeat of Mak's outburst of violence, though how much of that was thanks to Ardek keeping his distance was hard to tell. He wasn't so much fearful as wary, speaking to and helping her as necessary but watching his words and keeping a careful eye on her whenever they were close. And Mak must have gotten some small catharsis out of it, because after that night, a little of the quiet strength I remembered returned to her eyes, bit by bit.

If Ardek was holding a grudge I wanted to know, but when I asked him about what had happened he didn't look angry or anything. His face fell and he shrugged. "I'm not an idiot. She was pretty clear about why she did it. It's not like she's wrong either. It just surprised me, that's all. She's good at hiding her anger."

"You didn't even try to defend yourself," I said. "She's a lot smaller than you. Aren't you embarrassed?"

"Like I said, I'm not an idiot. This is more or less a gang, right?

I narrowed my eyes at him, but he stuck to it and continued quickly. "A small one, but basically a gang. I don't know what else to call it. I've been in a few gangs, and one rule is always the same: If someone higher up than you decides that you need a beating, you take it. Fighting back gets you beat worse if you're lucky. If you're not lucky, you're dog food. Or fish food, if the gang's turf is near the water. Then you either fuck off, you swallow your pride and keep going like nothing happened, or you find a way to kill the bastard."

He looked across the small clearing we were in, at Mak napping in the sun. "I can't go anywhere. And I don't want to hurt them."

"You would die," I told him. It was that simple.

He paused. "Probably, yeah. And she's right. I didn't do anything. I don't think I could have. I might've gotten killed if I tried. But yeah. I was there, I knew what was happening, more or less, and all I did was look away."

He had a thin, green stick in his hands, and started peeling the bark with his thumbnail. "You know, when we were offered to join, it was the best day of my life. We'd made it, you know? Berek and Ava and me. The Night Blossom, she's one of the big ones. She doesn't run a gang. She runs an *organization*. No ganger fucks with you when you work for the Night Blossom. And all we were supposed to do was guard her businesses, run messages, maybe move some less-than-legal stuff from one place to another. Nobody ever told us about any slaves or any torture prisons or shit like that.

"I won't lie to you, boss. I'd like to just run off and pretend that none of this ever happened. Maybe use my stash to buy passage to Tavvanar or Marbek. But I can't. When I think about skipping out on you and the ladies, it's like . . . I feel sick in my soul. Know what I mean? I owe them, for being part of all that, and I owe you, for letting me live when there was nothing stopping you from killing me. I'm not going anywhere. Can't say I love being out here, though."

"You'd better get used to it. I won't feel comfortable sending any of you back to Karakan until Tam and Val are back, and we don't know when that'll be."

"That's the brother and his man, right?"

"Right. They're the swordsmen of the team. The frontliners. Once they return, I'll probably send you all back."

"I think I've seen the brother before. At one of the Night Blossom's gambling places, down by the harbor. Not many 'teki in the city, you know, and the merchants don't speak Karakani like a native. Luckiest bastard at dice I've ever seen. The house boss banned him after a couple of nights. Wanted a couple of us to rough him up to really get the message across, but there was a guard patrol passing by and he slipped away."

"Lucky you. If you tried to lay hands on Tam, Val would have fed you your own spine. Possibly in the company of some of the Gray Wolves. I thought the Tekereteki adventurers were fairly well known?"

"I'm sure they are in the Adventurers' Guild. Maybe among the guards too. But it's a big city. Why would anyone know anything about them who doesn't need to? Besides, the house boss is an asshole. He barely tolerates Barleans, and he's half Barlean himself, or so they say. I'm sure he was overjoyed to have an excuse to give a 'teki a beating."

"This isn't the first time I hear about Tekereteki being disliked here, though I haven't seen it. Is there an actual reason for that, or is it just assholes being assholes? You're not at war with them, are you?"

"I mean . . . war? Nah. Not right now. But Tekeretek and the League have little wars all the time. Next one is probably just over the horizon. But even when we're not at war, there's always 'teki pirates attacking ships and raiding fishing towns for slaves. I wouldn't be surprised if that's who the Night Blossom was selling her prisoners to. So, you know they're villains, right? In stories and theater plays and all. Plus they enslave anyone with magic just for having it, which is just uncivilized, isn't it?"

"Karakan enslaves people who can't pay their fines. That's sick."

I could see that he wanted to argue, but instead he said, "Maybe. But enslaving someone because they got magic as an advancement, that's just . . . It's supposed to be something to celebrate, you know? They twist it into something ugly. There has to be something wrong with people like that."

"Herald and Mak's parents would have agreed with you. They were refugees who fled Tekeretek, from what I've been told."

"Yeah? But to most people that won't matter. When you see a 'teki who speaks our language like they grew up here—"

"Which Herald, Mak, and Tam did. They're all citizens. Herald was born here."

"Sure, but nobody's gonna know that. You see a 'teki with perfect Karakani, you figure they're a spy. I don't know what else to tell you. I mean *I* know, *now*, that they aren't. Because they're not, right?"

"Not as far as I know," I said flatly. He was clearly aware of the hole he was digging, and was trying to find a way out.

"Yeah, yeah, of course, but, uh, where I was going with all this was that there are real reasons people wouldn't like 'teki—"

"Can you say the whole word? I'm pretty damn sure that what you're using is a slur."

"What, 'teki?"

"Yeah. Stop."

"Uh, all right. So, yeah, there are real reasons someone wouldn't like 'teki— sorry, *Tekereteki* people, I mean—like if they have friends or family on the sea, or on the coast. They could have lost someone, you know, or they're worried that they will."

"Are the Tekereteki pirates the only ones?"

"Nah, there's lots of Barlean pirates, too, and they usually have crews from all over the League, I think. Any sailor desperate enough could become a pirate, I guess."

"Yeah. Ardek, if you're not already, I want you to convince yourself that Herald and her siblings are neither spies nor pirates. Understood?"

He nodded meekly. "Yes, boss."

"And when we're back in the city, if you could try to help their reputation without getting your ass kicked, I want you to do that too. Maybe point out how these three particular Tekereteki were instrumental in saving three or four dozen Karakani citizens from slavers, stuff like that."

"That . . . I mean, I'll try, boss. I'm not a lawyer or a politician, but I'll try."

"Come on, where's your self-confidence? People like you, right?"

"I don't know if that will help, if I'm trying to talk up someone they hate. But I'll try, boss. I'll try."

Five days after I'd brought them all to the mountain I had their days all turned around. I'd told them what I was doing. They agreed with my reasoning, and as far as I could tell they were being honest, though Ardek had been pretty uncertain until I told him about Mak's night vision spell. After the second night, they'd started sleeping just inside the gate, and I had gone back to sleeping in my nest. I'd started worrying more about someone setting up camp and seeing the gate open when we came out than I did about Ardek betraying us, and I wanted to be able to check the situation out before opening.

On that fifth day I woke them a few hours before sunset. That night we were going hunting, and the humans had spent most of two previous days preparing wooden racks that Herald told me were for drying skins and meat. I'd offered to bring them fresh meat myself, but Mak and Herald had resolutely refused. Mak because she thought that a hunt would be a good activity for them as a team, and Herald because she just enjoyed hunting, which she couldn't exactly justify doing if I did it for them.

"*Besides,*" Herald had said when I talked to her about it, sitting away from the others, "*Ardek can reliably hit inside the lines from a hundred feet now, even with the awful practice arrows I make to replace the broken ones. I was hoping that we might find a deer, and he could take a shot at it.*"

"*And if he misses?*"

"*Then he can look for the arrow in the dark. It will be good practice for him.*"

"*You are taking his training seriously.*"

"*I do not see the point in teaching him if I am not going to be serious about it. And I feel bad for him. I could so easily have been in his position.*"

"*Really?*"

"*Yes. I was practically a street kid myself, though I at least had a roof and a warm meal to return to in the evenings. Mak and Tam worked themselves to the bone to provide me with even that. If they had been a little less determined, or caring, or lucky, I might have ended up like Ava.*"

"Ava . . . that was—"

"The woman you killed coming out of the prison, and Ardek's friend. Yes." Herald sighed. *"It turns out that I knew her, once. Not well. She was with one of Mag's friends a few years ago, and she was not on the street when I knew her. I did not even realize until a few days ago when I was talking to Ardek and he mentioned her. I do not know what happened, but it must have been shortly after I stopped seeing her around that she joined the gang that Ardek was in. Perhaps her parents were ruined or died without leaving her an inheritance. Such things happen."*

She looked at me sadly. *"My point is, that could so easily have been me. Neither her nor Ardek were there because they were bad. She could be rude and condescending, but she could also be funny, and kind. Ardek told me that Ava couldn't look when they brought me past. I guess she must have recognized me. And it is true that neither of them did anything to intervene, but they had few options and less to fall back on.*

"I suppose I want this to be a second chance for him, which Ava will never get."

"Is that why you asked me to spare him to start with?"

"I have no idea what I was thinking back at the house. I remember very little from when you rescued me. When we spoke in the cellar, I suppose that it had some part in my motivation, but I meant what I said. I really do think that he will be useful. He knows many places and faces connected with the Night Blossom, so if we are to find her, having Ardek's loyalty and cooperation will be a great help. And I think that he is sincere in his desire to help."

"I got the same impression," I said. I wasn't the greatest judge of character, and I wasn't too proud to admit that, but as far as I could tell, Ardek had been honest with me. *"But he knows everything there is to know about Mak and myself. If he betrays us . . ."*

"If I even suspect that he might, then I will kill him myself," Herald said solemnly. *"So take his continued survival as a sign of my confidence in him."*

I looked at the seventeen-year-old in front of me, the girl who wanted nothing more than to be taken seriously as an adult and an adventurer, who had just declared that she would murder a man only two years older than her if she even suspected him of being disloyal. A young man who, according to himself, had an ability to make people like him. It wasn't that I doubted Herald's determination or sincerity. It certainly wasn't that I doubted her ability and willingness to kill when necessary; she had killed men in front of me. But this was different, and if push came to shove, I wasn't sure that she could do it—kill a man in cold blood like that. And I wasn't sure that I wanted her to, necessary or not.

"If you suspect something, come to me before you do anything about it," I said, not wanting her to think that I doubted her. *"If you catch him in the act, use your judgment."*

"As you wish," she said with a small shrug. I might not have hidden my concerns as well as I'd wanted to, but if she didn't want to make a fuss over it, I was happy to call it there.

The hunt went about as well as could be expected. We all went in a group, of course, and Ardek showed a remarkable inability to learn from his earlier mistakes, crashing through the trees like a drunk moose. At least that's how it felt compared to the rest of us, who all moved like cats. Perhaps he was still distracted by his amazement at Mak's spell, which let him see in the dark. Herald and I, of course, didn't need it, since there was plenty of moonlight.

Once the stars aligned and Ardek managed to move quietly enough for long enough to get within sight of a deer that I'd sniffed out, he took his shot. The first one missed so wide that the deer was barely alerted, only briefly looking up and around before going back to stripping leaves off a bush.

The second shot hit, but poorly.

Herald had talked for a long time, using sketches about where to aim on a deer and a boar, the two types of prey we were most likely to come across. The area you wanted to hit was smaller than I'd thought, but still fairly large, covering most of the upper torso where the lungs and heart were located. Ardek's arrow struck two feet off target, hitting the poor deer somewhere low in the gut.

The deer, of course, jumped and ran. Was the hit lethal? Probably, on a long enough time scale. It could be hours before it bled out or, in the worst case, days before it died from massive infection if no major blood vessels had been hit. And the deer would be in horrible pain the entire time. Luckily, Herald and I had talked about this ahead of time. When she'd learned to hunt, Lalia had shot her own arrow at the same time as Herald, so that if Herald's shot was bad, Lalia's was likely to kill the animal quickly. We only had one bow, so we couldn't secure the kill that way, but we had something better. Me.

The moment the deer ran I went after it. It was entirely instinctive; even if we hadn't discussed it, I'm certain that I would have done the same. The prey ran, and I pursued. That was just how it worked. When food or fighting was in the cards, the dragon came out in full force. I'd felt it slowly growing stronger all night, and now it was let loose.

The deer ran for its life, not knowing that it was already as good as dead. It ran full tilt, and it was hard for me to keep up with it, but the smell of deer and blood was strong, and it was easy to follow. I used my wings for bursts of speed whenever possible, sometimes keeping the deer in sight and sometimes not, but it was a matter of endurance, not speed. Thanks to my fortitude advancement, I had endurance in spades as long as I didn't sprint dead-out, and the deer couldn't keep up its pace for long, not with an arrow in it.

It didn't collapse, but it did slow steadily, and in the end I ran it down. I felled it the way I'd seen big cats do on TV, getting my claws in its hindquarters and knocking it off balance enough to make it stumble, which let me tackle it to the ground properly. I didn't want to make a mess of it, so I sunk my teeth into its throat and tore it open, veins, arteries and all. God, gods, Mercies, or whoever, it felt good! I thought back on my first kill, an injured mountain goat, and I almost laughed. I had been so . . . maybe not weak, but soft. I'd cried, actually cried, when I killed the poor thing. Why? It had been in pain, as good as dead, and I had been hungry. Sympathy is one thing, but to cry when I had been practically doing it a favor, ending both our suffering at once? That was just sad.

Humans can be so weak, I thought fondly. *That's why they need dragons to look after them.*

CHAPTER TWENTY-ONE

An Ill-Considered Visitor

When the others caught up with me they, or at least Herald and Ardek, were in a much better mood than I'd expected. Mak was keeping her expression carefully neutral as she scanned our surroundings, on guard in case the sound and scent of the hunt attracted unwanted attention.

I had to fight down an urge to warn them off from my kill, but the little voice reminded me that they were my humans. They needed food, so I would provide.

"I will not pretend that it was a good shot," Herald told Ardek, "but it was a hit. That's better than many manage on their first hunt. Of course, if we had not had Draka to help, we would have had to track the deer down to finish it, which might have taken hours if we were unlucky. And then we would have had to carry it back from wherever we tracked it to, which would have taken longer, only with the added burden. I suggest you thank her for sparing us all that."

He ducked his head toward me. "Right. Thanks, boss."

"Thank me by shooting better next time," I said lightly. "I won't run the next one down for you. All that tracking and carrying are a great way to motivate someone to get better, right?"

I was, of course, bullshitting. I'd loved running that deer down, and I'd do it again in a heartbeat. It was like winning a race with my friends watching, and the prize was that I got to eat my opponent.

Herald took my words at face value and looked less than enthusiastic. "You do realize that we will have to go with him in that case?"

"I like walking in the forest with you all," I said. "But if you don't like the idea, then I suggest you make sure that Ardek gets better. With all that motivation I don't see how he could fail."

Herald sighed but didn't argue. If she wanted to keep him and train him, I was going to make sure that she took her role seriously.

"What about your arrows?" I asked.

Herald crouched by the carcass. "This one might be recoverable. We will see once I cut it out. We can consider the other one lost. As much as I would love to have Ardek look for it, it is more important that he is here to dress the deer."

"What's that?" Ardek said.

"You've got to get the blood and guts out," Mak said from off to the side. "Or do you want to carry all that extra weight back to camp, and then have a pile of deer guts, full of deer shit, next to where we spend our time?"

I couldn't tell, my night vision being all grays, but from the expression on Ardek's face, I'd guess that he paled at that. "No," he said. "I guess not."

"Then we may as well get started," Herald said, pulling out a short, very sharp-looking knife. "So, you want to start with a cut around the butthole . . ."

By the time the deer was dressed and tied to a pole Ardek had thrown up twice. But to his credit, he'd come right back each time and did what he was told to. He almost ran off again when I chowed down on the deer's lungs, but he kept himself composed that time. There was hope for him yet.

Herald and Ardek, being the closest in height, carried the pole, with Mak taking Herald's bow along with her own spear. The bow was too long for her, but not so bad that she couldn't shoot it if necessary. And while she wasn't anywhere near as good a shot as Herald, she was still better than Ardek.

While Mak kept watch and Herald tried to make Ardek sick again by describing how they'd skin and butcher the deer when they got back, I walked along, feeling fat and happy. It wasn't to the point of needing to sleep it off, but I'd eaten a lot of the wobbly bits that Mak and Herald didn't want, and it had added up. I would have loved to take a nap, but Herald insisted that the deer needed to be taken care of as quickly as possible, and she'd been less than amused when I offered to just spray it down with venom to keep the flies off of it for a couple of hours.

Loose and relaxed, I joined Mak at the front. "Let me know if you see any signs of a bear," I said softly. "I keep smelling one, but I haven't seen one."

"Do you think it's the one you and Lalia fought?" she replied at the same volume.

"Nah. That was much farther south. Although that bastard was good at hiding, so maybe? Hope not, though. I am not ready for a rematch, and none of you have horses to escape on."

"Was it really that bad?"

"Like I told you. I'd've been bear food if Lalia hadn't come back for me. I got the hell out the moment I got a chance. Oh, and there's at least one more of those monsters in this part of the forest. With cubs! Can't smell the difference between a monster bear and a regular one, so it could be one of those, or it could be a basic bear."

"Out of curiosity, what is your plan if we run across a bear?"

"A regular one? Kill it. Between Herald, you, and me, it shouldn't be a problem. A monster? Shit . . . Dump the deer, hope it's happy with that? Otherwise, I'd try to lead it off while you guys climb the tallest tree you can." I lowered my voice even further and switched to Tekereteki and said, *"Maybe use the boy as bait, hmm?"*

That got an amused snort and an actual smile out of Mak.

"If necessary, I would like to do it myself," she said in the slow, careful way that she spoke the language. *"But feeding him to a bear . . . acceptable."*

We didn't run across any bears that night, and I lost the scent when we got closer to the mountain. When I thought about it, I hadn't smelled any wolves for a while either. I didn't want to assume I'd been lucky enough that they'd just decided to abandon my mountain. They'd be back, I was sure of it. But it was nice to have one less thing bothering me, and we could always go looking for them if we got bored one night.

Back at the mountain Herald asked Mak to get a nice big fire going, while she and Ardek got to work skinning and butchering the deer. There were apparently a lot of steps involved in preserving the skin and the meat, but I honestly wasn't all that interested. I figured I might grab some grilled venison from them when they got to that point, even though I'd already eaten enough for the next two days, at least; but otherwise, they were doing human things that I had no use for. Instead of trying to learn anything, I picked a nice, tall tree with a good view of the area. Telling the humans to shout if they needed me, I climbed about three quarters to the top, found a great place to comfortably wrap myself around some branches—I was getting bigger, and good trees to sleep in were getting harder to find—and finally took that nap.

I snapped awake. It was early morning, about time for the humans to go back inside to sleep. Someone should have awoken me already. Something was wrong.

I looked at the camp. The fire was burning, making a lot of smoke, with a large rack full of long strips of meat over it. The combined smell hung thick in the air, making my mouth water. Herald had warned me that dealing with the meat might take well into the day, so that was probably why no one had awoken me. Mak and Ardek were there, sitting on either end of one of the logs, which served as seating by the fire, but they were silent. They had their weapons prepared close at hand and were looking south warily. At first I couldn't see Herald, but then I spotted her behind a tree fifty feet from the others. She had her bow ready and an arrow nocked, occasionally throwing a glance my way.

Something was wrong, but they hadn't called for me. That should mean there was no immediate or obvious need for violence. I stayed silent, but moved to make myself more visible and waved to catch Herald's attention the next time she looked. Once we made eye contact she nodded once, then returned her attention south.

"Hello, the camp, and good morning!" a man's voice called. "Do you mind if I approach?"

The voice was familiar, but there were too many trees in the way for me to see the speaker with how high up I was. I was sure that I recognized it, though.

"What brings you out here?" Mak called back. "And are you alone?"

"I am. As for what brings me here, I was hoping to use this campsite for a day and night. Mind if I join you?"

"We came out here for some privacy."

"Did you? Well, a young couple like you. I won't impose. I can make my camp back on the other side of the stream if I must. I don't suppose it makes any difference if I'm a fellow Guild member? I must admit that I recognize you. I don't suppose Valmik is around? He could vouch for me."

I saw Herald shift uneasily when the man said he recognized Mak. I didn't like it either.

"Come closer," Mak called. "Let me see you! What's your name?"

"Barro," the man said as he stepped into the clearing, leading a donkey. Or a mule. It wasn't a horse, anyway. As soon as I heard the name, I could place the voice, and sure enough, the man that approached was the one who'd been in charge of the scholars' guards. I recognized him by his lanky build and his long, messy hair before I even got a good look at his face.

I was displeased. I had made it clear that they were not to return. That included him.

Herald had not stood idly by. She'd been circling, staying hidden, and around the same time that Barro walked into the clearing, Herald stepped in behind my tree. Fighting the morning light I deepened the shadow of the tree and shifted, gliding down silently and shifting back next to Herald.

"*That man,*" I hissed, "*is not supposed to be here. I thought I made myself clear.*"

"*Who is he?*" Herald asked. "*What do you want us to do?*"

"*Remember the scholars? He was in charge of their guards. And when I ran them off I told them, in no uncertain terms, that they would not enjoy the consequences if they came back.*"

"*Do you want us to—? I mean, it does not feel right.*"

I ground my teeth in frustration. Or I would have, if I had any flat grinding teeth. She was right. I couldn't ask them to clean up my mess, especially not when it was a man who hadn't done them any harm.

"I recognize the name," Mak was saying. "And I don't know that I've heard anything bad about you. You may already know, but I am Makanna. This is Ardek. We are *not,*" she said sharply, "a couple. You can join us for some fresh venison if you haven't had breakfast, but then we really do want some privacy."

It was probably the right choice, though I didn't like it. Mak refusing hospitality would have probably gone against her reputation, and would look even more odd than her being out here in the first place.

"Go, join them." I told Herald. *"I will figure out what to do about Barro."*

She nodded and returned her arrow to the quiver on her hip as she approached the others. As she did, I began to stalk around the area, making sure that Barro was as alone as he said. And it turned out that he was being honest. There was no sign of either the guards he'd had with him or the scholars. I could only assume that he had a great deal of confidence in his ability to keep himself safe.

I had no idea why the hell he was there, though, *especially* alone, so I stayed close enough to listen to the conversation going on by the fireplace.

Barro didn't look surprised to see Herald coming out from the trees. "Ah, hello. I thought you might be around," he said, after turning to look at her approaching footsteps.

"And why is that?" she asked.

"You're all quite well known around the Guild," he answered with a small shrug. "You're even more recognizable than your sister, as I'm sure you know already. And from what I've heard, the four of you rarely go out unless you're all together. Speaking of, again, I don't suppose Val is around here somewhere? We know each other since years back, and I haven't had much opportunity to speak with him lately."

"He and Tam are busy on another errand," Mak said.

"And you, Ardek was it? Are you a new member of the team then?"

"Ah, not exactly," Ardek said, but he was interrupted by Herald.

"We will see," she said. "Someone asked us to look after him for a while. He is in some trouble in the city."

"Ah," Barro said, giving Ardek a knowing look. "So what did you do? Get a girl in trouble? Duel the wrong man?"

"Neither," Ardek said. "Turns out my boss was a criminal. Well, a worse criminal than I knew of, anyway. And she's not going to forgive me for running off."

"A man of conscience, then? Oh, thank you." I guessed that someone must have handed him some of the grilled venison. "The world can always use more men like you, Ardek. Though you'll have to be skilled and clever to survive and get far, I'm afraid. Like Makanna here! We may not all know her name, but everyone in the Guild knows that our Tekereteki members are reliable!"

At this point I was satisfied that there was no one else hiding among the trees, so I took a position in the bushes behind Barro's back where I could watch the camp.

"Now you know why we are out here," Mak said slowly. "Other than flattering us, what's your business here? This place is rather out of the way, far from any road. What brings you to this campsite?"

"There is something in the area that I was hoping to get another look at," Barro said, and even without seeing his face, even if I hadn't already had a pretty good idea of why he was here, I would have been able to tell that he was being evasive. "I helped set up this site, several weeks back, but my employers returned to the city before I felt done here." He gnawed a bone, perhaps a rib, for a while. "Oh, but that's good! Thank you again. How did you find this place then? Like you said, it's rather out of the way."

"We have friends who go all over this forest. It is easy to find if you just travel along the hills," Herald said, not nearly as smoothly as she might have wished. Sneaking, she could do, and surprisingly well considering her size. Deception, not so much. But Barro was too smooth or polite to comment on it, simply acknowledging Herald's explanation with a grunt.

"If you're looking for something, why don't you just tell us what it is?" Mak said. "We can tell you if we've seen it."

I couldn't see Barro's face, but from behind he seemed to sag a little. "I really don't know if I should be involving you folks in my troubles, especially not after you've invited me to your fire and shared your food with me. I'm a Sorrows-damned fool as it is, chasing my nightmares out here."

Herald suddenly laughed, long and loud. It was, perhaps, not the politest thing to do after such somber words, and she was clearly well aware, covering her mouth, then turning away when she couldn't get herself under control. "Sorry! I really am," she said, then broke into another fit of giggles. "But do you expect us to be dissuaded by mysterious pronouncements of doom and gloom? We're adventurers, man! We have delved into the hearts of the mountains to rescue enchanted people from the clutches of monsters, and you try to scare us off with maybes?"

Mak just shook her head, and I scarcely heard her mutter with mock disgust, "I'm suddenly surrounded by poets."

Barro took it with good humor. "I don't blame you for laughing. Maybe I was being a little overly dramatic. But I mean it when I say that what I'm doing is foolish. I just can't help myself. What I saw out here haunts me. I keep thinking about, dreaming about it. I'm risking my life to face it, and . . . I'm doing nothing to dissuade you, am I?"

"Nothing at all!" Herald said cheerfully. "So why not simply tell us what it is you are after?"

At that Mak simply abandoned all pretense at politeness and spoke to Herald in Tekereteki. "*Sister, is it good to speak like this? We have secrets here.*"

"*He has been in the mountain,*" Herald answered her sister just as brightly as she'd just spoken to Barro. "*Our scaly friend told me about him. He was with the scholars I mentioned. We need to find out what exactly he thinks that he knows.*" She turned to Barro with a smile. "Apologies," she said. "This will only be a moment."

"Oh, no. Take your time."

"If he is a threat to you-know-who, then we will have to deal with him, one way or another." Herald continued. Mak frowned unhappily.

Ardek sat down next to Barro and murmured something, to which Barro just shrugged and shook his head.

"You know that I am right, Mak," Herald said softly.

Mak sighed. "Fine," she said, to both Herald and Barro. "Go ahead."

"I don't believe that I have actually agreed to share anything yet," Barro said, but Ardek cut in from the side.

"Oh, come now, Mister Barro!" he said. "You'd be a right bastard to leave us wondering after what you've already said. I don't peg you as a man who'd dangle a mystery in front of someone's face like that and just snatch it away."

"Does it have anything to do with the pit someone dug against the mountainside, a stone's throw north of here?" Herald asked.

"Of course you would have seen it already, if you're camping here," Barro sighed. "Yes. It does. When I was last here my employers had myself and my companions dig that pit over quite a few days. Very carefully, I should add. They went over the stone face with brushes, if you can believe it."

"And they found what they were looking for, did they not?" Herald pressed. "The gate."

Barro straightened in his seat. I was getting really tired of not being able to see his face, so I started circling back among the trees to try to get a side view instead.

"You know about the gate?" Barro said. "Is it open?" He was leaning forward, his voice suddenly eager.

"Perhaps you don't know this, Barro, but we were the ones who discovered the gates. We can recognize one pretty easily," Mak said. I could give her that. It was partially true. At least they'd found *a* gate, and they were the ones to tell the council about them.

"And yes, it is open," Herald said. "We have been camping just inside."

"Then you may already be in danger. Please say that you have not gone deeper!"

"Oh, should we not have done that? We have our main camp at the end of the tunnel, in some kind of nexus. We only sleep near the gate to make it easier to go outside."

"Oh, Mercies! Please, listen to me." The concern in his voice was touching, really, and earned him more than a few points against the debt he'd incurred by coming back. "You have to move your camp outside, the sooner the better. There is something in those tunnels, and it does not want us there! As one adventurer to another, I promise you that I have only your safety in mind. I have my own reason for why I must go in there, but if the thing that lurks in there does not know you yet, you may still have a chance!"

"I do not see what the fuss is about," Herald said innocently. She was doing a much better job of deceiving this poor man than I would have ever expected from her, though his excitement probably helped. "Whatever this thing is you may have seen, it has not bothered us, and we have been here for days. I suggest you come inside with us once we're done smoking and drying this meat, and you can see for yourself! What do you think, Mak?"

Mak shrugged. "He may as well, if it will calm him."

"I guess that you will have to see it to believe me," Barro sighed. "But I'll come with you, if only to help you break down your camp and carry your things when it drives us out."

"That is a very kind offer, Mister Barro," Herald said, and smiled.

CHAPTER TWENTY-TWO

Come Into My Parlor

Well, *what do you think?"* Herald asked me with a yawn, having stepped away from the camp to "pick some flowers." It was mid-morning at that point, and the meat still needed at least another hour or two above the fire, according to Herald. She looked badly in need of sleep.

"I think that you were rather unsettling, and that if he were not so distraught he might suspect you of trying to lure him into a trap."

"Really? I was trying to look relaxed and unconcerned. But I mean, what do you think about Barro?"

"He seems as terrified as I wanted him to, which only makes me more annoyed that he did not do as he was told and stay away!"

"What about me inviting him inside the mountain? I pretty much made it up as I went."

"I think I like it. At least this way we will have him under control. I will close the gate behind us, and then, as you say, we will make it up as we go."

"Draka . . ." Herald fidgeted, her voice uncertain. *"I do not want you to kill him."*

"Any particular reason?"

"He seems genuine and well meaning. He seems to be protective by nature, and I am using it against him. I feel rather bad about it, even if I think that it is necessary. And if it is true that he is an old acquaintance of Val's, I would prefer to hear from him before harming Barro."

I sighed. She made a fair point about Val, but I didn't like restrictions. And I'd told him what would happen if he came back. I didn't like backing off on my threats, and even the little voice wasn't complaining.

"I have long suspected you of being a decent person. Really, I am surprised that you tried and succeeded in deceiving him at all. I can promise that I will try. His concern for you does lessen my anger somewhat. I suppose that we could just shut him in there instead of killing him, since I do not see how he would get out, unless he has some kind

of magic and figures out the gate. But I would remind you that not wanting strangers in my mountain was the reason I drove them off in the first place."

"I know. I just do not feel that it would be right to harm him unless it is necessary, like if he intends to reveal you or what is inside the mountain."

Not right. She did not think that it would be right for me to kill a man who hadn't done anything to hurt anyone. Perhaps she was right.

I sighed. *"You are not asking anything unreasonable. I have become . . . colder recently. It is good that you remind me of the human perspective."*

"It is a relief to hear that. Thank you." She fidgeted, then made a vague gesture into the woods. *"Speaking of relief, I really do need to . . ."*

"Oh! Yeah, go on. Do not torture yourself. And when you are done, try to discreetly get Ardek out here so I can tell him what is happening."

It was about noon when the meat was dry, cooled, and packed away. They left the skin on a simple frame. Herald had scraped all the flesh and fat off it, and I figured it was drying or something. I hadn't bothered to find out. Much like earlier, it simply didn't interest me, though I felt like maybe it should. It was the kind of weird, useless knowledge that would have fascinated me six months earlier.

The humans stowed away the drying rack and put out the fire after lighting a pair of torches, then led Barro to the gate. We kept it open for convenience as long as we were right outside, and when they got to the edge of the hole and the gate came into view, Barro's step faltered as though he was reconsidering. But he pressed on, and no one else seemed to notice. I stayed in the shadows, not wanting to risk being seen in the bright midday light, so I lost sight of them as they descended. They kept talking, though, and when their voices quickly faded, I knew that they were inside. Barro had left his donkey untethered, probably so it could run if something came to try and eat it, and it brayed and backed away nervously as I approached the hole. I ignored it, figuring that paying any attention to it would terrify the poor thing. And I was still full of deer, so it wasn't interesting as prey either.

I shook my head at the thought. Donkeys and horses were not food in the first place.

I gave the humans a moment to put some distance between themselves and the gate, then followed them inside, closing the gate behind me and following them at a distance where I could just hear their voices echoing down the tunnel. When the thick stone slabs folded together, there was a finality to it. In the next hour or so, Barro's life was going to change. Whether that change would be terminal or not depended on what he said and did during that time.

Part of me wished that I hadn't been so soft and had just killed him and the scholars instead of scaring them off. My instinct was to correct that mistake immediately, and my human side seemed happy to let the dragon take the lead, but Herald had asked me not to, and that complicated things. It wasn't as though I had to obey her wishes, but she was my friend, and I owed it to her to at least take those wishes into consideration. That, and I had messed with her head in some way, which meant that I owed her even more.

Damn it, I *did* have to obey her wishes. I really couldn't kill the guy unless she gave the okay.

It was frustrating, but at the same time I was glad for the excuse. I didn't want to kill him. It was the smart thing to do, but like Herald had said, it didn't feel right. It wasn't fair. As angry as I was with Barro, he didn't deserve to die for defying me.

If he made himself a threat, though . . . If he intended to lead others to the mountain or tell anyone about me, then I would have no qualms about ending him there in the dark. I knew that Herald would support me. She had made it very clear how high my safety rated among her priorities.

That pretty much settled it. I trusted Herald to make the right call. Perhaps it was unfair to put that responsibility on her, but in many ways she was more mature than I had ever been. I'd mostly coasted through life, focusing on doing things that I enjoyed and that made me happy. She had struggled, growing up as an outsider, setting goals and working to achieve them. I could probably trust her to consider the consequences of any choice better than I could.

I should especially trust her over myself when it came to life-or-death decisions, now that I found myself needing reasons to not just default to killing someone. I could remember telling myself not so long ago that killing someone for my own convenience was a line I couldn't allow myself to cross, but in the past week it had been hard to feel it. It had been the same with Ardek. When we were leaving the house he was injured, and I didn't see any further use for him. Why not just kill him? When we were at the Wolves' base and I had questioned him, and I'd made my mind up to leave, I was pretty sure that the Wolves couldn't keep him. I couldn't let him go, and taking him with us seemed like a hassle, so why not just kill him? Problem solved. No man, no problem, right?

Although, wasn't it Stalin who said that, or something? If I was using his reasoning, I should probably think again.

"Here we are!" I heard Herald declare loudly from up ahead, and then the vast space of the hub opened up in front of me. I shifted and moved in closer, circling them until I found a vantage I liked, where I would be able to see and hear well but where I'd be completely hidden in the darkness, no matter how closely Barro looked.

Herald was walking around with her torch, a small island of light in the darkness. "Look," she said, her voice loud and harsh in the stone chamber. "There is nothing here, like I said. Whatever you saw, it is gone now."

"Like I told *you*," Barro said, standing among the piled bags of dried food and other goods, "this system of tunnels stretches for miles and miles. We first saw far from this chamber, in a small set of rooms that my employers were exploring. It followed us here, but it could be anywhere."

"You still haven't told us what you saw in here," Mak said from the darkness behind Barro. "'The thing in the darkness' is not the most useful description."

"Because I didn't want you to think that I'm mad, though by the way you're clearly humoring me, I see that ship might have already sailed, struck a reef, and been lost with all hands. To be completely honest, I barely saw it, but what I did see—and I beg you to believe me—was a moving darkness, like a shadow taken form. I don't know how else to describe it. The one time I saw it directly it was . . . it was like an invisible creature passed me only feet away, but all I saw was its shadow on the wall behind it."

"And it spoke to you. Threatened that the darkness would take you if you returned here, or even told anyone about it."

"Yes," Barro sighed wearily. "It did."

"Yet here you are. Telling us about it, in the place you were told not to return to."

"I told you that what I'm doing is foolish and dangerous."

"So you did. Though, if what you tell us is true, 'suicidal' sounds closer to the truth."

"Why did you come here, if it is so foolish and dangerous?" Herald asked, approaching Barro. "And what do you intend to do now that you are here?"

"I had not thought that far ahead, to be honest. If the gate was closed, my plan was to set up camp where I found you and see if anything happened. If it was open, well, I don't know. I suppose I would have had to go in sooner or later."

"Why?" Herald pressed him. "You still have not answered the question of why you are here."

"Like I said before, I'd rather you didn't think that I'm insane."

"No one here will think that you're insane," Mak said, her tone firm. "We're adventurers. Strange things happen, and sometimes you see something you can't explain. And I get the feeling that you want to tell us. That you want to tell someone. So go ahead. You say that you know me by reputation. I promise you that we won't ridicule you, or tell anyone what you tell us. Whatever it is that you're keeping in, that's driven you here to a place you say you should not be, just let it out."

"It's in my head!" Barro blurted out. "Calling me. When I sleep I dream of it, telling me to return to the mountain. Telling me that I belong here. When I'm awake I feel the pull of this place, all the time. I've resisted for over two weeks, and I'm proud of it, because you can't imagine how hard it's been. But I'm tired. I can't hold myself back any longer.

"Perhaps it's a message from the gods, or perhaps the thing in the darkness really is calling me back. Or it could just be that my mind's gone. I have to know. I don't think that I can rest properly until I do. I barely sleep. This is the most relaxed I've been since I returned to Karakan. I . . . whatever happens, I need to face this. To lay it to rest or to face whatever might be waiting for me here."

"And then what?" Herald prodded. "Once you have faced the darkness, what then?"

"Then, if I'm still alive and sane, I will put this all behind me. I will keep it to myself, trusting Makanna's word that you all will keep silent, and I will do my best to forget this place. If I'm wrong and there's nothing here, if the three of us here had some kind of shared hallucination caused by . . . I don't know, a gas pocket, maybe, then there is nothing to tell. But if I'm right then the thing in the darkness is here, and real, and its threats must be taken seriously. I've already defied it, coming here and talking to you about it. Once I've faced it, if it spares me, I would be truly insane to do so again."

"That is all?" Herald asked earnestly, getting closer to Barro and looking down at him intensely, like she was searching his face for any kind of deception. "Whatever the thing in the darkness is, you do not want revenge on it for driving you out of this place, embarrassing you in front of your employers and disturbing your rest for weeks afterward? You do not want to seek fame or glory as the one who revealed a mystery to the world, or slew an unknown monster deep inside the earth? You risk your life simply to know, and would be content with that even if you die, or if it turns out that you are mad?"

"Even then," Barro replied, his voice soft but carrying across the chamber. His face twisted in a wry smile. "Besides, I swore to my employers to keep this place and what they found here secret. Your sister is not the only one who takes her reputation seriously."

I could see by the soft set of Herald's face that she had made up her mind, but the outcome had already been clear halfway through Barro's explanation. "Then I owe you an apology," she said. "I brought you in here under false pretenses, and I do not like lies or half-truths. Barro, my sister and I know much more than we have led you to believe. Do you truly want to know the truth about the one in the darkness?"

"More than anything," Barro said, his face desperate in the torchlight. "If you know something, please tell me! I have to put this to rest, or I'm afraid I'll break!"

That was my cue. I stepped out from my hiding place and began slowly and silently making my way toward the group.

"In that case you should speak to the one who knows best. Draka!" she called into the darkness. "Would you speak to this man?"

"Draka?" Barro asked, looking around. "Who is—"

"Hello, Barro." I interrupted him as I stepped into the torchlight, trying to match my voice from the last time I spoke to him. A familiar mixture of wonder and fear painted his face. He barely had time to realize what was happening, his eyes going wide as I pounced and drove him to the ground.

CHAPTER TWENTY-THREE

All The Right Answers

D*raka, careful, please!"* Herald said urgently as I pounced on Barro.

"Douse the torches," I growled as I looked into Barro's staring eyes. He lay still and limp beneath me, not making the slightest attempt to break free as my weight pinned him to the stone floor. Without saying a word Mak picked up Barro's torch from where he had dropped it and smothered both it and Herald's, plunging the chamber back into absolute darkness. A heartbeat later I saw the glow of magic as Mak used her darksight spell, first on herself, then on Herald, and Ardek in turn.

"There," I said, blinking my own vision over to my shadowsight. "Much better."

With no light there was no point in keeping Barro pinned, and I stepped off him, watching him look around blindly in the sudden darkness. "Come on," I told him. "Speak. Since you were so eager to talk to me that you'd defy my command to never return here, I'm curious to hear what you have to say."

"What . . . what are you?" Barro said, his voice quavering. He'd sat up, supporting himself on one hand as the other one groped around in the darkness like he was trying to touch me.

"Come on. You got a good enough look, didn't you? Take a guess."

"A dragon," he whispered. "A dragon on Mallin. It shouldn't be possible."

"And why not?"

"Because there are no dragons here! They're seen flying in the distance, far out at sea sometimes, but no one has reported a dragon on Mallin since the Collapse!"

"But here I am."

"Here you are. Talking to me, instead of tearing me apart. Why?"

"That's easy," I said, circling him. He turned where he sat, tracking me by sound. "I promised someone that I'd give you a chance, and I haven't made my mind up yet. You should thank her."

"Is it miss Makanna I should thank, or miss Herald?"

"Herald. Though . . . Mak, what do you think? Should I kill him?"

"No," she answered quickly. "I don't see any reason why you would . . . or should, rather."

"There. You can thank both of them."

"Then, thank you, Miss Makanna. Miss Herald," Barro said, looking around in the dark. "Thank you for giving me this chance."

"I really am sorry," Herald said. "I am sorry for luring you in here under false pretenses. But we have to be sure."

"Who are you then? Besides adventurers of excellent repute? Are you part of the dragon's cult?"

Herald snorted, smirking with amusement. Mak, though, looked thoughtful.

"Nobody here worships me, I can tell you that much," I scoffed. "If they're a little overprotective it's because we care about each other. I guess Ardek could qualify as an employee. Or, I don't know. What do you think, Ardek? Do you worship me?"

"Sorry to say, boss, not at all. Fear and respect, yeah. But you're too solid and present to worship."

"There we are. Not a cult. Herald and Mak are here because we've fought and bled together, and Ardek because he made some unfortunate life choices. That's it. But we are here to decide about you. I heard your explanation for what you're doing here. From what you said I can't really blame you, but I hope you understand why I need to be sure about you."

"You're a dragon. They'd kill you."

"They'd try, yeah. For money or out of a misplaced sense of heroism or just to say that they did it. And what usually happens to dragon cults, or anyone suspected of belonging to one? The people close to me?"

"They'd be rooted out. Exterminated."

"And since I plan for me and my friends to live long and happy lives, I need to be sure that anyone who knows about me won't be spreading any rumors. So, I will tell you this. I played it up pretty hard when I scared you and the scholars away from here, but I was very serious about not wanting anyone to know about this place. Other than to protect myself and my friends, I don't want to hurt anyone who doesn't deserve it. I don't want to rob anyone, or extort anyone. I don't want to lay waste to any villages or steal away any young women, or young men, or anyone else for that matter. Anyone who isn't a monster and who leaves me alone has nothing to worry about. I hope that you still being alive is enough to convince you of that. Do you believe me?"

Barro paused before saying, "I do."

"That's nice to hear, but I doubt that you'd say anything else. Mak, Herald, what do you think? Is he being honest?"

"He is," Mak said, followed by Herald's, "I agree."

"Well. Congratulations, Barro. I guess that means you get to live, so long as you swear on your life that you will keep my secrets."

Barro didn't hesitate. "I swear it."

"Mak?"

She nodded.

"Great!" I said. "That settles that. You're here, you know, and you're still alive. Couldn't have gone better for you."

A long breath left him, and he lay back on the stone. "Of all the things I imagined might happen if I returned here," he said after a long silence, "nothing was close to this." He paused, then said, "Does that mean I can have some light again?"

"Oh. Right. Mak, would you . . . ?"

"Sure." Mak undid her spell on Herald and Ardek, then took out one of the light-balls from a bag. We hadn't needed them since Ardek had become fully aware of what Mak could do. Since Barro had no idea about any of Mak's abilities, she charged the ball inside the bag, making it look as though she'd only uncovered it.

"There," she said, placing the ball on a bag, then doing the same with the second ball to light up a larger area.

"Those are amazing," Barro said, his face shifting from relief to almost childlike wonder as he looked at the stones. "Light without a flame, in such a small package! Where did you get these?"

"Loot from killing valkin," Mak answered. "You could say that Draka got them for us. No idea what they're worth. Lots, I assume. Too useful to sell, though. Besides, they need to be charged with magic, so that limits them somewhat."

"Draka, that's . . ." He looked at me.

"That would be me, yes. The dragon has a name," I said, looking down at him. I could look down at almost anyone except Herald now. It felt good. "Did I hurt you?"

"Hurt me? Ah, no. No, you didn't. I'm sturdy."

"Good. It would have been embarrassing if you'd knocked your head open on the floor or something."

"Learning to fall is part of learning to fight." He looked a little out of it, though it was probably from the fast turns rather than anything else.

I could use that.

"Now that we're getting along so nicely," I said, "how do you feel about helping me with something?"

"I can hardly refuse, can I? But whether I can do it depends on what you want."

"I want to get in touch with the two scholars you came here with." I could see him immediately start to think about how to refuse me safely. Or, considering he'd said outright that I was in his head, perhaps he was trying to justify helping me despite his professional duty to keep his previous employers safe and confidential.

I pressed on. "I need to know what they know. How they found this place, what they know about its history. I can promise you that I don't intend to harm them. I don't even intend to meet them directly if I can avoid it. But I need to know."

Barro relaxed visibly. He was either not even trying to hide his emotions, or he was not very good at it.

"Well . . ." he said, "I might be able to get a message to them. But they're secretive with their studies from what I've seen, and I don't know what their heads are like right now. No guarantee they'll answer me, or give the answer you want. Once we got back to the city they went their own way, and me and the guys I'd contracted got our pay by messenger. I haven't heard from them since."

"If you do get in touch with them I'd be very appreciative. I take care of the people who help me."

"I won't be coy here. That sounds like a good position to be in."

"Much better than the opposite. Which brings me to something else I'd like your help with, if you're willing."

He looked at me with a mix of apprehension and interest.

"What do you know about the Night Blossom?"

"Not much. It's a false name for some rich woman, I think. At least everyone assumes that they're a woman. Runs a bunch of brothels and gambling halls. Some taverns. Seedy, but nothing illegal as far as I know. Why?"

"Since you've been so open with me I'll be honest with you. She captured two of my friends and tortured them. Then she captured me, and I think that she intended to sell me, alive or in parts. I'm going to kill her, and I need help gathering information."

Barro blanched. "And you want my help with this?"

"I do. Does any of this bother you? My plans and your potential place in them?"

"If what you say is right, then you certainly sound justified. I doubt that you or your friends could get justice through the court. But I don't know what I could do to help. I'm no investigator."

He didn't say that he didn't want to help. He had no reason to. I had threatened and attacked him, and the kindest thing I had done to him was to spare his life. But he didn't say that he didn't want to help me, he said that he didn't think that he could. Of course, that could be him just being careful and trying not to anger me, but the guileless way that he said it, the open expression on his face as he looked at me . . . I doubted it. I was in his head, just like he's said.

I had no idea how, and I wished that I did.

No matter how it had happened, I was going to exploit this man as much as I could without putting him in clear and present danger.

"I'm not asking you to go out and ask dangerous questions, but you're an adventurer. I'm sure that you're resourceful." I told him. "Just keep your eyes and ears open. Maybe press a little if someone brings up the subject of the Night Blossom, or maybe try to find out who owns a house on . . . Cloud Street?" I looked at Herald and Mak, who both nodded. "Right. A house on Cloud Street that was torn up by some kind of wild animal."

"That was you, I guess."

I grinned, showing plenty of teeth. "They tried to *cage* a *dragon*."

Barro leaned back just a bit, his lips thinning as he pressed them tightly together. "Right," he said. "What did they expect to happen?"

"What, indeed. But, Barro, I don't want you to put yourself in any danger. Just let me know if you hear anything, or find anything, and I'll compensate you for your time. That's all I ask."

"All right. Say I do find something, or I get in touch with the scholars. Should I come back here? What if the gate is closed?"

"No need. Are you familiar with the Gray Wolves mercenary company and their headquarters?"

"Oh, sure! Their company hall is down near the harbor. I have some buddies there."

"Right. Just go there, and tell them that you have a message for Garal or Lalia from Makanna and Herald's friend. That's all."

"Garal and Lalia. All right. I can do that."

"You have all the right answers, don't you, Barro? But you're surprisingly willing to help someone who threatened to murder you not long ago. You're not concerned about that?"

"Well, no? Should I be? Something brought me here, you or the gods, and I can only assume that it was to help you. And I'm not committing to anything, or promising to do anything illegal, or immoral . . . Thank you for your concern, but I'm not worried, no. If anything, I feel much more at ease now that I've spoken to you than I did when I walked in here."

In other words, I thought, *he's completely whammied*. That, or he was just a really steady guy. Good to know.

"In that case, I think we're done here. You're welcome to stay, but to be honest we were up all night hunting and taking care of that deer, so we all need some sleep."

"Right. Well, I've done what I came out here for, and much earlier than I could have hoped. I don't suppose I could have some company back to the gate?" Barro looked back into the darkness, where the tunnel back to the outside was barely visible to me as a deeper black. I doubt he saw anything at all, in which case he must have been very good at orienting himself.

"We're all going," I told him. "They all sleep there anyway."

"Not you?"

"Have you not been paying attention? I'm a dragon. I have a *lair*."

"Oh. Of course."

The walk back to the entrance was much less tense than on the way in. Mak and Barro especially got along well, talking shop and swapping short anecdotes about Val. There was just an awkward moment when we reached the gate and Barro realized that it was closed.

"Had to be sure about me, right?" he said, giving me a look.

"It's nothing personal."

"I should have known. It's just a little disheartening to know that even if I could have outrun you through the tunnel, it wouldn't have mattered."

"I can see how it might be, yes. Now, everybody, back up. If there's anyone outside, I don't need them seeing you all before I run them off."

I put my hand on the gate and willed it open. The afternoon sun spilled in, causing us all to blink painfully, but there was no one there. I waited for my humans to run off into the bushes if they needed and said my good-days while Barro brought his few things out. Then I closed the gate on them.

"So," I said to Barro. I stayed silent and just looked down at him until he squirmed on his feet. "You are welcome back if you want, as long as you don't lead anyone here. The others seem to like you well enough, and between Herald's and Mak's opinions of you and your acquaintance with Val, I think I can trust you. And I will be thankful for any help you can give me. Make yourself my friend and I will treat you as one, and I look after my friends. Or simply leave me and mine in peace, and I will leave you alone. All right?"

"I like the sound of that," he said with a wary smile. "I feel like there's a 'but' coming, though."

"*But*. Betray me in any way, or cause harm to anyone I care for, and there is no place on this island where you can hide from me. No matter where you go, I *will* find you, and you won't even know I'm there until you meet a messy end. Understood?"

"There it is," he said, his voice thin. "I understand you just fine, uh, Madam?"

"Draka is fine."

I sniffed the air and waved a hand. "Your donkey's over that way, I think. Hard to say from this distance, but I don't want to risk scaring it off."

"Thanks. I knew she wouldn't wander off, good girl that she is. Never gave me any trouble the whole way out."

"Well, I hope you have a good walk back. You might be able to make it before midnight if you set a good pace and don't stop too often."

"I just might. Mercies watch over you, Draka."

"Goodbye, Barro."

With that I spread my wings. I leaped into the air and climbed, circled once for no reason other than to show off, and headed for my nest.

It was another six days before we heard from Karakan.

Those days passed uneventfully. Herald resumed her efforts at making me fully literate. While I could read fairly fluently, I hadn't bothered much to practice my writing, and she was determined to use the days in the forest to correct that, scratching away in the dirt with a claw until my letters were least somewhat legible.

Mak and Ardek nearly went back to the way they'd been before Mak's outburst, though Ardek still watched his words around her. I suspected that a big part of it was that I allowed Mak to take out her aggression on me during our sparring sessions, which began the night after Barro's visit. Mak had found herself a couple of poles the right length and thickness to make good substitutes for her spear, and I was badly mistaken if I'd thought that her fear and respect might make her go easy on me.

Fighting Mak was educational to say the least. What she lacked in raw strength she made up for in speed, maneuverability, and just plain skill. It's not like she was perfect, and I won an exchange every now and then, but usually I ended up getting poked, prodded, or simply popped on the head. She had some kind of combination of speed, reflexes, and agility that allowed her to keep her 'spear' between herself and me, however I tried, and when I tried to swat it away to make an opening, she just swept her weapon out of the way without ever pointing it away from me. The first time I gave in to my frustration and tried to charge her, she planted the butt end of her pole in the ground and the tip at the base of my throat, and I hit it hard enough to bend, then snap the pole. The force was enough that even with my fortitude I was left coughing, and if it had been a real spear, the damn thing probably would have come out the other end. Lesson learned.

Mak, meanwhile, had danced away and drawn the 'sword' she kept in her belt, giving me a solid whap on the snout with it while I was busy wheezing. "That's a point to me, I think!" she said, grinning viciously.

"You know I'm supposed to be learning something, right?" I said once I could speak again. "I'm not just here for you to brutalize."

"You did learn something. At least I hope so. Don't charge right at someone who's got a spear on you."

"Any suggestions besides 'don't do that'?"

Mak looked at me thoughtfully for a while. "It'll probably go against your instincts, but against a spear I think that what you need to do is to lead with your head. You're too focused on getting your claws on me when your mouth is full of teeth. And it's a moving target, so you should be able to get it under the point of the spear and then push the haft with your neck."

I tried, and got jabbed in the throat for my effort. I tried again and got smacked on the side of the head. Mak, mercifully, didn't gloat, though she wasn't at all reluctant to criticize my attempts.

"It would have worked if you waited for me to be committed. I'm not sure what you were thinking, trying that when I was in a ready stance. Look, when I'm like this," she took her regular stance, sideways to me, feet apart and the pole extended toward me, "if you come at me, all I have to do is . . ." She drew her arms apart, sliding the pole back in her grip much faster than I could approach. At the same time she moved back, then slammed the point of the pole forward where my head or neck might have been if I'd been coming at her.

"You need to draw out an attack, wait for me to extend, then come at me."

"What I need to do is spit venom in your face so that you choke and die," I growled.

"And as much fun as I'm sure that would be, I know that you only have so much venom. Come on."

I have no idea what the score stood at, but her suggestion did work after several attempts, and I called it quits there. Mak agreed cheerfully. "No point in you being too bruised to continue tomorrow."

"I'm going to eat you one day," I muttered, feeling thoroughly beaten.

"Promises, promises."

She gave me some quick burst of healing, of course. Then once she'd cooled down she became a little more careful, probably worried that she'd pushed me too far, but that didn't stop her from going back to being cheerfully irreverent the next time she had a chance to knock me around. I just took my lumps and comforted myself with the knowledge that I was, at least, learning something. And that it seemed to do Mak some good, which felt a lot more important to me now than it had two weeks earlier.

I hadn't forgiven her, but I felt responsible for her, just like I did for Herald and Ardek. They were my humans, and I took care of what was mine.

CHAPTER TWENTY-FOUR

Truce

Six days after Barro had come and gone, late in the afternoon, I was gliding low over the trees. I'd been looking at how the trees were turning yellow in spots. Summer couldn't last forever, and I'd been wondering what fall and winter would be like here, when I saw a thin smudge of smoke rising from the campsite by the gate.

I landed a short distance from the clearing, like I usually did, and sneaked the rest of the way in the cover of the trees, but my stealth turned out to be unnecessary. By the fire, grilling what looked like a rabbit or hare, sat Garal. Melon was wandering a couple dozen feet away from him, grazing on the thin grass. I grinned. He looked focused on his dinner, so I silently crept closer, circling around to approach him from behind. I left the trees. Closer, and he didn't react. Closer. I was only a few feet away. I gathered myself to—

"*Koh-ahp!*"

Something small, though not very hard, bounced off my back. I whirled and looked at the pine cone on the ground next to me, then up in the trees where Rib was loudly laughing her butt off, then back to Garal who was grinning at me.

"If it helps," he said, "I didn't notice you until you were right behind me."

I waited for Rib to climb down from her tree. She approached us with her arms wide, the same shit-eating grin I'd gotten used to plastered across her face, and said, "I win again!"

"Did you not see me pull a man's head off?" I asked flatly.

"Yeah, but you *like* me."

I snorted. It wasn't like she was wrong. Something about her irreverence amused me.

"Where are the others?" Garal asked. "I was hoping to meet them."

"Wait here. I'll get them."

I descended the grade, Rib coming with me despite what I told them, and willed the heavy double doors of the gate open with a touch. They had barely begun opening when I heard a choked, "Oh, gods!" and Ardek practically flew out the opening, running off into the trees with a hurried, "Good morning, Draka!"

"Poor guy has been about to piss himself for half an hour," Herald said, strolling out after him and blinking in the sunlight. "Good afternoon, Draka," she said, then looked past me and waved happily. "Rib!"

"Hey, Herald!"

Mak came out behind her sister. "Hello, Draka. Rib, any news from the city?"

"Yeah, but I'm just along to see where you all live. I'll let Garal tell you. He's busy burning a rabbit I shot," she said, raising her voice loud enough for Garal to hear.

"I'm not burning it!" he called back from up the grade. "You just like them nearly raw!"

"I get that," I said, turning to give Rib a nod. "Doesn't that make you sick, though?"

She shrugged. "Hasn't so far. And meat tastes better rare."

I nodded agreeably. "I like some char on the outside. Should be nice and bloody on the inside though."

"Hah! Thought you might think so, dragon."

I let the humans eat and catch up before we got down to the meat of it. For the Wolves it had been mostly business as usual, though they'd had to increase their patrols south because of increased bandit activity.

"That's one of the things we need to talk to you about," Garal told me before moving on.

Rallon's traitorous interrogator had been found floating in the harbor shortly after we'd left the city. The assumption was that the Night Blossom or one of her men had decided that his past services didn't outweigh the risk of him getting nervous. The other guy who'd gone with him was still unaccounted for, but no one really expected him to be captured. If he was alive, and smart, he may not even be in the city anymore.

Herald and Mak were of course disappointed that there was no message from Tam and Val. Garal and Lalia had checked at the inn, but the innkeeper denied that anything had arrived. Still, they all agreed that it was too early to worry, with the men being overseas.

"Did a guy named Barro come by this week?" I asked. It was early, if he even intended to help me, but it was worth a shot.

"Barro? The same Barro that Val used to run with? Haven't seen him for months. He used to come by to see some friends among the men, but Rallon doesn't allow outsiders in the barracks anymore. Uh, barring special cases like you all, I suppose. Why?"

"He may have a message for me if he comes by. Don't worry about it."

"So you've decided to trust someone new?"

"It was that or kill him."

"I'm glad you didn't go with that option. Val will be too."

"Yeah, that was part of it. That and he seemed genuinely trustworthy. Or at least the others said so." I nodded to Herald and Mak.

"You trust their judgment?"

"I mean, yeah? I've known them for months, and I don't think they'll steer me wrong. Not again."

I don't know if anyone else caught the look I shot Mak, but she looked away and wouldn't meet my eyes for a long time.

"I'm glad for that too. You were . . . unsettling back at the barracks. You seem better now."

"What he means is you scared the piss out of my cousin and everyone else there," Rib added seriously. "It didn't get much better after you left either. We know some people in the guard. We've heard what they found in that house on Cloud Street. That started with you chained up, did it? And you just butchered everyone inside."

"Ardek and the housekeeper are still alive," I protested.

"Yeah, well, I think cousin Rallon was worried that you'd gone feral. He was relieved after we all talked, but I don't think he relaxed until he heard that you were out of the city."

"But now he wants something, right?"

"Right," Garal said. "He wanted me to be clear that he knows it's bad manners to call in a favor so soon after it's been offered, but that's what he wants to do."

"And he sent us because he's pretty sure you like us enough not to eat us if you feel insulted," Rib added. "He might have sent Lalia instead of me, but . . ."

Garal grimaced. "I'd prefer if you didn't suggest that my . . . friend . . . ?" He looked at me.

"Yeah, I guess," I said.

". . . that my friend would kill and eat my sweetheart."

"Nah, I wouldn't do that. As long as she keeps her damn head on straight." I paused. "And anyway, I wouldn't *eat* her."

Garal frowned. "Well, it's reassuring to hear that if you *did* kill my sweetheart, you'd at least leave something for me and her family to bury."

I rolled my eyes at him. "Fine, I'll stop joking about killing Lalia. You know I wouldn't. She says something without thinking, I threaten her, she backs off. That's as far as it goes, all right? It's our thing."

"See, I keep believing that, but then you say something like, 'I wouldn't *eat* her,' and the emphasis makes me uneasy."

"Yeah, okay." I sighed. "You have my solemn promise that I won't kill, or even harm Lalia, as long as she's not trying to harm me or mine. Does that make you feel better?"

"A solemn promise from a dragon?" Garal made a show of thinking about it, then smiled. "You know, yes! It does!"

"If we are done talking about my two closest friends killing each other," Herald said impatiently, "what does Rallon need Draka for?"

"Well." Garal leaned forward, his elbows on his knees. "The bandit trouble in the south actually started about two weeks before the awful things that happened to you all. At first it was just reports from the far south, but it gradually crept north until our patrols began to find raided villages. These last two weeks, though, it's gotten much worse. We've found several burned out hamlets and villages in just the last ten days, but we haven't found any sign of who's behind it. We've had some luck, though. Some of the survivors of one of the latest villages to be raided were retired soldiers, and according to them, the raiders seemed far too organized and disciplined for common bandits. We suspect that is also why they've been so successful at avoiding our patrols and covering their tracks."

"I'm guessing Rallon wants my help finding them."

"That's right. Rallon hopes that you, flying at night, may be able to find their camp, or camps, without being detected. Then we could strike them in force and wipe them out."

"You say they're too disciplined," Mak said. "You don't think they're bandits?"

"That's the fear. Nothing has happened on the southern border yet, but the rhetoric is getting hotter and hotter. Lots of saber rattling going on. Rallon and the council suspect that the duke is using his cavalry, professional or irregular, to raid deep into Karakan's territory under the guise of banditry. To weaken the city by disrupting the harvest or lowering morale, most likely, since there's little of value for them to take."

I looked at my humans, then back at Garal. "Could you take in my people while I'm away? I don't like the idea of leaving them out here."

"Are we your people now?" Herald asked. The words sounded like an accusation, but the tone didn't match, and she looked pleased at the idea.

"If I have any people here, you're it," I told her, and she smiled.

"If they want to come, I'm sure that we can take them. And with you away there's no reason for any real secrecy either."

I looked at Ardek. "Can I trust you to stay put with the others?"

"I'm pretty sure that I was last seen leaving the Wolves' barracks with two Tekereteki women. If I go back to the Night Blossom I'm a dead man." He said it calmly, and with absolute certainty. "It's only a question of how long my dying would take. I'll keep well inside and away from any windows, don't you worry about that, boss."

"Good. Herald, Mak, would you be okay with it? Going back to the city and being cooped up in the Wolves' barracks until I'm back?"

"I sure wouldn't mind it," Mak said. "As . . . nice as this all has been, I look forward to talking to some new people. Maybe playing some cards and having a chance to take an actual bath."

Herald nodded along to her sister's words. "I agree with Mak. I've enjoyed these two weeks, for the most part. But going back to Karakan, even for a few days, would be good."

"All right, that's settled," I said. "We can start packing up now, if you two don't mind traveling in the dark. Otherwise we'll leave at sunrise."

"Night's fine," Rib said. "I've got my little helpers!" She pulled out one of her little vials and wiggled it eagerly, while Garal grimaced but ultimately agreed. I suspected that she was happy for any excuse to use those things.

"We'll rest the animals while you pack up," Garal said. "We have two horses but they're lightly loaded, so if we walk them it shouldn't be a problem."

We didn't bring everything. Herald and Mak decided to just leave much of the camping gear, figuring they could afford to replace it if they had to and only taking a few favorite pieces, like a small pot that was "just the right size." For what, I didn't know. Then we were on our way.

Garal and Rib had only had a couple hours' rest, having arrived a little after noon, so it was rough on them and their horses, and we stopped frequently. In the end it was well after midnight when we arrived at the Wolves' headquarters, with me following the group in the shadows from half a mile back before the city gates. Instead of going through the whole song and dance of clearing the bottom floor, where there were always people no matter the time of day, I was let into the same upstairs room as the first time.

Garal offered to send for Rallon immediately, but I asked him not to. Since I'd unsettled him so badly the last time we met, I figured some humility was in order. Of course, it probably didn't count as humility if it was a calculated attempt to manipulate him, but at least it would look good and he'd meet me after a full night's sleep.

I didn't expect my humans to come and keep me company, so I resigned myself to a boring rest of the night. Fortunately, I was *fantastic* at napping, so I settled in on the floor, strategically placing myself behind the door in case someone tried to come in. I had barely closed my eyes when someone knocked on the door, opened it a sliver, and hesitantly whispered my name.

"Come in, Lalia," I grumbled, moving so that she could open the door and slip inside. Her hair was loose, and she was unarmed and wearing only simple linen nightclothes, looking the most vulnerable and uncertain I had ever seen her.

I sat up straight and looked down at her, waiting for her to speak. She slowly looked me up and down, then muttered, "Gods, you're fucking big now."

"You should have seen my father," I said dryly. I could vaguely remember him now, an impression of something black and sleek and so big that he seemed to fill the whole world. I'd probably been tiny then, though.

As though she'd heard my thoughts, Lalia said, "The first time I saw you. When you . . . saved Garal. And, you know. Thank you for that, by the way. I guess I never said that. I don't know what I would have done if I'd lost him. You were about the size of a dog back then. You must be one-and-a-half times as big now, and it's been what, four months?"

"Something like that."

"How the hell are you growing so fast?"

"You want to know a secret?" I'm not sure what inspired me. Maybe it was her uncharacteristic lack of hostility, or maybe it was that I had heard the words "Thank you" out of her mouth, but I felt an urge to be a little more open with her. Give and take, that kind of thing.

"It's not something you'll have to kill me over, is it?" she asked with a laugh that almost hid the seriousness of her question.

"Nah. Not unless you try to use it against me. But I don't think you will."

"So . . . what is it?"

I leaned in. She stood her ground admirably, and I whispered, "I'm not even close to full grown." I pulled back with a grin.

"Mercies preserve us all . . ." she whispered back, and I saw fear and something like awe on her face, as she imagined what the future might hold.

I let her think about that for a while, before saying, "Lalia, why did you come here tonight? Did Garal ask you to?"

"Huh?" she said, still lost in her own imagination. Then she blinked once and said, "Garal, the sweet, protective ass that he is, didn't even tell me that you were here. But it wasn't exactly hard to figure out, with him and Rib returning with your little cult in tow."

"Not a cult."

"If you say so," she said, but her tone told me that what she meant was "Keep telling yourself that."

"Garal doesn't know that I'm here. I waited for him to fall asleep. He'd either try to stop me or come with, and I wanted to talk to you alone."

"Here we are. What did you want to talk about?"

"You. Me." She sighed. "Mak and Herald."

"So everything, then."

"Pretty much," she said, then went and sat in the only chair in the room by the desk. "Two of my dear friends were taken and tortured because of their association with you, *but—*" She raised her voice a little and pressed on as I angrily started to protest. "—that is not your fault, and I admit that. They chose to be part of that mission, and the Night Blossom chose to target them. And you rescued them. Besides that, thanks to you they've made more money in these past couple of months than they have in the last few years."

As nice as that was to hear, she clearly had more to say. I waited, not quite staring her down but waiting expectantly.

"So, all right, good and bad, yeah? But the thing is, it doesn't matter how much I want . . . or maybe wanted you gone. I think we're stuck together. We have some people in common that neither of us is going to give up on. Herald fucking *worships* you, and I know, not a cult! You know what I mean. She loves you, adores you, whatever. She'd be glued to your backside if you'd allow it. And Mak . . ." She frowned. "Whatever happened between you and Mak, she seems to think that she deserves it. I know that she's not perfect, and I know that she's had some worries about you, so maybe she did something properly dumb. It wouldn't be the first time. But she's firmly in your pocket, yeah? Or . . . you have no clothes, but on your team, at least. So that means that we, you and me, we're gonna see a lot of each other. Especially since Rallon clearly wants to keep working with you."

"Looks like."

"Look, basically, I'm sorry, all right? I get protective. There used to be two brothers and a sister between me and Lahnie, yeah? They're gone. I don't want to lose anyone else, and I act without thinking. I know. It's a problem. It gets me into trouble. And I've heard a lot of nasty stories about dragons, which don't really match up to anything you've done. I'm sorry, yeah? That I gave you shit when maybe you didn't deserve it. Just . . . keep them safe. Please? And I'll try to be better."

The first thing out of my mouth was, "Shit, you're scared of losing people, and you fell in love with a merc?" which I immediately regretted as Lalia's face scrunched in anger. "No, forget that," I said before she could open her mouth. "You're reaching out, and I'm being a big, scaly bitch. You . . . probably don't deserve that."

I laid down on the floor instead of sitting up, so that we were more face to face. "Let me be clear. Herald is the most important person or thing in this world to me. I will sacrifice anyone or anything to protect her. That's not something you want to hear. I understand that. But I think you deserve the truth. Other than that, I will defend Mak, Tam, Val, Garal . . . Hell, you and Lahnie, maybe even Ardek, as far as I can. Good enough?"

"I mean, yeah. Same for me, with Garal or Lahnie. Them above anyone if I have to choose, you know? I'd hate myself, but yeah, I get it." She sighed. "I'd rather die, though, to be honest."

I believed her. She had a record of putting herself between me and people she loved, and I had no doubt that she'd continue to put herself in harm's way if necessary.

"All right. Here's what we'll do. You promise to try and be less of a bitch to me, and I'll promise to do my best to keep Herald and Mak safe. And I'll count to ten before I do anything if you say something hot-headed, so you can walk it back. Does that sound good to you?"

She snorted softly. "That'll work, yeah. But I didn't miss that it looks like I'm the only one in the wrong here."

"I mean . . ."

"All right. Yeah, maybe."

"For what it's worth, I think I would actually like you if you just chilled out a little. Calmed down, I mean. So, you know. Do that. And I'll keep in mind that it's not me. You're just being protective, and I can respect that."

She smiled. "That sounds better. Do you want to, uh, shake on it?"

She looked doubtfully at my clawed hands on the floor. Just to see what she'd do, I held one out, claws carefully in, and after a heartbeat's hesitation she stood, walked up, and hooked her thumb and closed her hand around mine. I carefully closed my hand, and she closed her free hand over our clasped ones, then released her grip.

"I'll go back to bed then. But, you know, I'm glad I did this. Good talk."

"Yeah, me too. Good night, Lalia."

"Good night, Draka."

CHAPTER TWENTY-FIVE

Briefing

I slept the last few hours of the night in front of the door to the small office. There was a constant low hum of activity in the building, but it didn't disturb me too much. I did wonder, before I drifted off, how many people there were in the company. There were a couple dozen beds, but patrols seemed to come and go at all times of the day, and I could only assume that the beds were shared.

Maybe I'd ask in the morning.

I was only bothered once. I was jolted awake by the door opening an inch and bumping into me. When no familiar voice spoke I shoved it closed, meeting a little resistance as I did so, and was rewarded by the sound of someone stumbling outside. A grumpy "Shove off!" sent them scrambling away, and I could go back to sleep. Damn mercs. I'd thought they had better discipline than that, but clearly curiosity could overcome anything. *Maybe I should tell Lalia*, I thought. Make it her problem. But, nah. I wouldn't be there much longer.

Rallon showed up what most would have considered monstrously early. But he was a military man, kind of, and waking up before sunrise fit my image of him perfectly. He had Lalia in tow, bleary eyed but looking much less hostile than normal, as well as Rib and Pot, who both looked chipper and downright friendly.

Rallon himself was unarmed and unarmored. Having only three companions with him and closing himself in such a small space with me must have been a big risk from his perspective. His tightly controlled expression and body language showed as much, as did the subtle but distinct scent of fear coming off him. This meeting, and what he wanted from me, must be capital-*I* Important to him.

"Lady Draka, thank you for coming to meet with me on such short notice," he said. We were back to "lady" now, apparently, up from "madam." I couldn't say that I disliked it. Maybe I could wrangle a "your eminence" sometime down the line? Rallon seemed like a decent enough man, but no matter what my relationships were with his people, the one between the two of us was all business. If he was a lord, it was gratifying that he put me on the same level. Although we both knew that I had good odds of being able to kill him before anyone could react, so he might just be trying to butter me up. Also something that I approved of. Flattery had always worked well on me, even when I was one-hundred-percent human.

I could try to be diplomatic too, if I had to. "Lord Terriallon," I said. "Rallon. I'm aware that I was a little intense the last time we met. I was not having a good day. I'm sure that you understand."

"Indeed. Then, to be quite honest, you did make me concerned. You were behaving much more like one might expect from a . . . well, a dragon. I've seen you as far more reasonable than the stories would lead one to believe, and it is good to see you more like what I hope is your own self again."

"Thanks. I do feel more like myself. But no matter how I behaved, I did one thing right. I promised you a favor for your hospitality, and I intend to honor that. It's a bonus if there are bandits or raiders involved."

"Ah, Garal gave you the basics then. Good. Let's get to it. Lalia, the map, please."

Pot and Rib were each carrying a large candle, which they set down on the desk, while Lalia rolled out a map twice as long as it was wide. It took me a moment to understand what I was seeing, but once I realized that they had the sea up and the mountains down on the map, it became clear. Going by the coastline and the mountains, it was obviously a map of the area south of the city. The north was bordered by the forest, and the south was marked "To Duchy of Happar." The focus of the map was on roads, canals, and settlements, with many of the settlements in the southwest, as well as many stretches of road, marked with red.

"This map shows every attack we know about in the last month, along with the dates of the attacks. You'll notice that the density of the marks is higher in the south, decreasing and becoming more recent as you move north. As I'm sure that you can see, the number of attacks is far too high for a single band of bandits of any reasonable size in such a short time. Reliable witnesses have also indicated that the attackers were better equipped and more organized than one would expect from regular bandits, leaving us with only two real possibilities. Either someone has gathered a large force of outlaws and equipped them in a very short time, or they've taken a long time but refrained from attacking, or we're dealing not with bandits but organized raiders, most likely from Happar. While Karakan is not at war with Happar, relations are strained at the moment. There have been some small skirmishes along the border, and I would not put it past them to send troops into Karakan's farmland under the guise of banditry. It might not even be a central decision. Their border commanders have always been an unruly lot. No matter who is behind this, it forces us to pull patrols from the north to reassign in the south, which we can ill afford with the increased number of refugees coming in from the untamed forest."

Skirmishes along the border? That was like small, limited battles, right? Should I tell Herald about that, or would Lalia already have done so?

And refugees? What?

Either way, first things first. "You want me to find them," I guessed.

"Correct. Our patrols have spotted groups of riders that we believe must belong to this force, whoever they are, but they always fall back, and I will not have one of my patrols lured into an ambush. While I intend to go south to deal with this problem, as is my duty to the city under our contract, I want to know as much as possible before I do so. Most importantly: where, how many, and how well supplied and equipped they are. I believe that you are uniquely suited to find some or all of these things."

"You're right. I am." And the fact that sending me meant that he didn't have to risk a single one of his own troops probably weighed pretty heavily as well.

We spent the next hour or so going over the map, with Pot, Rib, and Lalia describing the terrain as best they could and showing me which areas were farmland and which were hillside pastures or light woods. Mostly, we discussed likely areas for the raiders to be camped, based on where the latest attacks had happened. Or, more accurately, they talked and I listened. It wasn't as easy as just drawing a line from the edges of the raids to some point. You had to consider ease of movement by foot or by horse, following roads or going through different types of terrain. Since I knew jack and shit about things like that, I kept my mouth shut and tried to remember what the experts told me. I had intended to ask about the refugees in the north, but there was never a good opening. It wasn't really relevant to the matter at hand, anyway, and after a while it slipped my mind.

"So, you see why sending out scouts by horse would be a fool's errand," Rallon said. "In the area they've likely operated from these last several days"—that being the hills to the southwest of the city, not all that far south of where the road went that lead to the mountain village we'd visited—"it is easy for them to hide even a large camp, and their sentries would be likely to spot our scouts before the reverse. But you, ah, you're a whole other creature, aren't you? Flying by night you should be able to find them wherever they are, and I'm told you're stealthy enough that you snuck into a trolls' den while they slept. That is precisely what we need!"

"But, Draka," Lalia cut in, "just recon, yeah? If they start losing patrols, or if they get attacked in their camp"—she gave me a *very* pointed look—"they may either fall back or escalate."

"Lalia!" Rallon turned to her, looking less than pleased. "I'm sure that Lady Draka does not—"

"No," I interrupted him. "That's fair. I can't say I wouldn't have gotten rid of some sentries or a patrol or two if I got the opportunity. I don't like people who prey on the innocent. But no attacking them. Got it."

Rallon's expression softened at my defense of Lalia, and he turned back to me. "In that case, once you've returned with a location for us, we can discuss terms for you joining the attack, if that is something you might be interested in."

"I'll hold you to that. Just one question: Where are the other mercenaries in this? The Cranes?"

"The Cranes." Rallon's sour expression spoke volumes about what he thought of them. "They are patrolling the coast, 'guarding from pirates and sea raiders,' as Larrallan calls it. Useless cravens and a waste of the city's money, the lot of them. Needless to say, they will not be helping us."

"Didn't they deal with the first bunch of valkin that Mak and the others found?"

"Yeah," Lalia said. "And I heard they lost two men doing it. How the hell they managed that I can't imagine. It's probably better for us if they're not with us."

There wasn't much else to say. I would leave that night and stay out until I had enough to go on for the Wolves to strike in force, or until I gave up. Considering how bad that would be for my pride, I didn't see that happening. Rallon offered to clear the way for me to move into the cellar if I preferred. I told him no, with my thanks for the offer, but if they could get some of those fish Garal brought me last time I'd sure appreciate it.

They came through. Of course they did. Fresh as anything too.

Gobbling down twenty pounds of fish wasn't a great idea if I wanted to have a productive day, but it was only morning, and I was stuck in that little room until after sunset. The fish were just as delicious as I remembered, and I ate with relish and gusto, telling myself that this way I could just sleep the day away and then not need to eat during the entire mission. It was a win-win-win situation.

Of course, once I was done, splayed out on the floor and happily drifting off into torpor, Mak and Herald came to talk to me. Pulling myself together was hard, and clearing my head entirely was not happening, but I did the best I could.

Herald sniffed the air, looked at the long crate, empty except for the straw lining the bottom, and smiled at me with clear amusement. *I see that you had a nice breakfast.*

I'd gathered myself with a little more dignity on the floor and raised my head to look at them. *Mmm, Garal found me some great fish. Are you two here to talk about something?*

"You're going to be gone for a couple of days, right?" Mak asked, sticking with Karakani. She took the chair while Herald sat on the desk. Uncertainly kicking her feet, Herald looked uncharacteristically girlish.

"I'm guessing at least two days, yeah," I answered. I figured that if she didn't want to use her so-so Tekereteki, she must want to talk about something serious.

Mak took a quick breath and continued. "We know that we can stay here until you're back—"

"We want to go out!" Herald blurted. "We cannot be cooped up here day and night with little or nothing to do, not while we are in the city!"

"I . . . don't think that's safe," I said.

"It will be perfectly safe," Herald countered. "We will go out during the day, with plenty of people around, and be back here long before nightfall."

"And we'll have Lalia with us, or Garal, or both," Mak said. "You said that you'd be comfortable with us returning to the city once Tam and Val were back. Well, Garal and Lalia are as good at fighting as Tam and Val, probably even better against people. We'll be no less safe with them."

"I guess . . ." I really couldn't think of a good counter-argument. I was pretty sure that if I just told them no they'd do as I said, but I honestly wasn't comfortable controlling them like that when I couldn't justify it. "What about Ardek?"

"We figured we'd take him along."

"We may as well get used to moving around the city with him," Herald said. "If he is to become part of the group, we cannot very well leave him here while we go around."

"You're okay with that? Him being part of the group?"

"He's got a lot to learn before I'd count on him surviving a real fight," Mak said with just a little too much spite in her voice, "but until we've got the Night Blossom's head on a pole I think we need him."

"Yeah, all right. Fine. Just, be careful. At least two Wolves with you, arms and armor, stay around other people, all that."

"Yes!" Herald said brightly. "We promise!"

"Going to go check for a letter from Maglan?"

"As soon as I possibly can," she confirmed.

"And we need to talk to the innkeeper at the Favor," Mak said. "That's our inn."

"Herald's told me."

"Good. We need to talk to him about our mail. It's odd that there's been nothing at all these past weeks. Tam and Val aren't the only ones we're expecting letters from."

"All right, just, again, be careful. If there's one place anyone would be looking for you, it's there."

"But it's also a popular place to stay for adventurers, many of whom know us by name or by reputation. There's no need to worry. I promise."

"You don't need to keep laying it on, I already said okay," I said and laid my head on the floor. I wasn't sure how I felt about them coming to ask permission in the first place. Herald, at least, was supposed to be a free woman. But at the same time, I couldn't deny that I savored the respect and deference they showed, and that was hard to ignore.

I did still worry about them. I didn't know how vindictive and reckless the Night Blossom and her people might be. I knew practically nothing about them. But, between the girls taking their equipment, taking skilled fighters with them as escorts, and staying in public places, I really couldn't argue against them. And they'd go stir crazy if I insisted on them staying inside for days with the city just outside.

Herald hopped off the table, happier than I'd seen her in weeks, and knelt by me. I lifted my head slightly to look at her, and she grabbed me by the cheeks and kissed me right between the eyes. *"Thank you, Draka,"* she said, *"for everything. Be careful, will you?"*

"Do not fight, please," Mak added. *"Only scout."*

"Everyone seems to think that I am addicted to fighting," I grumbled. *"I will not reveal myself unless I absolutely must. I promise. Now let me sleep, I have a long night ahead of me. Are you not tired?"*

"We had a nap," Herald said, *"and now Rib is . . . helping us stay up."*

"Be careful with those vials. I do not like how attached Rib is to them."

"We will. Come, Mak. Let her sleep."

With that they left the small office, and I drifted off.

"Draka. It is time."

I woke slowly to the sound of Mak's voice. She was not in the room with me, I realized, and I felt a pressure against my feet. Blinking my eyes open, I looked around and found myself again splayed out across the floor, my feet against the door, which Mak had pushed open a crack to be able to speak to me.

Outside the open window the sky was dark, the opposite wall warmly but faintly lit by the streetlights.

"Mmm. Awake! Thank you, Mak," I said, and got my feet under me, stretching to relieve the slight stiffness in my back and limbs. I wanted to stretch my wings, but the room was too small. *"Where is Herald? I would like to say goodbye."*

Mak opened the door the rest of the way once I had moved. She grinned at me. *"Stuck in a game of cards. She will not admit that she has lost every hand, and will continue to lose. I will get her."*

Mak left and soon returned with Herald in tow, who looked very annoyed. *"I will learn that game,"* she insisted.

"You know the rules well, and some strategies. But you cannot bluff, so you will lose. When your cards are good, you look like a child given a new toy," Mak teased her.

"Then I will learn to deceive," Herald said, frowning.

"You have not learned in seventeen years. But I wish you well."

"No face for cards?" I asked.

"Face, hands, shoulders . . ." Mak said. Herald just kept on frowning.

"I am going," I told them to change the subject. *"Were you out today?"*

"*Yes,*" Mak said, suddenly a little cagey. "*We have things to tell. But they can wait.*"

I looked at Herald, who gave up her frowning and nodded. "*Nothing important enough for you to worry about on your mission.*"

I began to order them to tell me, but cut myself off. "*I trust your judgment,*" I said instead. "*We can talk when I get back.*"

Mak went to check outside the window, while Herald walked up to me and put her hand on my neck familiarly. She looked worried. "*Be careful,*" she said. "*No fighting. Or at least, come back immediately if you get hurt. Promise?*"

"*Yes, fine. I promise. If I get hurt in any way, I will return as fast as I can. And you two be careful. If you feel at all threatened outside, return here.*"

"*We will,*" Mak said from the window. "*The alley is clear.*"

"*I will see you two soon then. Be safe.*"

"*You too,*" Herald said. Mak nodded.

I heard Mak take a deep breath as I shifted, the only sign of her surprise. It was still fairly new for her to see, and I was curious what it looked like from an outside perspective. I drifted over to the window, and instead of going down into the alley and making my way from there I pushed, making a bridge of darkness between the window and the neighboring roof that I stretched across.

Once there, I looked back to the window where the sisters stood, looking after me. I shifted back, bobbed my head at them, and spread my wings. With a leap I was airborne, climbing in a spiral up over the city. Most of it lay dark, with only some buildings, squares, and the largest streets lit. The Wolves' headquarters was one such building, with its lit yard and the large lights in front of the entrance. It would be easy to find upon my return.

To the south the sky was covered in a mass of clouds. Even here the stars were hidden in patches, the moon in and out of cover, but there was enough for me to see by. When I'd reached high enough that the roofs blended together into a dark mass, I turned south and then west toward the mountains. I was excited. For all my worries about my humans, I still looked forward to this. I couldn't touch the Night Blossom yet, but these bandits, or raiders, or whatever they were, I could find them. I was sure of it. And they were going to get what was coming to them.

CHAPTER TWENTY-SIX

Raiders

Finding the raiders was not exactly effortless, but I hadn't expected it to be. It would have been nice to just lazily fly over the foothills and spot them immediately, but the area was large, and I needed to stay fairly high to be sure that nobody saw me. Herald had great night vision to go with her general hawk-eyedness, I knew that, and any organized force was sure to have at least a couple of people among them with similar advancements. Fortunately, I was in no rush. I had all night, and the next night, and the one after that, if necessary. I would find them. Nothing else was acceptable. Neither justice nor my pride would allow it.

The moon was a fat crescent as I reached the hills north of the search area, but it soon vanished behind the heavy oncoming clouds as I turned south. I soon flew into wind and a light rain, which gradually got heavier but, mercifully, never reached the level where it became unbearable.

My strategy was simple: If I saw a gathering of lights, I'd approach low and check it out. Since we didn't know if the raiders had a camp or were operating out of villages they occupied, I'd have to get in close and make sure. I doubted there were many people alive who could do that with my level of stealth. My shadow form wasn't invisibility, but at night it was close enough to make no difference.

I got a lot of training doing stealthy approaches that night, and the clouds and the rain helped. The hills were dotted with small villages and hamlets, surrounded mostly by orchards and open pasture, but most of them could easily be dismissed. We knew that the raiders were mostly or all mounted, so I kept my eyes peeled for any large concentration of horses. Hiding that number of horses without, say, a barn wasn't going to happen, so any place without large structures only got a cursory flyover. I did find one little place that had a large herd of horses wandering almost free in the hills around it, but when I went around the place, it was clear that it was just a peaceful village that happened to raise horses, and nothing else.

I'd lost count of how many places I'd inspected by the time morning broke. Boredom and frustration had me glancing at their livestock, but I held myself back. I wasn't hungry anyway. I'd flown back and forth over the area where Rallon suspected the raiders might be camped, and the area appeared to be rich because there were a *lot* of little places. What had surprised me was how many of those places looked completely undisturbed, even in the southern end of the area. I'd seen a few burned-out husks, empty or surrounded by poor souls trying to rebuild, but most of what I found was untouched. If the raiders had passed through, and if they were thought to be riding long distances to raid, why were they leaving so many little settlements alone? It just didn't make sense!

During the night I'd scouted out a nice, inaccessible cave high in the hills, and when sunrise was getting close I headed there. It was small and smelled like bat crap, but darkness and shelter from the weather were all I needed, and it served me well enough. The rain continued throughout the day, providing a pleasant background noise for sleep. It was always nice to listen to the rain when I myself was nice and dry.

The next night the rain and clouds had passed, the moon was bright, and I went right back to my flyovers. Because the terrain was mostly steep hills separated by valleys and dells, a decently hidden camp would have been easy to miss unless I flew directly over it, so all I could really do was cover the same terrain again, only on a different route. This time I went in a zig-zag pattern north to south, then turned around and did the same heading north.

With sunrise only a few hours off, I found them.

They'd been hard to find, and no wonder. Not only were they tucked into a valley, its sides so steep that it was practically a canyon, but it was a wooded one as well. It was blind luck on my part that some of the trees had begun losing their leaves early, letting me spot their fires shining through the empty patches and drawing me in for a look. When I snuck up in shadow form, I found the place calm and silent, except for one sound that piqued my interest—muted crying.

In the center of the camp was a stockade, and inside the stockade were a half dozen prisoners. They couldn't be anything else by the state of them. They were being generally mistreated, wearing worn clothes and sleeping on the ground with only the most basic of bedding to keep the cold away. The source of the crying was a man, probably in his mid-twenties, who lay crying softly with his head in the lap of a man perhaps in his late fifties. Unlike the prisoners traded from the valkin by the slavers, there was no pattern among these captives except that they were all adults. They were a mix of ages, both men and women. One of the men was missing a hand, but the injury looked old, not anything that had been done to him when he was captured.

I needed to know more. I had no idea why these people had been taken, and it wasn't like I could speak to them. While the older man with the boy in his lap seemed to be awake, his hand slowly stroking the boy's hair, there was a guard who was sure to hear any words that might be spoken. And there were other things I'd been asked to find out.

The first was easy. How many of them were there? After leaving the camp and shifting back to rest, I returned and started counting. Some slept in tents, some in the open. A few were awake, guarding the prisoners, the camp in general, or the horses. All in all, I counted twenty-five raiders, with sixty horses and six prisoners. While I counted them I also got a pretty good idea about their equipment, and while they weren't wearing any kind of insignia, it was pretty clear that this was some kind of professional force. Their weapons and armor, their tents, even their saddles were too similar to be just a hodge-podge of the best each man could afford. They weren't identical, but there was a definite uniformity to them that suggested they could be interchangeable.

They could still be bandits, of course. They could have deserted from that duchy in the south, taking their equipment with them and going north to avoid their own land's justice, but I doubted it. It was the prisoners that convinced me. They wouldn't take, feed, and guard prisoners if they didn't want them for something, and if these were bandits, well . . . I would have expected most of the prisoners to be young women.

Maybe it was a little paradoxical, but the fact that they had a middle-aged man and an older woman in that stockade was reassuring. They should, hopefully, be in less immediate danger of anything horrible happening to them. This fact made it far easier to keep my promise to refrain from violence.

It was far too close to sunrise for me to head back to the city. I could have made it back to the cave I'd used easily enough, but now that I knew where the camp was, I wanted to keep an eye on it. Not literally, unfortunately. I couldn't find a suitable tree with a clear sightline to the place, and instead had to settle for one where I could see the edge of the area where they kept their horses.

The next night I would move in as early as possible. The commander of the group had been easy to find—a big, scarred woman sleeping alone in one of the larger tents—and I hoped to hear some of what was said in or around that tent before everyone bedded down for the night. Then I could return to Karakan, report to Rallon, and lead the Wolves back here. It would be a goddamn slaughter, and I would enjoy every minute of it.

I curled up among the branches, hidden by the still dense leaves of the tree. This was getting harder, I noted a little sadly. I was getting too big to sleep way up in the crown and was going to need to settle for lower, sturdier branches soon. But that was tomorrow's problem, and I might as well enjoy this while I could. I drifted off to sleep with visions of bloodshed dancing happily in my mind.

I woke to pre-dawn twilight and the sounds of people saddling and packing horses. I hadn't slept long, an hour at most, and I could have gone back to sleep despite the bustle of the camp if I'd wanted to, but curiosity got the better of me.

It was still dark, and in shadow form I glided from tree to tree until I got a good look at the camp. There were two distinct groups preparing to ride out, it seemed. One, made up of about half of the raiders, were checking their gear or saddling their horses. The other group was already mounted, and consisted of five raiders, one of whom looked like some kind of officer by his finer dress and general attitude, and the six prisoners. The prisoners were tied to their saddles, the reins of their horses tied two to each of three of the raiders' saddles.

Three things came to mind. First, I couldn't do anything about the larger force except harass and disrupt them, but then I would be exposed to our enemy. Second, the smaller group looked to be taking the prisoners away. Maybe they were going to a different camp, and maybe they were going farther than that, but they were moving them, which meant that third, these raiders would likely be alone. Separated from their herd, so to speak. Vulnerable.

I could take five. In the open and with surprise on my side, it shouldn't be a problem. Surely they wouldn't be missed for a while? And I had only promised not to fight if it wasn't necessary. This definitely counted as necessary. This might be the prisoners' last chance for freedom, after all. And I'd be back before nightfall, so I could still gather more information before returning to Karakan.

I didn't even try to argue myself out of it. Instead I curled up in the best cover I could find where I still had a clear view of the smaller party. Just as the first rays of the morning sun hit the highest peaks of the mountains, as though that were the signal, they started moving. The passage of horses had worn a narrow path into the floor of the wooded valley, running right below me, and the raiders and their prisoners followed it south and out into the hills.

Following them among the trees was easy. The sun was low and it was still dark among the trees. It became more difficult once the woods ended and we were among the hills, which were covered in nothing more than grass, scrub, and low bushes.

I tried keeping up on foot, but while they weren't pushing their horses too hard, they still kept up a pretty good pace, faster than I could comfortably go for any length of time. The solution I settled on was hopping from hill to hill. I'd sit at the top of a hill and wait until the landscape inevitably broke my line of sight. Then I'd fly up just high enough to spot them, close in, and settle down to wait for them to disappear again. Sometimes they'd follow a ridge for a while, and then I'd have to improvise. I'd sneak along whichever side I thought I was less likely to be spotted, and if they saw me I'd just have to go.

I had followed them like that for about three hours, I'd say, when they stopped by a small stream to rest and water their horses, eat, piss, and whatever else they needed to do. They had the prisoners dismount as well, so they could tend to their own needs. That was good. I didn't want someone disappearing over the horizon on a panicked horse.

Sneaking up on them wouldn't be easy since the terrain around them was so open, but I didn't need to. I sat at a distance for a while, watching them spread out a little to tend to their needs and listening to them talk loudly to each other. Whoever they were, they weren't Karakani; it was obvious by the language. The language wasn't even similar, as different to Karakani as that language was to Barlean. Although, come to think of it, there were a lot of similarities to Tekereteki, in the way that, say, Spanish and Italian were similar. In appearance, the raiders were pretty much indistinguishable from their prisoners or any other average Karakani. That didn't mean much, necessarily, but it made me curious. I'd have to ask someone about it back in the city, but first I had some people to kill.

I barely reflected over how easily that thought came to me as I launched myself into the air, beating hard to pick up speed. I aimed for a woman at the center of the dispersed group, by the water, and she turned just in time to begin a scream before I hit her with a wet crunch. Feeling someone crumple against me was as satisfying as the last time. Unlike last time, however, this time my target was less massive than I was, and instead of going down together in a rolling heap, I managed to recover and stay in the air while she flopped bonelessly to the ground.

The only sound so far had been me ripping through the air, my victim's aborted scream, and our collision. The world stood still, waiting for anyone to react. Then the horses panicked and scattered, and the shouting started behind me.

"By the hells, what—?"

"Maraga? Maraga!"

"Oh, gods, preserve us! Oh, gods!"

"What is that thing?"

"Gods, no! Maraga!"

"To arms! Quickly, together!"

"Oh, gods! A dragon! Oh, GODS!"

An arrow zipped past me right as I wheeled around. I hadn't gone far, but the remaining raiders were trying to put together a defense. Well, three of them were. One just stood with a lance in their hand, the point resting on the ground, apparently too terrified to even move. The prisoners were nowhere to be seen.

I identified the archer and dove for him next. An arrow passed right through the membrane of my left wing, and it stung like a paper cut from hell but didn't seem to do any significant damage. He got off one more arrow, but I saw it coming and rolled slightly, making it glance harmlessly off my scales. He realized quickly that he wouldn't get another shot and dove to the side, but I turned with him and managed to grab him with one hand and my feet, dragging him into the air. I hadn't done that since my first big fight, against the gremlins! Despite how much I'd grown and become stronger since then, this was no gremlin, and I was *not* going to be doing any fancy flying with my hollering cargo. Slow and careful, maybe, but this was no time for that. Besides, when I looked down the guy was already pawing for a dagger at his belt.

Well, shit. Be that way, I thought and dropped him. From sixty or seventy feet above the ground and going as fast as I was, I doubted he'd make it. I'd have to check on him later to be sure, even if the way his scream cut off sounded pretty final. I didn't want any miraculous survivals coming back to bite me in the tail.

The two raiders who were still fighting had gotten together near the third. They had the right idea, I thought, staying close together with their lances pointed in my direction. I'd need to be careful. I'd gotten some solid advice from Mak, but we'd still only trained for a few days.

I landed near them and advanced, wings out and body held low to the ground. They clearly didn't know that I could understand them, because they were talking to each other, trying to decide how to tackle me.

The third remaining raider—a woman, I saw now, and not much taller than Mak—had dropped her lance and stood empty-handed on the grass. "Just surrender, you fools," she pleaded hopelessly with the two others. "Please! It's a dragon! You can't fight it!"

"Shut up and help us, coward!" one of the two men—the one I'd pegged as an officer—roared at her, though his eyes never left me. "By the Warrior, once we are done, I will execute you myself if you do not step forward!"

The woman actually took a step or two before stopping herself. Some kind of command advancement, maybe? I wondered what else they had. Certainly not speed; they were both considerably slower with their weapons and less quick on their feet than Mak. Something to do with riding, maybe, since they were cavalry?

Meanwhile, I was trying to coax them into attacking so I could counterattack the way I'd practiced. Going against one spear had been tricky enough, and now there were two of them, and these lances were longer than Mak's spear. The problem was that while they probably wanted me dead, I was pretty sure they would be almost as happy for me to just clear off and leave them alone. They were fine with just keeping me at a distance until I . . . I don't know, grabbed one of the bodies and flew off with it? That's probably what they expected. They still got some glancing or non-penetrating hits on me as I feinted an attack, and I was getting annoyed. I definitely needed to spar more.

"Please!" The unarmed raider was almost in tears. "I don't know why it wants us dead, but if we—"

At that point I realized that I was being an idiot. I'd been approaching this the way I sparred with Mak, which meant that I wasn't going all out to kill them. I'd been holding myself back so effectively against her that I'd forgotten one of my most effective weapons.

I gave the two raiders a good, long spray of venom. The woman at the back yelped and leaped back, while their simultaneous shouts of surprise turned into choking coughs and sobs of pain as it got in their eyes, mouths, and noses. Instead of trying anything fancy, I lunged, grabbed the shafts of their spears, and jerked them toward me. The officer held onto his and was pulled forward, where he was met by a clawed foot that brought him to the ground. I stepped off him to close on the other man, who'd let go of his lance and was scrambling backward, trying to see through searing eyes as I lunged forward, my teeth closing over his neck from the side.

His hands closed over my face, trying to pry my jaw open, but I simply braced my hands on his head and shoulder and jerked my head back, sharp teeth sawing through muscle, tendons, and gristle. The taste that filled my mouth was far too pleasant to think about, and I forced myself to spit the chunk out as I turned around to finish off the officer, who was trying to rise to his knees. He wasn't breathing, though his chest jerked spasmodically. He made it halfway to his feet, staggered, and fell again. *Good enough*, I thought.

There was only me and the last raider left in the gully. She was sitting on the grass, her legs beneath her like she'd just folded onto the ground, her hands at her sides. Just one left, no fuss, and then I could go find the prisoners.

"Please," she said, speaking to me directly. "I surrender. You're a dragon. You're intelligent, right? Please! Even if you don't understand my words, please understand me!" As I got closer she closed her eyes, tears trickling down her face as she started to beg. "Please. I don't know what we did, but I'm sorry. I'm not a warrior. You don't need to kill me! I surrender! Please!"

I hesitated. I wasn't sure why. One swipe with my claws and I'd be done, and I could go find those prisoners. I needed to round them up so I could get them back to a village somewhere, maybe send them toward Karakan to report what they'd seen, and then get back to the raider camp.

The woman was crying in earnest as I reached for her throat. She choked as my claws touched her skin but quickly recovered and kept repeating, "Please! Please! Please!"

God dammit, why did she have to beg?

I let go of her neck and knocked her over with a shove to the chest, then pinned her to the ground. "Why?" I growled in her language, standing above her with my face inches from hers. "Why do you deserve to live when so many villages have suffered? Did you think retribution wouldn't catch up to you?"

She opened her eyes and looked at me. Her mouth opened, but all that came out was a shuddering breath as she stared into my eyes.

"Nothing to say for yourself?"

Her mouth worked, and the words spilled out in a babbling, stuttering torrent. "I . . . I had nothing to do with that. I'm not a cavalryman or even a soldier. I never hurt anyone, I swear. I don't want to be here; they made me. I'm a bonded healer; I don't raid, I don't fight. They make me carry a weapon because *everyone* has to carry a weapon, but I'm only here to heal and tend to the prisoners, I swear, please don't kill me, please!"

I looked at her, then sniffed her. She stank of sweat and fear and desperation, but that was no surprise and didn't tell me anything new. I looked around. No prisoners. No horses. Nothing moved except flies and water.

I should kill her, I thought, even as I stepped off her. *I should get rid of her so that I don't need to worry about her returning to her company. It would be so easy.*

I couldn't do it.

"Stay here," I told her, turning away in frustration. "Don't bother trying to run. I can fly faster than your horses can gallop."

Then I took off in search of the prisoners.

CHAPTER TWENTY-SEVEN

Captives

The prisoners were smart. They had stayed together, and they had followed some of the horses. They tried to hide when I flew over them, of course, but the scrubby bush they found wouldn't have done much to hide *me*, let alone six human adults.

They broke and scattered when I approached on foot, but when I barked "Stop!" in perfect, if slightly hissy, Karakani, four of them came to a stuttering stop and turned to look at me. The remaining two kept running for a while but stopped when they looked back and saw that I wasn't chasing anyone.

"I am here to help you," I said as loud as I could. "You are free to go, but I want to speak with you first."

"You speak," the man with one hand said, barely loud enough for me to hear. I rolled my eyes. This again.

"Yes. I speak. You know what I am, or you should. And I need to speak with you. I swear that I mean you no harm, so if you come back with me, you can take the raiders' stuff, answer a few questions, and be on your way. If you will not come with me willingly, I will pick one of you, and we will talk whether you want to or not."

I was quite satisfied with my tone. It was very "this will happen." *Probably my command advancement helping me along,* I thought.

"What do you say, Dorten?" the man in his fifties said to the younger man who'd been crying in the night. Dorten closed his eyes and, even at a distance of a few dozen yards, I saw a flash of magic in my direction, first weak, then stronger. It barely touched me, and then it was gone, as though I'd absorbed it.

I considered my options. I did not like having magic thrown in my direction, but I hadn't felt anything. I settled on patience, for the moment. They were prisoners on the run, and frightened. I'd give them a chance.

Dorten spoke. "She . . . She? Yes. She means us no harm. Or, uh . . ." He swallowed nervously and looked in my direction. "She didn't, until I cast on her. I'm sorry." The last was directed at me.

"You can read minds?" I asked. This Dorten was entirely correct. I was not happy about him using magic on me, and even less if it was something that might mess with my head in any way.

"Uh, no, not really. I can feel what others feel. And, uh . . . change it, a little. I didn't try that on you, I swear!" he added hastily. "I only needed to know if you spoke the truth!"

"So will you return with me?"

"I, uh . . . I will. I think we all should," he said, more loudly to the others, and approached me. "Except maybe Valana and Parkon should keep following the horses?"

"Happily," the one-handed man, Parkon, presumably, muttered. Then he looked at me nervously and added, "Your pardon, uh, lady dragon."

"No, no," I said graciously. "I know what your stories say, and I did just kill a bunch of armed men and women with no effort. It's fine to be nervous. Go ahead, gather up the horses. The rest of you, follow me. At a distance, if you must."

I walked past them in the direction of the stream, not even looking back. I wanted to make it clear that it didn't even occur to me that they wouldn't do as I said, although inside I wondered how many, if any, would be behind me when I got there. One thing I was sure of was that my captive would still be where I'd left her. I knew the signs, now. She'd had the beginnings of the same feeling as Ardek and Mak, like she wouldn't dare disobey me. It was a . . . not quite a smell, but that was the best comparison I could make. Beneath the fear and the desperation there had been something that smelled like obedience. I couldn't describe it any other way.

It was the most wonderful scent I'd ever experienced. Even better than gold.

My captive, the self-described non-combatant healer, was indeed where I'd left her, though she'd taken the time to gather the three nearby corpses and lay them beside each other. She was kneeling by their feet and, by the look of it, praying. Again I hesitated, but this time I knew why. I owed her and her companions nothing, but it would still feel wrong not to give her a moment to perform last rites and say farewell. It wasn't like we would even be burying them.

Waiting meant that there was time for my aches and pains to make themselves known. I had hit an armored woman at something like forty or fifty miles per hour pretty much chest on and, while she had come out of it as a bag of broken bones, even magical fortitude could only do so much. I was going to have another bruise under my scales until I could rest it off on my hoard, that was for sure. And the little dings I'd taken from the lances weren't helping.

To take my mind off it, I turned my head to speak to the man called Dorten, who had approached within a few yards of me. "This one claims to be a healer," I said, "a non-combatant who never harmed anyone. Is she lying?"

"What will you do if she is?" he said apprehensively.

I let my silence speak for me.

"It's true, so far as I know. She tended us and offered what comfort the others would allow, though none of us could understand her. Her name is Bekiratak, or something like that. It's a little hard to say." He paused, then said, "Her treatments were too effective. I think she's a magic user."

Well, *that* was interesting!

"Like you," I said.

"Like me," he confirmed.

"And me, and the others," said the oldest woman in the group, who must have been pushing seventy but walked straight and proud now. "We are all different, but we are all magic users. They came for us, saying our villages would be spared if everyone with a magic advancement surrendered themselves."

She gave the raider woman a pitiless look. "They lied. They killed everyone. My neighbors. My husband. My children, those who'd stayed. My grand—" Her voice broke and she looked away, her hand over her mouth as she gathered herself.

"Thank you, dragon, for killing them. This group is a good start. May the Traveler leave their souls to rot."

They killed entire villages? Rallon hadn't mentioned anything like that. At first I couldn't quite believe it. I didn't see the point in butchering a whole village after you had what you came for. But then my more pragmatic side came out, and yeah, I got it. If you were going around capturing magic users for whatever reason, maybe you wouldn't want that getting out. Word would spread to other villages, and the magic users there would flee, maybe all the way to Karakan, where you couldn't touch them. Much easier to just butcher dozens, perhaps hundreds of innocents to cover your tracks. Throw in some less lethal raids and some attacks on travelers, and it would all look like bandit attacks.

"Do you know anything about the raiders," I asked after a long, sad silence. "Who they are, who sent them, things like that?"

"They're not Karakani, and they're not Happarans," a younger woman said. "I speak some Happaran. It's not so different from Karakani, just sounds a little funny. The words they use and the way they say them and such."

"Right." I came to a snap decision. "I guess I'm keeping this one. Can you all make it safely to a village? I can keep an eye on you until you're out of the hills, but I need to return to the city as fast as I can."

"If Valana and Parkon can bring back enough horses, we should be able to," Dorten said. "I have family near the coast. It's a long ride but you can all come with me," he said to the three others with him. "Anyone who . . . has no one left."

"And can I trust you all not to tell anyone about me?"

"For what you've done, I'm sure we can spin a tale that explains our escape," the older woman said. "To think that the council has a dragon helping them! I understand that neither they nor you want that to spread."

"Right," I said, not bothering to correct her. If they thought I was a state secret, so much the better. I turned to the raider, who had stood up and was looking at us. "You. Bekiratak. Take off your armor."

"Bekiratag," she corrected me softly, but she did as I said, beginning to loosen the straps of her layered leather hauberk.

"Becky. Once you're done, sit down and wait until the prisoners are ready to leave."

"Can I bury my dead?"

"No time. We'll be leaving as soon as possible. But there should be another one a couple of hundred yards that way," I said and gestured, "if you want to pray over him or anything."

"Beretog," Becky said and closed her eyes, then nodded. "He and Maraga were to be married."

I snorted. "Are you looking for sympathy? Regret? Pity? He put an arrow through my wing. Go get the murdering sack of crap, and lay him out to rest next to his murdering sack of crap betrothed if you want. Or don't. And grab their valuables while you're at it—coins, jewelry, anything like that. But don't waste time searching for something that none of you deserve."

She did go to fetch him. She struggled, dragging a man much larger than her across the grass. It took her twenty minutes once she found him, but she did it. She even found his bow and laid it on his chest, then put his and the woman's hands together. It might have been sad if I felt anything except contempt for the both of them.

The two prisoners who'd gone to fetch horses did a good job, bringing back eight of the original eleven. They were strong riders since, as I was told, they were both from villages that raised horses, but the others managed.

"Shall I run then?" Becky asked me when she was not offered a mount.

"Run? No, you'll be much too slow."

I saw a fearful suspicion begin to grow in her eyes. "But I . . . I'll fall behind," she said. She licked her lips, her eyes darting to the open hills beyond me. She was thinking of making a break for it, and she wasn't being very subtle.

"Don't worry about that," I told her. "And don't try to run. You won't like what I'll do if you run."

I turned to the mounted Karakani and called, "Get started! We'll catch up!"

"Turn around," I told Becky. "And lift your arms."

"No," she whispered. "Please! You let me live, you—"

"If I wanted to kill you," I told her, getting close enough for her to feel my breath on her face, "I'd do it like this. With you facing me, so I could look you in the eyes when I did it. Now turn around, and lift your arms."

She trembled visibly as she closed her eyes and turned, her hands shaking uncontrollably as she raised her arms.

"I've never tried this before," I told her as I got right up behind her. "Don't struggle, or I might drop you."

"What—" she began, but then I wrapped my arms firmly around her chest, kicked off hard with my legs, and clawed my way into the air.

Becky screamed.

I followed the rescued captives, flying lazy circles above them until they left the hills, getting on a small road which led them east. I pitied and admired them. They had all lost so much. I wondered if they would ever get over the grief and survivor's guilt. But they all soldiered on, at least for now, as I turned north and then east to skim the mountains on my way back to the city.

Becky had stopped screaming after a few minutes. Then she cried off and on for a while, before going completely silent, hanging stiff beneath me and holding on tightly to my arms while I held her with all four limbs, my arms around her chest and my legs around hers. I definitely felt her weight, but it wasn't more than I could handle. I would need a rest on the way back to Karakan, but we could have been back before nightfall if I wanted to.

It made me think. Becky was fairly small. But if I could fly for miles and miles with her, surely I could fly for just one or two miles with Herald? I could finally show her my hoard!

I laughed, and felt Becky tense to beyond rigid under me, her grip on my arms tightening even further. "Don't worry," I shouted over the wind, "I was just thinking how you're actually being useful! This is good practice for me. And being useful means that *you're* safe!"

"P-p-p-ple-ase d-d-on't-t—" she stuttered as loudly as she could, her teeth chattering, and I realized that she must be freezing. I'd been flying pretty high to avoid being seen, and hadn't thought about how lightly dressed she'd been under her armor.

"Shit, you're not dying on me, are you?" I shouted back.

"I—I—"

Well, damn. It occurred to me that she might have been going hypothermic. It was about time for a rest anyway, so I started slowly descending, keeping close to the mountains and looking for a good place to land.

"I'm going to set us down," I told her. "If I try to land normally with you like this you'll be smashed, so I'm going to slow down, hover, and drop you. So . . . try not to break a leg. It'll be a bad time for you to fly the rest of the way back to Karakan with a broken bone."

Becky trembled in my arms.

I found a fairly wide ledge on the side of a cliff. It would do as well as anything, so I started shedding speed and dropping quickly.

"Get ready!" I told Becky. I stopped and hovered above the ledge, slowly letting myself drop between each beat of my wings. Fifty feet up I released my legs, causing Becky to lurch forward with a terrified howl. The screaming started again, only this time her teeth were chattering so bad that it sounded utterly ridiculous.

I dropped to maybe six feet up, as low as I dared go in a hover, and then I let go of Becky.

Becky did not let go of me. She had a death grip with both hands on my left wrist, and dangled, only feet above the ground but acting as though she was hanging over the gates of hell.

I shook my arm, trying to dislodge her, shouting, "Goddamnit, Becky! Becky! *Bekiratag*! Let go!" But she refused. It struck me that I hadn't fully understood just how terrified she'd been during our flight until that moment, and I had to do something. I could see three options: Maim Becky until she couldn't hold on; climb again, with Becky dangling until she inevitably fell; or land the best I could.

With a resigned growl I braced myself, flared my wings, and dropped.

The hardest part was not crushing Becky. She hit the ground, not hard but unprepared, and would have fallen backward if she wasn't still holding on to me like I was her final lifeline. Instead she folded and crumpled onto the ground under me, and I had to jerk my arm quickly to the side to avoid planting it in her face or chest, throwing her hard on her side. I came down, trying to distribute the force so that I could absorb as much of the landing as possible with my joints, but I still felt a shock of pain lance up my right arm from my wrist. That arm folded, and I ended up on my side basically spooning Becky, who was alternately chattering, crying, and laughing hysterically. She still had not let go of my wrist.

I felt a furious rumble start deep in my chest, and Becky must have felt it too, because she went suddenly quiet and turned to look at me. "God. Fucking. Dammit, Becky!" I said, my teeth inches from her face. "I told you to let go!"

She went limp. "I-I'm s-sorry," she said, her voice somehow trembling *while* she chattered. "S-sor-ry! So s-sorry!" She just kept repeating that, going on and on about how sorry she was, and I was, finally, completely convinced that she was not a soldier. I didn't know if she was a coward, but she didn't handle fear very well, that was for sure.

She was kind of pathetic, really.

"Fine," I said, some of my anger evaporating in the face of her fear. "You're a healer, right? You have magic? Heal me. My right wrist."

"I . . . yes. I do! I c-can!" She finally released my left wrist, and I felt a rush of blood that I hadn't realized that I'd been missing, bringing with it pins and needles that I tried to flex away while Becky scrambled to put her hands on my right wrist.

"You'll need to push harder than normal," I told her. "I resist magic."

"Y-yes, okay, yes." I saw the magic gather inside her, then flow through her hands into me, just like when Mak did it. Becky did it silently, though, her eyes fixed on my wrist as she seemed to direct the flow exactly where it needed to go. She strained, and I felt the pain recede, replaced by a soothing warmth.

"T-there," she said, and looked at me, her eyes shining with hope. "Have I done good?" they seemed to say. "Do I get to live?"

"Do my wing too," I told her, opening up my left wing so she could get at the damaged membrane. I didn't like what I saw. The hole wasn't long, but I was pretty sure that it had torn a little at the corners as I flew.

"You're freezing," I said as she healed it. She was such a terrified mess that I couldn't even be angry anymore. At that point all I felt was pity. "Come here. I'll warm you up a bit before we go on."

I didn't wait for her to move. I simply wrapped my wing around her and pulled her in, curling up around her and holding her close while she trembled like a kitten, and went to sleep.

CHAPTER TWENTY-EIGHT

Flames

I awoke as the sun began its descent behind the peaks. I could tell that Becky was awake and wondered if she'd slept at all. Unlikely. She was probably as terrified as ever. At least she wasn't shivering any more.

I felt a twinge in my conscience. She *probably* didn't deserve what I had and would continue to put her through, but at the moment she was cargo, nothing more. I had the location of the raiders' camp, and I had a prisoner who hopefully wouldn't be missed, and who could tell us a lot about who they were and why they were doing what they were. I needed to get her to Karakan as soon as possible, and all she needed to be was alive and able to answer questions. Whatever trauma she suffered on the way didn't really matter.

Or so I told myself. I wasn't entirely sure if I believed that, but it made things easier.

"Are you awake?" she asked, her voice surprisingly steady considering the past several hours.

"Yeah. Time to keep going. We have another . . ." I looked at the landscape. I usually navigated by which peaks and valleys I could see, and from this angle it was hard to tell. "Another hour at the very least. Could be two or three, depending on how fast I can fly," I said.

"All right."

I realized that her voice wasn't just steady. It was tight, flat, and empty of emotion. She crawled out from under my arm and got to her feet a little unsteadily, not really looking at anything, and stood straight with her arms out.

Well. That couldn't be good. I might have gone a little overboard. But as I thought that, I saw a very interesting shine from under her shirt. The telltale glow of magic. And it wasn't inside her.

"Are you all right?" I asked, considering my approach.

"I'm fine," she lied in that same, flat voice. She was clearly not fine. I wondered if she'd checked out entirely. Which might make things easier, but I wasn't sure how that would affect the questioning once we were back in Karakan. Maybe Mak could do something about it?

"If you say so," I said, careful not to put too much weight on my injured wrist. The pain was gone, but I knew that it might not be fully healed. "Are you wearing a necklace, Becky?"

She looked at me. For the briefest of moments there was a spark of defiance in her eyes, but it flickered and died under my gaze.

"Yes," she said, looking down.

"Is it magical?"

"Yes."

"What is it?"

"It . . . The lieutenant had it. If you charge it, it will point you to its twin."

"Which is where?"

"The commander has it," she whispered.

"Shit," I growled. "Do you think she knows where you are now?"

"She keeps them in a chest. There's no reason for her to keep an eye on them. They're only so any group that leaves can follow the main company as they move."

"Great! Thanks for telling me this, Becky. If you're keeping anything else from me, I'll drop you. Do you understand?"

"Yes."

"Are you hiding anything else that's important?"

"No, I swear!"

"Good. Give me the necklace. Just put it on me."

Becky removed a small silver medallion from around her neck, the chain hidden by the high collar of her tunic. I should have been able to smell it, but the scent of her fear was so strong that it had masked the silver until she took it off. She hesitated before approaching me, then put it over my head, letting it slide down to settle against my chest. She had the other valuables I'd had her loot in a pouch, but I didn't want her carrying this particular piece.

"Thank you, Becky. Now it's time to go. Stand right on the edge," I told her, and she calmly walked up, raising her arms. With her arms out she looked like she was about to throw herself off.

Is it just me, I asked myself, or is she looking down?

"Let's not risk that," I muttered. I quickly grabbed her and leaped, spreading my wings and turning the fall into a glide then banking north. I'd considered going east of the nearest mountains to be able to stay a little lower and still avoid being seen, but decided against it. It would add at least an hour to our time, and I'd need to go pretty high over some of the passes anyway. Instead I stayed much lower this time, barely a hundred feet above the ground. If I happened to pass above anyone, I'd just have to hope they didn't get a good look at me. Becky hung limp and silent under me, which I had thought would make things easier but actually turned out to be really disturbing. At that point I was pretty invested in getting my prisoner back to the Wolves, and I kept wondering if she'd somehow died on me.

"Becky!" I shouted. "Are you alive?"

She stayed silent at first, but I felt her tense a little. Then, barely audible over the wind, I heard her shout, "Kira!"

"What?"

"Kira! Everybody calls me Kira! I don't like *Beki*!"

"Yeah! Whatever! Kira! You're not dying on me, are you?"

"I'm cold! But not like before!"

"Yeah! It gets cold above a few thousand feet!"

"Are you?"

"Not really! I'll stay low, though! I need you alive!"

"Oh! Good!"

Becky—or Kira, as she apparently preferred to be called—shouted her side of the conversation in a disinterested monotone, but at least I hadn't accidentally squeezed her to death or anything.

I had to stop to rest one more time, after the sun had set. Carrying over a hundred pounds—somewhere upward of half my own weight—really added to the strain of flying, and I was slowly getting worn out—wings, arms and legs. This time I set down by a hidden stream, and Becky or Kira, whoever she was, dropped obediently. She went to the stream for a drink, then sat down and just watched me for a while before laying back and looking at the stars.

"You're taking me to Karakan," she said, startling me from my nap.

I raised my head to look at her. She was still just looking up at the partially obscured stars. "I am."

"What will happen to me there?"

"You'll be questioned. Then, I don't know."

"Will they kill me?"

"Hard to say. But if you convince them that you're truly not a soldier, and that you didn't hurt anyone, I don't think that they will. Especially if they know that you can heal." I paused to think, and remembered what I'd been told about criminals who couldn't pay their debts. "You'll probably be indentured or something."

"Is that like being bonded?"

"I don't know. What does it mean to be bonded?"

"It's like being a slave. You can't choose where to work, or live. But with more rights, I suppose."

"Huh. I suppose so. Indentured servants are supposed to be released when they've worked off their debt. No idea how long that might be, though."

"Being bonded is for life." She giggled, but it had a disturbing edge to it. "So perhaps this is a good thing for me. Huh? What do you think, dragon?"

"Yeah," I said indifferently. "Maybe. It's too bad you don't speak any Karakani, or the Wolves might ask to keep you. I don't think they have any magical healers in the company."

"They are mercenaries, yes?"

"Yeah."

"I'm with a mercenary company too. Or I was until this morning, I suppose. The Silver Spurs."

"Hope you don't like them too much. The Wolves are going to come down on them like the fist of God once I tell them where your company is."

"No," she said sadly. "I only liked Magara. She was kind."

"To you."

"To me. Not to the Karakani, I suppose."

"What is this language we're speaking anyway?"

That made her finally sit up and look at me. "What do you mean? How can you not know what language this is?"

"I never needed to know what it's called. I just speak it."

"It's Tekereteki, of course!"

"No," I said bluntly and switched languages. "*This is Tekereteki. What you speak is some related language or dialect.*"

Kira's eyes almost bulged out of their sockets, the strongest reaction I'd seen from her since she went silent at the beginning of our flight. "You speak both classical and regular Tekereteki?" she asked incredulously.

"And Karakani, and Barlean, and anything else you can throw at me. But," I switched back quickly, "*this is what Tekereteki merchants speak, according to my friends.*"

She mouthed the words, going over them carefully, then said, "Merchants would speak classical, yes. Any Tekereteki merchant you meet in a foreign port would be a noble of some kind, and the aristocracy all speak classical Tekereteki, as does anyone from the city. Nobody else does unless we have to deal with the bastards."

"Huh. But you don't look Tekereteki."

Despite her fear she bristled at that. "What is that supposed to mean?"

"I know some Tekereteki. They're much darker than you."

"They've got their roots in the home provinces then. I don't. Doesn't make me any less Tekereteki. You're a dragon so maybe you don't get it, but being Tekereteki isn't about how you look."

"Yeah, all right, I believe you. It sounds like a sore spot." I couldn't tell if she was extremely offended or just self-destructive with the tone she took, but I'd brought her too far to do anything to her just because she talked back. And I honestly was embarrassed about my assumptions. I should have known better; I'd been a white woman who grew up with Lebanese and Kenyan neighbors. It was just . . . I was in a weird ancient-slash-medieval fantasy world. For some reason, I just expected every polity to be ethnically homogenous which, when I actually thought about it, was ridiculous. Most of the people I knew weren't even from Karakan!

Kira, of course, couldn't read the chagrin on my face. "Damn homers are always lording over the rest of us in the provinces," she said, almost muttering to herself, "even if they're poor and common like birdshit." She switched to what I considered Tekereteki, putting on an accent similar to how Herald usually spoke. "*Even if they do not speak the classical half as well as me.*"

"*You speak it better than some of my Tekereteki friends,*" I told her honestly. It wasn't perfect, I could tell that, but better than Tam, certainly, and more confident than Mak.

"They make you learn when you get bonded," she said. "In case your bond goes to a noble."

"So what did you do? Debt? Steal something? Unlicensed magic in the city? That's a thing in Karakan, apparently."

"What did I do? Why should I have done anything?"

"You were, what did you call it? Bonded. Enslaved but with more rights," I added when she looked offended again.

"Do you know anything about Tekeretek?"

"Not really. The people I know don't like it much and I don't plan to go there."

"It's beautiful," she said wistfully. "White marble, black basalt, and so much green from trees, grass, and jade that you'd think you were in a rainforest. And enough rain for it, too, obviously."

"The City of Rains. Right. So what did you do?"

"I didn't do anything. I'm a magic user," she shrugged. "When I got my advancement I reported to the Hall of Magic to serve the people, like any magic user should."

"You . . . enslaved yourself?"

"No," she said slowly, "I reported for bonding. If I'd tried to hide it and the Seekers had found me out later, then I might have been enslaved. There is a stark difference. I am still a citizen, just . . . less free in how I live my life. For the good of all."

"Damn, that's messed up," I muttered. "Are you ready to go? It's not far now."

"I'm ready," she said, though she said it like she was walking to the gallows. Maybe she was. I wasn't *entirely* confident that they wouldn't execute her once she'd been interrogated, though in my opinion, it would be a damn waste of a healer. And she probably didn't deserve it either.

Miles out from Karakan I could see flames. A pillar of smoke rose high into the air, lit with all the colors of the inferno below, and I knew, I just *knew* in my gut that it would be the Wolves' headquarters. Because what the hell else could it be? I increased my pace, not caring if I had anything left to give in my wings when I got there.

The Herald. *No*, I reminded myself, as I noticed myself slipping back into that possessive way of thinking, *just Herald*. I had to find her, make sure she was safe, and keep her that way. And Mak. Even Ardek. My humans. *My* humans. I should never have brought them to the city, because of course something like this would happen! The Night Blossom had infiltrated the Wolves once, and who could say that there weren't more of her people left in their ranks?

Faster, dammit! I had to go faster! I'd been staying high again as we approached the city, but now I spat on caution and went into a dive, feeling Kira tense beneath me as our speed increased to sixty, maybe even seventy miles per hour or more. Fast enough that she couldn't shout over the wind anymore, and so that even with my second eyelids closed I was starting to feel my eyes sting.

I wasn't worked up enough to just land in the street in front of the inferno, but it wasn't far off. I dumped Kira unceremoniously in a nearby alley, then heard her squeak and saw her back up rapidly on her butt into a stone brick wall as I shifted, still in the air, to swing around the corner and get a look at the people in the street. I felt a sharp, momentary pang of loss as the necklace slipped through me and hissed onto the ground, but I could deal with that later. I needed to find my humans!

My humans were not in the crowd. I glided closer, pushing the dark with me and using whatever natural shadows I could, but they were not among the wounded laid out down the street either. The only person I found that I knew was Lalia, who moved from group to group, and I couldn't talk to her in front of the others. There was only one thing to do.

I returned to the alley. Kira was still there, huddled among some broken boxes. She pressed herself into them when I approached in a cloud of shadow, making herself as small as possible out of some kind of useless, prehistoric instinct when faced with something terrifying and no way to escape. I shifted back right in front of her, and she went back to her babbling, most of the words completely incoherent. What I understood were mostly variations of "What are you? Oh gods, what are you?"

"Silence," I growled. "I need to find my humans. You will help me."

"Anything. Please. Anything!"

"There is a woman on the street. Her name is Lalia. She is . . ."

From around the corner I watched Kira walk unsteadily toward the crowd of mercenaries and gawkers. I'd described Lalia pretty well, I thought, and Kira went straight toward her. Nobody stopped her, which was pretty bad for security, but they were all busy staring at the fire, trying to fight the fire, or trying to help those hurt by the fire.

"Lalia?" Kira said loudly when she got close to her. Lalia turned to look at her, and not recognizing her gave her a brusque, "What? Kind of busy here."

"Lady . . . hmm . . ." Kira started in Karakani. She stumbled nervously over the words, trying to repeat what I had quickly drilled into her. "Lady in forest back? Talk you. Lady in forest talk you?" She waved toward the alley where I waited.

"What are you talking about, woman? Can't you see what the hell is going on here? Piss off!"

"Lahnie! Lahnie friend lady in forest talk you!" Kira insisted, taking two steps back and waving for Lalia to follow.

"Lahnie? What are—The lady in the forest! Oh! Oh, shit! Yeah, all right. All right. I'm coming." Lalia turned and said some quick words to a merc standing near her, then took a couple of steps toward Kira, who turned and jogged back toward me. Lalia followed at the same pace, though her eyes darted suspiciously and her hand never left the dagger on her belt.

While Kira just went straight into the alley, Lalia stayed well into the street. She walked up so that she had a clear sight down the length of the alley, then caught sight of me and ran in.

"Draka! You chose a shit time to come back! Not like I can blame you this time, though."

"Me being innocent never stopped you before. What happened?"

"What do you think? A fire broke out. Looks like it started in the mess, but it wasn't exactly easy to see while we were evacuating. Not too many hurt and no one dead that we know of, thank the fucking Mercies. Begging your pardon," she added in a lower voice, looking skyward.

"You think it's an accident?"

Lalia scoffed. "Looks like it, but no way. Nobody believes that. Although it's even money on whether it's the Night Blossom, the Cranes, or some other band of bastards. But you don't actually care about that right now, do you? You're looking for the girls."

"I care," I protested. "Just—"

"Not as much. And I get it. The girls are safe, all right? And that stray you picked up too."

"Where are they?"

"We sent them out of the city again, what else?" The relief that flooded over me at those words was immense, to the point where even Lalia must have been able to see it. "Hey, we're not going to let anything happen to them, you know that. Rib and Pot took them as soon as it became clear that the fire was beyond control. Almost two hours ago now."

"And Garal?"

"With the commander, talking to the Guard. Not that we expect anything. It's not like we can prove that it was arson. So, uh, who's the woman? Newest addition to your collection?"

"She's Bekira . . ." I trailed off and looked at Kira.

"Bekiratag," she said.

"Right. My prisoner. I was going to let you interrogate her . . . though she only speaks Tekereteki, so I'd have to translate, I guess. Not like that's going to happen now, though."

"Draka, you . . ." Lalia sighed and ran her hand down her face. "You were supposed to do recon, right? Figure out where their camp was?"

"Yeah, and I did. Then they sent a group south with a bunch of prisoners, so . . ."

"Right. So you saw an opportunity and you took it. Let's call it that. But you know where the camp is?"

"Yeah. I could probably show you on a map." I looked at the inferno. "If you have any left. But with this, I can't imagine that you'll be attacking anyone."

"Maybe, maybe not." Lalia frowned. "We lost a lot of equipment, but at least the stables were untouched and the animals are all fine. Can't exactly hold a prisoner, though," she said, looking at Kira. "She speaks Tekereteki? How's that work?"

"She says she's Tekereteki," I said with a shrug. "A mercenary, though she's more like an enslaved healer than anything else. But she's from the people doing the raiding. A Tekereteki mercenary company called the Silver Spurs."

"And you . . . carried her here?"

"Yep."

"How high?"

"Dunno. Five or six thousand feet, maybe higher? Until she started freezing to death on me."

"Six thou—Gods preserve us. Never try that with me, all right?"

"You be nice to me and I'll be nice to you," I said with a toothy grin that made Kira take half a step backward. The whole exchange probably didn't look great. Combined with the rather aggressive tone Lalia and I usually took with each other, I wondered what Kira expected to happen.

Lalia was used to it, though. All she did was shudder theatrically and say, "Deal." And only a month before I had been practicing smiling without showing any teeth at all. Trying to appear nice and friendly. Ridiculous. Anyone who knew me understood that I didn't mean them any harm, and anyone else would be best off showing some damn respect.

"Draka, I need to get back. Rallon didn't exactly leave me in charge, but someone's gotta keep that lot from falling apart. I've got people out securing lodgings and all that. I, uh . . . I appreciate the initiative, yeah?" She nodded at Kira. "Good thinking, bad timing. Any chance you can hold onto her for a while longer? Having to keep track of a captive that I can't talk to won't exactly make things easier."

"I'll keep her," I said. "I should go find my humans anyway."

"Your humans," she said with a grimace. "Right. Tell them we've got things under control, yeah?" She turned to Kira. "And you, you murdering little shit? You behave around the girls, or Draka here will be the least of your worries." The look on her face was enough for Kira to take a few steps back, putting me between the two of them.

"I'm pretty sure she didn't murder anyone," I told Lalia.

"She would say that, faced with you. Go on now. I'll come see you all in a few days maybe, yeah?"

"All right. But the sooner the better." I said, "Now, listen carefully. This is what I've found. The raiders are a Tekereteki mercenary company. The Silver Spurs. They're capturing magic users and sending them back wherever they came from. Happar, I think, but I'm not sure. I was waiting to question this one until I got back here, but that's not happening unless you've got someone who speaks Tekereteki. Do you?"

"Not that I know of," Lalia said. "Tekereteki mercs? Are you sure?"

"That's what she tells me. They're massacring whole villages, all right? They're camped in a wooded gorge near the mountains, about sixty miles south of here. We need to end them. You know where we'll be. Send for us as soon as you can organize a force."

"They're . . . All right. I'll see what I can do."

"And, I have this." I lifted the medallion, which I'd recovered from the ground. I didn't want to part with it, and I hesitated for a long moment, then held it out to her. Giving something magical and made of silver away was almost physically painful and I had to fight myself every inch. And I couldn't drop it.

"You, ah . . . you'll have to take it," I told her. My throat felt tight.

Lalia looked at me warily, then at the medallion. I'd turned my hand so it lay in my palm, the chain dangling.

"Take it!" I snapped, and her hand flashed out, snatching it from me before I reflexively closed my palm, claws out, and jerked my hand back, a growl escaping me.

Lalia flinched. Kira tried to merge with the wall behind her. Everyone froze.

Once I'd calmed down, convincing myself that Lalia was an ally and not a thief who should be torn to pieces, I spoke. "That, Kira tells me, will point toward wherever their camp is. Their commander has a bunch like it. But they may be able to use theirs to find this one, so . . . I'll trust the commander to know what to do."

"All right, yeah," Lalia said, looking at the medallion. Her voice only quavered a tiny bit. "Thanks. Seriously." With that, she headed back toward the fire.

"Can you tell me what all that was?" Kira asked me when we were alone.

"All you need to know is that I have nowhere to lock you up, which means that you get to come with me to see my humans. Stand in the street and hold your arms out. I don't have room to take off here. It'll be a rough start. I need to be quick."

"Oh," Kira said and deflated a little, clearly having looked forward to her flying days being over. But she did as she was told, and this time, she neither screamed nor emotionally flatlined on me. The woman was adapting quickly, I had to give her that.

On some level I felt pleased about having an excuse not to hand her over. In the short time since I'd picked her up, I'd slowly begun to think of her as *mine*, and this way I got to keep her without argument.

Now I just needed to figure out what to do with her.

CHAPTER TWENTY-NINE

Introductions

Finding the small group of travelers wasn't hard and it didn't take long. I flew low and fast over the road, staying just high enough to keep Kira from flinching whenever we passed a particularly tall tree. Since I could fly far faster than the humans could travel even on horseback, I caught up with them maybe ten or fifteen miles into the forest, well before they'd need to leave the main road to reach my mountain.

I spotted them riding at a trot in a tight group, Rib at the front and Pot at the back. As I approached I angled my wings, braking and making a little extra noise. There was no way they could miss me when I tore through the air so close above them, and I saw Herald turn, look up, and wave to me before I even passed them. A few hundred feet up the road I reversed course in a turn so sharp that I had to tighten my grip on Kira or have her ripped from my arms. I set her down, more gently this time, then landed and sat down to wait for my humans to arrive.

"That's a hell of an entrance," Rib called from down the road. Her voice lacked its usual irreverent cheer, but no matter her mood she couldn't help herself, and it was good to hear her at least attempt to take the night's disaster in stride.

"Are you all okay?" I called back. Lalia hadn't said that any of my people got hurt, but it might have slipped her mind.

"Yeah, all good," she said as they got closer. This took a little while, since the horses didn't know me and needed careful coaxing. "We were all out when it started, and your girls had their stuff ready to go, so someone got it into the yard before the fire got to it. Bad shit, though!"

"Who is this?" Herald asked. She took in Kira's generally shabby appearance, and her eyes narrowed suspiciously. I could almost hear the gears turning in her head before she shook her head, looking at me with exasperation. "Draka, you promised!"

Sitting tall in the saddle she towered over me, something I'd slowly become unaccustomed to, and I felt the full weight of her disapproval. It was a welcome surprise, in a way. I needed someone who could tell me off, even if it rankled me.

"I promised I wouldn't fight unless it was necessary," I said. "It was! And they won't even know she's missing!"

"When you say that it was necessary . . ."

"They were slaughtering villages to capture magic users and send them back to . . . wherever. So I stopped one of the deliveries."

Herald's face went slack. "That is sick!" she said after gathering herself, going quickly from dismay to fury. "And this woman—"

"Was a slave, more or less. A healer who was forced into the role of keeping the prisoners healthy, or so she says. Her name is Bekiratag, she speaks Tekereteki, and I want you and Mak to talk to her. To make sure that she's telling the truth and see what she knows."

"*This woman speaks Tekereteki?*" Mak asked haltingly in that language, not disguising the doubt on her face.

"*Better than you, maybe, Homer,*" Kira mumbled. It was the first thing she'd said since we left Karakan, and it was, perhaps, not the best first impression she could have given.

Instead of getting angry, though, Mak turned to Herald and said, "*Homer? Do you know what a Homer is?*"

Herald shook her head. "*The root word is home, but there must be some kind of context I am missing.*" She turned to Kira. "*Would you mind explaining what a 'Homer' is, and why you say it as though it is a pejorative?*"

Now it was Kira's turn to be confused. "*Pejorative . . .*" she said under her breath, clearly not familiar with the word.

"Insult," I told her in her version of the language, and she nodded to me with clear embarrassment. "*Thank you. Homer. You know? From the home province. Like the two of you.*"

Herald snorted, sounding more amused than insulted. "*I was born a Karakani citizen. My sister and brother were only children when they arrived, and grew up here. And our parents . . . I do not know where they came from. I always assumed the city, but they would not say, and they died proud citizens of Karakan. So save your insults. We are Karakani, nothing else.*"

"*Our parents fought too hard for this,*" Mak added, "*for you to lessen it.*"

"*Enough bickering,*" I told them. "*Kira, get up with Makanna. In front.*" I gestured to Mak. "I don't think that she'll try anything, but I don't want her behind you, all right? She's cavalry, so you should be fine."

We continued along the road, with me being the one holding us back. I didn't bother with running among the trees. It was dark enough, even with the group's lanterns, for me to simply vanish into the shadows if we met anyone, and I was feeling more and more fed up with hiding.

Trying to distract myself I said, "When I left Karakan you had things to tell me, about your day out. So? What happened?"

Mak's head snapped around and she started to say something, but Herald beat her to it. Beaming, she said, "I found Mak outside a bar, is what happened!"

Confused, I looked between the two. Mak looked mortified. "And why does that make you so happy?"

"Because," Herald said, looking at her sister proudly, "when she slipped away from us I thought that I would find her drunk off her ass somewhere. And do not look at me like that, Mak! You know what you are like when you are under stress, and these last few weeks . . ." Her voice shook at the end. She took a deep breath and continued. "So when we found her sitting *outside* a tavern, without having had a single drink, you can believe that I was proud of her!"

"Herald, why would you—?" Mak said. She'd been looking steadily more horrified as Herald spoke.

"You snuck off?" I interrupted her.

She couldn't look at me. "I did."

"And you were planning to get drunk?"

"Planning? No. I wasn't planning anything. It just happened. But then I found myself outside one of my regular places and . . . I couldn't go in. My feet wouldn't move. Just the thought of having a drink made me feel sick. But I couldn't leave either. So I sat there."

We walked in silence as she awaited my judgment. "Well done, I suppose," I said after thinking it over.

She looked at me. "You're not angry?"

"I'm not happy. You took a stupid risk. But you fucked up so much less than you might have that I'm mostly relieved. So, well done. Don't let it happen again, or I *will* be angry."

Once the conversation died down, Kira started up again, asking more questions about the sisters' background. She didn't seem at all satisfied with the answers she got. For all that she disliked anyone questioning her status as Tekereteki, she had a lot of trouble with the opposite. To her, anyone looking as distinctly Tekereteki as Herald and Mak couldn't possibly be anything else, which didn't exactly endear her to the only two humans she could speak with.

"Do you intend to keep her?" Mak asked me in Karakani after one too many attempts by Kira to figure out where their parents had come from. She couldn't seem to wrap her head around the idea that anyone might choose to leave.

"She knows things about the raids in the south, and she's a healer so, yes. We're keeping her, at least until the Wolves can take her."

"Do you mind if I make her join me for some sword practice?"

Ardek choked off a laugh behind us. It was good that he could laugh about it, at least.

Herald sighed. "Let us give her a chance first. I do not *think* that she means anything by it. She is just so weirdly patriotic that she does not *get it.*"

"This bonding thing she talks about . . ." Mak said. "I wonder if that's what our parents were fleeing."

"Were either of your parents magic users?" I asked.

"I know Mother was, but I don't know what she could do. They were very tight lipped about their advancements, even to us."

"Well, that would do it. Did they really never tell you these things?"

"I was too young to care while they still lived. Tam and Herald were even younger. Besides, they didn't like to speak of Tekeretek. I regret it now, but . . . well. I regret many things."

My thoughts went immediately to her betrayal. *I probably should forgive her,* I thought to myself. On some level I was even *glad* that she'd betrayed me the way she had. If she hadn't, who could possibly know what horrors the two of them would be going through? Death might be the best outcome, though it didn't seem likely. The torturer had been hinting to Mak that they were planning to sell her, probably both of them, as slaves when they were done with them. I couldn't imagine that illegally captured slaves would have a long or pleasant life to look forward to.

Even thinking about it made that comfortably familiar rage begin to rise again. It was a moment before I realized that the conversation had stopped entirely, and the horses were stepping away from me nervously.

Herald was the one to approach me. Of course she was. "*Draka,*" she said soothingly. "*You are growling. What happened?*"

I was. I forced myself to stop doing that, then slowed down, putting us behind the pack. "*I was thinking about what they did to you,*" I said. "*And what they might have done, if Mak had not . . . brought me there.*"

Herald nodded. She was trying to be strong in the face of her memories, but I could see her shrink in on herself a little, and I immediately regretted bringing it up.

"*I understand,*" she said softly. "*I think about it too. Often.*"

"*Do you talk about it? To Mak? Lalia?*" She didn't talk about it with me.

"*No,*" she said with a shuddering breath. "*I . . . even this is almost too much.*"

"*All right. But they say,*" I lowered my voice so only she would hear, "*back home, you know, that talking about it is the first step toward healing. If you are ever ready . . .*"

"*I know.*" It was as much acknowledgement as I could hope for under the circumstances.

"We will get them," I promised her. *"We will regroup at the mountain until Tam and Val return, and then you can go back to the city. Garal and Lalia are staying at your inn, and I can find a place nearby to hide during the day, and then we can really start getting back at the Night Blossom."*

"I will look forward to it," Herald said. She still looked haunted, but after that there was a hardness in her eyes that promised an absolute lack of mercy. I had seen the same look even before she and Mak had been taken and wondered if this had always been in her, or if it was my influence.

I didn't care much either way. I liked her the way she was, and she needed to be hard for what was to come.

"Right, so," Rib said when we stopped to rest an hour later, "dearest cousin Mordo didn't straight up order us to stay away from the city, but he did say that we should stay with you lot until we're absolutely sure that you're safe and secure, however long that may be. Now, I'm not suggesting that he's trying to keep his uncles on his good side by keeping us relatively safe in a time of uncertainty, but . . ."

"But he's definitely trying to pawn us off on you until things settle," Pot said, "which might sound insane, but we've been kind of working him in your favor." He grinned at me, and Rib nodded.

"Yeah," Rib said. "And you showing up all piss and dragonfire about fulfilling your promise and helping out did you all kinds of good in his book. I know that for sure. So, ah, do you mind if we stick around for a couple of days?"

Did I mind if I could steal two of Rallon's scouts, especially two as pathologically cheerful as the cousins? What kind of question was that? It was an absolute win in my book, even if I may have to suffer the occasional pine cone. I couldn't look too pleased, though.

"As long as the other humans are fine with it, I don't mind," I told them. "You'll need to get used to being up at night, though." I looked at Rib. *"Without* your little vials."

Rib sucked in her upper lip and gnawed it a bit, then said, "I can try?"

"I'm not asking you to give them up. They're useful. Just don't rely on them so much."

"Yeah. I'll try."

While I talked to Rib and Pot, Kira sat next to Herald. I watched her out of the corner of my eye, and wondered if she was about to finally snap Herald's temper, but she didn't say a word until I'd laid down and pretended to take a nap. Even then she waited a few minutes. She didn't say a word about the sisters' parents or origins. Instead she said, quietly, "Herald? *Is that right?"*

Herald looked up. She'd been taciturn since our short conversation, and didn't look eager to change that.

"*Yes.*"

Kira glanced toward me. "*You and your sister . . . Do you hold to the old faith?*"

"*What?*" Herald said, sounding more annoyed than curious.

"*Well, you . . . There is the dragon. I thought . . .*"

"*I do not know what you are talking about, so speak plainly. What does Draka have to do with religion?*"

"*Dragon worship,*" Kira whispered. "*You . . . Do you worship her? Like in the old days?*"

Perhaps I should have thanked Kira. Herald looked at her incredulously, then at me, then I saw her grin hugely before she covered her mouth and smothered a laugh. The others looked at her curiously, and Mak stood and walked over.

"*What do you talk about?*" she asked, not taking the time to correct herself before speaking. "*What is funny?*"

"*Dear sister, do you worship Draka?*" Herald said, still grinning.

Mak frowned. "*What is this question?*"

"*Do you?*"

"*Respect, yes. Obey, yes. Worship? That is crazy.*"

"*And you?*" Kira asked Herald. "*You avoid my question. Do you worship the dragon?*"

"*No. No, I do not. She is my dearest friend. I adore her and respect her and, like my sister says, I obey her wishes, within reason. But I do not worship her. Is that common where you are from?*"

"*No. It has been illegal for a long time. But it lives on, they say, in some small villages. Beyond the notice of the temples and the law.*"

"*Do you have many dragons in Tekeretek then? I do not remember reading anything like that.*"

"*No. None for a long time. I think that they pray for the dragons to return. Not everyone is happy under the king and the council. I thought, maybe, that was why—*"

"*This again,*" Mak said sourly. "*We have told you. We do not know why they left. To escape slavery, that is all they said. If they worshiped dragons, they hid it well.*"

"*But then—*"

"*But nothing. You are a prisoner. Perhaps you forget? Be quiet now.*"

"*At least stop asking about things we have already answered,*" Herald said a little more gently. Compared to Mak, she didn't sound or look the least bit offended. Amused, if anything.

"*I am sorry,*" Kira said, looking and sounding genuinely apologetic. "*I do not mean to offend. I just want to know about people. I like conversation.*"

"*If you want to talk,*" Herald said. "*Why not tell me a little about your home? I only know what I have heard of the city, and nothing of the provinces.*"

Kira was hesitant at first, but once she got going there was no stopping her. There was something about Mallinean refugees and vast plains, but I tuned her out at that point and mostly napped for the next half hour, or however long it was until Pot decided that the animals had had enough rest. But Herald and Kira got along fairly well after that, talking and even laughing every now and then as we continued on toward the mountain. They even managed to drag Mak into their conversation. No matter what she said, Mak was clearly curious about her parents' homeland, so long as she herself wasn't being badgered about it, and it wasn't like she could avoid it, seated behind Kira.

Meanwhile, Ardek was finding common ground with the young lord and lady. Probably because he was Karakani street trash, and they both wanted nothing more than to be just like him. Neither of them had talked to him at all during their short stints as his jailors, and they were making up for lost time, asking for pointers on how to properly pronounce some of the foulest and most obscure slang I'd ever heard. Some of it may not even have qualified as human language. I had no idea what a 'snipe licker' or a 'petty filch' were supposed to be, but at least their conversation made the long walk a little more interesting.

There wasn't much that listening to the others could do to alleviate my boredom, though. I couldn't really have a conversation with them since I needed to keep some distance from the horses, and I could only travel that same stretch of road, and that same path through the forest, so many times before it got old. Traveling on foot at all was frustrating. Humans were so slow! I'd never thought about it while I was still fully human, but now that I could easily cover a hundred miles in just a couple of hours, everything else was insufferably sluggish. My humans could only go so fast and they could only push their horses so hard. I was wasting hours of my life for the sake of these poor, wingless creatures. Even my slowest cruising speed on the wing was a gallop for a horse. But, it would look bad if I abandoned them because I was bored. I wanted to be a leader, and a leader didn't *get bored*. A leader *showed patience*.

Or whipped everyone on so that they'd pick it up, I grumbled to myself, but morale wasn't great as it was. Sure, they were all talking, but there was an edge to every laugh that told me the situation was fragile. I had my command advancement to thank for that little insight.

Of course they were on edge. Nobody believed that the fire had been an accident. It had been too sudden and spread too quickly. The mess had been set up to prevent and contain an accidental fire, and neither the great oven or the large cook fire should have been lit at that time of the night. No, the fire had been a deliberate attack for sure, which meant that either the Night Blossom still had people in the Wolves, or at least access to their headquarters, or they had another enemy to worry about.

Then there was the timing. The Wolves were planning an operation to get rid of the raiders in the south. How many people knew about that? My humans had recently returned. Who might have seen them? The rivalry between the Wolves and the Cranes wasn't exactly friendly. Would they do something like this if they could? There were too many unknowns, and the Wolves had lost too much for anyone to relax and feel safe. Even out here.

Kira and Ardek, of course, had their own worries.

Besides that it was getting close to sunrise and they were all exhausted. All except for Rib. She'd been hitting one of her vials when she thought I wasn't looking, but my peripheral vision was excellent. I didn't say anything, though, since it was good to have at least one person who was completely alert, especially a scout. I just wondered how much money she was spending on the things, and what would happen when she inevitably ran out. She could only carry so many.

Nobody wanted to think about what was going on, so they talked. Any topic of conversation was better than tense, worried silence, and if it was fun or interesting, so much the better. Personally, I was mostly frustrated. Not only would there not be any attack on the raiders for a while at least, but I had been hoping to use this return to the city as an opportunity to begin my campaign against the Night Blossom. Now I'd have to wait. Again. I was beginning to wonder if it was worth being so careful, or if I should just leave the others at the mountain and fly back into the city myself. Four of them were fighters. They could take care of themselves. And Ardek had told the Wolves a couple of locations that belonged to the Night Blossom. Maybe I could just go and hang out on a nearby roof for a couple of nights and see if any familiar faces showed up. Then I could follow them and do something terrible. It would send a message, and it would be very cathartic.

It was a terrible idea, I knew, but a girl could dream.

It was twilight when we arrived. The nights were still short, even though the leaves had begun to turn. I wondered if the summers were short here and, if so, how long winter would be. I'd noticed people dressing a little warmer lately, too, but I didn't feel the difference. Something about my biology, magic or otherwise, kept me comfortable no matter the temperature. Considering how cold Kira had gotten while we flew, that was a very good thing.

Being pretty much unaffected by the weather didn't stop me from enjoying the morning air, though. A light rain had started, not so much as to bother the humans but enough to bring out all the scents of the forest. Pine and moss, late blooming flowers, the vaguely pleasant smell of decaying wood and . . .

And blood, and that damned bear!

CHAPTER THIRTY

Unbearable

The scent of fresh blood hung on the breeze. We were just outside of the campsite by my mountain, with the wind coming in from the northeast. Something big had died nearby, for the smell to be so strong. And mixed with that scent, I smelled bear. I doubted that it was the bear bleeding.

"Everybody," I said, interrupting the two simultaneous conversations, "be alert. There's a bear around, probably the same bastard that's been staying one step ahead of me for weeks. And I think it's a big one. It's too smart."

Kira looked alarmed at my tone, so I told her, "*Big bear. It should avoid us, so probably no danger, but stay behind the others.*"

"The horses seem fine," Pot said, and he was right. The horses weren't skittish, or at least no more than they always were around me. Mostly they were tired, though, so that might have been affecting them.

"Still," I said. "I smell it. And there's a lot of blood on the air, like . . . a full-grown elk or a really big boar or something."

"All right, so we get a fire going. That'll keep it away, no worries!" Rib said, waving toward the campsite.

"The horses are going to be a problem. We'll need to watch them."

"Nah, these are good boys and girls. They won't run off anywhere."

"I'm more worried about the bear coming for them."

Rib blinked. "Oh. Yeah, right. That. But why, though? If it has a fresh kill, why would it bother?"

"Don't know. I've just had a bad feeling about this bear for a while. It's always around, never showing itself but never there when I've looked for it. Damn thing is . . . stalking me, or something."

"Sounds like it's dumber than your average bear then."

"I don't know. I'm worried it's the big bastard Lalia and I fought, back to finish what we started."

"How about this," Pot said. "We can get the nightcrawlers and your newest addition tucked away in those tunnels of yours, and Rib and I can stay out here napping with you up a tree or something. If it comes around, we'll deal with it."

"You two? Aren't you both dagger specialists? How the hell do you expect to fight a bear? Especially if it's that monster?"

"By distracting it so you can chunk it, mostly," Pot said. "That and poison." He dug a little vial out from a belt pouch. "Powerful numbing poison. Coat a blade with this and get a good cut or stab in and that limb'll be useless in seconds. Good stuff! Don't usually get to use it because, you know."

Because they'd usually sneak up and cut throats. I remembered the rest of the Gray Wolves following them and the other "scouts," with nothing but silence and dead sentries as we'd crept up on the bandit camp, months back.

"All right," I said, though I wasn't at all confident. *Though, worst case*, I thought, *we'll have to sacrifice a horse or two to get away.* "If it *is* the big bastard, though, and if it comes for us or the horses, I do *not* want you two fighting it. Lalia and I barely got out alive, and that was with her mounted and with a sword. Those knives of yours are going to do exactly jack and shit to that thing, and who knows if the poison will even work?"

"As you say," Rib said as Pot began to protest. "We're not monster slayers, either of us. Right, Pot?"

"Right," her cousin answered, his disappointment obvious.

The four others were silent, their eyes on me as they waited for me to tell them what to do. I wanted to tell them that they all managed fine their entire lives without me ordering them about, but that wasn't exactly fair. I had a hold on each of them, and for all I knew my command advancement might be making them more . . . deferential? "Subservient" came unbidden to mind. One part of me *really* liked that, and the other hated it. "Deferential" would have to do.

"All right. The rest of you, you know what to do. Mak, get everyone in there, but don't show the prisoner how the gate works. She's like you. Understand?"

Mak nodded.

"I'm leaving her in your hands. If she does anything stupid, subdue her. Bind her if you have to. We still want to question her."

"Right."

I turned to our captive. "*Kira, follow them inside the mountain. It will be dark and the exit will be closed, but it will be safe as long as you stay with them and do not wander off.*"

"*And if I do?*" she asked.

"*I could hunt you down, but I will not need to. You will die of thirst in the dark long before you find a way out. No one alive knows where those tunnels go.*"

Kira swallowed, then nodded. "*I will stay with Makanna.*"

"*Good.*" To the others I said, "Go on. I'm sure that you're all tired. Sleep well. I'll see you in the evening."

With four of the humans safely tucked away with most of the gear, I rejoined the two cousins. They'd set the horses free to wander the campsite, trusting them not to wander off. Oddly, I missed Stalwart the mule. He'd never warmed to me the way Garal's Melon eventually had, but he'd accepted me. There was something about domestic animals fearing me that my human side just couldn't accept, and which excited me in a way that I wasn't entirely comfortable with. Those problems went away when an animal stopped behaving like prey.

Maybe I should get a cat, I thought.

I woke up in the afternoon to a feeling of wrongness. At first I thought that it was because I couldn't see Rib or Pot, but I remembered that they'd followed my example and decided to get up a tree just in case. No, it was something else.

I couldn't smell the bear anymore. And the scent had not grown fainter and then vanished, I was sure of that—it was just gone.

The wind was slowly shifting. Maybe that was why? It had been coming from the northeast before, and now it was more easterly. I closed my eyes and tried to focus on just my nose. That was still unfamiliar but getting easier with experience, and as I . . . merged more and more with my dragon. I smelled the forest. Boar, perhaps. A faint whiff of blood, but nothing as strong as before.

A gust came in from the southeast and I smelled bear, strong, close, and fresh.

My eyes popped open and I shifted my neck around the trunk of the tree, looking in the direction of the scent. Nothing. I didn't hear anything either until a soft "Koh-ahp!" drew my attention to Rib, who gestured a question. I shrugged best I could and shook my head, then gestured southeast with my head. Rib's reaction was a shockingly eloquent, full-body "What the hell do you mean?" At least she turned to look in the right direction.

Two minutes later the thing lumbered silently out of the trees, going around the campsite. It was enormous, but a deer would have made more noise. It snuffled around, but its eyes were on the horses, who had for some reason not reacted to it at all. The thing was right there, and they just kept grazing! Then behind it came two brown, fuzzy lumps that by their size could have been mistaken for fully grown brown bears, but which I realized must be this monster's cubs. I was taken back to a sunny day months ago when I'd been learning to hunt, and a chance encounter had made me feel so small and vulnerable.

The mama bear and her cubs had found my mountain and, oh my, had they grown.

The draconic side of me wanted to fight on principle. If it had been a regular bear, even a big one, I would have gone for it, no doubt. If it had been the big bastard I fought with Lalia, I might have tried, for the sake of the horses. But this? A giant the size of a small elephant, with cubs? No. Sorry horses, but I valued my own hide far more than that.

While the cubs gamboled into the campsite and started pushing the log benches around, more curious than afraid of the fire, the mama stopped and sniffed. Slowly, she raised her head and looked up. I looked at her. So did Rib and Pot, whom Rib had woken up. The bear looked at all of us, then huffed loudly.

She lumbered up to the humans' tree, raised herself to her full height—she must have stood twelve feet!—and slammed into it. Rib and Pot hung on for dear life as the entire length of the tree shuddered and leaned under her weight. There was, perhaps, a chance that she only wanted to warn us, but I couldn't exactly risk it. They were climbing higher, but she could knock that tree down. I didn't have a single doubt about that. And I was not going to let two people I liked become part of the circle of life if I could help it.

"Look out!" I screamed and threw myself across the long gap between our trees. My wingtip clipped a branch, which smarted something fierce, but I made it, crashing into the cousins' tree a few feet below them.

"Hold on to me!" I said, and they looked at me incredulously.

"How—" Rib started, but I cut her off.

"I don't fucking care how, grab onto *something* that isn't a wing and hang on!"

"Shit! Right!" Rib looked at her cousin and said, "Back or front?"

"Front, you're thinner!" Pot said, and I nearly panicked when he *dropped* four feet to a branch below me. Luckily, I was distracted by Rib clambering onto my back, legs along my sides and her arms around my neck.

The dragon in me *hated* it. I had to consciously restrain myself from trying to bite her, grab her, or try to shake her off! Then I was distracted from *that* by Pot squeezing in under me and throwing his arms around my neck from beneath, which the dragon also did not like *at all*.

Looking down I saw that he'd hooked his legs over Rib's, like some kind of goddamn circus trick.

"Did you *rehearse* this?" I asked, as the bear slammed the tree again, almost making me lose my hold with the extra weight.

"Misspent youth, tell you some other time!" Rib shouted from my back. "Have you ever done this before?"

"Kind of, a couple of times!" I fibbed. I'd landed a couple of times while carrying Kira. That counted as multiple trips, I told myself. "Hold on, and be ready to run if I can't carry you!"

"What?!" Pot shouted from beneath me, and I kicked off.

I nearly hit the ground before my wings told gravity where to shove it and let me climb again, Rib whooping and Pot, who nearly ate it, screaming his head off. One of the cubs took a swipe at us, but it seemed more playful than serious. The mama was not happy about us getting anywhere near her cubs and came roaring after us, but I got us high enough to be out of her reach.

With Rib on my back and Pot held tightly in my arms I fought like hell to gain altitude. They were heavier than anything I'd carried, but not too heavy. Rib got in the way of my wings, but not too badly. I couldn't go for miles and miles and miles like I had with Kira, but I could go . . .

Really, there was only one place I could go. I'd never tried out of fear of dropping Herald—I'd never imagined doing this with anyone else—but having tried it with Kira and now having been kind of forced into action by a three-ton bear, I figured, why not? I needed to be able to get to my humans, and I couldn't exactly drop the cousins off anywhere and leave them. It was a flight of only a few minutes, made longer and far, far harder by the extra weight, but soon we reached the ledge, with its lonely little tree, and the cave. The grand entrance to my home.

"When I tell you to, I need you to drop!" I shouted to Pot.

"What?" he shouted back, eyes wide.

I stopped my momentum above the ledge. The extra weight made a controlled hover pretty much impossible, and I was jerking every which way as I beat my wings furiously, trying to get to a height where Pot wouldn't break his legs.

"I can't land with you on my chest!" I shouted. "You'll get crushed! I need you to let go with your legs!"

He looked down quickly, then back up. "Okay," he shouted to me. He did not sound okay at all, but he unhooked his legs from Rib's and dangled down my front, swinging every which way as I fought to stay somewhat still in the air.

"Right. When I tell you, I'll let go, and you do the same!" I let myself drop, then yelled "Now!" right before I beat my wings, letting Pot fall the last nine or ten feet as I shot back up. Looking down, I saw him hit the ground and roll backward like an acrobat, then get unsteadily to his feet and let out a loud "Woop!"

After that, landing was simple, just a matter of bracing a little extra.

"Oh gods!" Ribs moaned as she slid off my back. "Oh, sweet Mercies! Blessed ground!" She got on her knees and touched her forehead to the thin soil.

"It wasn't that bad, was it?" I asked, not entirely sure if I should take her seriously. She'd sounded like she was on a rollercoaster for most of the flight.

"Nah," she said, getting to her feet with a weak smirk. "I could even see it being fun! Just . . . with some warning, you know?"

"I'll let you know in advance the next time I schedule a bear monster, how about that?"

"That'd be great, yeah," she said. "Really, though . . . Mercies, you get to do that whenever you want. I never envied the birds until today. Or you, I guess."

"Never really knew what you were missing, huh?"

"I call 'back' next time," Pot said.

I led them inside. Perhaps I could have left them on the ledge to watch the gate and wait for the bears to clear off but, for all that I trusted them, there was no way I was leaving them alone with a clear line to my hoard. There were limits to how far I'd trust *anyone* except, perhaps, Herald.

The light dropped off sharply, as always, as soon as we got past the first bend of the cave system. All the cousins had to see by was the glow slime. I wondered how I'd get them down there without breaking their necks slipping on a wet stone, but they were prepared. As soon as it got properly dark, Pot produced a small vial, drank half, and gave the rest to Rib. "Health and honor to you," she said, raising it to me and shooting the contents, then blinking as her eyes not only dilated but took on an almost catlike sheen. "Interesting place you've got here," she said, looking around the narrow, sloping tunnel.

"Yeah, it's an alternate route inside," I told them evasively. "I'll get you to the others and then I can let you all out when it's clear." I was pretty sure they'd figured out where we were, but I wasn't going to confirm anything. As we descended they told me a little about that "misspent youth" Rib had mentioned, one that was probably still in full swing considering I doubted that they were above twenty years old, twenty-one at the very most. Part of that involved increasingly risky methods of sneaking out at night and doing what was pretty much really stupid circus acts, including one where one of them rode on the back of a horse and the other clung to its front. A shattered leg had put a stop to that particular trick.

"Here," I told them as we reached the crack in the wall. "I need you to squeeze through there."

"Looks easy enough," Pot said, eyeing the stone. "But, uh . . ." he gestured lamely at me. "What about you?"

"Just you worry about yourselves for the moment, all right? And mind the pit on the other side."

Pot shrugged and began sidling, with Rib right behind him.

"All right," Rib called from the other side, looking back at me. "Now what?"

I wasn't worried about letting them in on my secret. They didn't have that obedient feeling that Mak and Ardek did, but I still felt that I could trust them and, again, I was so tired of hiding. And frankly, I was counting on a mix of respect, honor, and fear to keep them from doing anything stupid, like betraying me. Besides, it wasn't like they could go anywhere if they didn't agree to keep my secrets.

"Now," I told them, "I just need the two of you to not freak the hell out. Maybe sit down first, I don't know. And I need a promise from each of you that you'll never speak to anyone about what you're about to see, except Herald and Mak. And Ardek, I guess."

"Uh, sure?" Pot said.

"I'm serious. I need a promise."

"All right," Rib said. "Whatever secret you are about to reveal, I swear that I will not speak of it to anyone except those you've mentioned. On my honor as a Tavvanarian and a member of House Terriallon, and on my life and that of my cousin Poterio."

"Hey!" Pot said. "But yeah, same here. On Rib's life. Good enough?"

"Yeah," I said. That was probably as serious an oath as either of them could take. Then, without further delay, I shifted.

"Whoa!" Rib shouted and fell back, nearly going off the ledge. "Oh waves and stars! What the—?"

Pot, meanwhile, was sitting exactly where he had been, staring slack jawed at me as I flowed through the crack and shifted back next to them on the ledge. He just kept staring at me in silence for a long while, then said, "That's impossible."

"Dragon magic," I countered.

"Magic is like—No. What you just did—Rib? What was that?"

"That's impossible," Rib agreed from behind me.

"Come on, Herald took it much better than you. Mak and Ardek too."

"The three people who follow you around and do whatever you say?" Rib asked. "Herald who loves you, and Mak and Ardek who are absolutely, utterly terrified of you?"

"I mean—"

"Invisibility is not a thing, Draka," Pot said. "It's something you see in heroic plays or hear of in myths and legends. Shapeshifting, or whatever you did, same with that. It's not something that anyone can actually do. Magic doesn't *do* that!"

"Dragon magic does," I said, and shifted, then shifted back. "Now come on, we need to get down there before Mak opens the gate to pee and gets eaten."

CHAPTER THIRTY-ONE

Little Fears

S o," Pot said, peering into the pit. "We're going down there?"

"Yeah." I felt a knot of dread in my gut. I hadn't wanted to think about this part. "We're going down."

"Looks pretty dark," Rib said. "This cat's eye potion needs *some* light to let us see. I don't even see any glow slime down there."

"Right! Wait here!" I said, and fled from the chamber.

How could I forget about the pit, and how it made us, me, whatever, feel? I'd stood on that ledge, and what I'd felt wasn't just the little bit of human anxiety and the reflected fear from the dragon. This was the full, gut-churning near panic that I had forced my dragon, my other half, to face. And I had to do it again, because there was no way I could back down in front of Rib and Pot.

I was still almost pathetically grateful to have an excuse to leave and scurry down to my nest to fetch my light-ball. Of course, now it would be explicit that I had at least some kind of stash here, if not my whole hoard, but I'd just have to trust them. And it wasn't like anyone could get up here stealthily. Or so I hoped.

The trip to my nest was quick, but I took a moment with my hoard to gather myself. It had been a little while and, even if I didn't have time for a nap, every minute I could spend there calmed and centered me. It was all too short. I dragged myself away, light-ball held in my mouth, and returned to the crack.

"One of you, get out here," I called into the chamber, wiping the stone orb on my scales to get the saliva off. "I can't carry anything when I shift."

"Uh, right," came an echoing call. It was Rib. "About that . . ."

"So, Rib bet me—" Pot called.

"I didn't bet you, I challenged you!"

"—challenged me to climb down. And then when I managed it, I challenged her. And—"

"Yeah, so we'll need a minute to get back up, is what we're saying."

Children. I was dealing with children. The fact that I might have done exactly the same thing less than half a year ago was irrelevant.

All right, I said to myself. *I'll just have to find my stick. Or maybe try to roll the thing?* Then I remembered a conversation with Herald, down in the depths. I'd tried it with a small stone, hadn't I?

I looked at the light-ball. It was fairly large . . . but I'd once swallowed a whole goat's leg, just choked it down. Surely . . .

I put it in my mouth. Really shoved it in there. My teeth continued way back on my jaws, but I had a fair space between them before my actual throat opened, where I lodged it. I closed my mouth, pressing my lips together when my jaw wouldn't go all the way. It was not comfortable at all. Then I shifted, and to my relief the light-ball didn't immediately smack onto the stone floor and roll away somewhere. I passed through the crack onto the ledge and continued down. The dread didn't vanish entirely, but I'd done it before, and now I had two idiots waiting for me at the bottom.

When I shifted back, the two humans startled away from me but relaxed when their brains caught up with their reflexes. "Where'd you go?" Rib asked, then made a disgusted face as I opened my jaw wide, put my hand in, and dug out the light-ball. It scraped on my teeth a bit.

"Ugh!" I coughed, ignoring her question. "You two had better appreciate this." Then I charged the ball, and their faces lit up as it began to give off its warm glow.

"Oh, a lightstone! From the valkin, right?" Pot said. "Just like Mak has!" He took the thing, shook it, then wiped it on the seat of his pants.

Lightstone! That was so obvious, and so much better than light-ball! "Yeah," I said, trying not to show my chagrin over their superior naming abilities. "Same haul. How'd you manage the climb down?"

"Wasn't all that hard," Pot said. "There's some decent holds in the stone if you feel around carefully. Bit slick, though."

The casual way that he said it didn't make me bitter *at all*. I scowled at them internally.

"Let's go."

I wanted to get moving as fast as possible. Not because I was worried. I didn't actually think that Mak would open the gate unless they absolutely had to get out. No, the reason was that the dread was creeping back in, and I had a feeling that if I didn't move and keep moving, I might just flee back up onto the ledge. So I went, and the two cousins simply chose not to be left behind. We set a good running pace that I could maintain. They had not been inside these tunnels before, and didn't want to stay longer than necessary, and I just wanted to get away from the pit. It rankled that it still affected me so much, but my dragon's trauma was my own now, and it wasn't like I could just 'get over' something like that.

As we descended, the cousins grew quiet. Maybe it was the monotony that did it, miles of featureless stone, always the same. For the longest time there was only the echo of our steps and their rhythmic breathing, but then Pot asked, in an uncharacteristically sober voice, "Do you think the horses made it?"

Rib's voice was gentle and calming. "I'm sure they're fine. They're fast and they're clever. They'll come back, or return to Karakan, you'll see."

I didn't tell them what I thought. I'd seen the other monster bear running down Windfall at a gallop, and he, as I understood it, was a fast horse. Best case, I figured all but one of the horses would be fine.

Pot seemed to have reached the same conclusion. "Poor things," he said quietly, and remained silent for the rest of the run.

We soon reached what I thought of as the lift chamber, above the throne room. "Now what?" Rib asked, peering through the hole. "I am not, by all the hells large and small, dropping down there."

"Now you get to ride the dragon again," I said. "Don't worry. We only need to land this time."

"Great," Pot said, his voice dry and flat. "I don't suppose you could do it in two trips?"

"I'm honestly not sure I can get back up here," I told them. "I'll try, but I'm not risking one of you being left up here."

"You can go on her back this time," Rib consoled her cousin. That was fine with me. Rib looked a decent bit lighter anyway, which would be easier on my arms.

"Climb on," I told Pot, then to Rib, "And you, stand by the edge."

"I don't like this at all," she told me, but she did it. "Don't even joke about pushing me right now."

"Don't tell me you have a problem with heights," I said as Pot clambered onto my back. "You spend half your life up trees! Are you secure there, Pot?"

"Good as I'm gonna get."

"Yeah," Rib was saying, "but trees have branches, and the forest floor is soft. Kind of. It's not a . . . what, hundred-foot drop, onto bare stone. If I slip or if you—"

I grabbed her and dropped.

Seconds later I was stretched out on the floor with Pot seated beside me, both laughing our tails off as Rib screamed, "You bitch! You crazy bitch! That wasn't funny! That wasn't fucking funny!"

"I never—" Pot wheezed, "I never heard you *shriek* like that before!"

"Not. Fucking. Funny!"

Rib forgave us quick enough. And she couldn't deny that if I'd done the same thing to Pot she would have been the one laughing. Spirits somewhat raised, we made our way to the hub, where the small storage pile still sat untouched in the remains of the camp, and then on toward the gate.

I'd been right not to worry. Mak was the only one awake, and she was sitting with her back against the wall between us and the others. Her spear was next to her, pointed up the tunnel. Her posture looked relaxed, her face was concerned.

"How?" she whispered urgently. "How did you get in, and what are you doing here? What happened?"

"Biggest damned bear you ever saw," Rib answered for me.

"We may have lost the horses," Pot said, getting glum again.

"I'm sorry to hear that." Mak sounded genuinely sympathetic. "Was this yours and Lalia's bear, Draka?"

"No. But I might have seen it before. It's a female with cubs."

"You couldn't have tried to lead it away or something?"

"Damn thing nearly knocked down a tree to get to us," Rib said. "Pretty sure it would have eaten us if Draka didn't get us out."

"And that damned thing had some advancements for sure," Pot added. "We didn't know it was there until it was right on top of us."

"Might explain why the horses weren't worried about the bear smell," his cousin continued. "Maybe it's got some kind of stealth that makes prey just . . . not notice it?"

"Can that happen?" I asked.

"Monsters certainly have advancements," Herald said sleepily from behind Mak. She'd sat up, and Ardek and Kira were stirring as well. "They are not well understood, but it seems that they have as much variety as humans. Though, whether they get to choose, and if so how, is unknown. An advancement like that does not sound impossible."

Mak nodded. "We know that goblins get advancements based on their existing strengths, but that they don't get a choice. There's no reason to assume that a monstrous animal should be the same as a goblin, though."

"Why not?" I asked. "They're all monsters."

"Yeaaaaah, *but* . . ." Rib said. "All goblins get advancements, right? But regular animals don't get them. We'd know by now. Only animals that get turned into monsters or born as them get advancements. So they're not the same."

"And then there's . . ." Pot gestured to me. "How about you?"

"I get choices," I said. "Several, in fact."

"Not just two or three?"

"Five." And maybe none for my majors, but they didn't need to know that.

"Damn," Pot said softly. "That's so unfair."

"*What is unfair is the rate at which she gets them*," Herald grumbled in Tekereteki. Then she looked quickly at Kira, who looked like she was barely awake, before turning an apologetic look at me.

I shrugged at her. Anyone who heard and understood could just be jealous.

"As interesting as this is, I should get back out. Do you all have enough water?" I asked.

"We should be comfortable for a few hours, if we're careful," Mak said. "Beyond that . . ." she shrugged. "We'll live. Probably best if we sleep as much as we can."

"Good," I said. Then as almost an afterthought, I added, "How's Kira been?"

"The woman likes to talk," Mak said drily, "but she's behaved. I don't think she means us any harm, or that she's going to try anything."

If Mak said it, I believed it. And it wasn't like I'd expected any trouble out of Kira. The woman could argue if she got riled up, but I didn't think that she had much violence in her. She was a talker and a helper, not a fighter.

I left the humans there, to sleep or talk or whatever they wanted to do, and made my way back up the tunnel. I was not looking forward to the next part. Even thinking about going back up had me anxious, and I was glad not to have any humans with me. I was sure that they'd be able to tell, especially Mak or Kira, and I didn't want anyone to see me in a moment of weakness. I had my pride, after all.

That anxiety grew into a jagged little lump of dread as I entered the throne room and looked at the ceiling high above me. I wasn't worried about making it through the hole back up to the lift chamber. That should be fairly easy, really. But the whole idea sparked old memories, fuzzy and only half mine, of being trapped and confused, throwing myself against the bars of my cage as I was lifted up, up to that place that none of my siblings had ever returned from. I'm not sure that I had even had a concept of death, but I understood fear well enough, and the fear that I remembered had been all-consuming.

I shuddered, and found that I'd pressed myself low to the ground, flattening myself in an attempt to hide from . . . what? The past? It was embarrassing, and stupid besides. An obsolete instinct when I could much more effectively hide by shifting into the shadows.

Even with no one to see me my pride was terribly injured. Still, I stayed there, small and unmoving, staring at that rectangle in the ceiling and trying to will myself to act. Then, soft and gentle, I heard the little voice. Calming, soothing, telling me that no one could hurt me anymore. That it might not seem like it, but what had happened had been long ago, and all those people were long dead and forgotten. Even the lift was dust. There was nothing to fear. The pit was just a pit, not a prison, and I could come and go as I pleased.

And, it reminded me, I had a foe outside. A bear that thought that it could just waltz around in my territory as it wished, eating my game, attacking my friends and killing their animals. That could not stand, could it? Surely I had to get out there so that I could keep an eye on the thing.

I knew exactly what the voice was doing, and dammit, it worked.

With a surge of will I launched myself upward, not allowing myself to think as I clawed my way straight up toward the hole. I forced myself to focus entirely on the problem of getting through the opening, which mostly meant the right angle, and enough speed. I needed to come from below, I needed to go fast and, despite how high the ceiling looked, I didn't have much distance to work with.

I got my angle as right as I could. Four hard beats of my wings was all I had time for before the final moment where I shot into the opening, folding my wings at the very last moment so that I didn't clip the tips.

When I entered the lift chamber and kept going, I realized that I might have overdone it. My speed carried me upward for another full second-and-a-half, but that was three times as long as I needed and I saw the ceiling approaching uncomfortably fast, forcing me to spread my wings to stop my climb. A little confused tumbling and half controlled maneuvering later, and I was sitting on the floor of the chamber. I'd done it.

I looked at the tunnel that led to the pit, and a disgustingly fearful sound left my throat. But I couldn't stop there. I had to press on. Even though I knew, theoretically, that there were other ways out, I had to do it. Not only because it had taken three days to find my way out last time, but because I simply couldn't tolerate the idea of surrendering to fear like that, not again. Sitting there, cowering before the darkness, mewling like a newly hatched whelp—

That's right, the little voice said. *You're stronger than that. Be proud, dragon! Conquer your fear, and let's go!*

"Yes," I hissed into the empty tunnel. "I am stronger than you. I am stronger than fear. I am a God and Mercies and Sorrows damned *dragon!*"

I took one step, and then another. They were slow and heavy, but I fought my way forward, building a momentum that was more moral than physical, until it became impossible to stop and I was running up the tunnel, screaming out my anger and my wounded pride.

I was a dragon, and I would not let fear rule me!

CHAPTER THIRTY-TWO

Loaded for Bear

When I stepped out onto the ledge in front of my cave, the mountain shading me from the late afternoon sun, it was a struggle not to launch myself into the air and go after that bear, monster or not. A deep-seated embarrassment burned inside me. I knew, rationally, that I could not have fought it. Not without any real warning and preparation. Maybe, *maybe* I could have distracted it while Rib and Pot fled, but more likely they would have done something heroically stupid and we would have all died. But I didn't want to be rational. I had *fled*. I had surrendered what was mine, the horses, my territory, to a beast, not even a human or another dragon, and the shame of it *burned*.

It didn't matter if it had moved on. I had been angry about it and its kin's presence in my territory even before it challenged me. Now I had to defeat it. I couldn't tolerate anything else. Even if it had wandered on, it knew now that it could return whenever it wished, and I had to show it that it was very, very wrong, even if that meant luring it back so I could fight it.

We need to be clever about this, the voice told me, and I agreed. No matter how satisfying it might be, fighting the bear directly, tooth and claw, was not an option. I needed to use my strengths to harass and misdirect, strike from the air and the shadows too suddenly and too fast for the thing to strike back. Even better if I could free my humans to help me, especially the . . . especially Herald. If I could put her somewhere safe with her bow, she should be able to hurt the thing with impunity. The others would have to remain inside the mountain or act mostly as spotters, since it would be foolish to risk their safety when it was unlikely they could hurt the thing.

The poison, the voice reminded me, and it was a good point! If it could be made to stick to an arrowhead that would give us an edge. We'd see how the monster liked not having the use of a leg or two!

But first, I needed to find it.

Of course the damned thing was gone when I reached the campsite. I walked around, sniffing the air and the ground, and caught their scent easily, following it south along the tree line. It made sense. Since there was no blood and no horse carcasses around the campsite, the horses must have fled, and they would have gone where the trees were least dense, I guessed.

It didn't take long before I found bones with most of the meat stripped from them. Poor thing. The bear's scent led me northeast through the forest. I followed its trail stealthily, weaving my way among the trees and bushes.

I found them as twilight was setting in. In the middle of a glade there was a giant tree. Like a fig given tree steroids for a few hundred years, the trunk split into branches several yards thick that stuck out along the ground in every direction before curving upward. Each of the branches had a multitude of roots growing off it, and among this massive root system there was a den large enough even for the mama bear. I found her lying on the forest floor outside, still alert, her cubs presumably sleeping inside.

Good. Now that I knew where to find her, I just had to go through, and succeed, with the rest of my barely formed plan.

It was dark when I arrived at the gate. I'd stopped every so often to make sure that the bear wasn't following me—it had been too stealthy and clever—and I was secure in the knowledge that I was alone. When I opened the gate, I was met with one extremely urgent question from Mak: "Is the forest safe?"

"As far as I can tell, yeah."

She immediately turned to the others and said, "You heard her! *Kira, we can go!*"

To my great amusement the humans rushed out of the tunnel and into the forest without even a word to me, gathering at the campsite once they'd done what they had to and then continuing in a group to the stream to drink and refill waterskins. Only then did I actually manage to talk to them, telling them about my plan for the night.

Pot took the bad news about the horse I'd found stoically, but there was a fire in his eyes when I brought up my ideas for evening the odds. "If the poison works at all, it should work on arrowheads as well as on a dagger," he said. "It will take some preparation, but it should work, especially if you aim for the limbs."

"That's not the concern," Mak said. "Draka, are you certain about forcing a fight like this?"

"This is my territory," I told them, making sure that my tone allowed for no argument. "The bear has challenged me. It can flee, or it can die, but I will no longer tolerate it walking around *my* land."

Herald, meanwhile, looked almost giddy with excitement. "Draka, do you realize what this means?" she said.

"What?"

"I get to fulfill my promise! We are finally going on that bear hunt! It took a little more than the two days that I said, but . . ."

Dear, reliable Herald. Of course that was what she'd think about. Not the danger, or whether it was necessary. She had made me a promise, and however late, she was going to keep it.

I grinned. If the others hadn't been around, I probably would have wrapped my neck around her, but I had an image to protect, and cuddling wasn't exactly fearsome. "It's about time, isn't it?" I said. "Let's find a good place for you to shoot from, Herald. Pot, prepare the arrows. Rib, you're on guard duty. And all of you, stay close to the gate, just in case. I don't trust that bear to stay put, and it may not be the only monster around. I never saw those wolves either. Don't hesitate to shut yourselves in, Mak."

I got some nods and nobody argued, which was good enough for me.

"*Do you have any ideas?*" I asked Herald as we walked. "*Concerns? Suggestions?*"

"*The first would be to ask how you plan to draw the bear to me,*" she said. "*If it has two cubs, I do not see it being easy to separate it from them.*"

"*I will just have to make it angry enough,*" I told her. "*I have some ideas for that. They mostly involve the cubs.*"

"*That is cruel, Draka,*" Herald scolded. "*They are innocent in this.*"

"*They are also already hundreds of pounds, and will grow into true monsters just like their mother. I cannot afford to have them around my mountain. But I do not need to kill or maim them for my plan to work, only threaten and frighten them enough to enrage the mother. And we do not even need to kill the mother, necessarily, if that is a concern, though you should remember what a threat all of them are to anyone living in this forest.*"

"*Ugh, I know, it is just . . . they are only babies.*"

"*Again, Herald, these babies are the size of fully grown bears. I am sorry, but killing them may be necessary.*"

"*Yes, fine,*" she said, but just because she gave in didn't stop her from pouting. It was surprising, honestly. I would have expected her to be more pragmatic when it came to dangerous monsters, but clearly the human love of fuzz balls transcended worlds.

"*We will need a tall rock or a ledge,*" Herald said, "*But something that is climbable. Something that I can climb, rather, but the bear cannot. I am not the strongest climber, but I have some practice.*"

"*The Terriallons did not tell you?*" I asked.

"*Tell me what?*" she asked, all innocent curiosity.

Oh, that made me excited. She had no idea! "*Climbing will not be a problem,*" I told her with a grin. "*Nor will escaping, if it comes to that.*"

"*I know that grin,*" she said. "*What are you not telling me?*"

"Oh, this is wonderful," I told her, grinning even wider. *"I was afraid that I would not be able to surprise you. I never thought those two would be able to keep their mouths shut!"*

Herald screwed up her face in mock outrage. *"Tell me!"* she demanded, hands on her hips.

"I will show you, as soon as we find an appropriate place for you," I said happily. *"We should not go too far, though. If we manage to wound it, I want to bring the others to help finish it off, at least Mak with her spear."*

"Ugh, fine," Herald said, but she kept looking at me suspiciously after that. She was going to love it when I finally showed her, I just knew it, and the anticipation made it so much better.

"How high do you think you can shoot from, accurately?" I asked a little later, considering a deep notch on the stone face. A section of stone had broken off, leaving a tall column with a wide, flat top.

Herald followed my eyes and considered. *"It depends mostly on how close you can bring the target, and how much it will be moving around. If we are looking at the same place, I would say that it is perhaps fifty feet up, so from there . . . a target a hundred fifty to two hundred feet away should be doable. That is well into the trees, so that would add another complication, but doable. Though I am not sure how you expect me to . . ."*

Herald's voice faded out as she looked at me. Her eyes flicked to my wings, then back to my eyes. She licked her lips and looked at my wings again, then back.

"No."

"Yes," I said, grinning.

"No?!" She grinned right back.

"Oh, yes!"

"That is how . . . you flew Kira here from the south! And . . . your nest is above the throne room! You flew Rib and Pot up, brought them from above!"

"They screamed their heads off!" I laughed.

"Finally?" she asked, kneeling next to me and taking my head in her hands. *"I have been hoping . . . I did not want to ask in case you said no, and you were so small before, but now . . ."* Her face split with a fierce, anticipating joy. *"Really?! You would not joke about this, would you?"*

"I would not. I told you that I want to take you to my nest. To show you my hoard, and what I have done with the place. I think I can do it now."

"I will get to ride a dragon," she whispered. I could see actual tears in her eyes. It was amazing.

"Well . . . for this, right now, I will have to carry you. I do not think that I can land there properly to drop you off. But when we are done here, yes, I think that I could carry you on my back. You can ride me."

With Rib and Pot, having someone on my back had been uncomfortable and somewhat demeaning, but I tolerated it because it was necessary. With Herald, I was looking forward to it. I had been looking forward to it for months, and the fact that I felt this need to deal with the bear first annoyed me no end, making me even angrier at the thing.

"*Shall we try then?*" I said. "*Are you ready to fly, if only for a few feet?*"

Herald *squealed*.

"*Stand up and face the cliff with your arms out,*" I told her. She did.

"*Stand on your knees, with your arms out,*" I corrected myself. She looked back and laughed at me, then knelt.

"*Now,*" I said and wrapped my arms tightly around her. "*Hold on to my arms, but be ready to let go and try to push forward when I say 'Drop!' We do not want any accidents here.*"

"*Just go! Just go!*" Herald said, wiggling excitedly.

"*Hold on!*" I kicked off as hard as I could, our shared excitement giving me strength to launch us both several feet into the air before I even beat my wings. Herald was a tall, strong girl, but she didn't weigh as much as Rib and Pot together, and I rose quickly enough that I had to break almost immediately to not smash us both into the rock.

"*Legs down!*" I shouted to Herald as I hovered erratically in front of the ledge. She understood my intent perfectly, and with her legs down and a little forward, knees slightly bent, I descended forward as carefully as I could.

"*All right! Wait for it . . . DROP!*" I shouted, releasing my grip on Herald as she simultaneously let go of my arms and boosted forward with her hips, back pushing against me. This got her comfortably onto the ledge while I was pushed back and away from the rock.

It was damned perfect.

I hung in the air, swaying left and right as I beat my wings, and Herald spun around where she stood, laughing, before facing me. "*It was like I leaped fifty feet straight up!*"

"*Glad you liked it!*" I called back. "*It worked well! Now we just need to get you down!*"

She looked over the edge, then at the rock face to either side of the ledge. "*I could slide, I think, if I had to. It would hurt, though. Help would be appreciated!*"

Getting Herald down was a little trickier than getting her up there, simply because landing on the ledge in a way that didn't end up with me falling backward took several tries. I kept chickening out, until finally Herald decided the situation for us by throwing herself into my arms and wrapping her arms around my neck while I screamed in surprise and called her a lunatic. Fair enough; I got her to the ground in one piece, but I was more than slightly shaken by the experience. She, meanwhile, was just giddy with excitement, and there was no way

I was going to do anything to dampen the sheer childish joy that poured off her. I couldn't even bring myself to be angry with her for scaring the crap out of me. All I could do was sit there and smile while she laughed and hugged me.

"All right. All right." She broke into a fit of giggles. *"All right, we have a job to do. Oh, Mercies, that was fun! Let us get my bow and get me up there,"* she said, her eyes shining, *"and then you try to bring the bear over. And then we can fly again!"*

I would have flown her to the gate and back again, but I wanted to save it. I wanted our first real flight to mean something, and there was only one place I had been dreaming of taking her. So we walked in happy silence, our steps light.

Back at the gate the others were calm but watchful. Pot had stretched his poison to cover the heads of a full dozen arrows. Rib, Kira, and Ardek were playing some kind of card game, although the "cards" were thin pieces of wood, and I wasn't sure how they managed without being able to speak to each other. Mak sat by herself a little ways off, and came up to us while we were speaking with Pot, who wanted to know if we'd seen any sign of the horses. We hadn't.

"Draka," she said softly, "once you are done with this bear, I need to talk to you." I got the feeling that whatever she wanted to talk about was serious, so I nodded.

"I'll come find you," I told her. "What is it about?"

"Kira. But it can wait a few hours. She's no threat, I'm sure of that."

"I'll take your word for it," I told her, and I could have sworn I saw her swell a little at that expression of trust.

Herald and I returned to the ledge we'd chosen. It was dark and chilly, but we'd prepared with Mak's darksight spell and a blanket, so at worst Herald should be bored up there. Flying her up was a little more precarious than the first time, for several reasons. Mainly because she was wearing the armor she'd ordered way back, before we went north. She'd brought it with her when we first left Karakan for the mountain, but this was the first time I saw it, and it was, well, flattering. Both in the way it looked on her, and for me. I'm sure that it was an effective suit of armor, but I couldn't possibly ignore the style. Made of thick, flexible leather covered in hard overlapping scales and dyed a midnight black, the suit so clearly resembled my own hide that I couldn't do anything but bear the extra weight with a smile. It included a skirt of overlapping leather plates to protect the thighs, greaves that went all the way up to the knee, and a crested helmet with cheek guards, which she chose to leave behind. She also had her bow and arrows, as well as her light pack, and the sword on her hip didn't make things easier. I'd questioned her about it, but she'd been very clear that *"I am not leaving my Sorrows-beloved sword, and that is that!"*

Happily, it only took one aborted attempt before we managed. With a promise not to forget her up there, I headed off into the forest, almost completely sure that I could find my way back to the bears. I didn't remember the way exactly, with the forest not being full of distinguishing landmarks, so after a while I resorted to moving in a large, zig-zagging pattern until I picked up their scent on the ground and surrounding foliage, which led me to them quickly.

The bears were sleeping. They lay in their den under the massive tree, warm and cozy and safe, the cubs with their mother, who was secure in the knowledge that nothing on this island could possibly be foolish or arrogant enough to bother them.

She didn't know me.

CHAPTER THIRTY-THREE

Unbearably Close

The bears' den was a simple thing, a space large enough for three huge bears dug out among the huge tree's roots. As I circled the tree, I saw that much of the excavated dirt had been packed in under the branching trunk, filling gaps here and there, as well as around the opening of the hole, which created a sort of wall. I wondered just how clever this bear was, because while I couldn't know what the purpose of that was, if there was one, it damn well *looked* like a levee to keep water from flooding the den during heavy rain.

I wondered what the hell it was with me and running into clever monsters. Had that first gigantic boar I ran into been some kind of piggy genius too? The fact that it ran off when I got some venom in its eyes instead of just going wild like some other creatures I'd fought, certainly suggested that it wasn't entirely dumb. Although I was pretty sure that I'd heard something about Big Beardy and his party hunting down a monster boar in that area, so I probably didn't need to worry about it.

Speaking of venom, I didn't expect it to do much against the bear. But I was damn well going to try. If there was one thing that I could always be sure of, it was that anything that didn't die from my venom was going to be in a very, very bad mood, and that was exactly what I needed. And if it got the cubs, too, that would only make the mama angrier. Hopefully angry enough to get careless.

Not wanting to take the slightest chance of waking them, I stayed in shadow form until I was just outside the den. The mama lay curled up, effectively blocking the entrance. Looking at her and considering how big the cubs were, I marveled at just how much dirt she must have shifted to make this den. Then again, as big as her paws were, and as strong as she undoubtedly was, perhaps it wasn't such a big deal for her. And it didn't make a lick of difference as I took a deep breath and gave her the longest, most concentrated spray I could muster. And boy was it effective!

Not that it disabled her. Not even close.

It started with a snuffle, then a sneeze. Then, not even awake yet, she started rubbing her nose with her paws, and then in the dirt. She slowly opened her eyes, and the venom in her furry face got in and started irritating them, which had her blinking and rubbing her whole face on the floor of the den.

She was several times my size, but all my instincts were screaming for me to attack while she was blinded. The rage inside me, aimed at her specifically, was so strong that I nearly did it. The only thing holding me back was the voice, which always got louder and more insistent the angrier I was.

I knew that it was my human side doing its best to hold me back when the dragon got too strong. I knew that listening to it was a good idea, and I did, even if I didn't always like it. But did it have to be so annoying?

Not yet. Stay back. You know that it will kill us, the voice said. Yes, fine, that was true. But I didn't like that she felt the need to point it out. It was insulting. I didn't need to be constantly told what I already knew.

I started forward. *Stay! Back!* the voice scolded me, and I was forced to admit that clearly I *did* need to be told. It was just so frustrating. My enemy, the one who had invaded my territory, was right there, partially disabled. If I could only get on its back, really get my claws in it . . .

The bear looked at me, its eyes apparently clear enough to keep open, and even with only the little bit of moonlight that filtered through the trees, I could tell she saw me.

I hissed. It roared, and I felt it in my chest.

I fled.

My plan to drag it back toward Herald was simple. As it scrabbled furiously out of the den while the cubs whined in confusion, I made a wing-assisted leap into a nearby tree. When the bear rushed the tree, I leaped and shifted across to the next tree in the right direction, hissing and screeching at the bear to keep its attention.

As I had hoped, the bear was angrier than it was clever. It took a couple of risky steps on the forest floor to keep it thinking that it had a chance of catching me, but I managed to drag it all the way back, the cubs following at a distance, confused and curious about what was going on.

I knew I was getting close when an arrow zipped in and thunked into a tree right where the bear had been moments before. *"Get it closer!"* Herald's voice was hard to hear over the distance and the angry noises of the bear, but I did as she said, taking the massive risk of throwing myself onto the ground and taking two running strides before launching myself into the air where the trees thinned out enough to fly safely.

The bear came charging after me, and I had a heart-stopping moment as I headed straight toward Herald. She had her bow fully drawn with a look of intense concentration on her face, and I, still between her and the bear, barely managed to shout *"Careful!"* before she loosed an arrow. It passed just below me, close enough that I had just enough time to pull my body up when I saw it coming. An angry roar behind me as I turned sharply suggested that she'd hit. When I came around, I saw an arrow wobbling around, stuck in the thick skin around its neck, and a glance at Herald showed her nocking another arrow, not so much calm as she was absolutely focused.

The bear roared at me as I made a low pass to distract it, but while I was coming around, I heard Herald shouting, *"Shit! Oh, shit! Draka!"*

What I saw seemed impossible. All however-many tons of bear had thrown itself at the stone face below the ledge and hung ten feet up. It was a seventy-degree incline at least, but the thing's claws *dug into the stone*, and as I watched, it pulled, kicked, and gained another two or three feet! Herald bravely stepped up to the ledge, firing down at the bear at an awkward angle, but even though she hit the thing on the head, her arrow just glanced off its thick skull, leaving only a cut behind.

"The limbs! Aim for the limbs!" I shouted, stopping in the air near her, and then I was off again. I put some distance between us, turned, and began building speed thinking to myself, *This is going to hurt.*

I expected the voice to argue, to try to talk me out of it. I did not expect it to scream, almost frantic, *Get her! Faster! Get her away from Herald!*

I came in at the same speed that had turned Kira's friend into a bag of broken bones. An arrow took the bear in its left forelimb just before I hit, and for a moment it felt as though I could have counted the individual strands of the fletching.

I hit. I did not break, and the bear lost its grip on the rock, sliding back down to the base. Those were the only good things about it. When I hit the bear, it only lost its balance, while I bounced off it, continuing forward and to the side, a dazed and confused lump. Luckily, I had the presence of mind to pull my wings in before I hit the ground, skidding and rolling for a good long while before I came to a stop.

This is becoming a bad habit, I thought groggily as I forced myself back on my feet. Every time I fought something bigger than myself, I ended up one big bruise. I'd have been dead several times over months ago if not for my fortitude advancement.

I heard Herald calling my name. I looked up. Then I was rolling again, my shoulder on fire from being slapped by the bear.

Instinctively, I shifted. It took a second, but a second was all I had before the bear was on me, passing *through* me, which was a horrible feeling, like being beaten on the inside. I had to get away. I had to regroup. I couldn't be on the ground, or the bear would tear me apart, shadow or not. In a repeat of my fight with Tiny the Troll, I went for the closest tree, flowing up into its branches.

I couldn't even guess how, but the damned thing tracked me, slamming into the tree. Herald screamed my name again, and another arrow hit the bear, right in the butt. I looked up and saw something that made me groan. Herald was on her feet, nocking another arrow. She was favoring her left leg as she approached.

Herald was on the ground.

She'd put herself in harm's way for me. She must have slid down the slope, hurting her leg on the way. There was no point in berating her for it. It was done.

Another arrow struck the bear before it even reacted and stopped trying to either climb or knock down the tree I was in. Another as it turned, and another as it faced Herald. She was much too close, a few dozen feet at most, close enough that I could see the cuts and scrapes on her arms and her shins from sliding down the rock.

I leaped from the tree, landing on the bear's back just as she started for Herald.

It said a lot about the monster that she could straight up ignore two-hundred-plus pounds of dragon on her back, and I was pretty much reduced to hanging on. I bit and I tore, but it was all skin and fat and did nothing. A helpless terror filled me, the seconds stretching as the monster sprinted at my best and, possibly only real, friend in the world.

Herald, wide-eyed and grimacing, dropped her bow, drew her sword, and threw herself to the side just in time. The bear's mass carried it past Herald, and it tried to swipe at her in passing, but the movement was sluggish, and it stumbled as it put its front paw down again. I didn't have time to hope, but seeing that drove me forward. I latched on around the bear's neck and shoulders and tried to actually do some kind of damage, but her ears were apparently not very sensitive, and her eyes were too deep set for my teeth. The bear still ignored me, clearly wanting to deal with the easier target first, and turned to have another go at Herald.

Herald had not done anything so sensible as trying to climb a tree. Although, considering the way the tree *I* had climbed was leaning, perhaps she was the sensible one. Instead she stood her ground, her stance low and her sword high and ready to strike.

The bear took one lumbering step forward, shaking its whole upper body in an attempt to dislodge me, then another, then it surged forward and swiped one enormous paw at my friend. Herald, God bless her reflexes, leaped back and to the side as her sword slashed down, and the bear pulled its paw back with a pained bark. Then the damned too-clever thing *feinted*, making as though it were going to Herald's left to circle her but aborting its movement and going straight for her as soon as Herald began to move, forcing her to scrabble backward and putting her in a terrible position.

I saw how this would play out immediately. Herald was moving backward, her balance off, while the bear was sure footed and going straight for her. She couldn't get out of the way once it put some force into it, and she'd be smashed, bitten, or simply crushed under its weight before she could change her movement.

I did what I could. I leaned forward over the bear's head, and bit her right across the snout.

That, finally, got one hell of a reaction. Not only did I get some of my teeth in her nose, but now I was blocking her sight. She roared, aborting her charge to rise on her hind legs and swat at me, but I'd been ready for that. I knew what happened after I bit something in the face. I'd been there before. Instead of letting her grab or claw or smash me, I pushed off her with my wings, letting the force tear my claws out and rising a few feet into the air above her before settling back on her, getting a new grip, and repeating. I was barely doing more than scratching her, but now I had her full attention, which was exactly what I needed. On top of that, I could feel the swell of my venom glands again. When I sprayed her, it didn't do much more to her breathing than the first time, but now she had a bunch of cuts and bites for the venom to seep into and irritate besides her eyes.

All in all, it only served to make her mad, but it also kept her attention on me. So I began a series of short swoops, harrying her, nipping at her from the air while Herald assessed the situation, sprinted the short distance to her bow, and started pumping arrows into the maddened creature.

At one point, one of the cubs worked up the courage to make a timid charge in Herald's direction, but a quick swoop and a screech from me sent it running back into the trees while the mama only became more determined to bring me down.

Finally, after what felt like hours but couldn't have been more than two or three minutes since I'd first brought the bear to Herald, she started backing off. She had nine or ten arrows in her at that point, though most of them swayed uselessly from her loose skin, and she was stumbling on limbs that clearly didn't work the way they were supposed to. Herald's quiver was empty, and she'd resorted to screaming and menacing the monster with her sword while I roared and screeched, swooping at her from the air. We were all tired, and I didn't see a way of finishing her off without taking some serious risks, but we didn't have to. She was clearly as done with the fight as we were and only wanted to get her cubs and go. With some careful positioning and coordination we used her cubs against her, threatening them and herding them south, forcing her to follow, which she did readily, almost gratefully. With a few screeching swoops and a nip at her tail, they finally broke into a lumbering run into the hills.

I didn't feel great about letting her go. My gut was telling me to finish her off, to end the fight once and for all, and the human voice was unhappy about making her someone else's problem. She was terribly dangerous, after all, and the further south she went, the more people she was likely to come across. But both sides of me knew that we had to quit while we were ahead, before a mistake born of fatigue or overconfidence led to something terrible.

I returned to where Herald had stopped her pursuit and landed. She was sitting in the dirt, breathing heavily, the skirt-plates of her armor splayed out around her. Her eyes were closed, but when I approached, she opened them, then crawled over and put her arms around me.

"*We did it,*" she said.

"*You were amazing,*" I told her. "*How can you be seventeen and fight like that?*"

"*I had to,*" she said. "*I thought that you were going to die.*"

"*I did not,*" I said, wrapping my neck around her tightly. "*You saved me.*"

"*I thought that I was going to die!*" she said with a shaky laugh.

"*You did not either,*" I said, "*You are too damned good to die to a bear.*"

"*I am too damned good to die to a fucking bear!*" she said, half laughing and half sobbing. "*But it took most of my arrows with it! Those were good arrows!*"

She needed to cry a little after that, and she kept going on about her arrows. I understood. She wanted to focus on anything except the fact that she'd been one bad dodge, one single moment where she was too slow, from death. I had feared just that, but she'd impressed me once again, and I was almost delirious with relief and happiness. We had won. The bear was gone. She was going to think twice before coming to my territory again, and if she did, I would be bigger and stronger, and Herald would be more experienced.

Hell, Herald was still growing. *She'd* be bigger and stronger too!

"*All right,*" she said after her shakes and sniffles had subsided. "*Let us get back.*"

"*Do you want to tell the story, or should I?*" I asked as we got to our feet.

"*I, of course. You are too dramatic.*"

"*I am not!*"

"*You cannot tell a story without making it sound like life and death, or the fate of the world!*"

"*This was life or death,*" I pointed out.

"*So you would make it sound like it was about the fate of the world,*" she countered, and I gave in.

"*Fine,*" I said. She really was better at telling stories than I was. "*Do you want to ride back?*"

"*I would love to,*" she said with a grin, "*but I want to save that for when we visit your home.*"

"*That sounds good,*" I agreed, and we began the walk back.

CHAPTER THIRTY-FOUR

What The Hell Happened Here?

What the *hell* happened here?!" I roared at the scene before me.

I'd been tipped off by the smell of blood as Herald and I approached the gate. We'd picked up the pace, and when we arrived we were met by two bodies, a few spent arrows, and a solid stone face, with no sign of the opening that led into the mountain, save half of a bloody handprint where a shimmering line marked the middle of the two doors.

The bodies were of a man and a woman neither of us recognized. They were rough and dirty, if not absolutely filthy, and had wounds from a sword and a spear, respectively. They also had nothing of real value on them. They were wearing simple, damaged armor, but it looked like any weapons they might have been carrying, their belts, and even their boots had been taken.

I opened the gate, the smell of blood and worse becoming even stronger as the doors swung open, and was faced by Rib and Pot, holding Mak's sword and spear respectively. Behind them stood Ardek with a dagger, and behind him Mak sat pale and groaning against the wall of the tunnel as both Kira and herself pumped magic into her. Her clothes were a mess of blood from her waist down.

That was right about the time I had a small conniption.

"Mak!" Herald screamed and rushed in, fast enough that if Rib and Pot hadn't put up their weapons when they saw me, Herald might have skewered herself.

"Hey, baby," Mak said with a weak smile as Herald took her hand.

"Mak, anyone, what happened here?" I asked, feeling a very real fear rise. "Is Mak going to be all right? *Kira, is Mak going to be all right?*"

"*Draka!*" Mak said, her eyes barely focusing on me. "*I got a sword in the gut, really bad. How about that?*"

"*Hush, woman!*" Kira said, but there was only fatigued concern in her voice. "*I told you to sit still and rest! Dragon, she will live. She has a potion in her and I am healing her. And she is doing some herself, I think, despite what I keep telling her. She will need a lot of food, especially as skinny as she is, but she will recover."*

"We're pretty sure that they were bandits," Ardek said, speaking at almost the same time. "Too rough to be the Night Blossom's people."

"We drove the fuckers off," Pot said. "Mak got one, but then another one got her real bad before Rib got him. The rest cooled off after that. Let us retreat into the tunnel, and I guess they must have fucked off if you didn't see them."

"Draka. Draka!" Mak said insistently, dragging my attention back to her. *"I need to tell you."*

"You are not dying, Mak. You can rest and tell me whatever it is when you have recovered."

"No, no, Draka. You need to know. Kira is a good woman. You need to know that." I could see Kira blush slightly as Mak continued. *"She just wants to help. She has too much love for the city that made her a slave, but she is good. Do not let them hang her, Draka. Please. Or make her a slave again. Can we just keep her? Not give her to the council or the Wolves or anyone? She is too good."*

"I will see what I can do," I said, with a sideways glance at Kira. I'd been thinking just that myself. *"But we need to find out what she knows."*

"Just need the right questions," Mak said. *"No need to hurt her for that. Right, Kira?"*

"I will not go against Tekeretek," Kira said carefully, *"but the Silver Spurs are mercenaries. I have no love for them . . . those that remain. I will answer questions truthfully, and tell you what I know."*

"See, Draka?" Mak said, *"We just need someone to ask the right questions. No need to hurt her."*

"Yes, Mak, I will see what I can do," I said, trying to be patient. I wondered if it was just blood loss and the alcohol in the potion that made her want to tell me this so urgently, but there had been something she wanted to tell me about Kira before. *"Now rest! I am not asking, I am telling. You have done well, and I need you to recover. Herald needs you to recover,"* I said, looking at the younger sister.

"Please, Mak, do as she says," Herald said, backing me up. *"You are out of danger. There is no need to strain yourself."*

"All right," Mak said, capitulating and relaxing back against the tunnel wall, then lapsing back into Karakani. "But don't hurt her, okay? She's so damned afraid and lonely, and she doesn't deserve that. Just talk to her, you'll see." Her eyes fluttered shut as she whispered, "You'll see."

"Can she lie down?" I asked Kira.

"Perhaps, but I would not do so. The skin and muscle have closed, but much damage was in the guts. I would prefer not to move her at all for some time."

I could tell that she was flagging. Her eyes were sunken, and there was a sheen of sweat on her face. Whatever Mak had said, the fact that Kira was putting so much into helping Mak was earning her major points in my book, and in Herald's as well, judging by how she was looking at Kira.

That made me suspicious, though. Perhaps it was unfair, but the fact that I suddenly felt so positively toward her, together with the fairly excessive way Mak had praised her, made me wonder what kind of advancements Kira had, besides the obvious. Ardek had something to make people like him, so I knew it was a possibility, but in his case, it wasn't strong enough to keep Mak from beating the crap out of him, and I would still only feel kind of bad if I had to get rid of him.

But that was not important at the moment. What was important was that my people had been attacked, and I was very unhappy with the situation. I'd returned triumphant from running off the bear, only to step into another problem. I was hurting and I was tired, and Mak was injured, even if she should recover, and I was angrier than I would've thought about that. I had come to rely on her to keep things under control and running smoothly.

It was a problem that I had to solve as soon as possible. I didn't need a group of bandits to worry about.

"So, you killed two," I said to the group at large, "and the rest ran off, meaning they know where to find you if they want to come back for revenge. How many of them were there?"

"Six," Rib said. "Two dead and four survivors."

"And which way did they go?"

"North, along the hills," Pot said.

"And do they know that the gate closes?"

"Yeah," Rib said. "Mak had to close it before she collapsed, and the survivors were stripping the bodies when she did."

"All right. At least four bandits or other violently desperate people who know too much," I said with a sigh. "Rib, Pot, can you see in this darkness, or do you have more of that potion?"

"We'll be fine," Pot said, giving me a curious look.

"Good. I want you two to go out and look for them. I'll do the same from the sky. Once we know where they are, we need to get rid of them."

"Yeah, not much choice, is there?" Pot agreed. "What's the plan?"

"Pretty simple. If there's not too many more of them, I take them out. You two make sure that no one gets away."

"On your own? Isn't that—"

"No, it's not," I said firmly. "Unless they're an organized force of strong fighters, four or a few more of them won't have a chance against me. I just don't want them scattering into the forest where I can't get them. Can I count on you? You're not mine, but I still hope that I can ask for your help."

Rib and Pot looked at each other silently, then Rib said, "Yeah, you can count on us."

"Herald, will you be all right?" I asked, making sure she followed my eyes when I looked at Kira and Ardek.

"Shut the gate, and *we* will be fine," she said, chiding me gently. I felt a flash of annoyance, but it passed. I needed to rely on her and Mak when it came to judging others, especially when I was annoyed or angry. She had clearly deemed Ardek and Kira safe.

"Right," I said. "We'll be back as soon as we can. Hopefully we can deal with this tonight, and then we can relax again. And perhaps tomorrow we can do that thing we talked about."

"I hope so," she said.

Rob and Pot didn't need much in the way of preparations. "How do we get in touch if we find them?" Pot asked.

"If *you* find them, go out in the open with a torch or something and I'll find you. I'm not sure how to handle it if *I* find them, though. Any suggestions?"

"Why don't you just fly low over the trees and, I dunno . . . roar or scream or something? Anyone else out here would be freaked out and confused, but we'll know who it is. Then we can do the torch thing."

"What if I do that birdcall Rib likes?"

Rib and Pot, like so often, shared a look.

"We'll know it's you," Rib said diplomatically, "so that's good."

Meaning that I was pretty shit at it, but it didn't really matter. Like she said, they'd know that it was me, and anyone else who might hear could wonder what it was, look up and not see anything.

We split up, Rib and Pot setting off at an impressive pace through the dark forest and me taking to the air. Finding the "bandits" was not actually hard. They had a rough camp just a few miles north. The hills there were lower and densely wooded, but from the air their camp was easy to make out, set up in a natural clearing. It looked so clearly divided that I was immediately curious. The camp had two distinct parts separated by thirty feet of emptiness with the feeling of a no-man's-land, each with a fire and four or five tents. There were clearly more than four people there, but the look of the camp made me confident that there was nothing to worry about. In fact, the whole situation looked so non-threatening that I decided to take a closer look before going to find the cousins.

At each fire sat a single sentry, staring at each other across the dark no-man's land as though they expected the other side to attack at any time. It didn't look at all like an organized camp. Blinded to the outside, they wouldn't have stood a chance if anyone or anything fell on them from the darkness. They had no idea how lucky they were that a certain bear had gone south instead of north, because she would have ripped half of the camp to shreds before anyone even had a chance to react.

Besides that, the sentries also didn't have any armor on, and their weapons were rough. One had an old, worn sword and the other what looked like a regular axe, for felling trees or splitting wood. If these were bandits, they were not only divided, but very new and woefully unprepared.

I'd seen all I needed to. Killing them would have been entirely effortless. I still left to find Rib and Pot, flying low and slow over the forest making my "Koh-ahp" sounds, which didn't sound the least bit like a bird, even to myself. But they heard me, and as Rib had predicted, they did know that it was me. I found them waving a torch in a dip between two soft hills after about half an hour.

"We're not killing anyone tonight," I told them. "There's a bunch of them, but they're pathetic. They've barely even got a camp. I'll show you where they are, but then I want to keep an eye on them for a while and see what's going on."

"What did you find?" Rib asked. "They looked pretty rough from what I saw, but the two we killed knew what they were doing."

"Nine tents, so there might be a bunch of them, but they have a bad camp, bad equipment, and there seems to be two factions who are suspicious of each other. I could have walked right into either side of the camp and they would never have noticed. Whoever they are, as long as I keep an eye on them, they're no threat to anybody. I could take them out whenever I want, and that's if they don't do it themselves first."

"So you want to just stay and watch them?" Pot asked. "You don't want us backing you up?"

"I wouldn't mind it. But until Mak's recovered I want you there to back up Herald, just in case."

"In case of what? Another attack?"

"In case Ardek or Kira—"

Rib cut me off. "In case they do what, exactly? Ardek wants you all to like him more than anything, and Kira is a pacifist who can't stand to see anyone hurt. Don't you know those two?"

"I . . . haven't really had any deep conversations with them. They both *say* that they'll behave, but they're both here against their will."

"Kira, maybe. Ardek could have slipped away in the chaos when the fire broke out, but he was right there helping to pull people out. He's not going anywhere, and I doubt that he wants to or could fight either Mak or Herald. He's scrappy, but he's not a trained and experienced fighter the way they are. And Kira isn't going to hurt anyone. Mak talked to her, and I talked to Mak. The way Mak tells it, working with those mercenaries was slowly killing her. And she's too smart to try to run. Where is she going to go?"

"And," Pot said, "after the fight *you* couldn't have held her back from Mak. She was holding Mak's damn guts in while she started healing and Rib poured a potion down her throat. She's a helper. It's who she is."

I frowned at them. I didn't like the fact that everyone seemed to have the same opinion about Kira. I'd killed . . . maybe not her friends, but her companions, and

I had dragged her here against her will and put her at risk of death. Hell, I'd pretty casually threatened to kill her myself a few times. I just couldn't believe that she wouldn't try something, given the chance. At least Ardek seemed angrier at the Night Blossom than he was at me, and I'd promised him money. Kira had nothing to look forward to except possibly survival as a slave for much of her life.

Although, thinking back on what I'd seen of her interactions with the others, she seemed to be on good terms with everyone. Once she'd stopped interrogating Herald and Mak about their parents, the three women had gotten along just fine, and while Mak had tried to stay cool toward Kira, she had obviously more than warmed up. And, even though she could only speak to the sisters, the others seemed to like her well enough anyway.

Everyone treated her well, and she was respectful and helpful in return. The only person she had any reason to have a problem with was me.

That displeased me in a way that made no sense. What did it matter if she got along well with everyone but me? If it kept everything running smoothly, I shouldn't give a single discount damn about what she thought of me. I was her jailor, not her rescuer or her friend. I wasn't really responsible for anything, but if I were, it would be for her life and her availability for interrogation, not her happiness.

I still had a petty, nagging feeling that it was somehow unfair. Perhaps if I were to have a real, somewhat friendly conversation with her, I could make her see me with something other than fear.

"Maybe you're right," I conceded. "I guess I could just go back and tell them that it's going to be a while. I still think you're going to be bored, though."

"Let us worry about that," Pot said. "Show us where this camp is and we'll keep an eye on them until you get back."

I could have argued with them, but I didn't. I felt that I could trust those two, and if I wanted anything more than a professional relationship with them, I should show that. Fear and respect were all well and good, but if I wanted to make friends, they weren't enough. So I brought them to the bandit camp. It didn't take long, and the same two men were still sitting guard, still looking suspiciously at each other. I left the cousins to find their own hiding spots, and returned to my mountain and the gate. A wide, freshly disturbed patch of soil at the edge of the tree line showed that Herald and Ardek had not been idle while we were away.

Herald was understanding when I told her the new plan. Of course she was. She could be hard and vengeful when she needed to be, but the one who'd hurt her sister was dead and she trusted my judgment.

And I needed to trust her. "I'll shut you back in," I told her. "But if you need to get out while Mak is still resting, I'll leave it to you to decide if you want to tell Kira how to do it. You all seem to trust her to behave, so . . ."

"Yet you still avoid speaking Tekereteki in front of her," Herald chided me with a little smile.

Kira had been dozing nearby, not used to the inverted hours I'd forced on them, but she'd looked up sleepily when I said her name. Come to think of it, she hadn't gotten much sleep when I flew her in, and then we'd marched out to the mountain through the night. I had no idea how much she'd slept in the tunnel while I waited with the cousins, but then they'd been attacked and she'd taken care of Mak . . .

I turned to her. "Bekiratag," I said in her own dialect of Tekereteki. "Kira. How are you doing? Did you eat? Sleep?"

"Makanna and Herald have been very kind," she said with a dainty yawn. "We all ate before the attack. But sleep . . . not so much, no."

"I'll leave you to your rest then," I said, then hesitated. "Thank you, Kira. For helping Mak. Rebatia and Poterio told me what you did. I wouldn't have expected you to volunteer like that."

"Oh," she said, clearly surprised and with not a shred of deception that I could pick up on. "Of course. She was hurt, so . . ."

"Still. She's important to Herald, and to me. Thank you," I said, and left.

CHAPTER THIRTY-FIVE

Belonging

W hen I returned to the "bandits'" camp it was no surprise to me that I didn't spot Rib or Pot until they showed themselves, safely hidden away up one of the more densely leafed trees. I wasn't happy about it, but I wasn't surprised.

The tree was far enough away from the camp that they wouldn't be able to hear anything that was said, but that hadn't been the goal. Nor would the sentries have been likely to hear us if I talked to the cousins from the ground, but rather than do that, I walked up to the trunk, shifted, and wound myself up until I joined them in the branches. It felt *so* good not to hide what I could do from them, and I got some petty satisfaction from how they instinctively pulled back when I suddenly appeared next to them.

"Have you seen anything interesting?" I asked once they'd taken a second to recover.

"A big fucking lizard just appeared out of the shadows and I almost fell down and broke my neck," Rib said. "That was quite something. Other than that, not really. They changed sentries shortly after you left, and the new ones are just as suspicious of each other."

"Don't know how many weapons they have," Pot added. "The guy with the sword handed it over to the woman who relieved him, though the guy with the axe was replaced by a new guy with a hammer."

"Another tool, not a weapon?"

"Yeah, like a carpenter's hammer," Rib said. "Come to think of it, other than the two dead idiots, the ones who attacked us all had forestry axes. I didn't think much of it at the time since we were busy staying alive, but seeing it like this, I wonder if those swords were the only ones this group has."

"Yeah," I said. "These are not bandits. Maybe they're trying to be, but these are just . . . people, aren't they? Too desperate or stupid to know better. And now they've run into a group much badder than themselves and they've lost two people, possibly their best fighters, and everything's falling apart."

"That sounds about right, yeah," Rib said, and Pot nodded.

"Well," I told them, "I'm going to get in there and see if I can hear anything."

"What if they see you?" Rib asked.

"What if they see me? What are these people going to do? I'm going to want you two to confirm that you recognize the survivors of the group that attacked us, but I'm pretty sure that I don't need much to justify just wiping them out if they so much as look at me funny. What happens if they see me depends entirely on them."

It was early twilight, but still dark enough for me to shadow pretty effortlessly. Neither of the sentries noticed as I entered the smaller half of the camp, moving silently among the tents but hearing only the sounds of restless sleep. It was the same when I moved on to the larger half, just the crackle of the fire and the occasional sounds of the sleepers.

Near the tents there was a dense thicket of bushes, and rather than return to the cousins, I decided to hole up there. I found a sizable hollow within that smelled like something had lived there for a while. It was almost large enough for me, and while I must have made at least a little bit of noise when I shifted back, my form pushing out anything that was in the way, no one reacted. There were some thorny brambles in there that couldn't hurt me, but also a lot of fragrant late-blooming flowers. It felt almost like a nest of sorts, and was really quite cozy.

As sunrise slowly approached and then arrived, the camp slowly filled with the sounds of people waking from restless sleep to a new day of hardship, with groans and grumbles instead of the satisfied sighs that I was used to. It made me that much more convinced that this was no organized group of bandits. With the way that the camp was divided, I got the feeling that I was dealing with a tenuous alliance of two groups, and with how poorly they were outfitted and prepared, I wondered if they weren't refugees, though from what I didn't know. I remembered Rallon mentioning refugees from the north, and kicked myself for not asking more about them or the situation.

I became more convinced that they were refugees when I saw the kids. There were three of them, a boy and a girl of maybe five or six, and I could see a baby in the smaller half of the camp that couldn't have been more than a few months old. Between the five tents in the closer half of the camp and the four in the farther one, there were a total of eighteen people, but only six of them looked like they'd be able to put up any kind of fight if it came to it.

The mood was, to put it lightly, shit. In such a small group I could only assume that each of them could claim one or both of the dead as a friend or family member, and many of them moved in that mechanical way you see in people who have just seen too much grief.

Between that and the children, my plans changed pretty drastically. I was not going to be wiping this camp out. I was not going to be killing any kids. That was a hard no. Neither half of me wanted any part of that; nor was I going to be making any orphans. As for the others, they couldn't really hurt me, so I shouldn't need to kill them either. If Mak or the others wanted to mete out their own justice for the attack, that was a whole other thing entirely, but I was in a mood for mercy.

I didn't learn anything useful. I heard some names, some short snatches of conversation relating to the doings of the morning, but whatever had brought them there didn't come up, either because it wasn't important or because it was something they didn't want to talk about. Either way I decided to check out the smaller camp to see if they were more talkative.

The people in the camp were keeping busy, and the undergrowth was fairly high, so I didn't expect to have any trouble staying hidden despite the brightening sunshine. The opening I'd used to get into the thicket was too narrow for me while I was still solid, but I made an attempt at just pushing through before I strained myself to shadow out despite the light. Even turning around made a slight rustle, and I only got my legs out of the hollow before the rest, especially my wings, caught and started making more noise than I was comfortable with. Oh well. It wasn't that much of a hassle to darken the existing shadow enough to let me shift, nor did I need to hold it long. As soon as I was out of the thicket, though, I shifted back and crept along toward the other group of tents, keeping low to the ground.

Either I hadn't been as stealthy as I'd thought, or the small amount of noise I'd made had been enough. As I crept away, I heard the unmistakable sound of a child's voice calling, "Mama! Mama! I saw a snake, Mama, in the bushes!" It was enough to cause a minor commotion and make me stop and look around, but no one seemed to be looking for me. They were more concerned about a snake in the bushes by the tents. "It was black and big like this," I heard the boy insist from behind me, loudly enough that I saw heads popping up from ahead of me. That did it. With some annoyance I pushed and shifted again, gliding along as a patch of shadow around the edge of the clearing.

There were no convenient bushes near the smaller camp, so I considered posting up in a tree. Finding a dense enough tree wasn't always easy, though, and I couldn't find one that suited me. Most leafy trees in the forest were types that spread their branches wide with leaves only at the ends, and the ones with much denser foliage, which I preferred, weren't common at this altitude. Rib and Pot were in one that had a good overview of the camp, but it was too far away to hear anything. The conifers that were dense enough were usually too short to climb, though they were good for hiding under on the ground; but the ones in the hills were mostly pine with tall, limbless trunks and open crowns.

With no bushes and no convenient tree to hide in, I ended up just slinking into the shadow of one of the tents and staying there in shadow form, listening.

It was still a bit of a strain to maintain, and it was getting too bright for me to see anything without shifting back, but it was any potential conversation that I was interested in anyway.

"Just one more Sorrows-beloved thing to worry about," a defeated male voice said. "Snakes. I hate snakes."

"It's no worse than up north," said a woman firmly. "We're still alive, aren't we? More than we can say for most."

"Aye, like Tork and that Sweet Creek woman he fell in with," the man replied. "Would that I could have talked them out of it . . ."

"And would that none of this had ever happened. Young braves with their heads full of stories. No one blames you but you, husband."

"Them Sweet Creekers do. They think we should have all piled in, fools that they are. Never seen a killer a one of them, and that's what I saw, and that's what they were. And now Tork's gone, poor young fool."

The woman's voice turned soft and comforting. "Come, Jek. Here, hold Alda and feed her her mash. Your brother doesn't need you anymore, but your daughter does. I do."

That was all I needed. I would have the humans take over and decide what the next appropriate step would be, and then we could put all of this behind us and get back to what was important. I needed to report what I'd found in the south to Rallon. Kira needed to be properly questioned, though I'd decided to listen to Herald and Mak and not let anyone actually hurt her to force any answers. Then we could get back to utterly destroying the Night Blossom, and I could be rid of the anger that kept bubbling inside me and relax properly.

We also needed to be back in the city for the men's arrival, which couldn't be far off. It was odd to the point of suspicion that nobody had heard from them for a while, but I wasn't worried about their safety. They could take care of themselves. It would just be nice to know when we could expect them, ideally on which ship. And how much money they were bringing. Couldn't forget that.

With all that in mind, I scooted back out among the trees, circled around, and picked up the cousins. Rib saw me at the base of their tree, and through some awkward sign language, I got across that I wanted them down. Pot was sleeping but roused easily enough when Rib poked him, and without a word they both shimmied around to the side of the tree most hidden from the camp and climbed down that way.

"So, family groups," Rib said when her feet were on the ground. "Kids and all. Not your typical outlaws, I'd say. Did you hear anything?"

"They're from two different settlements," I told them, "and they don't seem to trust each other, if the separate camps weren't clear enough. Sounds like the two dead ones might have been a couple or something, probably all that was holding the two sides together. Gods only know what'll happen now. Either way I want you all to talk it through and decide what to do. I'd be fine with just letting them go."

"So do you want us to come with?"

"Yeah. Let's leave it until evening. Even if these people break camp, they won't get anywhere fast, with the kids and all."

"I'm honestly glad the bear came our way," Pot said, paralleling my own thoughts from earlier. "I don't like to think what would have happened if it came across this lot."

It wouldn't have been pretty, I knew that much.

We covered the few miles back to the gate quickly. It was closed, so I opened it to let Rib and Pot through and found all the others sleeping, or just having been woken up, in the case of Herald and Ardek. I quickly told them what we'd found and what I wanted, got Herald's reassurances that everybody had behaved perfectly, and then shut them all back in and returned to my nest to sleep. As much as I wanted this whole bandit/refugee situation dealt with, and as much as I preferred to get the humans there before sunset to make the whole situation a little less dramatic, I was still in pain from fighting that damned bear, and I needed some proper rest and recovery. If that meant oversleeping and dealing with everything another day, so be it. I was satisfied that they were no threat, and they were not my responsibility, so I didn't much care about what happened to them.

When I awoke, feeling whole and rested, I had a fresh perspective, a problem, and a feeling that I didn't know what to make of.

The problem was that I wasn't as indifferent as I'd thought I was when I went to sleep. These people were in my territory, and in a way that made them my responsibility. I was unhappy about their situation, especially the kids'. Besides that, they were running from something, and I needed to know what, in case it became a threat.

The strange feeling, in a word, was Mak. I could literally feel her, somewhere to the south. It wasn't much, just a presence, a feeling of distance and direction, but it was more than enough to make it obvious that something had happened. Something had changed, but whether it was in her or in me, I couldn't tell.

I still didn't rush to get back to the humans. I needed time to consider what to do, and when I got to the ledge, I could see the barest blush of dawn over the sea.

I must have been banged up worse than I'd thought, because I'd slept a whole day and night away. I was hungry, too, so that would have to be the first thing I dealt with. Being hungry made me more draconic, and I needed a rational and somewhat compassionate mind.

Once I'd hunted, brought my prey back to the ledge, and eaten, the sun was well above the horizon. This was the last of the weaker old goats in the nearby population. I was going to need to go farther afield in the future, I mused, and let the local goats recover.

As I flew down, my sense of where Mak was grew stronger, to the point that I could have gone the last few hundred feet straight to her with my eyes closed if I didn't mind smashing my face into the rock. I hoped that my people weren't all asleep yet. I was sure that none of them would complain if I woke them, but they'd still be annoyed, I was sure of it.

Thankfully the gate was open. Ardek and Kira were sleeping just inside, but the sisters were sitting outside in the shadows that the trees still cast across the place. The sun was still too low in the sky to light the pit and would be for at least another hour, judging by how slowly it was creeping down the rock. As I flew over, Mak waved a greeting, Herald turning around to face me as well.

"You certainly took your time," Herald said with a smile and a quick pat on the neck.

"I needed more rest than I thought," I told them. *"What about you two? Mak, how are you feeling?"*

"Quite well," she said. Something was obviously up with her; her shoulders were hunched and she seemed to have trouble looking directly at me. *"The pain is gone, and everything has healed right. I only need to eat and rest. Herald told me how you spoke to Kira. Thanking her for healing me. I admit I did not expect that. Thank you."*

"Everyone else seems to trust her well enough. I will bow to your collective wisdom," I said, trying to sound dismissive about it.

"That is good to hear." Mak lowered her head. Then she seemed about to say something, but remained silent, her eyes flicking to Herald.

"She needs to know," Herald said gently.

Mak sighed. *"She does. Draka, there are two things I need to tell you. First, I believe that Kira might know something about the Night Blossom."*

"What?" I said, leaning forward. *"Why do you think so? What does she know?"*

"We have no idea what she might know," Herald said, *"only that she seemed to recognize the name when we were speaking to Ardek. Then the attack happened, and we have not had a good opportunity to speak to her about it. But that is not what you need to tell her, Mak."*

"No, it is not, is it?" Mak took a long, slow breath, visibly forcing herself to relax. *"The other thing is that I got an advancement as I slept."*

I sat up straight at that. This must be what had changed, and I felt a rush of curiosity and excitement. *"That is great!"* I told her honestly. *"Congratulations! Should you not be celebrating this?"*

"Perhaps. Probably. Yes, yes I should. And while it is a minor advancement, I am sure that it is a strong one. Life changing, I would say. I have been speaking to Herald about it."

"Do you intend to keep me guessing, or will you tell me?" I asked, trying not to sound too eager. *"You say that I need to know."*

"*Yes.*" She closed her eyes and said, "*I got two choices, as we always do. The first one does not matter. I considered it, but it was not really . . . me. I saw myself as a warrior, tirelessly striking down my enemies. It seems easy to interpret. Better strength and endurance, probably. But the other relates to you.*"

"*You are still making me guess,*" I chided lightly.

"*Yeah. Apologies,*" she said, then opened her eyes and looked at me with a grain of confidence. "*I saw myself in your shadow, Draka. Very literally. Going where you go, growing as you grow. I chose that path without hesitation.*"

Now, *that* was something. I didn't know exactly how I felt about that, but it was all good, that was for sure!

"*I believe that I have bound myself to you,*" she said, her voice and posture growing steadily bolder, "*drawing on your strength in some way. I would say that I hope that it was not presumptuous of me, but I can feel that it was not. I can feel that you are pleased with my choice.*"

"*Are you sure of what you have done? What it will do for you, and to you?*" I asked. I sure as hell wasn't, but I could guess. And if it meant that me getting stronger did the same for her, she would have a vested interest in my growth. Not that I expected her to betray me again, but still.

"*I am as certain of my choice as I have ever been of anything. I already feel stronger and more resilient,*" she said, "*and the Tekereteki comes more easily, I think, although that might just be practice. For those benefits alone, I am very satisfied. But more than that, I could feel you coming.*"

"*I can feel you too,*" I admitted. "*Ever since I woke up today, I have known where you are.*"

Mak smiled at that, nodding in acknowledgment. "*Before that, perhaps an hour ago, I could feel your satisfaction, distantly, and it gave me peace. I can feel how pleased you are with my choice, and it makes me happy. I can feel how you trust in my judgment, and it makes me trust in myself. When I say that I am bound to you, I do not only mean that I benefit from your strength.*

"*Draka,*" she said, her eyes bright and certain, "*I am yours.*"

And this, I told myself, full of smug satisfaction, *is how a cult is born.*

CHAPTER THIRTY-SIX

Subordinates

I had thought about Mak a lot over the past several weeks. About what she'd done and how I'd reacted. I knew why she'd done it. I understood. I hadn't forgiven her; I still couldn't think about it without needing to tamp down a flare of anger and spiteful satisfaction at the misery she'd gone through since, but I understood.

That morning I was pretty damned happy with her. She'd done a lot in the month or so since her betrayal to try and get back in my good graces, but if there was one single act that showed she was truly willing to do anything, this was it. As much as your acts and your beliefs, your advancements were what defined you in this world, and she had chosen one that bound her to me. There was no going back from this. No possibility that she was just waiting for an opportunity to turn on me again. She had made me a part of herself, as essential as her own magic. She had, willingly and unprompted, made herself *mine*.

She was being a little intense about it, but skin-in-the-game Mak was a lot easier to feel good about than sad-and-repentant Mak. With any hope she'd just be overcorrecting for a while and then come back to some kind of balance, but if not I'd still be far happier than I was before. She had a sense of strength and purpose about her that hadn't been there for a while, and it was great to see.

"*Are you not worried?*" I asked Herald after we'd stepped away to talk privately a little. "*I do not think that I could free her now, even if I knew how. She would not accept it.*"

Herald looked at me and smiled, shaking her head. "*She is so much happier now than she has been since we were taken. Almost herself again. I know that it is not the same, and that she has given up much of her freedom. But really, has she not just confirmed what we already knew? She already could not deny you anything. How is this any different, other than her being stronger and happier? She was already yours.*" She stopped, and so did I, as she looked at me seriously. "*Just as I am.*"

It was something I already knew, but to hear her say it made my heart flutter. My instincts, ones that had nothing to do with the dragon, told me that my face should be burning. *"Herald,"* I told her, looking way. *"Let us get your sister."*

That close to Mak I could tell exactly where she was, which was a feeling I wasn't used to. When I'd told the sisters about it, Herald had said it was *"Very useful, but quite creepy,"* and Mak had simply accepted it as though it was natural and only to be expected. They knew that I could feel the direction of my hoard, and Mak, as far as I could tell, simply lumped herself in with my *other* possessions. Which was disturbing in a way, considering how readily she did so, but also just felt right. And as long as she was content with it, I wasn't going to argue.

We found her back inside the gate, sitting against the tunnel wall across from Ardek, who looked somewhere between concerned for her and afraid for himself. She was, amazingly, apologizing.

"I was just always angry at you," she was saying, "and I never trusted you. I saw you as sharing the blame for what happened to Herald and me, even though I knew better. I could tell that you meant us no harm, that you felt guilty and wanted to make things right as far as you could, but I didn't listen to what my own instincts told me."

"It's really no problem," he said, "I get it, right? It's fine."

"No. I was dishonest, and I was cruel. I let you think that I'd forgiven you when I hadn't. I treated you with kindness and made you trust me, and then I turned around and violated that trust. And for that you have my apologies, and my promise that I'll be more honest with you from now on."

"Uh, right. Accepted. Thank you?"

"Listen, Ardek. If it helps, I'm telling you this as much for my own sake as for yours. I can't say that I will always be completely open with everything, but I need to know that you believe me when I say that I won't lie to you, and that I won't mistreat you for something you had no control over."

Ardek's eyes flicked toward Herald and me as we approached, a silent plea for help.

"Mak," I said. "I need to talk to you and Herald, together."

She turned and looked at us, then rose smoothly from where she sat. "Of course," she said, then spoke over her shoulder as she went with us. "I mean it. You didn't deserve the way I treated you, and I'm sorry."

"Yeah, thanks," Ardek said, relaxing more the farther Mak got from him. "You're forgiven and all that. Really!"

"All right. We'll talk later," she said, then spoke to us in Tekereteki. *"He does not quite believe me, but I cannot blame him. I would not believe me so quickly either. What did you want to talk about?"*

"Let's walk," I said, starting out and letting the sisters follow. I didn't feel like dragging them through the undergrowth, so I led the way along the rock face,

contemplating the scrubby bushes as I put my thoughts together. I needed to do this right.

"Are the bushes telling you anything interesting?" Herald asked after several minutes had passed, breaking me out of my thoughts, *"Come on. You are the one who asked us out here. As much as I enjoy spending some uninterrupted time with you, I believe that you had something you wanted us all to do today."*

"She is nervous," Mak said, sounding uncomfortable. *"What is wrong, Draka?"*

"Nothing is wrong," I said. *"I just do not want to express myself clumsily. This is important, and I do not want to give you the wrong idea or offend you. Herald, you are my dearest, truest friend in this world. Mak, we have had a difficult month. I will not pretend that there was not a short time when I hated you, and would have killed you or thrown your life away if it became more convenient or useful to me than keeping you alive. But before then, I believe that we were slowly growing close, and I hope that we can get back to something like that.*

"You have each said that you are . . . mine. I love that. I cannot describe my feelings any other way. Hearing you say that gave me so much comfort and satisfaction that, in a very selfish way, it almost makes what I went through worth it, even if I cannot ever forgive the Night Blossom for what she did to you.

"But Herald, Mak. I feel that you have offered yourselves to me as some sort of servants. Mak more than Herald, perhaps. And I do not want that. I think. In general, perhaps I do, at some level. Having servants sounds nice."

Herald laughed very politely.

"But you two . . . what I really need you to be to me are friends. Advisors and allies. As satisfying as it is to have people simply obey me, I need people who question me, who are honest with me about any concerns they have about my decisions and my behavior.

"I am not always constant in how I look at or think about things. Mak, Herald already knows why, and I will trust you with this as well. Will you swear not to speak to anyone about what I am about to tell you, except your sister?"

"On my life," she said. *"I swear that anything you tell me in confidence, I will take to my grave."*

"Good."

And so I told her. I told her about falling as a human only months ago, and as much as I remembered about being trapped and put into stasis as a dragon centuries ago, and waking as a single individual. I told her about the dragon speaking to me for a long time, and the human sometimes speaking to me now, and how different circumstances brought out each side of me—fear, stress, and anger, the dragon; and comfort and pity, the human.

"My greatest concern," I told them, *"is that when I or what is mine is threatened, when I even think of it, it becomes difficult to think of anything but destroying*

whatever offends me. Then, more than ever, I will need you to remind me of the human perspective, and of the long-term consequences of short-term satisfaction."

Mak had stood, then sat in stunned silence as I told her my tale, but she took my silence as an invitation to speak. *"Draka,"* she said, *"I knew that something was different about you. Besides the obvious, of course. What you tell me is incredible. Amazing. But so is everything about you and this . . . this explains so much. Why you speak the way you do. Your intelligence and your maturity despite your size. But I must ask, in the Night Blossom's prison, which part of you was that? I expected to die. Which part of you spared me?"*

"I had not fully understood or accepted my nature, but I am pretty sure that was all the dragon's doing. It is strange to look back on my own behavior, to think about why I did things, but I honestly think that you were lucky that it was that side of me. It was not mercy that made me spare you, but greed and spite. If my human side had been at the forefront, I might have just killed you." I glanced at Herald before looking back at Mak, and I was human enough in that moment to feel a small measure of shame. *"I am not proud of it, but I was hurting, and I wanted you to hurt too. I could not see past my own pain to how much you were already suffering. When you broke, when you stopped resisting me before I could decide how to kill you, when it seemed that death would be a release for you, that was when I decided to spare you."*

Mak visibly shuddered at the memory, and Herald put one arm around her sister, holding her until she was ready to speak. Her pained expression mirrored my own feelings. *"As unpleasant as that is to remember, it is still good to know that even the dragon in you saw fit to let me live, no matter the reason. She is clearly not a mindlessly destructive beast, which is what dragons are all too often depicted as. Thank you for telling me."*

Herald, for her part, looked equal parts relieved and horrified. *"Every time I hear about what happened between you two, my heart breaks,"* she said when I looked at her curiously. *"I am so . . . I do not know what to think. Draka, I cannot imagine your pain, and I cannot blame you for anything that you did."* She snorted softly. *"I think am literally unable to. But if Mak had not done what they asked of her, if you had not been captured and brought to the place where we were being held, I do not know if either Mak or I would be alive now. If we were, I doubt that we would be sane. Every moment that I can remember was full of fear and pain and . . ."* She looked away and pulled Mak closer to herself. *"I am sorry but, in a very selfish way, as you said, I am glad that Mak handed you over to them. As much as I love you, I cannot blame her either."*

"Yeah," I said. *"In the end, I do not think that any of us can truly blame anyone but the Night Blossom. But I had something important I wanted to say. Herald, Mak, if you want to give yourselves to me, I will promise to do all that I can to keep you safe and to help you prosper. And I will try to treat you as trusted friends and allies, not as servants. Subordinates, at worst. And I want you to know that this is all of me*

speaking. The dragon recognizes your value to us—to me, I mean, just as well as the human does."

And she really did. She had long recognized the value of Herald as a go between and representative, beyond the purely emotional benefits of having a close friend. But Mak had proved her competence and usefulness over and over since we'd met her, and while the dragon didn't need friends as such, she definitely recognized the benefits of having competent people bound to us. Hell, she'd been going on about the four adventurers serving us for months.

Herald side-eyed me and scoffed playfully. *"Servants, indeed! You are certainly arrogant enough, whether there is a human side to you or not. But you know that I am your friend, forever, and if you want me to promise to always be honest, even if the truth might hurt, then I will do so without hesitation. So long as you will make the same promise."*

Mak looked, well, not quite crestfallen. I'd seen her face fall as I said that I didn't want servants—not a great sign of her mental state. But she rallied, her face passing through a series of emotions from despair to disappointment to something more like uncertainty. Being able to feel the intent behind my words must have helped. *"I am prepared to serve you for as long as it takes to work off my guilt, a year or a lifetime,"* she said. *"Since you have asked for our honesty, I do not know if I am ready to be your friend, because I do not know if I deserve it. I have not forgiven myself, and I do not know if I ever will. But if you think that you could go back, that you would have me as a friend again, then I will do all that I can."*

"I am sure that you will have plenty of opportunity to convince yourself in the near future," I told her. *"Now, as good as this whole conversation has been for me, we have an immediate problem to deal with. Have Rib and Pot filled you in on the refugees?"*

"Our supposed bandits. Yes, they have," Mak said.

"They have told us all that they saw and what you talked about," Herald said. *"For me, I am inclined to simply let them go their own way, but it was Mak who was injured, and who had to kill them. Well, Rib killed one, but she seems to take such things lightly."* She wrapped her arm around her sister as Mak seemed to shrink in on herself at the mention of killing.

"Was this the first time you killed someone?" I asked Mak.

She fidgeted a little, picking at the skin around her nails. *"It was. It was my first real combat against people at all. I have been in fights, but nothing life-or-death."* She closed her eyes and took a slow breath, then straightened herself. *"I agree with Herald. If what we have heard is true, they do not deserve any more hardship. The two main offenders are dead; the others in the group were reluctant to fight us in the first place, and withdrew as soon as they could recover the equipment of their fallen. Let us talk to them, find out what they are running from, and send them on their way somewhere they will be able to start over."*

"*Then that is what we will do,*" I told them. "*Where are Rib and Pot? I would like them to show you the way. I have only flown, so I am not sure of the best way by ground.*"

"*Oh, they are . . . around. Somewhere in a tree, probably,*" Herald said, waving her arm in the general direction of the trees. "*Listening to us, for all I know, though I have no reason to believe that they understand Tekereteki.*"

"*Yeah, they are good at skulking, are they not?*" I said. "*I can barely even smell them at the best of times.*"

Herald started surreptitiously scanning the treetops. "*I can usually find them, given a little time. Just pretend that we are talking about something important.*"

After a few minutes of idle chit-chat she said, "*I found them. Behind you and a little to your left there are two short kala trees, with a tall, dense dura between them. They are halfway up the dura, Pot watching us and Rib keeping an eye on the forest.*"

"*The what?*" Several months in and I did not actually know the names of any of the trees here, so that meant nothing to me.

"*A leafy tree between two trees with needles,*" Mak explained.

"*Right,*" I said. "*Well spotted. Let us go get them then. Mak, do you want to do the honors?*"

Mak thought, then made a good attempt at a grin. "*Sure.*"

I didn't take us straight toward the tree but at an angle, all of us chatting pointlessly and none of us looking at the tree or the two cousins. I had no idea what Mak had planned, but the idea had clearly raised her spirits. I was both surprised and impressed when she suddenly broke into a sprint, covering the short distance to the tree before I knew what she was doing and then leaped up to grab one of the lowest branches and hauled herself up. The branch was nine or ten feet off the ground. For such a little woman it was quite impressive. And she was climbing quickly, too, her grip sure, hauling herself up nearly one-armed in some cases.

I don't know how surprised the cousins were, but they loved it, laughing and cheering as Mak climbed. She stopped a little below them, having covered fifty vertical feet in just a few seconds. It was enough to make an old climber jealous.

"Come on, get down!" Mak said loudly, looking up as she stood on one stout branch while holding onto another.

"All right, all right!" Pot laughed, loud enough for us to hear on the ground. "You could have just asked!"

"And yet I didn't!" I could hear the grin in Mak's voice. Whatever that advancement was doing to her—and I had a very good guess—she was clearly enjoying it.

"*Showoff,*" I muttered as they joined me and Herald.

Mak just grinned. "You're impressed, aren't you?"

I snorted, but it wasn't like she was wrong. "Let's get Ardek and Kira, get you all ready, and go deal with these transients," I told the others.

"Why them?" Rib asked. "Can't we just leave them here?"

"We could . . . but then we'd have to either shut them in or leave the gate open for them, and one would be pretty unpleasant for them and the other unsafe. They're coming."

"Yes, ma'am. Understood."

For all that we hoped that this would be a somewhat friendly meeting, the humans did not take it lightly. Herald and Mak both had their armor on, Herald wearing her helmet this time, which made the whole effect seriously imposing. Over six feet of angry woman in night-black scale armor wasn't something anyone could ignore. Rib and Pot, however, didn't wear much in the way of armor, or anything else that reduced their mobility. Ardek got Herald's bow and her few remaining arrows—Mak insisted that we needed to show him some trust, and after what I'd just said about wanting to listen to their advice, I didn't want to refuse. Kira just looked kind of anxious about the whole situation, even after we explained that we didn't want or expect any violence. With everyone mostly awake, geared up, and ready, we set off through the hills.

The cousins had mapped a nice, easy trail to get to the refugees' camp, and while we couldn't move at their speed it still took less than an hour.

"How do you want to do this?" Mak said softly to me as we got close. "You feel tense."

"I just want this to go well," I told her, "which means that I'm pretty sure that I shouldn't follow my instincts here."

"Which are?"

"To march into their camp, terrify them to death, and tell them that I'll wipe them all out if they don't fuck off immediately. So instead, I want you and Herald to go in and handle this. I'll stay in the trees, out of sight, with the others. I'm sure they'll be smart enough to assume that there will be others with you, so even if they get any stupid ideas they shouldn't act on them. Especially with your sister looking the way she does in that armor."

"Impressive, isn't it? I'll tell you what she spent on it if you want to know, but I think you're better off not asking. We all thought it was worth it, though. First impressions with clients and other adventurers are important, and she's going to make a Sorrows' first impression."

"Give her your spear and *I'd* think twice about taking her on," I agreed. "And you didn't even see how she handled the bear. The girl can move."

"She did grow into quite the little warrior, didn't she?" Mak grinned. "I used to worry so much. Well, I still do, but . . . she can handle herself, can't she? At least in a fight." She laughed. "It still took her hours to work up the courage to read her letter, though."

"She got a letter?"

"Oh, she didn't say? She got a reply from Maglan. Do you know what she wrote to him? She won't tell me, and all she'll say is that everything is fine."

"No," I said, glancing back at Herald, who was talking to Kira, "but she was anxious about getting something back. Strange that she'd put it off."

"Well, you know how it is. You must have sent letters and messages when you were . . . before. Sorry. It's still strange to think of, you being—you know. But you must have waited for an answer before, worrying what it might say, or that none might come at all."

I thought back on messages left on "Delivered." Or worse, messages left on "Read." Bloody torture.

"I guess, yeah," I said.

"At least whatever he wrote seems to make her happy."

Ahead of us Rib raised her hand, signaling "Halt!"

We had arrived.

CHAPTER THIRTY-SEVEN

Submission

I asked Rib and Pot to keep an eye on the periphery of the camp. I didn't want any surprises. As I waited among the trees with Ardek and Kira, the sisters approached the refugees.

A ripple of fear passed through the small camp when Herald and Mak strode up, armed and armored and grim faced. For all the lack of rancor that they had expressed for the people here, the sisters were determined to establish the pecking order firmly from the start.

They had approached the larger half of the camp, and they made no secret of it. Some of the refugees were probably out hunting or foraging or things like that, but everyone there stopped what they were doing to watch the sisters approach, with the children being shooed into a tent and out of sight.

"Who is in charge here?" Mak called out and turned her gaze to the other half. "That includes you in the other camp. Come out. We need to talk."

A few people slowly drifted in, with the members of each camp making two distinct groups that eyed each other suspiciously. There was a clear nervousness, however, that was shared by both groups.

"I assume that some of you are away," Mak said. There was a hard edge to her voice that I wasn't used to. It suited her. "That doesn't matter. I recognize one face here at least, so I know that I have the right people. You, there." Mak pointed to one of the men, no older than herself, with her spear, holding it straight and steady. "Come forward!"

The man hesitated, and when he began to move he was stopped by a woman's hand around his arm. I guessed that they were the two I'd listened to earlier.

"I promise that we mean you no harm," Mak told them, "but you were with the group that attacked us. We want to talk to you. Now!" The last word was barked with a force that made some of the small crowd flinch. The man gently removed the woman's hand, kissed her on the forehead, and approached the sisters, stopping a dozen feet in front of them.

"I'm Jekrie," the man said, his voice unsteady but loud enough for everyone to hear, "and I speak for these people as much as anyone. We have no leader, but you're right, I was in the group that attacked you. For that, I'm sorry."

"Where are the others?" Herald asked, her hand resting on the hilt of her sword.

"Hunting, Miss," Jekrie answered. "We have little food."

In the trees, Ardek leaned in and whispered, "They had two archers, but they were right shit shots. I don't know how much luck they're likely to have."

"You injured my sister gravely, and terrified our companions," Herald said. "You have angered our patron. Why?"

"Your patron, Miss?" Jekrie shuffled his feet, but continued when the silence dragged on. "We were desperate. We still are. The woman you killed, Madalie, it was her idea. And Torkel, my brother, the man, he was her sweetheart, and he went along with it. And they convinced the rest of us. We could tell that you had so much more than us and we . . . I'm sorry. I am sorry, and I am ashamed. We're desperate, and that is all."

Somewhere in the camp a baby started crying, and the woman who had tried to hold Jekrie back looked at him desperately before ducking into the tent behind her.

Herald and Mak looked at each other, and Herald spoke. "You are fleeing something," she stated, "and you have children with you. The woman who instigated the attack, and your brother, who injured my sister, are both dead. Our patron . . . she is not without kindness or mercy. She is willing to forgive you, so long as you swear that no one in this band will try their hand at banditry again, and to answer all our questions completely and truthfully."

There was a visible shift in the mood of the refugees. Some, but not nearly all, of the tension slowly relaxed, the fear shifting toward fragile hope. From where I watched, I even thought that I saw some careful smiles.

But all was not well, that much was obvious. The immediate threat might have passed, but there were still two armed strangers standing before them. Back on Earth a large group might have easily been able to overpower two experienced fighters, but here advancements were large, unknown force multipliers. And these two women were still making demands of them.

Those from the other half of the camp especially were talking softly amongst themselves, though that might be because they were already bunched together. What bothered me was that I couldn't quite figure out what the problem was. All Herald had asked for was information. She could have demanded reparations and been well within her rights to do so. Silver, food, their weapons, none of these would have been unfair, but she hadn't asked for anything like that. She had only asked for honesty, and that, for some reason, was still a problem.

One that needed to be dealt with, and while I trusted the sisters to do what they thought best, I wanted this dealt with my way.

"Go to them," I told Kira, "and tell them that I want to talk to Jekrie."

She looked anxiously toward the camp, then nodded to me and walked out. There was some murmuring from the camp when she walked out of the trees, and despite the fact that she was unarmed and dressed in simple clothes, the new tension remained. They had probably guessed that Herald and Mak were not alone, but now the refugees could see that with their own eyes. In this newly nervous atmosphere, Herald turned to Jekrie and said, "You are coming with us. Our patron wants to speak with you."

"Why?" The voice that called out was strong but thick with fear. The question came from Jekrie's woman, who'd come out of her tent with their baby in her arms. "Why does he need to go anywhere?"

I got annoyed. It was obvious that she was just worried for the man who was presumably her husband. The father of her child. But I just wanted the whole situation to be over so that I could focus on other, more important things. And when I got annoyed, Mak *snapped*.

"Because he," she said, punctuating the word by pointing at Jekrie with her spear, "watched his brother cut my guts open! And now my *patron*," she pointed back my way, "needs to make her mind up if you all are free to go on your way!"

"But why must he go? If this woman is watching us, which she must be, sending someone to speak to you, why can't she just come out and talk to him where we can see them?"

"Tinir—" Jekrie pleaded, but Mak cut him off.

"You don't want that," she said darkly. "We are here because *she* does not want to deal with you. She is already annoyed. Don't make her angry!"

"But—" the woman started desperately. The whole camp fell silent when Mak started marching toward her. I was becoming increasingly fed up, which fed into Mak. And the way that Mak had snapped at Ardek had taught me that she could bear a grudge. Mak, I thought, was about to lash out again.

Jekrie quickly got in front of Tinir, backing up with his hands up and careful not to touch her. "Please, Miss! She worries for me! I'll come and make no fuss. Please don't—"

At the same time, Herald caught up and put her hand on Mak's shoulder, stopping her. She said something to Mak that I couldn't hear, then raised her voice. "He will be back. Unharmed. You can believe me, or not, but I swear it."

Tinir didn't protest anymore, but the anxiety didn't leave her eyes. Jekrie turned back to her, grasping her shoulders long enough to place a tender kiss on her forehead, then came with Herald to where I was waiting. Mak brought up the rear without a word, but I could see the irritation on her face.

I'd known in a detached way that she could feel what I felt, and that it affected her. She'd told me as much, and I'd seen it myself. But I hadn't quite understood how it affected her, and the way she'd reacted just then, on the edge of violence just because a worried woman had questioned them, that was a little extreme. We'd need to talk about that . . . sometime. At the moment, I had this Jekrie to deal with.

I walked a little farther away from the camp, leaving Ardek to show them which way I'd gone. I found a nice little clearing not too far away, where I climbed a tree and waited. I didn't try very hard to pick one where I'd be well hidden, and I didn't bother with one I could climb in shadow form either. I picked one of the ridiculously tall ones, where the branches began fifty feet off the ground and I had to either fly up or climb it by claw, hand over foot. I'd made it about two hundred feet up—I could climb pretty damned fast if I wanted to—when the humans walked into the clearing and Herald and Mak, knowing me, stopped and looked around.

And I, obviously, pushed off from the tree, letting myself drop for a hundred feet before I braked hard. I hit the ground a little more heavily than I might have liked, but it caused a satisfying *thump* that probably made me seem larger and heavier than I was.

Jekrie gaped. Then he tried to back away, but Mak held his arm in a firm grip and dug her heels in, and despite her size, he could not escape her. Well, if he really strained he could have probably lifted her off the ground; no matter how much stronger she had become, she was no heavier than she'd been. If anything she was a lot lighter from all the healing she'd done, and he looked quite strong. But it looked like just the act of holding him back was enough for him to stop struggling, and in a moment he just stood, struck by fear and awe.

Meanwhile, I sat up to my full height and opened my wings a little, for the sake of drama. I waited until he'd gone still, then spoke.

"Jekrie," I said, and he jerked in Mak's grip. "You've attacked my people with no provocation, and wounded one so gravely that only the efforts of two healers saved her life. I know your reasons, and I sympathize, to some degree. I am willing to put all of this behind us, and leave you to mourn your dead with no further consequences. All I ask is that you answer some questions. Can you do that for me?"

"You . . . are you a forest demon?" Jekrie stammered.

That annoyed me, which annoyed Mak. She tightened her grip on Jekrie's arm, and he stifled a groan.

"I am *not* a *demon*," I growled. "I am a *dragon*. I'll leave it to you to decide if that's better or worse, but it *does not matter*. Will you answer my questions, or will you keep wasting my time until I stop being nice?"

"Dragon," Jekrie whispered, staring at me as though he expected what he saw to change.

"Take your time," Herald said. "Just not too long. She has been rather annoyed lately."

That snapped Jekrie out of it. Instead of answering my question, his approach was to fall to his knees in the leaves and raise his hands in supplication. "Please," he said. "My people. They are innocent. They—"

"Are safe," I told him bluntly. I couldn't deny that I enjoyed seeing him crawling in the dirt before me, but I was just done with the whole business. "As are you, as long as you just do what I tell you and answer a few simple questions!"

"Yes. Yes! I will tell you anything you want to know!"

"Good!" Finally we were getting somewhere. "Why were the other group—the Sweet Creek people, I guess—why were they so unhappy about you answering some questions?"

"We . . ." Jekrie hesitated. All that and he still hesitated! But a look at my unamused face was all it took for him to spill.

"We are outlaws," he said heavily, then quickly added, "for no crime of our own! Our forefathers refused to pay the council's tax, and when the collectors came they fled north. Council did nothing for us, why should we give a single coin, you see? And we were fine, living in peace outside the law. But now the monsters are growing more numerous, and bolder, and we . . . we lost so many. So many."

"Since when? And what kind of monsters?" I asked brusquely. Since he didn't seem to respond to patience and gentleness, I chose to be harsh.

"Only animals, to begin. They've been getting more common over the years, but some months ago they began to come far south in numbers like we'd never seen or heard of. Then goblins. Fresh ones, and wild, not like the tribes we've dealt with before. They steal and destroy, and make no bargains, and we think there must be a nest somewhere near our village, perhaps more than one."

"So the goblins were what drove you out?"

"No. We could have handled them. There were more of us, and some of us skilled hunters and fighters. But then . . ." Jekrie's voice shuddered, "then the trolls came. That was a week ago, I suppose. Some of us tried to fight, but all who stood before them died. Sweet Creek they laid to ruin, and my village, Piter's Clearing, they made that their home. We who survived took what we could and ran. A brave few of us came back the next night, as they slept, and took a few more precious things. Then we went south."

Mak, Herald, and I shared a look. Trolls. The ones we had encountered had been farther south than normal, according to my companions, and that was many miles north of the farthest known human settlements.

"How far north of here is Piter's Clearing and Sweet Creek?" I asked.

"I honestly can't tell you for sure," Jekrie said. "The going was hard, with so much baggage, and the children, few though they are. We had little food, and hunting and foraging along the way was necessary. We would have been lucky to make ten miles on the best day, and far from all of that southward. If I were to guess . . . forty miles, perhaps forty-five, if you pardon my ignorance."

Trolls. First the scholars, then a big fuck-off bear, and now this. More trolls. Big, stinking bastards who collected shiny things like magpies. Forty miles or less north of my mountain, and possibly moving south. "God *dammit!*" I growled. I wanted to rage. I wanted to disembowel Jekrie for bringing me this news, and throw his corpse into the camp to show how displeased I was with their very presence and what it represented. I wanted to fly north and find the trolls, and fight them and kill them, *now*, without delay. I wanted to *destroy*, to lay waste to the countryside until the council brought me the Night Blossom in chains to vent my anger on until whatever fueled it was sated.

I did none of these things. I spread my wings and growled and did . . . something, something that caused Jekrie and Herald to fall to their knees and Mak to grit her teeth until her jaw creaked, but I stayed where I was. I did not rush off like a lunatic. I did not kill the person I had promised safety. Instead, I sat where I was, closed my eyes, and said slowly, "I just want to deal with the Night Blossom. I want to take her gold, display her shredded corpse in the main square, and fly back home to spend the rest of the year just relaxing with my newly wealthy friends. Is that so much to ask? Why do I have to deal with these constant goddamn *interruptions?*"

I staggered as a spike of pain smashed through my head, accompanied by a wave of fatigue and nausea. This happened at about the same time I noticed that we were all shrouded in darkness in the middle of the morning. I had *not* meant to do that. It had just kind of happened, and that just angered me further. Things outside of my control kept throwing me off. Now I was having trouble controlling myself, and it was infuriating.

The darkness around us deepened. "*Draka,*" Herald groaned from her knees. "*Please!*"

That made me realize what I was doing. Herald. I was hurting *Herald!* I released my shadows, snatching my tendrils back. I would have been forced to do so in a few moments anyway, when either the pain grew too strong or I passed out from exhaustion, but I did it consciously. And like *that*, everything went back to normal.

Well, the light came back, and Herald slowly got to her feet. Mak, however, was looking at me slack-jawed, with what I could only call adoration in her eyes. I wouldn't have been surprised if she'd fallen to her knees next to Jekrie, who had prostrated himself before me, his head in the dirt as he fought for words. I liked that. My head was pounding, but that display of fear and respect, that . . . oh, that was good.

When Jekrie found his words, what he said was, "Please! Great one! I beg you. For myself, for my family, for all those who are with us. Great one, mighty dragon! I beg you for your mercy and protection!"

And through the haze of fatigue and lingering pain, all I could think to say to his submission was what was in my flattered heart.

"Yes!"

Something fell into place inside me, a feeling of wholeness and rightness. And while I couldn't tell if Jekrie knew what he had done on behalf of his group, I did, and as I grinned, I could see on Mak's face that she did too. There was apprehension there, a worry about stepping into the unknown, perhaps, but also a satisfaction that mirrored my own.

There was no walking this back, for either Jekrie or myself. Whoever this little band of humans had been, and whoever they were now, they were *mine*.

CHAPTER THIRTY-EIGHT

Sympathy

While Herald and Mak returned to the camp with Jekrie, I remained among the trees. I didn't feel that it was the right time to reveal myself to the group at large, but it would need to happen. The only question was whether it would be sooner or later.

"What happened?" Kira asked me as I joined her and Ardek. "What did you talk about?"

"You should start working on your Karakani," I told her. "We're going to have some new guests at the mountain."

"You're taking them in?" Her tone told me that she hadn't expected that outcome at all, but by the way her lips curled, she was clearly pleased. I told myself that I shouldn't be surprised. I'd been told several times that she cared about people, no matter who they were. Seeing the pitiful state of the northerners must have twisted her heart.

"Jekrie asked for protection, on behalf of the others. I decided to grant his request."

Kira thought about that, with a look in her eye that I found hard to decipher. "I cannot imagine what you might gain from this that's of any value to you," she said after many long seconds. "But you have more mercy in you than I would have expected."

"They're neither slavers, bandits, nor raiders," I said, pointing out the obvious for the sake of contrast to her own group, which I'd destroyed with extreme prejudice. "Some of them made an incredibly stupid mistake, but that sin punished itself. The rest of them . . . I don't know. It felt right."

I wasn't about to tell her, of all people, just how good it had felt to *claim* these people. She'd been anxious about dragon worship as it was. Better not to give her any ideas that hadn't occurred to her already.

"Does helping them salve your conscience?" she asked.

I snorted. "My conscience is clear, no matter what you may think." It wasn't entirely true, but it was close enough as far as she was concerned.

While we talked, Jekrie and the sisters walked into the camp to deliver the terms I had laid out for him. "I have made a bargain," Jekrie announced, raising his voice so that all of the gathered people, who'd returned when word went out that he was back, could hear him. "The . . . patron of these two women has offered us a place to make a new home, and protection from man and beast. She can deliver, of this I am sure. In return, we must obey her, unless her demands are cruel."

That was the one concession I had made.

"Choose for yourselves. Come with me, or go your own way. Know that once you accept this bargain, you cannot back out. But know also that there is no other place in the south that is safe from the law of Karakan. We have until sundown."

"None of this is negotiable," Herald added, her tone brooking no argument. "You either accept the terms, or you leave our territory. There are many villages scattered around the forest, with good people. They may take you in, if you are lucky, or they may treat you as the outlaws that you are, fair or not. But if you go, do not expect to be easily welcomed back. My lady does not look kindly on those who refuse her generosity."

After that we waited. The refugees broke camp, since it was clear that no matter what decision they reached, they would not be staying where they were. Two small groups returned from the forest during the afternoon, and once they did, Rib and Pot joined Kira, Ardek, and myself. Herald and Mak stayed with Jekrie, helping to break the camp and talking about things I couldn't hear.

There were many things I could have done with the time. I spent some of it napping, but there was one thing I wanted to do that I hadn't found the time for until then.

"Kira," I said, getting her attention. She'd been listening to Pot, Rib, and Ardek telling increasingly dirty jokes, with no sign of understanding.

"Yes?" she said, turning on her rock to face me.

"The others told me that you recognized the name Night Blossom. Tell me about it."

A thoughtful look crossed her face, and she said, "That is true, in part, at least. I remember hearing the commander mention someone named Blossom, though I do not know or recognize *Night*."

"What was the context? What was your commander talking about?"

"Something about interrupted deliveries, I think. I assumed that it was about logistics, and it did not seem to affect us, so I didn't listen too closely. It was when we had only recently crossed into Karakani territory, I remember that much, and that the commander was annoyed and ordered one of the lieutenants to contact this Blossom. I didn't think much of it. But then I heard someone mention the same name and I wondered if it was Karakani, so I asked if it was a common one. Since you're asking me, I'm guessing it's someone important."

"You could say that," I told her. "She's a crime lord who tried her hand at slaving, and someone I want to find very, very much."

"I don't suppose you'll try to convince her to change her ways," Kira said, looking down at my talons. I followed her eyes and realized that I'd been unconsciously scratching long, deep furrows in the dirt.

"You're right about that," I said, stilling myself. I'd never been a fidgeter, but these last few days had me on edge. "This woman doesn't deserve any second chances. As soon as I get my hands on her, she can start counting her remaining minutes, and hoping that there aren't too many of them."

Kira sighed and looked away, clearly uncomfortable with how sanguine I was. "You said she'd taken slaves?" she asked after a while.

"Yeah. Whole villages. Keeping children and young adults, discarding anyone who was too old or with permanent injuries. Her people told the . . . suppliers to deal with them however they wanted."

"That's awful," Kira said softly, and I could see her own guilt on her face. She was barely more than a slave herself, but she'd still been a part of the same kind of cruelty.

"Yeah, it is," I agreed. "That would have been reason enough to get rid of her. But then she decided to hurt my friends and insult me, which got her bumped from 'deliver for public execution' to 'try to leave some identifiable chunks' in my book."

Kira turned a little green, and that finally *did* ping my conscience just a little.

"Kira," I said. "This woman is a monster. I don't know how much the sisters have told you, but what she had her people do to them . . . Think about this: She calmly told one of her men to break some of Herald's fingers if Mak wouldn't stop crying. All right? And that's where you can start from. It only gets worse. There is nothing I can do to her that she doesn't deserve."

"I see." Kira kind of folded in on herself, and something stirred inside me. She looked . . . what? Sad, sure. Resigned, maybe. Tired, sure, though this was the middle of the night for her, so that was fair enough. But mostly she just looked very small in that moment. Like she'd been through a lot of shit that she'd had no control over, and that she didn't deserve. And like she knew that it was going to keep happening, and there was no way, no matter what she did, that she could stop it.

Some of that was my fault. It was done in anger, and I'd felt completely justified, but I doubted it made any difference to her.

She'd made a choice, once. She'd wanted to do the right thing, to help her people, and I got the feeling that that was the last real choice she'd been allowed to make. And then they'd made her a party to unimaginable suffering. She, who just wanted to help. To help anyone and everyone in front of her, even the people who'd abused her.

I did the first thing that came to mind. I couldn't tell how welcome or not it would be, but I walked straight up to her and wrapped my wing around her, pressing her against my chest. I would have used my neck, but she looked so small that it didn't seem possible without lying down on the ground, and whatever I felt in that moment, I couldn't do that. Not in front of her. She stiffened, then seemed to realize what this was and relaxed a fraction.

"I won't ask you to do anything, yeah?" I said gently.

"If you say so."

"I really won't. I promise you that. This is something we have to do, Herald and Mak and me, but I won't ask you to hurt anyone. Or to help us hurt anyone. That's over. Okay? I can't let you go, but . . . I won't ever ask you to be a part of that. You'll never have to help hurt anyone again, as long as you're with me. If nothing else, I can do that for you."

I felt her lean into me, slowly, tentatively. Just a little, but enough that I felt it. "Thank you," she said, so softly that I barely heard it.

"I'll have Ardek and the cousins take you back to the mountain to sleep, yeah? You know how to open the gate?"

"I do, but . . . can I stay a moment?"

I looked around, and immediately felt like an idiot. What was I worried about? My image? Rib and Pot were off somewhere. Ardek had seen the whole thing, though he presumably hadn't understood a word of our conversation. He sat with his back to a giant tree, carefully whittling at a branch he'd picked up. He was studiously avoiding looking at us, but, what? Was he going to make fun of me for showing a crumb of empathy? Not likely.

"Take all the time you need," I told Kira, and wrapped my other wing around her. "There's no rush."

I filled in Rib and Pot on what Kira had told me about the Night Blossom. Then I sent Kira home with them and Ardek, just like I'd said I would. They couldn't talk to each other, but Kira didn't need that to get along with people, and Rib and Pot were good with gestures. They'd be fine.

By the time sunset rolled around no one had loudly denounced me and stormed off, but there were definitely some differences in opinion among the refugees. Both Herald and Mak had popped in among the trees to talk a few times, and their combined opinion was that we'd lose a handful of people, but not many. And they were right. Two young men and one woman—a brother-sister pair and her husband, I thought—took their things, said their goodbyes, and vanished into the forest. They preferred their undisputed freedom over safety, and I could respect that. None of them were among the party that had attacked us. They knew neither who I was, nor where we were taking the rest, so I let them go in peace.

I agonized over that for a moment or two, but at that moment it seemed like the option I'd be happiest with in the long run. I considered following them and putting the ever-living fear of me in them, but that would just invite one or all of them to grow some gonads and a hero complex in the future, which might invite all sorts of trouble. And *that* possibility meant that if I suspected any one of them of not being entirely, irreversibly cowed, I'd have to kill all of them. And I just didn't feel like I had it in me. It would be practical, sure, but it would be utterly monstrous. On a different day, that might not have been a problem. I still swung between the extremes of my combined self, depending on the circumstances. I had days when I felt no concern about the possibility of becoming a completely pragmatic, practical monster. But after spending most of the day watching a small group of people gather the remnants of their shattered lives, and after my little moment with Kira, this was most definitely not such a day. So I watched them wander off in the general direction of Pine Hill and a bunch of other small settlements, and silently wished them well.

The remaining refugees, unable or unwilling to leave the group, decided to trust Jekrie and take a chance on me. Or rather, on Herald and Mak's mysterious patron, whoever that may be. They'd find out soon enough, but for the time being I was content to let them wonder. I'd let them settle in and get comfortable before I showed them what they'd gotten themselves into.

In the end, as night set in, Mak and Herald led twelve adults—five men and seven women—of various ages through the trees toward the mountain and the gate. With them came one boy of about six and two girls, one maybe four years old and the other Jekrie's infant daughter. Having kids around changed the game a little. Not that I'd been planning on throwing any lives away, or even making them needlessly uncomfortable, but I had a soft spot for kids. I'd never wanted any, but I'd always found them fun to be around, as long as they weren't mine. All of the fun and barely any of the responsibility was exactly how I'd liked it.

With the kids around I felt a little more motivated to actually live up to my side of the bargain. As they walked among the trees, I kept watch over them from the shadows. It might have been excessive, but they were mine now, and I'd be damned if I let any of them stray or get eaten by wolves or something like that.

I was going to set them up at the scholars' campsite outside the gate to start with, and then we'd start looking into setting up more permanent homes for them. It was a good spot. Plenty of game and forage around, and a stream nearby large enough to have fish in it meant that they wouldn't go hungry, and there was plenty of stone and timber to build with. Fields might be a problem, but since they were from the far north, I doubted they'd done any large-scale farming anyway.

And there was, of course, the gate. I'd said that I'd keep them safe, and being able to put several tons of rock between them and any threat if necessary would go a long way toward that.

It wouldn't be fair to say that I was second guessing myself, but I was very, very aware of the fact that this would change things significantly. I had been relying partially on secrecy to keep my people and my stuff safe. That wasn't really going to be possible anymore if I set up a small village right at my doorstep, and especially not when that village was made up of outlaws. While I was sure that detail could be fixed, any village invited visitors. At a minimum, once people became aware of the village's existence, there would be adventurers showing up looking for resupply, and there was always the possibility of the council's taxmen, which had been the thing that drove these people's forebears north in the first place. And it wasn't like this place was entirely unknown. Enough people knew that there had most definitely not been a village there as little as a month or two ago, so someone would start asking questions.

I'd had a problem foisted on me, and my solution was to invite a bunch of new problems. So, I wasn't second guessing myself. Second guessing would lead to doubt, and I had too much shit going on to be able to afford that. But a big part of me was asking, trying to figure out, rationally analyzing, really, why the hell I was doing this.

As we neared the mountain Herald dropped back, out of earshot of the group, and said, "*I truly cannot wait to hear what your plan is here.*" It was pretty impressive how she found me in the darkness.

"*I am flattered that you think I have a plan,*" I said wryly. "*I did the only thing that felt right. Beyond this moment we will need to take things as they come.*"

"*We, is it?*" Herald said, radiating eagerness.

"*You approve,*" I said, and she gave me a single firm nod.

"*I believe that they will be useful more than they will be a nuisance. As long as we can keep them in line, of course, but I do not see that being a problem. And, well . . . it was the humane, if not necessarily the human, thing to do. I was glad to see it.*"

"*That is a relief,*" I told her. Her opinion meant the world to me, and having her support made me even more certain that I'd made the right choice.

"*That was quite a trick, by the way. Back in the clearing. But I would thank you to never do it again when I might be affected. Part of me wanted to scream and run, and the rest of me hoped desperately that if I just sat completely still and silent you might not notice me in the dark, insane as that idea was. And I know that you love me! I cannot imagine what it was like for Jekrie, and Mak . . . Based on what I felt, I am beyond impressed that she remained on her feet.*"

"*Have you told her?*" I asked.

"What, and let her get a big head about it?" She smiled. *"But you are right. It is good to see her proud again, and I should encourage that. Though I assume that her new advancement has something to do with it."*

"You may be right," I agreed. *"Or it may simply be that she no longer fears me. Or the dark, perhaps. Still, you really should celebrate her advancement."*

"Do you know what it does?" she asked, though I got the feeling she already had an answer of her own and just wanted to know what I thought.

"Based on what she has told me . . ." I said, thinking about it. *"She is stronger, clearly. More confident. And she says that Tekereteki comes more easily to her. I would be surprised if she was not more resilient and stealthier as well."*

"Yes?" Herald said, waiting for me to state the conclusion she had already come to herself.

"I think that she has the effects of all my minor advancements," I said. It just fit. Her vision of growing in my shadow, the effects she'd reported . . . *"Reduced perhaps, but that is what I think. And you, I see, have drawn the same conclusion."*

"I have," she said, her smile turning into a full-toothed grin. *"And I could not be more pleased for her. It is an amazing advancement. Do you think it will work as you grow?"*

"I can only assume so based on what she saw," I mused. *"I should think about that next time."* Then I remembered something, and it was my turn to grin. *"One of the choices I have had, ever since my first threshold, is physical greatness. Improving all my physical attributes at some unknown cost. Including size. Imagine if I take that, and it affects Mak?"*

"You would not dare!" Herald said, her face stormy with mock outrage. *"She is my sweet, tiny little big sister, and I will not have some lizard with delusions of grandeur ruin that!"*

"Lizard with . . ." I sputtered back. *"Those are brave words for someone in head-ripping range!"*

"Try it!" she challenged, then reached out and scratched the scar where my left horn had been. My remaining horn curved back over my neck and was about as long as Herald's palm. I leaned into her hand. It wasn't like it itched or anything, but the scritches felt really good.

"I accept your tribute, mammal," I purred. *"All is forgiven."*

After a bit she stopped scratching and instead ran her thumb with some firm pressure over the scar. *"You have a little bump that has not been here before,"* she said, leaning in to look closer in the dim moonlight. *"I wonder if the horn is growing back."*

"I almost hope not. One horn missing looks fearsome, in a way. One big one and one tiny one is going to look dumb."

"I think it will look cute," Herald declared.

"*Cute*," I repeated flatly, trying to make that gel with what I knew of my appearance. Nine or ten feet from my nose to the tip of my tail. Powerful, batlike wings. A snout full of wicked teeth, brutally strong limbs that ended in hands and feet with claws that could shred flesh without a second thought. All of this covered in sleek, matte scales of *just* the right black to let me vanish into deep shadow or against the night sky.

If a tiny horn could look cute on that . . .

I bumped her shoulder with my head. To my great satisfaction it made her stumble. *"I'll take it."*

CHAPTER THIRTY-NINE

Most Precious

When we reached the gate—or "The Gate," as I'd started thinking of it, being the most important of them—I hung back to make sure that there was no immediate trouble. Everyone was tired, but it looked like the advance party hadn't been idle. Ardek must have been shown where we'd stashed our supplies, because he, Rib, and Pot welcomed the refugees with a meal, which immediately improved the mood of the ragged group.

I was lying on the rocks looking down at the camp that was springing up around the fire, with Herald sitting beside me. "*Go eat,*" I told her, as I heard her stomach growl. I wasn't sure, but it might have been over a day since she'd last eaten. And I hadn't heard a single complaint out of her. "*Then tell Mak that she is in charge, and come back here. And bring one of the lightstones! I will take a nap.*"

She gave my head an affectionate rub, rocked onto her feet, and ran off without a word.

I woke to gentle snoring. I blinked and yawned as I cleared the sleep out of my head, and felt a pressure against my side. Herald was stretched out half alongside me, half laying on me, with my wing covering her from shoulder to mid-thigh. I must have covered her up unconsciously at some point.

"*Hey, wake up,*" I whispered and rustled my wing a bit. She groaned unhappily and snuggled in closer.

I snaked my neck around so that my mouth was right by her ear, and said, "*It is time to go flying!*"

The back of her head nearly caught me in the chin as Herald shoved herself up to look at me. "*Really?*" she asked, looking torn between excitement and anxiety, like she wasn't sure if what I'd said was true but desperately wanted it to be.

"*No time like the present,*" I said, and went to rise. "*Let me get up, then climb on my back.*"

Herald scrambled to get on before I changed my mind.

"All right," I said, *"you are . . . a little taller than Rib, but this should be fine. Try to . . . Right, lock your arms under mine. Good, now see if you can hook your legs over mine."*

Herald held on as best she could without getting in the way of my wings. Her torso wasn't quite as long as my entire body, sans neck and tail, but she was undeniably big. I tested my wings and found that I could move them without too much trouble. Flapping jostled her a little, but not enough to be dangerous, and as long as I didn't try anything too aerobatic, there wouldn't be any problems.

"We will be going to a thousand feet," I told her as I approached the edge, *"maybe twelve hundred. I am not completely sure, to be honest. It does not look so high from down here, with thousands of feet of mountain left to go above our destination, but I think that you will find it plenty high enough."*

"And if I do not? If I want to go higher?"

"Then there is always tomorrow, and the day after, and thousands and thousands of days after that. Let us not get carried away. I am still not used to this."

"I will consider that a promise," she said giddily, and pressed her cheek against my neck. *"Go on! Fly! I have waited long enough already!"*

"How old are you, twelve?" I said, but I loved it. I was as excited as she was. This was something I had been wanting to do ever since I first began to consider Herald my friend, and only the fear of hurting her had been holding me back. Now that I'd had a successful test run—several, in fact—it was about damn time!

"Hold on!"

I leaped.

This time I was ready for the extra weight right from the start, and my wings beat powerfully, driving us up and over the camp below. Herald locked in, her arms around my neck and her legs behind my own squeezing hard enough that even through my fortitude and my natural resilience, I had to fight the urge to tell her to ease up, because that was one thing I definitely did not want her to do. As I went higher and faster and began to turn she gave off a high-pitched, jaw-clenching "Iiih!" that went on and on, a noise of excitement, fear, and absolute, exhilarated *joy.*

I could feel how securely she was holding on. Barring something terrible and unforeseen, she wasn't going anywhere, and I binned any idea of holding back. I beat harder and faster, picking up speed, even as I climbed and passed the point where I should have turned for the cave. Instead, I kept going north and climbed another thousand feet before I leveled out and made a long, lazy turn. Herald laughed and whooped as I began a gliding descent that gradually became steeper until we were hurtling downward at well over a hundred miles per hour, the sound of my locked wings tearing through the night air loud enough to drown out Herald's maniacal screaming. I only leveled out again as I hit the highest treetops, the forest a dark blur beneath us as we approached the mountain at a speed that, to me, was familiar by now but, without a doubt, was several times faster than Herald had ever gone in her life.

My approach was near perfect. I had almost enough momentum to carry me to the ledge, but with Herald on my back I wasn't quite as sleekly aerodynamic as I might have been. Instead, I had to work for the last few hundred feet, setting us down in what would have been a textbook landing if anyone had ever written a book about dragon flight.

Herald didn't so much climb as roll off me, and lay on the thin soil of the ledge kicking and hiccupping with laughter for over a minute before her brain switched back on completely and she sprang to her feet.

"Thank you!" she said, beside herself with the whirlwind emotions our short flight had stirred up. I could see tears in her eyes. It might have just been the wind, but that seemed unlikely. "Oh, gods and Mercies, Draka, thank you! That was . . ." She wiped at her face and gave a shuddering laugh. "Thank you."

Then she fidgeted, like she didn't know what to do with her hands, before grabbing my head and kissing me hard right between the horns. "Incredible doesn't . . ." She pulled back to look at me, her normally careful diction gone. "I can't—I just can't! Thank you!"

As for myself, I was almost giddy with happiness. All I could do was grin back at her. Our first flight had been everything I'd wanted it to be, and more. Nothing had gone wrong, she'd been mad with excitement the whole time, and now she was overflowing with love and gratitude. What else could I possibly hope for?

I stepped up and wrapped my neck around her, and just stayed like that until I'd calmed myself. "That was just the beginning," I promised her once I could talk again. "Then there's tomorrow, and the day after that, and thousands of tomorrows after that."

"You promise?"

"I promise. But that was only half of what I wanted to show you!"

"Your lair?" she asked, just as excited as she had been for the flight.

"Lair, nest . . . my home. And my hoard! God, you've got to see my hoard!"

"Promise that you'll let me leave?"

"Funny." I said it as drily as I could manage while still grinning like a big, scaly idiot. "Come on. It's this way."

Herald was suitably impressed with my lair. She'd sat down on the mat of coins, idly picking up jewelry and knick-knacks that I'd found in the bandits' loot or the Night Blossom's stash. *"I knew that you must have a pretty good stash of coin by now,"* she said dreamily as she ran her fingers through them. *"And I suppose that there was probably more than this in the chest we found. But seeing it all spread out like this . . . Oh!"*

Her voice rose in delight as she picked up a nodule of stone and silver. I kept them all collected in a little pile where I could see them easily. *"This must be from the mines where we first met!"*

As for me, I was having trouble answering. The moment I'd led Herald into the bulge on the tunnel where I made my nest, there was a feeling of *rightness*. She had joked about me not letting her leave once she was there, and it had all been in good fun. But right then, seeing her there surrounded by my *other precious possessions*, was stirring up all kinds of distinctly draconic feelings.

"Yeah," I said. My throat felt dry and thick, like the humidity was too low. Which was ridiculous, of course, with water literally dripping off the walls. *"They are very important to me."*

"That is cute." She turned and gave me a bright smile, warm and sweet in the golden light of the lightstone. *"You are sentimental!"*

"I suppose that I am," I said, padding forward and lying down next to her, causing the scattered coins to rustle pleasantly. *"They remind me of how I met my first and best friend in this world."*

She settled in, draping one arm over my back and snuggling in tight. In the silence I heard her sniffle a little, then she said, *"I am so glad that I met you. And not only because we might have all died if you had not been there. Despite . . . what happened, I still would not wish for things to have gone any other way. I love you, Draka. You know that, right?"*

"I know, Herald. I love you too." Whatever influence I had over her, I had to believe that her love was real. Sometimes that was the only thing that kept me human. If I allowed myself to think that it was all just an illusion, some kind of magical manipulation messing with her mind and making her think that she cared for me, I might lose myself completely. And that idea was too sweet as it was. It would be so easy to abandon any thought of right or wrong or consideration of other people's feelings or wellbeing. To just take and kill and dominate as I pleased. To just let myself be a dragon, fully and forever.

"Goodnight, Draka," my dearest friend said as we lay in my nest, surrounded by my hoard.

I covered her with my wing and tucked my head in. *"Sleep well, Herald,"* I said. *My precious*, I added silently, then closed my eyes and let my worries drift away.

It was a struggle to let her leave.

We slept well into the morning. We were back to somewhat regular hours rather than the night shift I'd have preferred, but it couldn't be helped. Not with a whole little community of new people who needed looking after and guidance from my humans. I felt good, as I always did after resting in my nest, and Herald was spry and energetic from the moment she opened her eyes. Whether that was any effect of the hoard or if she just had a really good night's sleep, I couldn't tell.

The problem came when it was time to go. I planned to take her out the same way I had with Rib and Pot—through the pit. I needed her to see it, so that she'd have a picture of where I'd come from, and she was curious and eager to go. It was just . . . I didn't want her to. I had no problem leaving her, beyond the normal pang of regret that came every time we parted, but I didn't want her to leave.

The connection was obvious enough that even I couldn't close my eyes to it. There was nothing in the world dearer to me than her. She was my *most precious possession*, as unpleasant as that thought was. It was an enormous relief that I hadn't received an advancement when she stepped over the very fuzzy line that defined the border of what was considered my hoard. If that had happened, I didn't know if I could have handled it.

As it was, Herald must have wondered what the hell was happening. We had been awake for several minutes, she *knew* that I had been awake all that time, and I hadn't said a word.

"*Draka?*" she said in the dim light. Her voice was steady, but there was an undercurrent of tension in it. "*This is very cozy, and I do not want to get up either, but I think that it is about time.*"

The possessiveness, the urge to just keep her there, was so bad that I considered not charging the lightstone, in a lame attempt to keep her from finding her way out on her own. As though the light of the glow slime wasn't enough for her enhanced eyes. It didn't occur to me to use actual, physical force to prevent her from leaving—this was Herald, after all—but if she stayed on her own accord . . .

"*Draka?*" I couldn't look at her, but when she spoke my name I heard just the barest tremor.

It was like being plunged into freezing water. *What the hell are you thinking, woman?* I asked myself and grabbed the stone. With barely a thought I pushed some magic into it, illuminating the space for her. "*It is,*" I agreed, getting to my feet. "*Do you need anything? Food, water? I have firewood stashed at the entrance, and the steel and flint. I could get a goat . . .*"

I was stalling. I knew it, and I still kept going. The whole situation, being there with Herald, being in my home with a friend at all, was just too familiar. Too comfortable. It reminded me so much of what I used to have, something I hadn't thought of for weeks, maybe months at that point, and leaving it behind even temporarily was, frankly, scary. What if this was the last time, I wondered. What if I never got to bring Herald there again, and that was the last time I could feel, in some little way, normal?

"*No, that is all right.*" There was a relief in her voice, the lack of a tension that I never wanted to cause again. "*I can hold out for a few hours, if you still want to show me this pit and the tunnels. But if you would rather go for another flight . . .*"

She trailed off, and it was clear what her first choice was. Curious as she had been about the pit, she was as hooked on flying as I was.

"*We will go through the pit,*" I told her. "*We have the whole day in front of us. Do you have anything warm to wear? I could take you over the mountains, if you are brave enough.*"

She gasped in mock horror and swatted me playfully on the head. "*Do not impugn my courage!*" she commanded, and I cringed before her wrath.

"*All right, all right!*" I said placatingly, and we began the short walk to the crack in the wall and the pit.

Herald was not a climber. Not the way that Rib and Pot were, at least. She took one look over the edge of the pit and simply refused to go.

"*If you want me down there,*" she declared, "*you're taking me.*" And so I did. I leaped in there with her on my back, not daring to hesitate with her watching.

When she'd clambered off me she was grinning.

"*Was this just a ruse to ride me again?*" I asked her indignantly, and her grin grew wider.

"*Perhaps,*" she said. "*Although, I really am not very good at climbing rocks. And I remember you telling me how you ended up here. I would rather not see if it works the other way.*"

"*That is for the best. I do not think my people would handle a dragon showing up very well. Here is what I wanted to show you,*" I said, illuminating one of the stones ringing the pit so she could see the patterns carved on it. "*Do you have any thoughts about it?*"

"*This is definitely an enchantment!*" she said excitedly and took the light from me, moving it this way and that around the carved stone. "*I am not familiar with most of the patterns, although . . .*" She traced one of the lines with a finger. "*This links the stone to the next one, I think. Very common for large enchantments. I have mostly read about enchantments on items, but I have a book about famous enchanted buildings that has some diagrams. I should bring it here so I can compare!*"

"*Any time you want,*" I told her. "*And above the tunnel entrance?*"

She went over and looked as closely as she could at the keystone of the arch. "*Some kind of sealing, perhaps?*" she said uncertainly. "*Also linked to the other stones. I have seen an enchanted keystone used to keep heat in or out, but . . . that is unlikely to be what this one does.*"

"*Not much difference in temperature throughout these caves and tunnels, no,*" I said. "*But if you ever want to return here to study the carvings, just tell me. Anything you can tell me about them could help me understand what happened here.*"

"If I were an enchanter, I would have some intuitive understanding just from look-ing at the patterns," she said, her voice heavy with longing. *"But that is decades off."* She reached up and ran the tips of her fingers over the patterns. *"If ever."*

"You will get it. I am sure that you will. Now . . . it is a long walk down the tunnel."

We walked most of the distance in silence. It was rare for our silences to be uncomfortable, and the walk started out fine, but the mood shifted subtly until Herald spoke up.

"About what happened back there . . ." she said, clearly no more eager to talk about this than I was.

"In the pit?" I answered, knowing full well that wasn't what she meant. And she knew that I knew, so she just ignored me.

"Before. Was there . . . Was I in any danger?" She kept her voice carefully neutral, but I could smell just the slightest trickle of fear coming off her. It hurt, and I immediately got defensive.

"Do you really need to ask that?" I said, not looking at her. It was the guilt talk-ing, but on some level I had just assumed that she trusted me implicitly, no matter what. Or that dragon-magic fuckery made it impossible for her to think ill of me.

Actually, the fact that she could even ask that question was a small relief.

"I do," she said. The fear was still there, but she responded to my tone with firm confidence. *"I need to hear you say it."*

"No," I said. *"You were never in any danger. My mind was struggling to find a way to convince you to stay, but I would not have prevented you from leaving. I could not. Not you. Never you."*

I stopped, sitting down and looking at her. *"I want to be very clear, Herald. If I ever do anything to hurt you, if I even defend myself against you . . . if that happens, I am gone. I am not me anymore, and you need to get as far away from whatever I have become as possible."*

She searched my eyes for long seconds. *"You really mean that."* It was a decla-ration of faith, delivered with complete certainty.

"I do."

"You could not hurt me even if you wanted to. If you had to."

"No."

"Why? What makes me different from Mak, or anyone else?"

"You are . . . you." It was a lame answer, but how else could I explain it? I was as bound to her as she was to me. There was an undeniable imbalance of power, true, but I couldn't imagine abusing it, so did it really matter? When she deferred to me because she trusted and loved me? How could I properly explain just how important she had been to me these past months?

"From day one you chose to trust me," I tried instead. *"When the others saw me as a threat or an opportunity, you saw me as a potential friend. When they were gone*

and you feared for their safety, you came to me for help. When I approached you all, I appealed to your greed, and you, Herald, instead responded with genuine interest and curiosity and kindness. I barely dared to hope for anything and expected nothing, and you gave me everything."

Herald had listened silently, but when I paused for breath, a little hiccupping sob popped out of her. She wiped at her eyes, grinned at least as wide as she'd had after our flight, then threw herself forward to wrap her arms around me.

"What kind of monster could feel anything but love for you, Herald?" I asked softly, and my own tears began to fall.

CHAPTER FORTY

The Post

It took us a while to get back to the others.

I'd been keeping a lot of emotions bottled up. Whether I'd been doing so subconsciously or if it was still the dragon side of me suppressing things, once I started crying it was like a dam broke, and I had a lot to let out. Besides that, I was just so *goddamn relieved* that I hadn't messed everything up. Herald, on her part, was quite overwhelmed by my declaration that she was the best and most important thing in the world to me. We ended up just sitting there in the tunnel, hugging and crying, until the lightstone faded. It was nice. It had been a long time since I had a good, happy cry. And since dragons did not cry, it reaffirmed that there was still a lot of human in me.

But return we did, if somewhat reluctantly. Herald enjoyed the drop into the throne room just as much as I'd expected, and then it was back to the hub and down the tunnel to the gate. If someone was there who wasn't supposed to be, I figured I'd deal with that if and when it happened. But no one was. I could only suppose that they were too clever to go into the forbidden, pitch-black tunnel on day one.

The next two days weren't very interesting. I made sure to get some sparring in with Mak, but otherwise my humans were busy with the newcomers—getting to know our new neighbors, getting them settled in, and keeping them in line. Ardek, surprisingly—or perhaps not so surprisingly, given his "love me" advancements—became a useful link, helping smooth any friction when either of the sisters found it necessary to go dictatorial on them. He even had the two camps getting along better, stepping in to soothe tempers when things got heated between the people of Piter's Clearing and Sweet Creek. "It's like when two gangs join up, right?" he told me. "You've just got to get people working together and distract them from the bullshit."

Herald and I didn't have time to go for another flight. There was just too much to do, but whenever she knew that I was nearby, she'd sneak off to reassure me that things between us were better than ever. She was worried that I'd think she was avoiding me, which I thought was very sweet of her.

On day four, after I'd "invited" the northerners to stay with us, Lalia arrived. She came in not long after noon, looking harried and riding a lathered Windfall. I found this out when I was awoken from a wonderful nap by a commotion in the camp. The newcomers did not take the arrival of a hard-riding, armored woman calmly, with roughly half of them panicking and trying to hide the children, and the rest preparing to defend themselves.

Lalia's reaction, upon finding the beginning of an actual settlement where she'd expected a rough, possibly-but-probably-not occupied campsite, was to reign in Windfall and shout, "Someone tell me what the *fuck* is going on here, right now!"

It took the arrival of Rib to defuse the situation and convince the northerners that Lalia was at least nominally friendly. "I need to speak to Mak or Herald, immediately," Lalia demanded once she was satisfied that all was as well as could be expected. "Them, or you-know-who. It's about the boys."

I'd been watching this from a nearby tree. Lalia's general urgency already had me interested and a little worried, and the mention of what I could only assume to be Tam and Val got me really worked up. They had our treasure, after all. I was tempted to just drop out of the trees and talk to her, but I still didn't feel comfortable with the idea of showing myself to our newcomers.

Fortunately, Rib was pretty sharp. "Head north, around the bend," she said, loudly enough that she could be sure that I'd hear her. "I'll go get the sisters and meet you there."

Lalia gave her sharp nod, turned Windfall, and headed in the indicated direction. Rib looked up into the trees, finding me after a few seconds, and jerked her head after Lalia before heading toward the gate to inform Herald and Mak.

I followed Lalia and joined her the easy way, moving through the shadows. I would have gone the "descend from the sky with the thunder of wings" route, but I felt bad for Windfall. The poor boy looked upset enough after a long, hard ride. He deserved to relax a little.

And Lalia probably didn't need that kind of surprise either, even if it was always good to remind her of where we stood with each other. Another time, I told myself. I didn't even appear suddenly behind her, and felt pretty proud of my restraint! Instead, she got to greet me with a dignified "Draka," as I walked out of the undergrowth. She gestured back toward the camp. "I see your collection's growing."

"They asked for a safe place to live, and I granted it. No pressure, no coercion."

That only got me a raised eyebrow. "You're disposing of the city's territory now? Handing out charters?"

"We can talk about who controls this place in law and in fact, if you want to. But what will you do if I say yes? Fight me? Bring the rest of the Wolves? And if I say no, will you tell these people, who have already lost everything, that they can't stay here?"

She frowned. "You know that I won't."

"Then the answer to your question doesn't matter, does it?" I sighed. "Look, Lalia. They were in a bad situation and they asked for help. I couldn't say no. That's about it." I glossed over the details about them being outlaws and me terrifying Jekrie into begging for my protection, probably out of fear for all of their lives. It was better for everybody if she didn't know that.

Her eyes softened a bit at my words, and the atmosphere was a little more friendly after that.

"So what about striking back at the raiders?" I asked. "I've been hoping for days to hear that you're ready to go, and nothing."

"I know," Lalia said, looking oddly guilty. "We've been ordered to pull our patrols back closer to the city. Rallon was fucking livid when he told us, but the order comes straight from the council."

"Sounds like bullshit to me."

"Yeah. Good thing Rallon had some warning ahead of time, and had already sent out every Wolf in fighting shape, isn't it? But we didn't exactly have time to send someone for you, so . . ."

"You went without me?" I felt oddly hurt by that.

"Yeah, it was that or lose the chance. But the medallion you gave us led us straight to them, so you've done plenty!"

"How did it go?"

"Could have gone better," she said unhappily. "Light casualties on both sides. They saw us coming—good scouts, I've got to give them that. We had them well outnumbered, but they were already moving by the time we reached their campsite, and we only got some of their scouts and part of the baggage train. It should fuck them over pretty good, though, so that's something, but Sorrows take us if we try to do anything more now. Can't go against the council now that the order's been given, or we'll be violating the contract. The medallion's helping us keep track of them, and they haven't returned south, so we're keeping up patrols as close as we can to wherever they move. We've seen off one of their raids already."

"That's something." It was a small relief, at least. "So what do I do about Kira?"

"The Tekereteki merc who looks Karakani? Yeah, that's something else I'm here for. We didn't take any prisoners, so Rallon wants me to question her instead, if that's all right with you."

"I don't have a problem with it. She doesn't speak any Karakani, though, so you'll need Herald or Mak to translate."

"Not you?"

"No."

"Just, no?"

"I think Rallon would trust them more than me," I said matter-of-factly. "And she likes them. Besides, I'm feeling lazy."

"Yeah, fine. Although knowing those two, they may not give me the opportunity once they hear my news."

When I asked what was up with the men, she just told me that there had been a message, but that she didn't want to repeat herself once Herald and Mak got there. I figured I could be patient, so we just made small talk while we waited. The Wolves seemed to be doing all right, other than the fact that the officers were annoyed at being held back by the council. They had temporary quarters arranged in a different warehouse while the old one was being repaired, and most of the soldiers were housed there. The officers, though, were all staying in various inns, and it was clear that Lalia was *not* happy about the idea of having to give up the room that she shared with Garal to move back to a barracks. She didn't say anything outright, but hinted pretty heavily that they were making good use of their private room.

Ah, I thought. *To be young and in love and still human.*

"Oh, and that Barlo guy came looking for us at the inn," she said after I successfully steered the conversation away from her, Garal, and things that I'd rather not start missing.

"Who?"

"Barlo? Adventurer, long hair, kind of scruffy in a nice way? He came looking at the old place and the guards sent him our way. He said he had something for you, about some scholars or something like that?"

"Oh, *Barro!* I thought you all knew him?"

She scoffed. "Garal does. Am I supposed to keep track of all my man's drinking buddies? Anyway, he didn't leave a message. Wanted to tell you in person. I mean, he said that he'd been told to get in touch with Garal and that it was for 'an important lady in the mountains,' so it wasn't exactly hard to figure out who he meant."

"I was hoping that he'd get back with something!" I said. I'd have been more excited if I wasn't already so curious about what had Lalia all worked up. "Can you or Garal help set up a meeting?"

"Yeah, no trouble," she said with a dismissive wave of her hand. "He left an address and all."

Another person who'd been asking about me was Lahnie, apparently. I took the fact that Lalia was even mentioning her sister to me, instead of hoping that I'd forget about her, as a friendly gesture. It had hardly seemed possible a few months earlier, but our relationship wasn't entirely terrible anymore, ever since Lalia decided that she didn't have a chance in hell of taking me on. Soon after that, however, Herald and Mak came into sight, and Lalia wasted no time relaying her urgent news.

"There was a letter," Lalia explained, "from Tam and Val. We, uh . . . we read it. Hope you don't mind. I know it's a shit thing to do but we were really worried about them and thought it might be important. And it was, just, not as important as how we got it."

Mak frowned. "Yeah, kind of a shit thing to do, Lalia. Though I appreciate the reason for it. So what's got you so worked up that you rode poor Windfall half to death getting here?"

"Fucking innkeeper's been stealing your letters, that's what!"

"Reben?" Herald exclaimed incredulously, while Mak kept her anger to a scowl and a restrained "That bastard!"

"It's lucky the mail carrier came in from the harbor while me and Garal were at the door, or he'd have disappeared this one too. We heard who it was for, and it wasn't like he could keep it from us when you both had said to give us all your mail. And then the carrier commented on how that was two letters in one week, and wasn't that interesting? And then we beat the crap out of Reben for a while until he admitted that he'd been handing your letters over to someone. There's been three more that we never saw!"

"Wait," Herald said, "You beat up old Reben?"

"I mean, we didn't go straight to that. There was a bunch of talking first. He was being evasive, we caught him in some lies . . . You know Garal, he's good with that. Then we beat him up when he wouldn't tell us what happened to your letters."

"Bastard," Mak growled. "We've been waiting for word for weeks, and he's been stealing our letters! I'll see him thrown from the rock for this!"

I didn't know what "thrown from the rock" meant, but I couldn't imagine it was something that ended well for the treacherous innkeeper.

"That might be excessive," Herald said soothingly, putting her hand on Mak's shoulder. "I am as . . . nearly as angry as you are, but you know as well as I that Reben would not do something like that unless he was being coerced."

Mak just kept scowling silently.

"What did the letter say?" Herald asked, and Lalia stuck her hand inside her armor, coming out with a soft leather tube which she handed over.

"Here it is. But the summary is that they were supposed to be back already, but their ship was delayed by bad weather. We can expect them any day now."

"That is fantastic!" Herald said, smiling brightly. "I cannot wait—"

"And they've sold . . . whatever it was. Congratulations by the way. I expect I'll be calling you 'my Ladies' soon." Lalia grinned ruefully and went on, "But whoever has the letters knows about that too. And I don't think you'll have any trouble coming to the same conclusion we did about who that is."

The dragon rose in me at just the suggestion. We all knew who she meant. Who else could she be referring to but the Night Blossom? Who else had the motivation? And she knew about our treasure, and that Tam and Val would be arriving soon. There was no way she was not having the harbor watched. She would have expected them already, but surely she wouldn't pull her men back just like that?

No, we needed to go. Tam and Val would be walking into an ambush. If we were not there to help them, the treasure would be lost. I would leave a trail of corpses from the harbor to the north gate before I let that happen. I didn't care who saw me, and I didn't care about the consequences. Let the heroes and the adventurers and the monster slayers come, and suffer the consequences of their idiocy! I was *not* going to let the Sorrows-damned Night Blossom steal *my* treasure!

Or hurt Tam or Val. I couldn't lose track of that.

As the anger built inside me, it was joined by a strange kind of relief, an anticipation of cutting loose and releasing all the tension that had been building over the last few weeks. And I could see it mirrored in Mak. I could almost hear her heart speed up as the corners of her mouth twitched. She looked first at me—and we shared a moment of understanding—and then turned to Herald and said, "Get your things together, Herald. We're going, immediately. I'll tell the others. It'll be a long walk, so—"

"I have a better idea," I told them, cutting Mak off. "One that is much faster than walking, and that leaves plenty of time for Lalia to talk to Kira before we go." The three looked at me questioningly. Then, slowly, Herald's face split in a huge smile as she realized what I had planned.

"You said you wouldn't kill me!" Mak screamed in my arms. "You promised! I've done what you asked! I've served you the best I could! I bound myself to you forever! Please! You promised!"

Mak was not enjoying her introduction to the pleasures of flight.

We had left as soon as the sun touched the mountains and had been flying for perhaps thirty seconds when Mak started screaming. Herald was on my back, whooping and hollering as loudly as the first time, but Mak . . . she'd had her misgivings, sure. She'd expressed a slight discomfort with the idea of being carried in my arms as I flew the three of us to the edge of the forest, just north of Karakan. And, yeah, she'd been pretty stiff and she hadn't really been breathing, as such, as I took off. But I hadn't realized that there was a serious problem until I got to a few hundred feet up, and Mak opened her eyes.

Mak had never mentioned a fear of heights. Perhaps she hadn't known that she had one. Perhaps it was the fact that she was hanging under me, with nothing but my good will between her and a long drop followed by a very final stop. Either way, Mak was *not* enjoying her first flight.

A minute in, and I was thinking that I should have just put her in the big bag, where she couldn't see anything. She was small enough, and I was sure the fabric could take it. But it would have been so undignified! I couldn't do that to Mak!

Two minutes in, I decided that I both could and should do that to Mak. Herald seemed to have realized that Mak was not, in fact, screaming with joy and excitement, but the situation felt too urgent—and I was too proud—to turn back. At least by that point she'd gone from screaming to barely audible begging and bargaining.

About five minutes in, Mak had gone silent, from what I assumed was a combination of Herald's gentle, soothing touches and Mak's own grim acceptance of her fate. After that, the rest of the flight went pretty smoothly! Mak didn't weigh much, and while I'd felt the extra strain I could have easily made it the rest of the way into Karakan if I'd wanted to. The accomplishment, carrying two people for twenty-five miles or so, felt really good, Mak's lack of appreciation notwithstanding.

The whole flight only took us about half an hour, but judging by how profusely thankful Mak had been and the way she worshiped the ground once we landed, I was pretty sure that, if she had her way, she was done with flying forever. That, unfortunately, was not up to her. I checked on her, and she hadn't gone flat on me the way Kira had, so I was pretty sure she could soldier through if she had to. Letting her dangle like I had, though, that was not going to work, and I took the opportunity to ask Herald to think about some kind of harness for her. I refused to consider a saddle. That somehow made the difference between letting someone ride me and being *ridden*, and anyone who thought that I would tolerate the latter was in for a nasty surprise.

As Herald and I looked down the long, sloping road into the city, the sun dipped behind the horizon. *"I want you two to walk in through the gate,"* I told Herald. *"If the gates are being watched, I want them to know that you are back."*

"Is that not an unnecessary risk?" Herald objected. *"Would it not be better to fly us in after dark, so that they do not know we are there?"*

"No!" Mak exclaimed, having made it to where she was sitting on her heels and looking up wide-eyed at her sister. *"No, I . . . I need time. Give me that, at least."*

"No worries, Mak," I said. *"You are not flying anywhere else tonight. Perhaps it would be smarter, perhaps not, but if there is anyone watching the gate, I want them to see you. I want them to worry. Because they must understand that if you are there, I might be around. But they will not know for sure, nor do they know what I am capable of or willing to do. It complicates things for them."*

"If you are sure . . ." Herald said.

"*I am,*" I reassured her. "*I will make my own way in. Stay together and I will find you.*"

"*How—*" Herald began, then looked at her sister. "*Right. I need to learn to take that into consideration.*"

"*Yeah,*" I said. "*It is a strange feeling. Especially when you move around a lot, Mak.*"

"*I like it,*" Mak said, getting to her feet and rubbing her face. "*I find it . . . reassuring,*" she added thoughtfully. "*Knowing that you can always find me if something happens. It feels safe.*"

"*Huh,*" Herald said, looking from her sister to me. "*I suppose it would.*"

"*This does not disturb you?*" I asked Herald. She hadn't been entirely comfortable with the idea when I first told them. "*It could be the magic talking.*"

"*A little, perhaps. But it is far too late to worry about which of our thoughts are genuinely our own, and which come from your influence, is it not? Let us say that I understand Mak's perspective. If I were captured again, knowing that you could find me would certainly give me some peace of mind. And the satisfaction of knowing that whoever captures me is already dead, whether they know it or not.*"

"*Right,*" Mak agreed.

I couldn't argue with that, nor did I want to. She was right. It was too late, and I'd only said anything because I felt that I *should* be worried, but honestly, I wasn't. Just as I *should* be worried about the degree to which I was objectifying Mak in my mind, but I wasn't that either. Mak belonged to me. She had made herself very important to me, and it was nice to know where she was. And as long as she stayed with Herald, it meant that I knew where Herald was too. It was like having an AirTag on my keys in case I lost them.

I sent them marching off down the road, then took to the skies. It would be a little while before full dark, when I could safely approach, but we had the entire night ahead of us. We were all well rested, I had made sure of that, and we had much to do. I could hardly wait.

Gods and Mercies and Jesus Christ for good measure, but I was excited. I was angry, that cold, comfortable anger that I felt whenever I thought about the Night Blossom. And I was eager, almost impatient, to get to grips with helping out my friends and messing up my enemy's plans. But above all, I was *excited*, a feeling that grew as the light dimmed and the time to go grew closer. I had been on the defensive for too long, and lately I had started to *hate* it. It felt like most of what I'd done since we busted out and left Karakan had been me making the best of the situation, and I was tired of it. At least now when I reacted, I was reacting forward. I had been itching to go on the offensive, and the Night Blossom had given me the perfect excuse. There was a sense of urgency now, no reason to wait, no excuse to hole up and wait for better days.

It wasn't like I had a plan beyond "Rescue the dudes in distress, unleash hell on anyone in my way," but I was satisfied with that. I'd leave the strategy and the tactics to Herald and Mak, and the others once they arrived sometime the next day. I told myself that this was my command advancement guiding me, pushing me to delegate to those under me who were best equipped for such things, but it could just have been me being lazy.

Planning was never really my thing anyway.

CHAPTER FORTY-ONE

Returning

As the last light vanished behind the mountains, I took off. I climbed and climbed, reaching well over a thousand feet before I turned toward the city in a long arc. I must have reached two and a half thousand by the time I was above the city and began a swift, corkscrewing descent. I fell hundreds of feet in seconds, the wind tearing at my wings as I began to slow myself to pinpoint Mak's location, the streets getting closer.

There!

They'd made quick progress. Mak and Herald were halfway down the wide, poorly lit boulevard, which led to the huge central square—the Forum, the heart of the city as they'd explained it to me. I picked a tall, important-looking building ahead of the sisters, one with a dark roof, and set down gently. There was still a clatter of tiles, but nothing fell off, which I considered a good result! Then I shifted, becoming a liquid shadow that slid off the roof to that of a smaller annex and into a partially lit courtyard, and then over the wall into an alley.

There were two guys hanging about, drinking something, presumably wine, out of a skin. I doubted very much that they were a danger to my girls, since they weren't paying any attention to the street at all, so I let them be. Mostly. I let my shadows pass over them as I went past, and to my satisfaction both of them shuddered, then one with the wineskin nearly dropping it.

"I, ah, I'm getting a bad feeling about this place, Bor," he said. "How about we go somewhere with some light and . . . some people around, aye? Somewhere more lively?"

"Right, right, yeah," the man called Bor said a little shakily, though he was trying to put on a brave face. "Some music. Too quiet here, right?"

"Right," the first man said as they began moving out of the alley. "No reason to be hanging out here on a night like this. Temple's giving me the creeps, anyway, looming like that."

"Should be more lights on the temple at night, right? Disrespectful is what it is."

The two continued talking, agreeing that they both just wanted something more fun and lively that night, while nearly running out of the alley.

I was very happy with the result. It had been practically effortless, though that was partly thanks to the "disrespectful" lighting of the building, the temple, presumably, that the alley ran along. Still, knowing that I could cause fear and discomfort in different degrees, not just the outright despairing terror that I'd unwittingly inflicted on Jekrie and the sisters, delighted me. I could already see a multitude of situations where I could make good use of it. To be fair, most of those involved either clearing a space when I didn't want to reveal myself or messing with people, but I was sure that there would be situations where I might want to make someone fear me without the explicit threat of violence.

And it had been *so* satisfying to see Jekrie fall to his knees. If I'd still had hair, the memory would have given me goosebumps. I wanted more of that. What the hell was the point of being a dragon if you couldn't have the weak prostrate themselves before you?

I had a sudden image of the Night Blossom, pale and wide-eyed with terror, begging for my forgiveness as I stood in judgment above her, with Herald and Mak by my side. Oh, that would be sweet. I'd still kill her if I had the opportunity, and she might get away, but if I could see her crawl . . .

My pleasant nighttime daydream was interrupted when I felt, more than saw, Herald and Mak walk past the alley, and I had to rush after them. I was about to shift back to call them into the alley, but I had the presence of mind to look around first.

Across the street and a ways back, two smaller than average figures crouched in the shadows.

Mentally, I smiled. It looked like the sisters had indeed been spotted, and even followed. And with a bit of luck . . .

I let the pair pass me, then drifted invisibly across the street and after them. And just as I had hoped, the two looked familiar. A little harried, and a little warier of dark alleys than the last time I'd seen them, but the two kids were definitely the same ones who had followed my humans out of Karakan when we left. I would have thought that I'd scared them off messing with these particular Tekereteki women, but in this case I didn't mind so much. I would need to have a word with them, that was all.

As I basked in my own smug satisfaction, up ahead Mak stopped, halting Herald with a gesture. That caused the kids to stop and duck behind a corner, and that was where I struck.

I didn't want them to run off anywhere, but I did want them nice and attentive. So, as I began to shift, I also enveloped them in darkness. I tried not to hit them too hard, but I had no real reference to work with, and I didn't know if it was an exact science anyway, so I went for "as hard as I could without straining myself."

I heard the girl's breath catch as some nameless fear gripped her, while the boy went dead still. Then, as I finished my shift, I grabbed them.

I could only guess what it felt like to have your shoulder grabbed from behind in the unbreakable grip of a clawed hand. Combined with the fear from my shadows, and the anxiety they must have already felt about the chance of running across me again, it resulted in two entirely different reactions.

The girl started crying. Silent, shuddering sobs with no attempt to either fight or flee. She just stood there, silently awaiting her fate.

The boy tried to run. Credit to him, he grabbed the girl's arm first, but it wasn't a very clever move. Of course, desperation isn't always clever. He got all of one step before he jerked to a stop and yelped as my claws dug into his skin. He should thank the Mercies that I had been expecting something like that and had them *mostly* retracted.

With both kids well under control and feeling Mak approaching, probably to check out the sound, I leaned my head in over the kids and said, "You're still following my girls."

The girl started frightened-child ugly crying. The boy stared and started babbling, "Oh. Oh, no. Oh, no, no, no!"

And I . . . was not sure what to do next. Their terror, as always, was satisfying, but the little voice was not happy at all. I wasn't angry enough to be cruel— although one might argue that traumatizing two kids was already quite cruel. Besides, their noises were getting annoying, and I wasn't sure how to stop them without hurting them.

I was saved by first Mak and then Herald rounding the corner, hands on their weapons. Mak didn't have her spear, of course, but she looked threatening enough with her hand on the hilt of her sword. They looked at me and then at the children I was currently terrorizing, and Herald gave me an exasperated look.

"*Was this really necessary?*" she asked, waving her arms at the kids.

"*They were following you!*"

"*Was that not what we wanted?*" Mak asked. "*I could feel that you were pleased. Why stop them?*"

I suddenly felt defensive. "*They were—these are the same kids who followed you out of the city.*"

Herald nodded sagely. "*Ah, yes. I see. Why does that matter?*"

"*They were* supposed *to be too frightened of me to risk messing with you again!*"

"*So your wounded pride is why you are terrorizing children?*"

The boy had gone quiet at that point, looking back and forth as we spoke, but the girl chose that moment to start whispering, "We're sorry! We're so sorry!" between her hiccupping sobs.

I briefly considered doing something to her, then recoiled as the little voice turned into what I could only think of as a mental snarl, making it absolutely clear that we were *not* hurting these kids any more than we already had. "*You take them then,*" I said hurriedly. "*I was hoping to find out who they report to, but I doubt they will be much use with me around.*" I glanced at Mak and saw that she knew exactly what had passed through my mind. The annoyance, followed by the urge for casual violence and then the horror I'd felt at myself.

"Come here," Mak said quickly, offering her hand to the boy on the ground. "She's agreed to let you live for now, but there's no telling when she'll change her mind. Go on, get up! Herald, take the girl!"

Neither of the kids seemed inclined to move, but when I drew back my shadows and growled a little they allowed themselves to be dragged along deeper into the alley and onto a street that ran parallel with the main one. From there I followed the small group toward the harbor and finally to a building that was unmistakably an inn, which they entered.

The sign read HER GRACE'S FAVOR, and judging by the surprisingly well-painted image on it, the favor referred to her bosom. The inn sat where a large road met a small square, looking much less well-to-do than the surrounding expensive-looking shops and trading houses, with their high roofs where hidden observers might lurk. While waiting for some sign from the others I made my way around, just in case, but my idea of spies hiding among the chimneys had perhaps been a little romantic. All there was up there was a steadily more bored dragon and a nocturnal bird or two.

Soon enough, though, as I circled the building, I found an open window with a familiar face looking out of it. Garal was hanging on the sill, looking down into the alley below, then up along the rooftops. I could have just gone in there. His room was lit too brightly for me to shadow in, but I could have fixed that by bringing my shadows with me. But there were two problems with that. One, only Herald and Mak knew what I could do, and I was trying to keep it that way. A sourceless shadow gliding in through his window followed by me suddenly materializing was not the kind of thing I could explain away. And two, if I did shadow in past him, I wasn't sure how he'd be affected. I liked the guy, and I didn't want to freak him out for no reason.

So, I settled on walking out of the shadows on the roof of the opposite building. He saw me soon enough, and had clearly been expecting me.

"The girls have the kids in their room," he whisper-yelled across the gap. "I'd invite you in, but . . ." He waved at the narrow frame of the window. His meaning was clear, and he was right. There was no way I'd get through there without a whole lot of racket, not unless I could, perhaps, change into a cloud of malleable darkness. Which I could, but he didn't know that.

"I'll come out," he continued. "Front door. Follow me?"

"Right," I said, and vanished back into the shadows.

When Garal came out the door a short while later, he didn't go into the alley. I followed him with interest. Looking like a man just walking home after a night on the town, he went down a side street, around a long bend, down some stairs, and under a small bridge, ending in something like a small, abandoned park or garden. There he stopped to wait, but since I was right behind him, he didn't have to wait long.

"Hello again, Garal," I said as I came into the little patch of wilderness. "I missed you, last time I was here."

"Well, I was a little busy," he said with a smirk. "Home on fire, unknown enemies, you know how it is."

"Did you find out what happened?"

He sighed. "No. No evidence, and no leads. It might've been an accident, but that seems unlikely. Still, we're not letting that whole mess slow us down. We've got new accommodations. The old place is still sound, but badly damaged, and there have been *some* perks to not having to sleep in the same room with all the others."

"Not you too!" I complained. "Lalia has already filled me in on how the two of you have been taking advantage of the situation. Too much information!"

"You can't blame her for bragging, can you?" he asked, with a glint in his eye. "But I take your point. It's good to see you again, Draka, though it would be nice to meet under better circumstances, for once."

"One day, yeah. So I hear you beat up an old innkeeper?"

"He's not so old. And Lalia did the beating, though I won't pretend I tried too hard to hold her back. She was furious when she found out that man had betrayed the girls. They've been staying there for months and have had a very friendly relationship. Still, he's not entirely to blame. He was being paid, but he was also being threatened, and he's sure that whoever it is would know if he confessed what he had done."

"It has to be the Night Blossom, right?" I said hopefully.

"Don't see who else it would be. He's supposed to hand the letter over tomorrow, so I'm glad you're here. I can't exactly go running after thugs. Patrols to make, you know? But with you here . . ."

"Yeah," I said with a grin. "That's good. That's really good! We can follow the bastard back to whoever he reports to!"

"Right. Hope you find something," Garal said with a nod.

"What about Tam and Val? Do we know which ship they're coming in on? When is it expected?"

"They've booked passage on a ship called the *Laughing Gull*. As for when they'll arrive . . . they should have departed already, and now it's a question of whether the winds are with them. Tomorrow, perhaps, or the day after that. I'll have a boy watching the harbor, and it wouldn't hurt if you do the same. We have to assume that the Night Blossom, or whoever, knows their ship from the previous letter. They'll be watching too."

"Any chance we can pick off their people before anything happens?"

He shook his head. "I don't see how. The eyes will just be regular dockers, street urchins, and prostitutes, not anyone that stands out in a crowd. The heavies will be waiting somewhere comfortable until the ship comes in."

"Right . . ." I said thoughtfully. I'd been looking forward to messing up some of the Night Blossom's people. But that could still be arranged. I just had to run it by the sisters first. I'd had the kind of idea that you don't just spring on people. "You couldn't spare some of the Wolves, I suppose?" I asked.

"Still can't act in the city," Garal said apologetically. "And that includes Rib and Pot, unfortunately, even if they're kind of on leave at the moment. Although, those two are damned sneaky. I'm sure that no one could say anything about them keeping their eyes open and their ears to the ground."

"Too bad. But thanks for the advice."

He nodded. "Of course, if anything happens . . . I mean, if we'd known about Mak and Herald . . . there are limits, you know? We would have gone, and damn the consequences."

"I know," I said. "You two really care about them, don't you?"

"Mak's a good woman, and a good friend to Lalia," he said. "And Herald . . . I think she reminds Lalia of her sister, the one that she lost. She was about Herald's age. And she's quite likable, isn't she? A little serious, but . . ."

"She can be fun!" I protested. "She just has a dry humor, that's all."

"No, I know! We all like her. She's like everyone's little sister. Although," he grinned, "I hear that we're not supposed to call her things like that anymore, now that she's all grown up."

"I don't think she cares what you call her, as long as you treat her as an adult. And she is, you know that. By your laws and by what she's experienced, she's as much of an adult as anyone can be at her age."

"I know, I know," he said, raising his hands defensively, then smiling. "It's really sweet, do you know that? How protective you are of her?"

I narrowed my eyes at him. "I am not *sweet*. I'm a dragon."

"A dragon who'll burn the world for her human friend. It's sweet. And . . . reassuring, I guess. Seeing you like this—up close, I mean—you're quite intimidating. It's good to know that you can care like that."

I blew some air out my nose. I could live with that. Garal grinned, seeing that he'd won the point.

"You know what, though?" he said suddenly. "We can't go running after criminals, of course, but if me and some of the others are off duty, there's nothing stopping us from going down to the harbor to welcome our old friends back. Once their ship gets here, that is. We'll need *some* deniability."

I liked the sound of that. If Tam and Val were to be attacked when they got off their ship, it would be good to have as many friendlies around as possible. And if not, I figured Tam and Val were the kind of people who'd be touched by a big welcoming party.

We said our goodbyes after that. I asked him to tell the girls that I'd be around and to come out before dawn so we could talk, which he said that he would. But as I was leaving, Garal spoke up. "Before you go . . . Mak. Is she going to be all right?"

"Haven't you talked to her?"

"I have, and I know what she and Herald think. I'd like to know what you think."

"We're okay again, her and me, if that's what you mean. Mak . . ." I hesitated. Would she be all right? Did I even know, myself? "Mak," I said again, "has chosen a path that she can live with. One that she hopes she can be proud of. And I'm going to do what I can to help her. But until she and Herald can close the book on . . . all of this. What happened to them—"

"You mean taking revenge?"

"Yeah, I mean taking fucking revenge! Don't interrupt me! I'm being contemplative! Anyway, Herald might be able to survive without it. She won't forgive anything, but she might be able to put all this shit behind her someday. But not Mak. Not after what they did to Herald, and not after what they made her do. Either we break the Night Blossom, or Mak breaks. I don't see it going any other way. But yeah, once we have our revenge—and I am going to put everything I have into making that happen—once we have that, I think that they're going to be okay, both of them."

"And what about you?" he asked gently.

That caught me by surprise. What about me? Was I going to be okay? Which side of me? All of me wanted to grind the Night Blossom under my heel, but the question was if that would be enough. Once she was gone, then what?

Sometimes it felt like the Night Blossom was just the most obvious symptom of a broader disease, one that I'd been suffering from since day one. A big part of me blamed the council, the Adventurers' Guild, the whole city for my self-imposed exile, for the secrecy that I had forced upon myself in the name of safety. Would I ever truly be okay as long as I lived in the shadows? I wasn't so sure.

"Don't ask me that. The answer is too long, and you won't like it."

CHAPTER FORTY-TWO

Down the Drain

There was one problem I needed to solve urgently. Fortunately, I had one idea and two fallbacks.

The problem was that I needed somewhere in the city to sleep. Even for naps I needed somewhere hidden, preferably somewhere dark, where I wouldn't be disturbed. My first fallback was the cellar of the Wolves' burned-out warehouse, but that wasn't a sure thing. I didn't know how intact it was, for one, or how actively it was being repaired, for another but, despite those two problems, it might be worth checking out.

My second fallback was to simply leave the city. I could fly back home, or to the edge of the forest if I wanted to save half an hour, or I could use one of the sea caves I'd discovered during my first ill-fated flight along the coast. All of those would remove me from the city during the day, when I couldn't cross the wall without the risk of being spotted. Which I could deal with, but I'd rather not. Not until it was on my terms.

My preferred solution was something I intended to spend the night investigating. During that same first flight I had discovered that the city had a functioning sewer system, and it emptied into the sea. During my time on the streets I had also seen several storm drains, which made perfect sense if they had the infrastructural know-how to make them work. The island of Mallin, or at least the central eastern part that we were in, was mostly all or nothing when it came to rain. There had been one or two light rains during my months there, but generally it had been weeks of drought punctuated by torrential downpours. I hadn't actually seen the city during such a rain, but with its wide, sloping streets, I couldn't imagine that it was pretty. Thus, the storm drains.

So, my plan was to become a sewer dwelling monster. Interestingly, I didn't find myself balking at the idea. As long as I could stick to the stormwater parts of the system, I should be fine. The sanitation parts . . . If I could avoid them entirely,

I would. My nose was off when I shifted into shadow form, but unfortunately, I had yet to find a way to maintain that while sleeping.

Finding a storm drain was easy. Finding one that met my criteria was hard. First, I'd prefer it close to the inn. While there were a few, this being an affluent area, they didn't meet my second criterion—accessibility. In shadow form I could thin out and stretch myself, but there were limits. And finally, if at all possible, the drain should be in shadow as much of the day as possible. That was the hardest part.

I never did find one that met all three criteria, but I got two out of three with some cheating, which would have to do. The drain I found wasn't in sight of the inn, but at least it was close. It was a hole in the ground covered by a grill, located in an alley with a dip between two small hills and toward which two larger streets sloped. By the lay of the alley it should be in shadow almost all day, except noon, so that was one of three. Where I cheated, well . . . I got frustrated, and I yanked the grill out of the mortar that held it in place. Being able to open and close it would have to do.

The well under the grill was barely large enough for me, but with a little bit of contortion, I fit. My wings with their long, thin bones were the worst, but I managed. Slinking in and pulling the grill in place above me before anyone might come to investigate the rather loud racket I'd made, I shifted and began my exploration of the stormwater system.

The tunnels I was in were long and straight, narrow and currently mostly dry. They were infested with rats and bugs, but those couldn't bother me in shadow form and would probably count more as snacks than nuisances even if I did choose to shift back. The system was extensive. There were a couple of main tunnels, which were wide enough for me to walk in if I shifted back, as long as I kept my wings tightly tucked in. Then there were many more smaller tunnels that drained into the main ones. Of those, most were too narrow for me to even try squeezing in without shifting, and some were just pipes, openings two or three inches wide in the walls of the tunnels. I wondered how they'd built them. Some parts were carved directly into the rock, and others were lined with stone brick, but that included tubes narrow enough that no one could have gotten in there to cut or line them. The ones that went through stone were so straight and smooth that they must have been done with some kind of magic.

Exploring the tunnels and pipes, I found plenty of openings to the surface in interesting areas, some of which were, if even just barely, wide enough for me to squeeze through. Sadly most of those would take a lot of effort in the form of bringing darkness with me if I wanted to use them during the day, but it was still good to know. Of course, I might remember half of them if I was lucky, but that was still much more than I'd known that evening.

I did also find a few places where the stormwater and sewer systems connected. If I understood the construction correctly, which was far from likely, it looked like it was built so that the sewer should be able to overflow into the stormwater system, but not the other way around, which seemed sensible to me. Nobody wants their waste water backing up, after all.

I resolved to try and find a path to the sea. If all the sewers drained there, it shouldn't be too hard; just follow the muck downstream. But I didn't know that that was the case, and I'd rather not get stuck in the stinking tunnels on my first night in the city. Perhaps I could start from the other end. Some other time, though. Some other time. I had already spent several hours exploring, and I needed to give myself time for a nap. At that moment it was enough to know that I had a hidden place to sleep comfortably . . . as long as it didn't rain too hard.

When I woke up and called it quits on my tunnel-ratting, there was still an hour or two left before dawn. I spent some of that time just wandering the streets near the inn. I was in shadow form, so it was more like drifting around, but it had the same feel to it. Part of it was that I was checking for anyone suspicious hanging around near my humans, but by then even the ladies of the night and the would-be muggers had gone to bed. It felt like I had the city to myself. Like it was mine, and mine alone. I liked it. It felt right.

I stayed near the inn, lurking in whatever dark places I could find, until Mak came out shortly before twilight. Knowing me well by that point, she started looking for likely hidden, shadowy places. There were a few people on the streets by then, moving hurriedly in the chilly pre-morning air, some of them dragging carts of boxes or barrels. Mak got a few odd looks, but nobody lingered. I was on a roof at that point, but it was easy enough to intercept her as she stuck her head into an alley.

She seemed to sense my presence, turning to look in the direction of my shadow before I even materialized. She looked a little anxious as she said, "*Good morning, great and mighty one,*" in a grave voice. "*Do all dragons love filthy alleys,*" she managed before her facade broke into a grin, "*or is it just you?*"

I was a little taken aback by that. Surprised, but amused. Mak had so rarely joked with me, even before she became mine. It took me a second to find a reply. But finally I decided that if she was in a good mood, I'd play along.

"*Oh,*" I said, matching her initial tone, "*does my lowly servant find it appropriate to judge my choices?*"

"*Not at all,*" she said, and at that point she had stopped even trying to be serious. "*This one only wishes to know if she should find a nice garbage heap for you to rummage around in later in the day.*" She broke into a short, sharp fit of laughter. "*I am glad you enjoyed that. I was a little worried.*"

"*Herald's suggestion?*"

She nodded. "*I was not sure, but she knows you better than I do, so . . .*"

"She does. But, really? A garbage heap?"

"Lowly servant?"

" . . . fair. How did it go with the kids?"

"They are terrified, but it is too late to convince them to stay silent about this. The boy confessed that he told anyone who would listen to him about the dragon he had seen, after the last time. No one believed him, of course. For now they are convinced that you can find them wherever they go, and that you will eat them if they go against you. Not that we said anything like that. Herald actually tried to make you sound kind. But they are children who were just faced with, well, you. So, we told them that if they help you, you will be most pleased, and they drew their own conclusions."

"I can accept that, I suppose."

"We thought so. In the morning they will lead us to the man they report to, a thug called Kosh. We were not intending to confront him, only to see who he is and where he can be found."

"Good. See if you can get any help from Ardek. The Wolves will not be able to help us, from what Garal said, but if you can keep them in the inn for extra safety, that might be for the best."

Mak nodded. *"Garal has already arranged a room for Rib and Pot. Ardek can stay with us."*

"And Kira?"

Mak stopped and blinked a few times. *"Kira? She is not coming, is she?"*

"Is she not?" That was news to me.

"She—what can she do? She hates violence, and she cannot fight. She can heal, but . . . We thought it best to leave her."

"With the northerners? She does not speak their language!"

"No. But she has a kind soul, and she is a country girl. She can help with many tasks. They already like her, Ardek made sure of that, and we told them that she is important to you. She will be fine. And we told her to work on her Karakani, which she will have little choice but to do."

I thought about it. What *would* Kira be good for in the city? Healing? Then we'd need to bring her with us everywhere. She'd be dead weight if no one was hurt, which would hopefully be all of the time. No, this was the right call.

"I knew I could count on you two. Well done," I said, giving her a nod, and she beamed at my praise.

Right, I reminded myself. She was linked to me much more deeply that she had been, than *anyone* had *ever* been, really. She had bound herself to me. She could read people's intentions, but with me she could straight up feel my emotions, even when we were far apart. She had made a choice to make me important to her. My praise was not just words to her, it affected her in a way that I needed to make myself remember.

"*Well*," she said happily, "*I should return. The sun is coming up and the others will wake soon, as will the city. Where can we look for you if we need you?*"

I gave her a quick description of the alley with the drain I'd chosen, and she said that she knew it. It turned out that she had a pretty good mental map of the area around the inn, the harbor, and the Adventurers' Guild in general, which made sense. Once a method of contact was established—throw something noisy down there and see if I show up—I sent her off, sending my love to Herald with her. She returned to the inn while I returned to the alley, drew back the grill, and descended back into the tunnels.

Brimming with energy, and with my sleeping pattern well and truly ruined by that point, I only napped for a few hours. The sun came in bright and strong through the drains I approached, the light coming through in negative to my shadow vision and reducing my world to a series of tubes that terminated in patches of infinite darkness.

Not content to sit and wait in case the girls wanted me—and I could sense Mak's direction anyway—I continued my exploration. I had avoided the tunnels that sloped upward to the northern and eastern parts of the city simply because I'd only had so much time the previous night and needed to limit myself, so that was where I went.

It didn't take long before I found the first of two interesting things, which was evidence that the tunnels were being used.

That didn't surprise me. Here I had a series of tunnels, large enough for me to walk through and which ran all under the city. The average citizen probably never thought of them, only having a vague idea that the waste must go somewhere and knowing that there were holes in the street where most of the rainwater went. But with no obvious way in or out, why should anyone worry?

Or maybe they were as intrigued by the idea of sewer-dwelling monsters as the average city kid back on Earth. I'd have to ask Herald.

Either way, as I went north, I found a place where the stone brick had been torn out, high on the wall, and a tunnel had been dug to a chamber the size of a fairly large studio apartment. The chamber was empty, but the dirt floor was scuffed. I noted the location and moved on. Further up the tunnel I found another, much more interesting chamber. There I found a table, a chair, a hook for a lantern to be hung, and some other simple creature comforts. And, more interestingly, a ladder leading to a trap door in the ceiling. I tried it, of course, but it wouldn't budge easily, and I didn't want to deal with the possible consequences of busting it open just yet. With how close it was to the harbor, the whole setup screamed smugglers' den, and if I stayed around for a while, I'd have to keep an eye on it in case anything interesting happened. And I'd have to see where that trap door led, of course.

The rest was more of the same tunnels that I'd started to get used to. Then, a few hours in and after I had started exploring the eastern parts, I discovered something important. To call it a game changer would be an overstatement, but what I found was a possible solution to some of my problems.

There was a wide passage, complete with carved steps, dug from the storm-water tunnels down to a natural cavern. And not just any cavern. A sea cave. Much like the one under the Night Blossom's prison-house, it was complete with a dock and a small boat with two sets of oars, and I could see a slight brightness in the water where a currently submerged opening connected it to the sea.

The cave was spacious and, while it was humid from the sea water, the connection to it sloped first upward and then down from the storm-water tunnels, in a kind of inverted U-bend. There was no risk of getting flooded out in case of a heavy rain, like there was in the tunnels. The cavern was connected to the sea, if I dared to risk an attempt at swimming, and the chambers I'd found in the eastern part told me that there were connections to the surface. I just had to find them.

I had, if I wanted it, the makings of becoming a real subterranean monster. I could set up a small lair here to operate out of when I didn't want to leave the city, with access for my friends and allies, and the only stumbling block was that I might have to deal with some smugglers or other criminals at some point.

A few criminals wandering the darkness of the tunnels? I was not concerned. In my mind the place was already mine. All I had to do was to claim it.

I was sorely tempted to celebrate with a well-deserved nap. I already had a likely alcove picked out, wide and flat and well above the high-water line. In the darkness and with my wings covering me, I'd be invisible. But instead I decided to do the responsible thing and return to the harbor area, near the inn, where I'd told Mak that they could look for me.

At that point it was sometime in the afternoon. I was getting sleepy and peckish, but nothing I couldn't handle. As I moved west from my new cave, I could sense Mak ahead of me, and as I got closer and closer, I felt a sneaking suspicion that I knew where she was. As I approached the agreed-upon spot I was proved right, as I heard a distant tinkling of bells. I came to the narrow pipe connecting the drain in the alley to the tunnels, and as I watched, a bunch of bells tied to a thick string plummeted onto the stone, making a ringing racket, and were pulled up jerkily, jingling and jangling all the way.

I shifted, pushed the darkness ahead of me, and emerged into the short shaft beneath the grill. I shifted back just in time to get half a pound of brass bells in the face.

"Ow," I said flatly, staring up at Mak above me, who jerked with the same mix of awe and fear that she always displayed when I shifted. Memories of the prison and the first time she'd seen me do it, no doubt. "What is it?"

"Thank the gods, I thought you wouldn't show up!" Mak said, looking around and then crouching to get a better look at me. There was no worry on her face, only excitement. "We thought you should know, and we may need you along. We've got a lead!"

CHAPTER FORTY-THREE

Simdal

The man to whom Reben, the innkeeper, had delivered the sisters' letters, had disappeared. Most likely, Mak said, he'd found out that Reben's duplicity had been discovered, so he'd cut his losses. However, when that door had closed, a window had opened.

The kids, the boy Relki and the girl Sana, had led the sisters to the thug they reported to. His name was Kosh or something like that. I didn't care much. After dutifully reporting that the sisters had entered the city and were back at Her Grace's Favor, they'd received a pitiful sum of coins and a slap for Relki for being late, after which the sisters had followed Kosh to a nearby, and incredibly disreputable, gambling house.

When they returned to the inn they found Ardek waiting for them. He and the others, traveling on foot, had arrived during the morning, Lalia and the Tavvanarian cousins having gone off to report to Rallon and leaving him there to wait. When they described Kosh, Ardek not only knew who he was and where he usually hung out, but he also knew who he hung out *with* and who he usually reported to. And *that* was who they, or possibly we, were going after, because he, Ardek was pretty sure, might know where the Night Blossom could be found.

Lots of uncertainty, but at least it was something to go on.

Our quarry, Simdal, ran the gambling house for the Night Blossom, along with a few other places. In a twist of fate, he happened to be the same racist bastard who'd wanted Ardek and some others to beat the living hell out of Tam for winning too much. Besides being a bigot he had a reputation as a hard-ass and a meticulous manager, making frequent rounds of the establishments he managed to make sure that not one bit went missing. *Supposedly*, he could fight, but he wasn't a heavy. And, again *supposedly*, he always knew if someone was lying to him. Unfortunately, that was unlikely to help him.

The plan was simple: Grab him off the street as he left the place that Kosh had gone to, take him somewhere nice and quiet, and question him as harshly as necessary. I would hopefully not be needed. Ideally we wouldn't need to risk revealing my presence yet. But we didn't know how much muscle Simdal would have following him around, and so I'd be lurking in the shadows, ready to swoop in and turn the situation into a bloodbath if necessary.

Simple.

It occurred to me that what we were planning should, but didn't, bother me. Completely ignoring the legality of what we were doing—it was definitely illegal—I had become almost entirely inured to violence. Every time I thought about that, it managed to surprise me, and I wasn't sure why. The first real sign that not only my body but my mind had changed was the first time I killed a man, on that forest road with Herald, and I felt nothing except annoyance at what a mess he'd made. Herald, Mak, and Ardek had grown up in a society that accepted violence as a fact of life, but not me. Or rather, not the part of me that kept bringing up such distracting concerns. What use were they? I should abhor violence. Fine. I didn't. What good would that do me? A crime lord had captured and *tortured* two of my precious humans, and taken me with the intent of displaying me, selling me, or possibly chopping me up for parts. We had no reason to believe that she wouldn't do worse as soon as she had a reasonable opportunity. And I figured you didn't get anywhere in her organization without being an unconscionable piece of crap. So why, I wondered, should I be concerned about violence?

Because making violence a first choice instead of a last resort is how you become a monster, I told myself. I still believed, despite all the evidence to the contrary, that humans were supposed to abhor unnecessary violence. And perhaps there was something in that, but the fact that I didn't bothered me less and less.

According to Ardek, Simdal made his rounds every evening. That was when business was at its peak. So once Mak had informed me of the plan, she left me to my own devices for the next several hours, with orders from me and a promise from her to return to get me when it was time. I spent some of that time exploring more of the tunnels, where I stuck to the ones that humans could reasonably move through and was rewarded with two more hidden paths to the surface. Again, I left them unexplored, not wanting to risk starting something when I had plans for the night. When I tired of that I returned to the entrance, where I slept nearby until the chiming of bells woke me. I stretched, yawned, and rose, excitement bubbling up inside me that I hadn't felt in a long time. It was time to go. It was time to embark on our journey of revenge.

I wasn't going to be digging any graves, though. Not with a perfectly good river right there.

This time I shifted back inside the well of the drain while Mak was hauling the bells up, so I avoided getting them dropped on my face again. Only barely, though, since she clearly wasn't ready for me and her grip on the line slipped when she jumped. But she caught it, so everything was fine.

Mak looked around, then pulled the grill to the side. "We're ready to go," she said. "Ardek's going to show us a place near the gambling house where we can hide out while he keeps an eye on the door. I'm not sure about good spots for you. Sorry."

"*What happened to your Tekereteki?*" I asked as I climbed out. "*It would be safer to use a language no one else knows.*"

"*Apologies. It does not come naturally to me, and we have been speaking Karakani for the sake of Ardek and the others,*" she replied with some chagrin.

"*That is all right. But try to remember. And you are getting so much better!*"

She smiled at my praise, and I loved to see it. "*Thank you. I will.*"

Together we put the grill in place, and then I shifted, following Mak out of the alley and toward the inn, where Herald and Ardek waited, armed but unarmored. Swords were one thing, and not entirely eyebrow-raising so long as they had their peace-ties—those little knotted leather cords around the hilt—fixing them in their scabbards. Armor would make them stand out far too much.

It was annoying that none of the Wolves could, or would, join us. But I understood their position. Of the Wolves we knew, two were officers, and two were cousins of the commander. If they were found to be involved doing something explicitly illegal, it would jeopardize the whole company's position, something none of them were willing to risk until the stakes were considerably higher.

And it wasn't like they weren't doing anything to help out. The cousins were keeping their ears to the ground for news of the boys' ship, and Garal and Lalia had secured Rallon's permission to welcome Tam and Val back at the harbor. With that handled, the rest of us could focus on other things, which was a big help in itself.

All told, I wasn't *too* bothered that they weren't with us. It only meant that if we found a situation where their help would have been needed, I would be the one to vent my frustrations on some unquestionably bad people instead.

Her Grace's Favor lay in the richer, eastern part of the harbor district. From there I followed the humans as they, in turn, followed the water west, sticking to small, decaying back streets with few people at this time of the evening, and fewer who would dare to hinder three armed individuals walking with confidence and purpose. A drunk in the street before them tried to catcall the girls, but he shut up when he realized that not only was one of the women approaching him half a foot taller than he was, but both had their swords loose in their scabbards, and neither they nor the man with them showed any sign of swerving or slowing down. He beat a quick retreat into a narrow alley at that point.

I watched this from the roofs, looking down into the soupy haze of the light coming out of destitute homes and the city's least well-to-do shops. The streets were clean and tidy, but the wood here was withering, the stone cracked, and the brick crumbling. Some had so many missing or broken slats or tiles that I could have crawled inside, shifted or no, and I couldn't imagine what it was like to live in those buildings when it rained, or in winter. Some of the villages and hamlets I'd spied on had looked poor, but this was something completely different. I hadn't realized that misery like that existed in the city, though perhaps I shouldn't have been surprised. I wondered, had any city ever been free of poverty? Perhaps. There had been a lot of cities throughout history back home, and here was a whole new world with its own past. But I doubted it.

As I considered the suffering of the people beneath me, my more practical side noted that there were plenty of places here to slip inside and hide. Sure, there may be some truly destitute people living under the leaky roofs, but those would be easy enough to get rid of. Just turn up the shadows and they'd probably leave without even being sure why. No fuss!

Among the rundown buildings there was one very literal spot of light. A bright lantern hung outside a sturdy door, guarded by a large, rough man who looked like he could stare at the same crumbling wall for days on end without getting bored. This was the door the humans staked out. Ardek opened an unlocked door and shooed the sisters inside, then took up a position in the shadows outside, where he could see who went in and out of what must be the gambling house. And there were plenty of people to watch. Every few minutes someone would come or go, singly or in pairs or small groups. While no one I saw was richly dressed, as such, there were some who were clearly better off than others, their tunics and coats finer—there was a notable lack of trousers inside the city—and notably lacking the heavy wear that I saw on most of the patrons. Some left in high spirits, others with a desperate, haunted look in their eyes. One was bodily thrown out, then given a disinterested beating by the bouncer when he tried to rush back in. He lay in the street for a long time without moving before slowly, painfully getting to his knees and crawling away through the dirt. On the bright side, someone stopped and helped him to his feet before he vanished from my sight, so that was nice.

I might have been able to just stay shifted all night. I'd come a long, long way since I first got this power, and as long as I was in deep darkness and didn't move, I didn't tire quickly. But I decided not to risk it. If I was needed, I wanted to be alert and rested, not groggy and fighting a headache. So I went back one building, where there was one of those nice, big holes where the roof had partially collapsed in a corner. I took a look inside and there was no one there, nor was there any sign of the space being used by anything but bats and rats, so I went inside and shifted back. Then I lay down and curled up with my head just barely sticking out of the hole, confident that I'd be invisible in the darkness.

All I had to do was wait.

Not too much later a man walked out the door. He was paler than most, his skin a light enough brown that it was almost a deep tan instead, and his hair was unusually curly. The bouncer gave him a respectful nod. This wasn't remarkable; a select few guests got the same treatment, all of them from the richer, or perhaps less poor, part of the clientele, and this man was among the best dressed I had seen so far. What really made me take notice of the man, though, was that Ardek stirred. He crouched in his shadow, quickly popping his head inside the door where the sisters were waiting. This, I concluded, must be Simdal.

Two others followed him closely, their behavior marking them as somewhat professional bodyguards. Something hung at their sides. I couldn't say if they were truncheons or short swords. Not that it mattered if I got involved, but I'd feel much better if I knew that there was no sharp metal being pointed at my humans. And, yeah, perhaps the memory of being stabbed under the wing played a small part too.

As the sisters came into sight, I shifted and left my hiding place. Simdal had started up the street, away from us, and I followed him, trusting the others to do the same. We kept pace, passing the gambling house at the same time, and I tensed mentally for a moment before relaxing. The bouncer took a look at the trio, but when they made no move to enter his door, he apparently marked them as Not His Problem, and settled back against the wall. Once away from him they sped up, slowly gaining on Simdal and his guards.

This, of course, was the tricky part. Ardek was not a fighter, and neither of the sisters would be fighting with their preferred weapons. Ahead of them were three armed men, all of whom could be assumed competent when it came to violence. It also wasn't impossible that Simdal, at least, knew that the sisters had been prisoners of his boss. They were quite recognizable, after all. So we couldn't count on the element of surprise unless they managed to set up an ambush. On that front, though, fortune smiled upon us.

Simdal abruptly stopped, barking out, "Tar, stay here. Dem, with me." He then stepped into a narrow alley, one of his men remaining vigilant on the street.

I passed over the alley, where Simdal was pissing against a wall, making obnoxiously loud noises of contentment. My humans closed in, passed, and just kept walking, speeding up when the guard on the street mean-mugged them and quickly disappearing around the bend in the street while I stayed behind with our quarry.

When Simdal emerged and continued up the street, they were long gone. Curious what their plan was, I went ahead as quickly as I could. That wasn't particularly much faster than walking speed, but I put a little distance between us, making sure to keep Simdal in sight. Thus, I saw my humans lying in ambush several seconds before Simdal and his men reached them.

Honestly, I might have missed them if it were only Mak. Even though I could see clear as day in the dark corner of a stairway where she was hidden, she still seemed to melt into the background. If it weren't for my spotting the others and knowing she must be around, I might not even have looked for her, and even then I might have overlooked her if not for my sense of where she was.

Score one for my "Mak gets all my minor advancements" theory, I thought smugly. There was no way she'd been that stealthy before surrendering herself to me.

The streets were clear. My humans had their weapons ready and were positioned so that they could strike from the front and the back at the same time. Mak being the strongest melee fighter, I assumed that she would go first.

Simdal and his guards reached, then passed Mak. She tensed . . . and nothing. She began to move, then fell back, pressing herself against the stone of the stairway. Herald and Ardek, clearly waiting for Mak to engage, stayed in hiding, clearly unwilling to go in without her. Simdal and his guards moved on, none the wiser, and that should have been that. It would have, if not for me.

We could have waited and tried again another night, after figuring out what happened. But I, for all my patience, did not want to wait. I had what was supposed to be someone with access to the Night Blossom right in front of me, and my blood boiled with the desire to learn just what he could tell us about her. So there, on a rickety roof in one of the poorest parts of Karakan, I shifted back. With my prey walking away from me, I launched myself from my perch, tearing up tiles as my legs shot me forward. One of the guards stopped as though to listen, but by the time the first tile shattered against the street I was already on them. I fell on them like a hawk on a trio of mice. Braking only enough to be sure I didn't kill the man I was after, I bowled the guards to the sides, knocking Simdal to the ground beneath me and grabbing him before they really knew what was happening. With the stunned man firmly in my grasp I took off, wings beating as hard as they could, and by the time he started struggling and screaming, we were already a hundred feet off the street and climbing fast.

He didn't try to reason with me. I felt more than a little miffed by that, for some reason. Sure, thinking about it logically, he'd just been grabbed off the street by a big reptile, one strong enough to fly off with him and whose claws were digging into his flesh. There was no reason he should assume that I was even remotely intelligent, unless he recognized me as a dragon. I'd just assumed, on some level, that anyone who was anyone in the Night Blossom's organization would know about me. But why should they? This guy ran some gambling houses, maybe a bar or a brothel or two. Why should he be in on everything that happened?

Ah, well, I thought as he stupidly tried to break my grip, maybe to get at the knife on his belt. I'd learn what he knew soon enough.

The whole thing had been kind of spur-of-the-moment. My initial plan if things went south had been to kill the guards and let my humans deal with Simdal, but when the moment came and he was beneath me I just kind of went with it. I had no real plan. I didn't know where to take him, and the guy was hollering pretty loudly, making me wonder how many people down below heard him. Possibly a lot. The waterfront was pretty lively, even at night. That . . . might cause issues in the future, but what was done was done.

Ideally, I should go somewhere in the city where the humans could find me, but I wasn't sure how to do that without alerting half of the population. I needed to shut the guy up somehow. But how—

I snorted at myself. "Shut up!" I growled, and when that didn't work, I hit him with as strong a dose of shadows as I could manage while still flying. It wasn't exactly something I'd done before, but I didn't see any reason it shouldn't work. Which it did, surprisingly well! Simdal went stiff in my grip and his voice caught in his throat as abject terror gripped him, and I took that opportunity to look down at him and repeat myself.

He was already silent at that point, and he stayed that way. It also had the bonus side effect of making him stop squirming. That was good, because if he somehow managed to get loose and fall a few hundred feet, I'd have to find someone else to question, and that would have been annoying.

Feeling very pleased with myself, I circled back, focusing on Mak. I could feel her down there, somewhere, but I needed to get closer to pinpoint her location. There was nothing for it, I decided. I descended, trusting that I wouldn't be *too* visible against the night sky, and headed in her direction. There was a small annoyance, in that whenever I let up on the shadows for too long Simdal would start getting ideas again, but another couple of doses together with casually digging my claws in put an end to that.

It seemed that they were heading back to the inn. Fine. I could work with that. I cruised along the street, on which I thought they must be, low and slow, until I saw them. When I got within perhaps two hundred feet Mak stopped and turned to look up, and our eyes met just as I glided by and continued toward the inn.

I did not, of course, go there. Instead, I went straight to my tunnel entrance, the grill-covered storm drain in the alley, where I pulled the grill aside and unceremoniously threw Simdal in. I wrapped him in shadow to the point where my head began to hurt and I was pretty sure he couldn't see a thing, and then I told him, "I will be watching. If you make a sound, I will punish you."

He stared up at nothing, not even breathing, which I took as a "Yes, ma'am." When the shadows lifted and he could see again, I was gone, perched on a nearby rooftop. There I waited, and watched.

It took half an hour or so, but the humans showed up, just like I knew they would. They came in the alley warily, and Mak fished out the bundle of bells from the loose brick where she'd hidden them. Meanwhile, Herald walked up to the grill and looked down.

"Huh," she said, and turned to her sister. "*I found the man. Now, where is the dragon?*"

CHAPTER FORTY-FOUR

A Friendly Chat

From where I rested on a rooftop, I watched the humans in the alley below. I could have just dropped down to them right then, but I was curious to see if they'd find me.

I was watching Mak more closely than Herald. She wasn't just searching every dark corner and scanning the rooftops like Herald was. Instead, she stood very still, relaxed, focused. She turned in my general direction, zeroed in, and then looked directly at me and smiled wide.

Well, that was another theory confirmed. She could find me as easily as I could her. We'd have to figure out how that worked soon, because each of us being able to find the other was too useful not to figure out the details.

Satisfied, I glided down into the alley, checked that there was no one in sight but my three humans, and shifted back. Herald had noticed me when I came down, but Ardek jumped a little at my sudden appearance. Although, to be fair to the boy, he had been watching the ends of the alley, so I couldn't exactly fault him for not noticing me earlier.

"*We have him,*" I said without preamble. "*Now where are we taking him?*"

"*The inn has a cellar,*" Herald said. "*The innkeeper has kindly offered to let us use it for anything we might need.*"

"*Is there a way I can get in?*"

"*There is a cellar door in the courtyard, around the back.*"

"*Excellent.*" I walked over to the well. After opening the grill I reached down, took a firm grip on Simdal's arm, and hauled on it. He groaned and clasped my arm with his free hand, and up he came, rolling in the dirt where I dropped him.

"Take him," I said to my humans. Then, leaning down so my face was just in front of Simdal's, I growled, "Go quietly and do what they say, and you may still be alive by morning. All we want from you is answers. Try to fight, or run, and me and you will go for another flight. Understood?"

Simdal clasped his arm with a grimace and nodded, his eyes wide and blood-shot. Slowly he got to his knees, then to his feet, and Herald and Ardek closed in on him. He was silent and compliant, but he still found the guts to give them each a dirty look before they slid a bag over his head.

"Mak," I said.

"Yes?" she answered apprehensively.

"We need to talk. Once he is secured, go to your room and open a window."

"Right," she sighed, and with that they left the alley, Simdal boxed in between the three.

I followed them along the street back to the inn, flitting from shadow to shadow. They avoided the few people who were out. Of those that saw them, no one questioned them. People, I'd noticed, tended to keep to their own business around steely-eyed women carrying swords, peace-tied or not.

If anyone recognized Simdal and ran off to tattle, I didn't mind. I wanted the Night Blossom to know that someone was going after her people. I wanted her to know that someone was coming for her. That reminded me that I should ask if Simdal's two guards were still alive. They had definitely seen me, and if they talked to anyone higher up, the Night Blossom might well know who exactly was after her, and soon.

The thought excited me. I was again struck by the urge to just go flying over the city, screaming for her to come out and face me. But, no, I reminded myself. We were doing it this way for a reason. Terrorizing a few criminals was one thing. If I started to spread fear among the general citizenry, though, the city would have to do something. And that would be capital "B" Bad.

I still wanted to do it.

Once inside the sisters' room at the inn, I was faced with a contrite Mak. The room was larger than I'd expected. It had two beds with some decent space between them, a table with two chairs, and a second, small table with a washbasin on it. It even had a wardrobe and some shelves! It was, however, fairly empty, with the sisters living out of their packs—they didn't know if they'd need to leave on short notice.

"*Well?*" I asked Mak. I wasn't angry, but I was annoyed. While I hadn't been part of the plan for their ambush, it had been obvious enough that Mak was supposed to be the one to spring it. And she hadn't.

"*I froze,*" she said. She said it with embarrassment, but she didn't make any excuses. "*I was about to attack, and I could not do it. I imagined those men lying dead in the street, their blood on my hands, and I froze.*"

"*You had no trouble fantasizing about killing Ardek,*" I reminded her. "*And you killed a woman a week ago. You did not freeze then.*"

"*That was different,*" she said. She slumped onto one of the beds, closing her eyes. "*With Ardek, I had so much rage in me that I was afraid to let it out, until it happened anyway. And with the northerners, they attacked us. It was kill or be killed, or at least lose our supplies. Tonight . . . I am sorry. I could not do it.*"

I snorted with annoyance, but I knew that she was being honest with me. No excuses. She was a killer in the literal sense, but that was it. She hesitated to kill another human unless she had to. She needed to be forced into it, to have no other choice, and that was that. Perhaps it was something we could fix, but for the moment, I couldn't count on her to kill in cold blood.

I sighed and asked, "*What happened once I left?*"

"Herald," she said, her voice small and tired. "*She . . . took care of it while they were stunned and staring after you. She and Ardek put the bodies in an alley. Tried to make it look like a robbery. There was blood all over the street, so who knows if anyone will believe it, but who will care?*"

Herald. Dear, reliable, capable Herald. How far she had come! How satisfying, and how goddamn awful it was that she could kill so easily.

"*Well, I am disappointed,*" I told her. She slumped even further, but then, as I let the silence linger, she straightened and looked at me. She could feel what I felt. I didn't know in what kind of detail she could feel it, but she certainly knew that I was not angry with her.

"*But not with you,*" I continued. "*Only that the plan, such as it was, failed. It does not matter. None of you got hurt, and we have the man. It is perhaps good that you are reluctant to kill, if Herald is not. And now that we know, we can take it into account. We will simply leave the killing to her.*"

I stopped there, letting my words sink in. I was not angry. But I *was* disappointed. And for all the steps she had taken to get back on my good side, I needed to be able to rely on Mak for anything and everything I might ask of her. I felt some little trickle of shame about using Herald against her like that, but there was truth in what I said too. While I wouldn't ask her to hurt anyone needlessly, I might need them to fight and kill in situations where I could not go with them. And while Herald had proven herself capable, she needed support. Who better to give it to her than her own sister?

Mak slumped again, almost falling forward, supporting herself with her elbows on her knees.

"*No.*" Her voice was low but firm. "*I will do better. I will.*"

Seeing the effect my words had on her was satisfying, but at the same time the trickle of shame turned into a stream.

"*You do not have to, if it is too much,*" I said, but she was determined now.

"*I do. I must. What kind of sister would I be to let her shoulder that burden on her own?*" She turned her eyes to me, and they were as hard as her voice. "*I do not want my sister to become a killer, Draka.*"

"*Very well*," I told her, wondering if it was already too late. I had seen the excitement in Herald's eyes when she fought. The first time she killed she had needed to process it, but since then it had seemed to come easily.

I didn't tell Mak that. I let her cling to whatever memories she had of the innocent little girl she loved, and I sent her down to the cellar to open the doors for me. It was time to talk to Simdal.

Interrogating Simdal was exhausting. Not because he wouldn't talk, but because once he started he just would not stop!

The man was used to being in charge. A flight with a dragon, repeated exposure to the clearly terrifying effect of my shadows, half an hour inside a well, and then being dumped on the floor of a small room in a cellar must have convinced him of just how little he was in charge, and it made him immensely uncomfortable. It didn't help that Herald had apparently told him that if we decided he needed to die, she'd leave it to me, after which she'd happily told him about the time I tore a guy's head off. The man could supposedly detect lies, and he believed her.

Simdal did not want to die, and he was a nervous talker. But, it turned out, not a stupid one. I wondered if you could have an advancement for blathering.

"We're all supposed to have eyes out for the 'teki girls, all of us, not just me! It wasn't my idea, the orders came from the Night Blossom—she wants them found. I don't know what you did," he said, looking at Herald and Mak in turn, "but she's really pissed about it, wants you captured and delivered to her alive. Doesn't care what we do to you, as long as it can be healed. But—but you—"

Just like every other time that he'd looked directly at me, his words deserted him. He'd need some encouragement to get going again.

"Yes?" I said. "You're wasting our time again. What about me?"

"You—you—nobody said anything about you! Nobody said anything about any Sorrows-beloved *dragon*! I didn't know! I just got some orders handed down to me from the boss to find and capture the girls, and I had some of my guys keep their eyes open, that's all! But you, I didn't know anything about you! Oh, gods and Mercies, you—" His eyes widened until it hurt to look at him. "That's it, isn't it? It was you! All of you! We all heard about the house on Cloud Street, how someone attacked it. It was you, wasn't it? That's why she's so pissed!"

The man talked a lot. The problem lay in getting him to say anything useful. Yes, it was interesting that the Night Blossom had kept me and the reason she wanted the sisters secret. And it was good to know that she had all or most of her subordinates keeping an eye out for us, not just this guy. It told me that

we'd need to be more vigilant. It also made me wonder if there had been other
people following us, and I'd only seen the kids because they were . . . well, kids.

But getting anything else out of him, anything about the Night Blossom, was
like pulling teeth, something I began seriously considering as we got into the second hour. Because for all of his babbling, the man was admirably loyal. He kept
dodging our questions, redirecting to prattle on about something else, but he did
it as though he was giving us something incredibly useful. I did not care about
who in the Guard was being paid to look the other way. I didn't care which gangs
occasionally did jobs for the Night Blossom, or which ones were on her shit list.
I . . . did care a little about how much money the places he ran pulled in. How
could I not? That was about silver, after all. But it didn't get me any closer to
my goal!

In the end it was Ardek who cracked him.

I wish I could say that it was planned, but it just kind of happened. We were
tired and frustrated, but neither of the sisters had wanted to go so far as to actually start hurting the man. I was pretty sure that I could do it if I just silenced
my nagging conscience, but if I did that I might just end up killing him in a fit
of frustrated pique. And putting the fear in him only shut him up until he got
going again, without making him say anything useful. I was becoming more
and more confident in my theory about blather advancements. The man was
infuriating!

We stepped out for a while to cool our heads. We left him in the small room
where we'd stuck him and went where the barrels of beer were kept. Ardek suggested that he might get the prisoner something to drink, and I off-handedly told
him to do whatever he wanted, without thinking much of it.

We'd been talking about anything except the odious man for about half an
hour when we realized that Ardek had never returned, and Herald got worried.
We hadn't heard anything, and there was no way for Simdal to get out without
going past us, but that didn't mean that nothing had happened. When we turned
the corner into the room though, we were met by an entirely unexpected sight,
which caused us to back up and listen rather than interrupt.

Ardek and Simdal were sitting on the floor, Simdal still bound and Ardek helping him drink from a tankard. Nothing too odd about that, except for the fact
that they were *laughing*.

". . . but honestly, I didn't recognize you," Simdal was saying. "Tark would
have new recruits sent around to the places I run, sometimes, to try them out.
Guess you lot couldn't do much damage in the shitholes they have me in." There
was a lot of bitterness in his voice, and I wondered if we could use that.

"Well, sir, it's honestly damn good to hear that they don't tell you high-ups
much more than us on the street," Ardek said. "Makes it easier to believe they
had us guarding the dragon. A handful of new guys and not a fucking heavy

among us. It's just . . . it only makes sense they wouldn't tell us if they don't tell no one shit, doesn't it?"

"It's my only complaint, really," Simdal said. "Fucking secrecy all the time, got to hear everything in rumors coming down the line. And I get told to do something and they don't tell me shit, and then my guys ask why, and I got to be the fucking bad guy telling them to mind their own business and keep their mouths shut when I want to know as much as they do. But the boss does good by us otherwise, so I won't be complaining."

"Yeah, until this," Ardek said darkly. "You didn't see her, sir. The dragon. Every poor bastard in her way, she just tore them apart. Piled them all in the pool in the atrium. Can't blame her after what the boss did to her, but Mercies' tits . . . every day I wake and I can't believe I'm still alive."

"Why are you? She killed ten guys in that house from what I heard. Why not you?"

"I ask myself that all the time," Ardek said. "She wanted me to show her where the Tekereteki girl was being kept, and then she, the girl I mean, she asked the dragon not to kill me. Dunno why, though."

Simdal snorted. "Fit young lad like you? It's not so hard to guess why the girl wanted to keep you around. Play your cards right and she'll be warming your bed soon enough. Not bad looking for a 'teki either, if you like 'em tall."

"Eh, I doubt I'm that lucky. Don't think either of the Tekereteki sisters like me much, and she has a betrothed, or something."

"Why's that stopping you?"

"There's her sister, for one. You haven't seen her temper. But Mercies, if I had the rocks . . ."

Wait, I thought. *Did he mean that? Was that actual regret in his voice? Still, emphasis on the full Tekereteki. Well done, Ardek.* The boy had listened to me. Herald was looking distinctly uncomfortable, though. Even with my excellent ability to see in low light, it wasn't quite bright enough to tell, but I could have sworn that she was blushing, which . . . I'd expected her to be annoyed, or angry. Not embarrassed.

Still young, I reminded myself. She's still young.

"The dragon, though," Ardek went on. "She really doesn't care about any of the Night Blossom's people. She wants the Night Blossom, and she wants Mister Tarkarran, and anyone else who was directly involved. As long as she gets that, everyone else is safe. You can tell when someone lies, right, sir? That's what they say. Am I lying?"

There was a long pause, then a tired sigh, and I knew that we had him. "No," Simdal said. "All right. I'll cooperate. But I'll need to lie low until this is all over, right? You, you're already dead if anyone realizes you're here and alive. I don't want to join you."

"Fair, very fair," Ardek said agreeably. "Here, finish this, then I'll go talk to them."

There was the sound of drinking followed by a satisfied sigh, then of Ardek getting to his feet. When he stepped out of the room and saw us, he startled but had the presence of mind to keep quiet, and we moved back out into the main cellar.

"So," Ardek asked apprehensively, "how much did you hear?"

"About my sister warming your bed, or the rest?" Mak asked flatly.

"I, ah . . . Miss Herald, don't listen to that old lech, yeah? I was just trying to . . . Not that I wouldn't . . . I mean, you're very . . ."

That time Herald most definitely did blush, her cheeks turning a darker, richer brown than I had seen them for months. She didn't look away from him, though, keeping her eyes locked until he withered under the sisters' gazes and looked at the floor, flushing almost as dark as Herald.

"Sorry," he mumbled.

Herald didn't say anything, though there might have been just a tiny hint of a smile once Ardek looked away from her.

"With that out of the way," I said, "good job. If this gets us somewhere, and if you don't die of embarrassment, I think you can be satisfied with your performance there."

"Thanks," he mumbled, still staring at the floor.

"Go upstairs and have a drink. A strong one. We'll talk to Simdal."

With another mumbled, "Thanks," Ardek scurried off. He didn't look at any of us.

I led the way into Simdal's improvised cell, the sisters flanking me. "So," I said, "Ardek tells me that you've decided to stop giving us the run-around. Good for you. I was starting to consider bringing you back home for a snack."

He didn't look like he fully believed me, but he had the good sense not to call me out. "Is . . . is it true, what the kid said? That you're only going after the ones who wronged you, and those who get in the way?"

I considered that. I might need to hit some of her people who weren't involved to draw her out or get information, so it wasn't quite true, but . . .

"I'm not going after anyone just because they work for her. And once she's dealt with, I'm not going after anyone who'll just walk away. That's all you get."

Simdal considered that. "If anyone knows that I talked, and I'm caught, I'm dead. Will you let me live and run if I've got to, once we're done?"

"Once you tell us what we need to know, as long as you keep your mouth shut and don't do anything stupid, I don't care what you do or where you go. Of course, if you keep being useless, or if you do *anything* that pisses me off, well . . . we'll see where my mood takes me."

The way his vile little face blanched at that was far more satisfying than I should have been comfortable with.

After that he answered our questions directly and without any obvious bullshit. He couldn't give us the Night Blossom; he'd rarely seen her, and he didn't know where she might be or even what her real name was. But he could give us Tarkarran, the weaselly little shit he reported to, who himself reported directly to the Night Blossom. The man I'd disabled in the forest, and who'd escaped capture afterward. The man who had tortured my friends. And that earned Simdal all the mercy he might desire.

CHAPTER FORTY-FIVE

Hide And Seek

We let Simdal go. We blindfolded him, and then I flew him out to the middle of a field in the starless night. It was mostly theatrics for his benefit, though, to keep him scared. He knew who'd held him, and he could have gone straight to Tarkarran or some other lieutenant of the Night Blossom's to rat us out, but Mak and I were in agreement that his survival instinct was stronger than that. Besides, he didn't know anything they could use that they wouldn't soon know anyway. Better to have him out there, potentially telling other flunkies that if they just cooperated, the big bad dragon would let them live.

Once he was gone and I was back, it was almost morning, and the humans had missed a full night's sleep. They went to bed, but I wasn't about to leave them unattended. Just in case Simdal *did* do something as monumentally stupid as bring people back to the inn for some revenge, or to try to capture the sisters like the Night Blossom wanted, I went with them to their room, entering through the window. I slept on the floor in front of the door, preventing anyone from getting in without going through me. I'd worry about getting out once everyone was rested.

Simdal, as it turned out, was not an idiot. That, or whoever he reported to was cautious. No gang of thugs stormed the inn, and no one tried to break down the door or climb in the window. Someone did knock on the door to our room in the middle of the day, though. Rib and Pot had been gone all night and returned at some point. After a nap they were very curious about what we'd been up to. The fact that I was there, and not hidden away somewhere, excited them to no end. We'd had a good six or seven hours of sleep by then, and the sisters decided that they may as well kick Ardek out, get dressed, and let the cousins in. It wasn't like Rib and Pot were likely to leave them alone at that point.

The two were not only there to satisfy their own curiosity, though. They also brought welcome news. The *Laughing Gull*, the ship we were expecting Tam and Val on, had been passed by a mail ship and was expected sometime later that evening or the next morning.

"What kind of a name for a ship is that?" Pot said. "Sounds like a cheap sailors' tavern. Anyway, they're sailing into the wind, so the mail ship overtook them easily. Oars and all that. No new messages from Tam or Val though, at least nothing they'd give us."

We told them about grabbing Simdal. I'd become much less eager to embarrass Mak after my talk with Herald and Mak's efforts to show how reliable she was, so I left out the part where Mak had frozen. Herald and Mak didn't bring it up either, for obvious reasons. With any luck the cousins would never need to know.

Once Rib and Pot left, the conversation pretty naturally turned to how—and how much—to tell the boys about what had happened while they were away. Personally, I was all for just telling them everything except what I'd done to Mak. They both knew the sisters well, and it would only be a matter of time before they started asking questions. If nothing else, they'd want to know why there was a young man sleeping in their sisters' room. It wasn't as though I was ashamed of my actions, even if I did regret some of them, but I wanted to give them some time to settle in before we gave them the whole story.

Herald and Mak, to my surprise, were a little less sanguine about telling them quite everything, at least at first.

"If we could leave out just how I was taken . . ." Mak said, turning her face to the wall in embarrassment.

"We will have to tell them about the Night Blossom and what happened," Herald said, "but I think we should leave out the details for now. Is it not enough that they know Draka rescued us? Telling them about . . . what happened between you, and how things are, will only confuse things. Let them think that you are merely grateful for the rescue, Mak, and we can let them know the full truth of it in time."

"That may or may not work, depending on how much the mercs know and if they can keep their mouths shut. Garal is good friends with them. Wouldn't he tell them everything if they asked?"

"He might," Herald said slowly. "But he does not know the details, only what he has seen. If we ask him, I think he would be willing to . . . not lie, but to let us handle any questions. As long as we let him know that we consider this to be a delicate subject, I am sure he would understand."

"And Lalia? The cousins?"

"They're impulsive," Mak said. "They may blurt something out, even if they don't mean to."

Herald sighed. "In that case . . ." She trailed off thoughtfully.

"We'll just tell them that I've sworn myself to you, Draka. Out of gratitude for rescuing us, and guilt for my part in getting you captured. It's not even a lie; it just leaves out one, admittedly large and important, detail."

"The dragon magic?" Ardek asked.

Mak turned to him, an unimpressed look on her face, and said, "Yes, Ardek. The dragon magic."

"Do they . . . What do they know about you, boss?" Ardek continued, undeterred. "Do they know you have any magic at all? The whole turning into shadow and that?"

"Not really," I told him. "Only you three and the cousins know about that. But they've sworn on their lives not to say anything."

"What about the village? The northerners, I mean? Should we tell Mister Tamor and Mister Valmik about them? Cause Jekrie is pretty sure that you did something magical when you scared the crap out of him."

"Huh." I hadn't thought about that. I'd bring them there soon enough, I was sure of it. They'd talk to Jekrie, and I hadn't really thought about what he'd taken away from our meeting in the forest. With him being such a respectful guy, he'd probably tell them anything they wanted to know. Not that it was anything compromising, but better they hear it from me first.

"Good point," I told him, and he straightened just a bit. "We'll just have to tell them before they find out."

Mak shook her head. "If they're going to be helping us with the Night Blossom—and we'll have to lock them up to stop them if we tell them what she did to us—they'll need to know what you can do before nearly anything else. How are you going to get anywhere with them around if you're trying to hide something like that?"

Herald nodded in agreement as her sister spoke, and added, "Besides . . . this is not for me to decide, obviously, but do they not deserve to know? They are our family, and they have fought and bled with you. We found the book together, and we are sharing the proceeds. I do not know if we will continue adventuring," she said with a sigh. "Not with the amount of money that we hope they'll bring. But whether we do or not, we all will still be a group, will we not? It will surely not be the boys doing their thing, and we girls doing ours."

There was still the concern of betrayal. I had thought that I could trust Mak, and that hadn't turned out great. If she'd known about my magic, we might all still be prisoners, or dead, or worse.

I must have glanced at Mak, or shown something on my face, or perhaps Herald just knew me, because she said, softly, "You can trust them, Draka. On my life, I promise that you can."

There wasn't much I could say to that. If I couldn't trust Herald's judgment, I was pretty much lost.

"All right," I said. "I'll show them. Not right away, but soon."

With the boys' arrival almost literally on the horizon, there was no point in planning anything else for the day. I would have liked to check out the secret rooms in the tunnels to see where the trap doors went, but that would have to wait. Nor was this the time to go after that little shit Tarkarran, as tempted as I was. No, we needed to be patient, bide our time, and make sure to be there when Tam and Val stepped off the *Laughing Gull*, whenever that might be.

To that end, the humans kitted up as much as they reasonably could in the city without arousing suspicion. Rib and Pot would be going with them. They'd be heading down to the harbor immediately. Hopefully Garal, Lalia, or both would join them before anything happened, but that depended on if they returned from their respective patrols in time. The Wolves may have been restricted to patrolling the areas closest to the city, but that didn't mean they spent any less time on patrol.

"There's a seafront tavern at the eastern end of the northern docks, called the Turtle," Mak said. "It's got a big sign, though the sign is a tortoise. Don't ask me why. That's where we'll be most of the day. It's popular with adventurers and merchants, so we won't look out of place there with our gear."

"A tavern?" I asked her pointedly.

"I'll behave," she said seriously, "and I'll have the others there to keep me honest."

"Besides," Herald said, "we are working. She never drinks when we are working."

I looked at them both and thought about it. It wasn't like Mak had been a raging alcoholic or anything. She drank to handle anxiety and stress, from what I knew, and she did seem a lot more stable now than she had a few weeks earlier. And, like she said, she'd have others there.

"All right," I said. "I trust you."

For a moment Mak looked like she might cry, before schooling herself. "Thanks" was all she said.

I continued. "I'll make my own way down to the harbor, somehow. I'll try to find some place close to the tavern. Mak, how close do I need to be for you to feel me?"

"I'm not sure," she said. "Fifty feet? A hundred? A mile? It's still very new to me."

They left the room to grab the cousins and head out. As for me, going out in the middle of the day was a big risk. The harbor wasn't far, but the streets were no less lively than any other day. While it wasn't quite the sea of humanity that I'd seen in major cities back on Earth, there were still lots of eyes to catch a shadow moving where it shouldn't. But it was a risk I'd have to take. If the Night Blossom or Tarkarran or anyone else was going to try to hit Tam and Val—to capture, kill, or rob them—fresh off the boat would be the time. And their lives, and the treasure they carried, was worth more to me than my slowly deteriorating secrecy. Besides, if someone saw me like that, they would only know they'd seen "something." Even if they had heard Relki's crazy story about a dragon stalking the alleys, they were unlikely to connect the two. If anything, they'd probably think they'd seen a particularly large rat or a cat.

It would still be dumb to take undue risks. The solution, I decided, was to try the drains. The tunnels were laid out regularly, and I was sure I could make my way to the right area without any trouble, and that way I'd only have to make a sprint for my entrance. Even then I'd have to be careful. The sky was cloudy, but it was still plenty bright enough to pose a problem.

From the partially open window I scoped out a good patch of shadow on the ground, where I'd be able to cross the wall enclosing the inn's courtyard to the alley beyond, and when there was a lull in the foot traffic, I went for it. Then it was a matter of staying on the shady side of buildings, moving between patches of shadow, and trying to stay behind boxes, stalls, walls, and fences. In the inverted light of my shadow vision, people walking the streets were visible mostly by their shadows, patches of light in a sea of black. I generally couldn't see where they were looking, and had to rely on waiting for an opportunity and moving as quickly as I could, stretching my darkness to connect to whichever new island of light I wanted to get to.

It was fun. Sneaking around, staying hidden in the middle of the day, was a real challenge. And since I didn't care too much if someone saw me in shadow form, the stakes were not particularly high, making the whole thing something of a game. An exhausting game that threatened to give me a headache, sure, but a game nonetheless. Ducking behind things, flitting around corners, sneaking right behind someone along a street, or just crossing behind them as they passed . . . It was oddly exciting! I was sure that if I'd been corporeal, I would have had a giant grin on my face by the end.

Nothing beat the moment when someone did a double take, staring right at the place I'd just passed, and even going so far as to saunter over and take a look. I had to scramble to get into a different cover before they—male, female, young, old, I couldn't tell—actually got a good look at me. I had been in several literal fights for my life, yet that moment made me feel incredibly alive. Clearly, I told myself, I'd been missing out!

But, as fun as it had been, soon it was over. I made it to my goal without any screaming, tired in a way that had nothing to do with my body, and with the beginning of a headache. I checked both ends of the alley, shifted back, drew the grate to the side, and—

"What the hell was that?"

The voice, high but male, came from just outside the alley. In a rush, I dove into the well, and as I was pulling the grate back into place, I heard quick steps, and the voice again, saying, "Did you see that? I swear I saw a tail go in that—"

I shifted as fast as I could, sped through the pipe connecting the well to the tunnels, and shifted back. And I was grinning like a goddamn fool.

While I was exploring the drains previously, I'd only gone far enough toward the harbor to be reasonably sure of where it was. Instead I'd focused on the north, where the gate to the forest was, and the east, where I knew there were sea caves and the sewers emptied.

This time, then, I went into fairly unknown territory. As I went I became aware that the tunnels had begun to slope ever so slightly, which made sense. They had to empty into the sea somewhere, so naturally they should slope in that direction.

The tunnels in that direction had fewer of the larger right-angled connections, but that was hardly a problem. My first order of business was to reach the sea, and then I could worry about other things. And reach the sea I did.

It began with a gradual brightening and then, seemingly out of nowhere, a spot of bright light in the distance. When I stopped and listened carefully, I could hear the soft sounds of the surf echoing, and there was the faintest scent of the sea. The bad kind of scent, of rotting seaweed, but the scent of the sea nonetheless. I kept going until I was met with the first deep water I'd seen down there, the slope of the tunnel taking it under the level of the sea at high tide.

Putting my feet in salt water brought back some unpleasant memories, and I stepped back unconsciously as I remembered thrashing in water, fishermen trying to harpoon me, and waking with water in my nose. I hesitated for a moment then, angry with myself, forced myself to press on.

By the time I reached the end of the line, I was shoulder deep in water, but getting along pretty well. I'd found that I could use my tail to help my legs along, whipping it side to side like a croc. It wasn't bad, really, and I really should get comfortable with swimming. I'd found two places in the city that exited into the sea already, and if I could swim comfortably, instead of madly scrabbling to keep myself from drowning, I would be much better able to make use of those spaces.

That was particularly relevant where I was. There were marks in the stone where a grate or grill had once been anchored, but it was long gone. I wondered if the whole system was a relic of the old Mallinean city on whose ruins the current city of Karakan was built, with no one maintaining it. If it was, whoever had originally built it had done a hell of a job. I hadn't seen any signs of repair, but neither had I seen any damage that hadn't been caused intentionally, and I wondered if there was some kind of magic at play, or just a ridiculous level of skill. Perhaps there was some kind of major advancement that let your work last forever. It sounded ridiculous, but Ardek had a minor advancement that made people like him, and Mak could literally heal people with a touch, so why not? Someone had built the stormwater and sewer systems. Someone had carved miles and miles of smooth, uniform tunnels in the mountains, with entire complexes of rooms and gates that were so well hidden they might never have been found if I couldn't see the magic in them. Merely making your work extremely durable seemed reasonable by comparison.

I stood half submerged in the sea. Carefully sticking my head out, I could hear gulls and human voices nearby, and I could see the main docks perhaps a quarter mile away to my right. To my left were some simpler fishing jetties, and beyond those the city wall extended into the water. I was facing southeast, so I didn't have the sun directly on me. Getting out that way unseen would be tricky, but it was, at least, an option.

Feeling quite satisfied, I returned to the darkness. I continued back up the tunnel until I was back on comparatively dry stone, then turned left, toward the northeast, the first chance I got.

It took a while, but I found what I was looking for. From my earlier finds I'd been pretty sure that I would. A few hundred feet up the tunnel, intersected with another one, and when I looked down the connecting tunnel, I could see stones on the ground. The wall had been cracked open, and beyond that opening was a two-foot tunnel leading to a small room with a ladder and a simple trap door.

I looked at the trap door, smug as could be, and whispered, *"Jackpot."*

Climbing was a little awkward, but I managed. I listened carefully at the trap door and heard nothing. There was something on top of it, but nothing too heavy, so I pushed it open just a crack, listening and sniffing the air. There were a lot of scents but nothing that I heard or smelled warned me of nearby people.

With a heave I opened the hatch the rest of the way, whatever had been on top thumping on the floor as it fell. I stopped and listened. Again I heard nothing, so I crawled up into the small room above.

The thing that had blocked the hatch was a barrel. By the feel of it as I put it back, it was empty, probably just there to cover the secret entrance to the tunnels. The small room I was in held dozens of barrels just like it, on the floor and on two-tiered shelves along the walls. They were all covered in thick dust. An empty doorway led into some kind of unused storehouse, filled only with empty shelves, dust, and broken crates.

Though, not completely unused. Besides dust there was a confusion of smells in the air, the aromas of spices and woods and even animal scents. And the floor was almost clean, the broken boxes shoved aside as if to get them out of the way. The large double door on one side of the building, where sunlight leaked in through weathered wood, was chained shut from the inside. But there was another door, four feet wide, at the back. Listening there, I heard the sounds of a distant crowd but otherwise nothing.

I tried the door. A chain rattled on the outside, and no one reacted. I slammed against it once, twice, three times, and something gave. With the sound of splintering wood and the chain clinking to the ground, the door opened a foot. I peered outside into a dark alley or side passage, covered by a leaky roof, and smelled spices and the sea. And just like that, I had a secret route to the harbor.

CHAPTER FORTY-SIX

Reunion

At some point, possibly soon, someone was going to realize that their storehouse, with its secret access to the stormwater system, had been broken into. Or broken out of, but they weren't going to realize that. I wondered if they'd be unfortunate enough to try and stop me from using it.

The roofed passage, accessed through the back door, connected a block of similar buildings, each with its own door. It was dark and deserted, but in either direction the passageway joined narrow streets that ran toward the sea, and these had quite a few people moving along them. Rather than repeating my people-dodging from earlier, I searched the roof and found a hole large enough to squeeze my shifted form through, bringing me onto the roof.

I went solid again and quickly looked around. There were plenty of tall buildings and a few towers nearby—I was in the lowest part of the city. By pressing myself as flat as I could and staying in the gutter that formed between the storehouses and the peaked roof of the passage, however, I could keep hidden from any casual onlookers. At least I thought I could, and if not, I would hopefully just look like a black splotch against the background.

There were five buildings on the block, built wall to wall, each with a peaked roof running at right angles to the one I was on. I could see the sea between them. Needing to orient myself better, I risked sneaking along the valley between two of the peaks to take a look.

The waterfront was bustling with activity. Against the pale tans and swirls of brown and pink of the sandstone that was so common in the city, woods and cloth stood out in a galaxy of colors. While greens and yellows were clearly the most popular for clothing, they were far from exclusive. Sails, drapes, and awnings in various hues, tones, and patterns were everywhere. To anyone who had never been to a city before, the colors alone would have been overwhelming.

I was on the eastern end of the docks, and from where I hid I could see two large ships, one with one mast and one deck of oars and another with two of each. The larger of the two was being loaded with wagons full of boxes, bags, and barrels, waiting on the long stone pier. I could hear the calls of the longshoremen as they carried the goods on board. Further out, in the circular harbor, a dozen other ships of various types and sizes lay at anchor. Along the street below me, people in simpler clothing, mostly cinched or belted tunics, hurried along or stood around talking to each other, while others in adventurers' gear, or what was unmistakably military uniforms—more than I'd expect, considering the situation in the south—or finer tunics, robes, or multicolored body wraps walked purposefully or strolled along, laughing with their companions. The sea air was fresh, and over that were the aromas of spices and woods and other goods that passed through the harbor for sale abroad or for consumption in or around the city.

I could have laid there for an hour. The sounds, scents, and colors, the variety of styles of dress and people was, quite simply, wonderful. But I had somewhere to be. I was in the wrong end of the district and needed to move west along the water to find a tavern called the Turtle.

The roofs seemed like my best bet, so that's how I made my way west. I could have gone back down into the tunnels and hoped to find another access point, but that might have been a waste of time. Besides, sneaking along the roofs just seemed more fun! Softly padding along, trying not to make a sound, staying low and shifting, moving from shadow to shadow at just the right time to avoid being seen, had my heart racing. And it wasn't just fun, it tested me to my limits. I had to find the best patches of darkness to shift, then strain to stretch across streets to another shadow quickly enough and at the right time, pushing both my abilities and my timing to their limits. There was no doubt in my mind that sneaking around a busy part of the city like that, in the middle of the day no less, was the best training I'd had since gaining my shadow powers, and I loved it.

There was no chance I would have done something like that without motivation. It was just too risky. I'd let myself get comfortable, complaining silently about feeling restricted by my need to hide but not doing anything about it. If it wasn't for the risk that the boys would be attacked somewhere between the ship and the inn, I would be sitting in the tunnels, waiting for someone to get me. Hell, I would probably still be at the mountain, watching the little village grow and waiting for someone to tell me that it was time to go hunt down the raiders in the south. Instead, there I was, having the time of my life dodging people and trying to keep track of sightlines, making my way slowly but surely to the western end of the docks.

I moved across roofs and across terraces. I shifted and dropped to street level and slunk behind walls and fences and, at one very memorable point, I snuck in *under* a cart as it made its way across a particularly wide and busy intersection where a small street met the main boulevard to the harbor. As I moved along, my sense of Mak's location grew more and more precise, until I could practically point at her on the ground floor of a three-story building up ahead, the first two floors built of the sandstone that made up so much of the city and the third of a dark red wood. I'd been keeping my eyes on the building since it stuck up above the roofs around it, and was glad that it was my destination. With any luck I'd be able to get up on the roof, which would give me a great view of the harbor.

It was better than I could have hoped. On the seaward side of the roof, a dormer with windows on the front and sides protruded to the level of the building's facade, and on the western side was a large, double chimney. The chimney and the peaked roof made a shadowy niche where I could sit, hidden from the buildings higher in the northern and eastern city, while the dormer blocked off the high city in the east. Meanwhile, I would have a lovely view of the harbor and the docks. It wasn't perfect, since there was still the slope of the roof to think about, but as long as I lay still it would be fine!

I made my way across the roofs to the building that housed the tavern, quickly checking that there was no one in the open windows. With the coast clear I shifted and stretched myself up onto the roof, then over the ridge and into the nook behind the chimney. Then I shifted back.

And I slid.

It was the barest movement as I felt the tiles under my hands move, but I nearly swallowed my tongue. Luckily, I didn't shout in surprise, instead taking a sharp breath as my tail whipped out to hook around the chimney while my right hand hooked all five claws deep into the wood of the dormer, stopping me from moving any further. The only casualty was the tile that had slipped under my hand, as it scratched and skittered its way down and then vanished over the edge of the roof almost immediately followed by the sound of shattering pottery and angry voices.

Well, I thought. *That could have gone better, or a whole lot worse.* On the bright side, there was now an exposed batten for me to brace against as I lay down, spreading my weight over more tiles. It felt secure enough. I was a little bit worried about what would happen when I needed to move, and my claws had left some hard-to-explain gouges in the wood, but at least the view was as good as I'd hoped.

There I stayed for about half an hour. I let myself simply enjoy the view until I felt Mak, below and behind me, start to move. I was close enough that I could tell as she got up, moved around something, and passed under me out the door and into the street. I carefully moved forward until I could see onto the street, and I saw her standing there. She was right by the edge of the quay with her back to the water, her hand resting on the pommel of her sword as she scanned the rooftops. Her eyes scanned for anything recognizable, slowly zeroing in on where I lay until they found me. Our eyes met, then she looked around the rooftop and nodded. She found my eyes again and pointed quickly to herself, then up, and then approached the building.

What followed was a little odd. While I returned to my hiding spot, Mak moved around the building, then entered it from some back door. Then she started moving in bursts, sometimes sitting still for almost a minute before moving only a few feet, other times moving slowly for several seconds before stopping, then starting again. She moved quickly at a diagonal upward, then went back to her stop-start motion, then up again, and then straight up, and then I could feel her almost next to me. There came a scraping from the dormer. The window facing me swung open, and I was greeted by Mak's grinning face.

"*I just had some fun,*" she whispered, and I grinned back.

"*Sneaking through the building, going places you are not supposed to?*"

"*Yes! It was amazing! My steps are so light, and it's like I blend into the shadows. It is . . . It must be from you, right?*"

"*You always had a pretty light step from what I have seen, but I think so. Now move over.*"

I shifted and, while she got the same awed expression she always did when she saw me use my powers, she did what I'd asked. I could probably have gone past her anyway, but it felt kind of rude to just push past someone, whether I was immaterial or not.

"*So,*" I said once inside, "*did you come looking for me for a reason or just to check in?*"

"*We have had word of the Gull. It has been spotted on the horizon. The boy Pot had at the lighthouse asked the spotter there, and he thinks it will be another five or six hours. It appears that they have given up on the wind and are moving by oar, and they only have one small bank of those. Then it will likely be another hour before anyone can come ashore.*"

"*Six or seven hours . . . It might not be dark yet by then, right?*"

"*Right,*" Mak agreed. "*But it is not like we can do anything about that.*"

"*I will just have to follow you the best I can then. Hopefully I will not be needed, but try not to move too quickly. Feel for me. Slow down if I fall behind.*"

"*We will. Now, the ship has three masts with gray sails. It has ten oars on each side and a large gull as a figurehead, so you should be able to recognize it fairly easily once it comes into the harbor.*"

"*Thank you,*" I said. I hadn't thought to ask, and I appreciated the thoughtfulness. "*Now, get back to the others. Enjoy yourselves. We have some long hours ahead of us. I will be here if anything comes up.*"

With that, and a nod from Mak, I went back out the window. She closed up, and I could feel her sneaking back down. There was a vicarious thrill in "watching" her go, and I found myself happy that we had something unexpected in common.

Then, with her back in the tavern, I settled in for a long wait.

I lay on the roof. I napped, and I watched the ships come and go. I saw more soldiers; there must have been quite a few of them in the city. A recruitment drive, maybe? Raising new regiments for the threatened war? I listened to short snatches of a hundred conversations. I didn't pick up on anything useful, but it brought me back to my days by the road, when I was alone in this world and just trying to find someone to connect with. I wondered what would have happened if I'd approached some other group. If I'd never met Herald. Would they have accepted me at all? Or would they have run me off and started a serious hunt for me? Who would I be, four months later, if I'd never made a single friend? If I saw every human I came across as a threat? What would I be?

I would be a dragon. That was the obvious answer, and I wasn't sure that I didn't like it.

Below me Mak sat, and then she moved. She went into the street and to other places along the docks, but she always returned, and she never came back up. The sun slowly passed across the sky, and on the horizon sails came into view. And, under one particular set of sails was a white figurehead, which I could see when it came closer, in the shape of a bird, its wings spread to the wind. The ship was slowly dragged along by ten pairs of oars, as someone aboard did some complicated things with the sails to try to claw just a tiny bit of speed from the wind. It was our ship, all right. And on board were two men who were hopefully still my friends, and they carried with them a sum of gold that should be enough to set their family up for life. And me . . . I very much looked forward to getting my claws on my share.

The ship passed the breakwaters and the lighthouse, gliding calmly into the harbor, and I wished that it would move faster, that it would dock *now*, that its passengers and their cargo would come ashore *now*. But I knew that I had to be patient. They would be here soon enough. The *Laughing Gull* anchored at a spot near the middle of the harbor, and the longest part of the wait began.

On the westernmost pier, an old wooden construction instead of the solid stone piers used by the larger ships, a small, single-masted boat with many oars lay. I watched it, trying to take my mind off the approaching treasure, and thought it was odd that it didn't set sail. It was quite far away and it was hard to make out any detail, but there didn't seem to be any supplies being loaded. I could see that there were a bunch of people hanging around, on the boat or waiting on the dock, so what were they waiting for? But then again, what did I know about sailing?

Herald, Mak, and the cousins, along with some people I didn't recognize, had come out of the tavern. They were standing on the quay, pointing and talking in excited, happy voices, waiting just like I was. They had been standing there for a little less than an hour, and there was still a twilight glow in the sky when I heard Herald exclaim, "A boat! They're lowering a boat!" and the excitement redoubled. And if I looked very carefully, I could see that she was right. Few others could have seen it in the deepening gloom, but there was a small boat—though it must have been fifteen feet long, at least—sitting in the water next to the *Gull*, a lantern at the . . . stern, maybe? The front bit. And another at the back. I watched with a growing hunger as the boat began to move, slowly approaching the docks.

Then something else caught my eye. The single-masted boat I'd been watching, which had waited so patiently for whatever it was waiting for, had left the docks at some point. It was perhaps three hundred feet out when I saw it. Six rowers were pulling it along with powerful strokes, and it was picking up speed, heading straight for the *Gull* and its launch.

I sat up and a chill raced along my spine. Surely this was a coincidence. The harbor was large, but going out the middle was surely the most direct way to get from the docks to the sea. But why would someone be heading out when it was getting dark? Could they be heading to the ship to pick up some cargo that couldn't wait for the ship to dock? But then, wouldn't that have been sent with the launch? And if not, why would the boat that was now racing forward at a tremendous speed have waited until the launch was in the water before they themselves left?

And why was it heading straight for the launch, its course changing ever so slightly to cross paths with it?

When they were within a few hundred feet, I couldn't deny it any longer. The two boats were going to meet. My humans on the quay had noticed the same thing and were scrambling to react, trying to get hold of a boat to go out themselves. It would have been too late, even if they'd reacted the moment the intercepting boat set off.

I could reach it in time, if I flew. But it wasn't dark enough. I'd be seen for sure, and even though it was getting late, there were still hundreds of people near the docks.

I could wait. I felt guilty for even thinking it, but I could. I could let the intercepting boat take the treasure, then follow them and take it back. That would be the safe thing to do, but Tam and Val would die. There was no doubt in my mind. I wasn't as close to them as I was to Herald or Mak, but they were two of the few humans that I liked and trusted. And they were useful. It would be a waste, letting them die.

And it would break Herald's heart.

I threw myself off the roof with a clatter of tiles. Shouting and screaming erupted behind me seconds later, unleashing a riot of emotions within me that

I had no time for. I ignored them. I beat my wings as hard as I could, turning myself into a missile cruising unerringly toward my target.

There were things in the world that mattered more than secrecy.

The two boats got ever closer. The launch had begun to turn, and as I hurtled through the air, I could see my friends and the crew scrambling to react. The harbor pirates on the larger boat, those that weren't rowing, stood braced with weapons in hand. Not one of them looked toward land, too focused on their rowing or on their target.

Two of the pirates raised bows. They nocked their arrows—drew—aimed—and loosed.

On the launch, no one stumbled. No one fell.

The pirates didn't seem to care. They looked so calm, so self-assured. They matched my own feelings perfectly. They had not the faintest idea of the hell they had invited upon themselves.

I crossed the last three hundred feet in less than four seconds.

The launch finished its turn, but it wasn't fast enough. The larger, many oared boat would soon be alongside it. The man at the rudder of the launch saw me and raised one hand to point, but there was no time for anyone to act.

The archers nocked—drew—aimed—

Too slow.

A few dozen feet out, I locked my wings, and the air whispered over them. There was barely a sound as I dipped to two feet above the surface of the water, turned up to clear the gunwale of the boat, and struck.

In the gathering dark, it must have looked to those standing behind the two archers as though a shadow had passed across the boat and just . . . taken them away. I didn't scream, or roar, or screech. I didn't make a sound. There were a pair of wet slaps, and by the time shock gave way to confusion and two bodies splashed into the water, I was a hundred feet away and turning sharply, my feet, knees, and hips mewling with pain. I had struck one man in the shoulder and the other in the head, and if either had survived the impact, I doubted they would be in any state to save themselves in the water.

I came around, taking out the turn so that I was parallel with the boat, coming up fast from behind and in full view of the rowers. One man, clearly choosing to believe his own eyes, had the wherewithal and the reflexes to throw himself into the sea. I graciously accepted his surrender. The others were not so lucky. As I tore past the boat, I let loose as strong a spray of venom as I could muster and, while it was not concentrated enough to kill, I doubted that anyone caught in it would be at their best in the fight that was sure to come.

My course brought me right above the length of the launch, and I had just enough time to see Tam, sword in hand, turn, catch sight of me, and gawp. Then I was past and turning again. When I came around, the boat, now a scene of utter chaos as men flailed and stumbled, had come up alongside the launch.

The three idiots at the prow still tried to board, seemingly not realizing that of the eight fighting men behind them, two were long gone, one had stumbled into the water, and the rest were struggling to see. Those three died quickly and unceremoniously under Tam and Val's swords. The rest were not so lucky.

I came down, braked *somewhat*, and crashed into two remaining fighters. What little I'd learned from Mak was lost as I just . . . let go. There was no need for skill or finesse. There were humans here. They were trying to rob me, to harm my humans and steal my treasure, and now they were all but defenseless. I abandoned all petty human concerns of restraint or mercy. There was no room for them on that boat.

Instinct took over. I let myself be a dragon, and I did what a dragon would do.

They had left the docks with seventeen men and women aboard. When the red cleared from my vision, there was not a human left alive on that boat. I think some threw themselves in the water. A little part of me hoped that they had, but if not, so be it.

The boat I was on glided past the launch. I looked at those on board. The crew stared at me in abject terror. One of them was on his knees, weeping openly. Val was his usually stoic self, and only gave me a quick nod, free of judgment. Tam gave me a nervous smile and a wave.

I returned a grin full of sharp teeth and flew off, grabbing one of the bodies and bringing it with me. For the sake of misdirection, I told myself, and not because instinct told me to bring my kill somewhere nice and calm. Not that I knew if it would do any good.

There was no coming back from this. I had revealed myself to dozens, perhaps hundreds of people. The dragon was out of the shadows, to mangle a phrase. I'd had a taste of freedom, and I felt completely and utterly alive.

CHAPTER FORTY-SEVEN

Out

Drunk on the carnage I had unleashed, on the fear in the humans' eyes, and on my own power, I left the harbor flying fast and low. I crossed the breakwater and turned north, dropping the dead man I carried, to be swallowed by the waves as soon as I was out of sight of the lighthouse. I'd only grabbed the body to give the boys some plausible deniability, but it was uncomfortably reminding me of the fact that I was hungry. In less than a minute, I reached the cave where the sewers discharged into the sea and there, proud creature that I was, I shifted and entered the least glamorous part of the city.

I didn't care. Nothing could assail my mood that night. A chain on my soul had been struck, and I was free. Too many people had seen me for their stories to be dismissed, and soon anyone who mattered would know. There would be no stories about wyverns, and anyone who'd seen a shadow move in the corner of their eye would wonder. They would know, and they would fear, and I reveled in it.

It was better this way. How can you fear what you do not know?

At that particular moment, however, what mattered was not what anyone might know or think of me. It was to rejoin my humans, and to make sure they were safe. As unburdened as I felt, I still wished to keep my association with them secret, as much as I could. Mak had told me all about her fears, what might happen if we were connected beyond doubt, and I agreed. I could only hope that tonight was not enough for that to happen, and that there was no ambush planned if the harbor pirates failed, but all the hope on Mallin and a peacock was worth a peacock. Thus, I needed to get out of the sewers and find them, wherever they may be, and make sure they were safe.

I could sense Mak, and I followed that sensation the best I could. Wherever two sewer tunnels joined, they grew wide enough for me to shift back and recover, which was . . . unpleasant. The air was barely breathable, but that was the least horrible part of it, and I considered myself truly blessed that anything that was not part of me fell right off when I shifted.

It took a few false turns and far longer than I might have liked, but I finally found a place where a high lip separated the sewer from the drains. Once I was over that, I felt more comfortable, back on familiar ground, as it were, and I started really following Mak. From what I could tell she had left the docks, but she had not returned to the inn, which they should have had plenty of time to do. Instead, they were heading northeast, and I had no idea what their destination might be. But they were moving at a steady walking pace, not running. That was a good sign.

Doing my best to take whichever tunnel would get me closer, I followed, keeping my eyes open for a break in the wall, but finally I got fed up and started testing drains, emerging into the street through the first opening that could accommodate me.

No alarm bells rang in the city. There was no panic. No crowds whispered fearfully in the street. Instead, a normal night was setting in. The streets had cleared as they always would, and slinking along on roofs and in the shadows was easy. That was good, of course. Convenient. Yet I couldn't help but feel somewhat disappointed. The memory of screams behind me as I threw myself out across the harbor was still fresh, and the pleasure it gave me was almost more than I could handle. I had felt fulfilled in a way that I couldn't have predicted, as though I had achieved a goal that I'd never known I had. As I moved along, getting ever closer to my target, I thought back on all the times I'd driven fear into the heart of some human and admitted that, yes, it had filled me with a base joy.

I remembered the way that Mak's spirit had broken under the weight of that fear, and a stab of shame snapped me out of my self-indulgent musing. Taking pleasure in the fear of others? Even those who had done nothing to me? What was I? That was a very draconic thing, I knew that deep down. And it was a part of me. But it wasn't *me*, not all of me, and it was something I would need to keep a close watch on. I'd let myself operate entirely on instinct ever since I left that roof overlooking the harbor, and it was far too easy, too comfortable, to just keep doing that. To relax, not worry, just take everything as it came and either destroy or dominate anyone in my way.

It was frightening just how *fun* I could see being a monster, and I couldn't let that happen.

I crossed a final block of roofs, and I found them. What I saw displeased me. My humans, or four of them at least, were being marched along inside a square of city guards, with Ardek, Rib, and Pot, along with others that I didn't know but thought were probably Wolves following along behind. Pot was carrying a familiar box of red lacquered wood in his hands. I felt oddly pleased that Tam and Val hadn't sold it, even though it was no doubt very valuable. The rest of what

I assumed was the boys' luggage was distributed among the group, along with all of my humans' weapons.

I had thought that I'd shed enough blood for one evening. Clearly I'd been mistaken. A furious anger rose inside me, and I prepared to leap into their midst to show, again, just what happened to those who'd steal from me. But, before I did, Mak found me among the shadows and rooftops. We locked eyes, and she shook her head, the motion small but her expression pleading.

I scowled, but nodded once. Fine. I'd trust her, and I'd give them a chance to talk their way out. Pot had what was presumably the treasure, so that was safe, at least. But my Herald, my Mak, and the boys were being taken somewhere, and I didn't like it one bit.

The place they were being taken to was a building made of solid sandstone, thick and sturdy, with a banner above the door bearing the city's emblem of a mountain rising out of the sea. The little family was brought inside. The Wolves, however, were denied entry, but Rib was not having it. She drew herself up in a way that I'd never seen before and, while I couldn't hear her exact words, she spoke in a clipped, confident way that made it entirely clear she was used to being listened to and obeyed. They let her in. Her young ladyship Terriallon Rebatia of Tavvanar was clearly not as easy to refuse as Rib the mercenary. She returned outside after a few minutes, looking no more satisfied than she had when she entered.

That made me even more displeased. But I'd give my people a chance to talk their way out. I understood. They wanted to hide their connection to me—and perhaps give the guards a chance—and I agreed. It was safer that way. But if I was not satisfied with their results, I would take charge, and I would do it my way. For the sake of the guards, I hoped they'd listen.

I spent most of my wait watching the Wolves and the lacquered lockbox in their charge. While I trusted the cousins well enough, I knew nothing about the others, or any of the few passersby. And the amount of gold and silver that we could assume was in that box . . . money can change people. I caught even Rib and Pot, certified aristocrats, throwing the odd, lingering look, and I kept my eyes on them until they came to their senses.

Mak only ever moved a little bit. I could imagine her pacing a cell or something like that, worried that I might smash my way in to free them at any moment. And she was right to worry. We were close enough that she should be able to sense that I waited, still as a statue but with little patience, my blood up and the desire to just pop off boiling inside me.

The idea of her fearing a rescue amused me for a while, but mostly I was relieved that I could still sense her. The idea that someone might try to quietly get rid of them was at the top of my list of reasons to simply go get them, but I held myself back. I had promised myself that I would trust Herald's and Mak's judgment, and if not then, well, when? I knew next to nothing about the law or keeping the peace in the city, and Mak had practically begged me not to get involved. And so, on edge and badly frustrated, I waited.

About an hour after Herald and the others had been brought inside the guardhouse, or courthouse, or jail, or whatever it was, a younger man exited and ran off toward the high city. Two hours after that the same man returned, accompanied by a large, elderly, and very unhappy woman, who was wearing an extremely expensive-looking robe. Trailing them were a number of burly men who had the look of personal guards. The men at the door scrambled to let her in, and she spent less than five minutes inside before leaving again, looking no happier but with a considerably faster gait than she'd come. Two minutes after she left, Herald stepped through the door, followed by the others. As soon as Mak came outside, her eyes found me, and she quickly touched her chest and bowed her head in thanks, drawing a few looks. She ignored them.

The group of Wolves was no smaller than it had been, and there were cheerful, if sleepy, greetings and congratulations all around before they all began moving in the general direction of the inn. I followed them closely on the rooftops, keeping low but unconcerned about being spotted as roosting birds fled before me. Tam urged the Wolves not staying at Her Grace's Favor to head back to their own beds, with his thanks, but not one of them did. Tam and Val, it seemed, had plenty of friends among the mercenaries, and they were determined to see the travelers safely delivered.

"I wasn't expecting to go back to jail quite so soon," Tam said to Rib when the conversation lulled.

"Yeah, most people don't," Rib said cheerfully. "Glad it wasn't longer, though. We were getting worried out here."

"Well, I heard that her young ladyship threatened to involve her cousin," he said as they moved along.

"I may have lost my patience just a little," she admitted.

"The lady justice Sempralia was not happy about being brought out so late," Tam continued. "Luckily for us, she was even less happy that it was because Mak here had been taken into custody. Apparently she remembers my sisters vaguely, but in quite a good light. *And* she was one of the councilors to vote in favor of granting our family citizenship, years back, so seeing all three of the city's Tekereteki citizens in custody . . . not happy."

"So . . . ?"

Tam grinned. "So she threatened to send the night commander to serve the rest of his career as a guard captain at a salt mine somewhere if he didn't either give a good reason, or release us immediately. Say what you want about privilege and corruption, but damn, it's nice when it works in your own favor!"

Rib sighed. "I do miss being able to just order people around sometimes. Cousin Mordo's gonna be pissed that I hauled my rank just to piss on some poor guard's boots, but beloved Mercies, it felt good!"

"They ever say what they were hauling you in for?" Pot asked. "Officially, I mean?"

"'Disturbing the peace,' they said. As though we had anything to do with anything. Even then, they had no standing to bring in my sisters."

"Well, Herald . . ." Rib said. "Anyway, not your fault those pirates pissed of Dra—" Rib barely caught herself. She threw a quick glance at the other Wolves, but no one seemed to have noticed. "That creature. Sorry. Hiccups. Too much stimulant."

"Don't worry, your ladyship," one of the Wolves said, dropping his voice. "It's the worst kept secret in the company. We know, right? Hell, the raid on those forest bandits in the north, half of us here were there! We've seen it."

"Uh, right," Rib said. It was hard to tell from where I was, but I thought she looked a little embarrassed.

"And the secret meetings the commander's been on? Garal clearing the hall for five minutes at a time? It's been pretty obvious that something's been going on. Maybe not this, but . . ."

One if the women weighed in. "I was at both the lake, after the nasty business with the camp there, and at the raid. You see a . . . what we saw once, you're not sure what you saw. Twice, you start to wonder, you know? Three times . . ."

"And always around you all," the first guy said, looking at Herald and Mak. "Or Garal and Lalia. We're not stupid," he said, laughing. "Just figured the less we said about it the better."

I wasn't all that surprised. I knew that plenty of the Wolves had seen me at least once. Rallon had ordered them to keep it secret, but it wasn't like that was ever going to stop a bunch of mercs from talking amongst themselves. I considered just jumping down there with them, to see what they'd do, but . . . nah. That would make it too obvious. I should probably talk to Rallon about a formal introduction to the company, though.

The group walked in silence for a block. We had probably all thought that the secret was better kept, but it didn't matter anymore.

"So," Tam said, breaking the silence, "you didn't miraculously give up your little vials while we were away then?"

Rib laughed. "Hah! Not on your life. I'd offer you some, the way you two look, but we're halfway to bed already."

"Sleep will be difficult as it is," Val said, but I wasn't so sure. The man looked asleep on his feet. "I fear the morning will be lost."

"And what do we need the morning for, love?" Tam said. "Let's sleep in! Live a little!"

"My forms—"

"Can wait, or you can miss one morning in a thousand. We're home! Besides, look at my sisters! We'll sleep until they get up, and then we'll have the most opulent breakfast imaginable to celebrate! What do you say, boys and girls?" He turned, taking in the whole party. "Spiced teas and fruit bread and honeyed fishes and anything else you could desire, paid for by your humble servant!"

"We're all on duty or patrol tomorrow," a Wolf answered cheerfully, "but if you can extend the celebration to the evening, we'll be there!"

"That's settled then! A fine breakfast around noon, and a fine dinner and drink in the evening!"

Val, off balance at the quick back and forth, just nodded, while the sisters behind them grinned.

Herald and Mak looked so happy to see the boys, back and free, that I almost didn't want to get involved. But unfortunately, there were things that we all needed to learn from each other, so half an hour later I was waiting on the roof of the Favor for everyone to get inside. I didn't need to wait long. The Wolves, other than Rib and Pot, said their goodbyes. There were renewed promises to meet up the next night without a location ever being mentioned, there were handshakes and hugs, and then my half of the group headed inside. I didn't wait. I simply shifted and drifted in through the same window I'd left open that morning.

I settled on the floor. Soon I heard cheerful, if muted, voices in the hallway outside, which ended with a "Come on in! Let's talk!" from Mak. Then the lock rattled, and Mak opened the door, greeting me silently with a rare look of mischief on her face. I grinned at her.

Tam *jumped* when he walked through the door and saw me. Val, who came in behind him carrying the lockbox and bringing the mixed scents of gold and silver with him, merely startled. That was a fairly strong reaction for him, though. "Draka, good to see you again," he said and gave me a simple nod.

Tam was less restrained. "Draka!" he said with a smile, his voice choked as he held himself back. "Traveler take me, but you scared me! You're here! In the city! And you were terrifying! Are you out now? No more hiding?"

Out. That was certainly one way of describing it.

"I suppose that I am," I said. "I will not be walking the streets openly or flying across the city during the day, but enough people must have seen me in the harbor that my existence won't be secret anymore."

Tam's smile softened to something fonder. "In the harbor? So that was . . . You were still hiding until just now? You threw that away for us?"

"Don't flatter yourself," I said. "For the treasure, of course."

"Clearly," Val said somberly. "Much effort and risk was spared, your way, instead of waiting for the pirates to take the treasure somewhere secret. A great inconvenience avoided."

"Can we talk now?" Tam asked. "Why were there pirates in the harbor, and why did it seem like you all expected something to happen? I tried to get some answers out of these two," he said, indicating Herald and Mak, who'd come in behind him, "but they kept telling us to be patient. Also," he continued, turning directly to Ardek, who stood with the sisters, "I feel like I recognize you, but can I finally get some answers about who you are and what you're doing here, with us? No offense, but you look a little younger than Mak usually likes 'em, and Herald was spoken for last I checked."

Rib and Pot came in, closing the door behind them, and with everyone crowded into the small room, Mak sighed. "Tam, Val, you two should sit down."

"Why?" Tam looked around, his smile slowly turning nervous. "Why do I feel like I'm not going to like this?"

"Here," Val said, putting his hands on Tam's shoulders and gently pulling him down to sit on one of the beds. "Listening to Mak would be best, I think."

Mak didn't ease them in. "A week after you left for Tavvanar, the slavers grabbed me off the street as I was stumbling home, blind drunk," she began, and Tam's face fell. "The next day they took Herald."

When we filled them in further, there was anger, and there were tears. Herald and Mak spared Tam and Val the details of what had been done to them, but Tam wouldn't let his sisters go for several minutes once he got his arms around them, cursing the slavers for what they'd done, the gods for allowing it, and himself for having left. Ardek had wisely chosen to position himself as far away as he could from Tam before Mak got to the part where he was one of the Night Blossom's guards. Tam still lunged for him. With two people holding him, and a dragon and two others standing between him and Ardek, nothing came of it, and we managed to calm him down by telling him how helpful and contrite Ardek had been since then.

We told them nearly everything. We told them about breaking out, though not how I got loose. About staying with the Wolves and leaving Karakan. We told them about the gate and my mountain, about Barro—who Val did indeed remember fondly—and about the raiders in the south and the fire. We told them about the bear, and about flying, which got some laughs and some appropriately impressed noises. We told them about the refugee camp, soon to be a village, and they both approved wholeheartedly with my decision to let the northerners stay. They were very disappointed with the innkeeper, but understood that there was little he could have done to resist.

Mak even told them about her new advancement. All that we left out, really, was just how bad it had been between Mak and myself, and the details of my relationships with Herald, Mak, and Ardek. They would need to know someday, but it was too soon.

They were a little uncertain about Kira.

"So this mercenary. She's, what? Your pet?" Tam asked me cautiously.

"Prisoner," I corrected. "And only until I hand her over. Or that was the plan, at least. Now I'm not so sure."

"So you're keeping her?"

"She's staying."

"But you're keeping her there, at the mountain. Your home. Because you want to, not because she asked to be there. But she's not under guard or anything. So . . ."

"She's not a pet!"

"But she is a young-ish woman that you abducted—"

"Captured! She's a mercenary!"

"Fine, yes, that you *captured*, and now you're keeping her at your mountain. But she's not a prisoner?"

"She's free to move around as she wants. She just . . . can't really leave. There's forest all around and she doesn't speak Karakani."

"So you'd let her leave if she wanted to?"

"She is mine!" I snapped. "She has nowhere to go, and your city will make her a slave, at best, if I turn her over. So, fine, yes! I am keeping her, and that is that!"

"All right, all right," Tam said, his palms up. "I just wanted everything to be clear. And Ardek . . . ?"

"I work for her, I just can't quit," he volunteered cheerily. "Paid me a dragon up front too! Better boss than the Night Blossom, so far."

Tam was looking pretty haggard at that point, with Mak on one side, Val on the other, and Herald holding him from behind. "Right. All right. Mercies, I need to sleep on all of this. Can we put off our story until tomorrow? It's nowhere near as dramatic as all this, but . . ."

"The story, yes," I said. "But there's one thing that can't wait. I've waited for too many weeks. Tell me. I have to know. How much did you get?"

"Enough?" Tam said. "Can we leave it at that? Enough that we should leave it in a room that has a dragon guarding it, just to be sure?"

I felt the irritation rising, and Mak must have too, because she stepped in. "Go on, Tam. Just tell us! What's the problem?"

"I just . . ." he began, but trailed off.

Val scrutinized his lover for a few seconds, then said, "There is a great deal of coin. I trust everyone in this room, except, and I ask your forgiveness, Ardek."

Ardek gave a *fair enough* kind of shrug.

"But you all have taken him into your confidence, and so shall I. Tam, is this because of what we talked about, on the ship?"

Tam looked back at Val, then sighed. "Yes."

"Then there is a solution. Draka. Will you promise to remain with us, or near us, until we can secure the treasure?"

"Yes?" I said, confused that they would even ask. "Of course I will."

"There will be no immediate departure, to take your share back to your hoard?"

"Oh."

That was actually a reasonable concern. Knowing me, I might have done just that. "I . . ." I said, and hesitated. Could I promise that? My share would not feel as though it was truly mine until I'd brought it home, but surely I wasn't that weak? Besides, my humans were still in danger, and I had to keep them safe.

"Yes," I said, confidently. "I can promise that."

"Very well," Val said. "Tam, do you wish to . . . ?"

Tam raised his head, and he was grinning. "You do it, love. Tell them."

"Five pounds," Val said, and began to grin. "Five pounds of gold was paid, or rather, its equivalent in gold, silver, and gemstones. Four hundred dragons, in various recognized coinages. Less our expenses for the journey, and a full sixth share set aside for the Three, sixty-six dragons each, and some eagles and peacocks."

Herald's eyes lit up. Her face split in a grin only matched by the one she'd worn after we flew together for the first time. Then she fell back against the wall, her feet kicking wildly to either side of Tam as she clamped both hands over her mouth and squealed with pure, avaricious glee.

CHAPTER FORTY-EIGHT

A Most Profitable Journey

Val had been wise to make me promise not to go anywhere.

"How many eagles?" I asked, my voice thin. I found myself suddenly having some trouble breathing.

Val smiled, then snorted, and then laughed, short but full and not holding anything back. "I suppose," he said, clearing his throat after getting himself under control again, "that it's best left to dragons to worry about bits, when silver's on the table. Very well. After expenses, split six ways, each take comes to sixty-six dragons, four eagles, twelve peacocks, and one bit, to give the exact number."

Sixty-six dragons. Nearly a pound of gold in theory. The reality was even better—several pounds of mixed gold, silver, and gems. And it was mine. I wasn't sure, exactly, but that might *double* my hoard, and I was itching, desperate to go, to bring it home where it belonged. There was no way this wouldn't get me another advancement as well, and mighty though I was, every advantage was welcome. Especially now that I had, to some degree, outed myself to the people of the city. It would surely draw would-be thieves and slayers, some of whom might actually pose a real threat.

As I worried about that, there were two other thoughts above all others, proud and arrogant. *Let them come*, I thought. *Let them try.*

A shameless rumble filled the room. Just looking at the treasure was a test of my honor and my resolve. Most of the value was in gold coins—a mix of dragons and others, with flowers or trees or fish or other designs on them—and small pouches of diamonds, rubies, emeralds, sapphires . . . all kinds of beautiful things. And then, of course, there were several pounds of silver coins, to make up whatever value the buyer couldn't come up with in more convenient currency. I wanted to take my share and leave. To be totally honest with myself, I wanted to take the entire box, but I was not going to stab my friends in the back, no matter how intoxicating the fortune before me was. I forced my avarice down. Besides, whatever went to the humans was practically mine anyway. Mine by proxy, as it were.

There was a very real desire in that small room to find some all-night tavern and celebrate until the sun came up, but in the end it was the fact that I couldn't join the humans that killed that idea. Instead, they all separated to their individual rooms, although Tam insisted that Ardek take his cot and move into his and Val's room. Herald rolled her eyes at that, and Mak gave her brother a very unimpressed look at how insistent he was, but they didn't argue. Ardek snored.

So, in the small hours we finally got to sleep. The humans were all exhausted, and the sisters were asleep in moments, despite their excitement over their new riches. I'd had plenty of time for small naps but, curled around the red box full of treasure as I was, the heady scents of precious things lulled me into a deep and relaxing sleep, full of sweet dreams.

Late into the next morning we woke to knocking, and Lalia's voice calling, "Hey? You girls in there?"

I got up, stretched, and, with some difficulty and great care, got the key off the hook by the door and worked the lock.

"Good morning, Lalia," I said, making her jump as I opened the door. "Where were you last night?"

"Draka! Hells, what are you . . . You know what? Doesn't matter. Double strength patrol with Garal, got stuck out, had to camp for the night. Just got back from reporting in." She stuck her head in the room, actually getting within a foot of me without flinching. "Girls! I met Val outside, and he says you haven't celebrated yet! Get decent and let's go!"

"Hey, Lalia," Herald called from her bed. She was still curled up under her blanket. "Just . . . gimme . . ."

Mak sat up, her blanket wrapped around her, and waved, then got up and started dragging a loudly protesting Herald out of bed.

Lalia turned to me. "You don't mind, do you? I don't really know any place we can go where we could bring you . . ."

"Market!" Herald exclaimed. "Let us just get some stuff from the market, good stuff, expensive stuff, and eat here!"

"It's fine," I lied. "I don't mind if you want to go somewhere nice."

Herald started to protest, but Mak spoke over her. "Draka, we wouldn't have found the book without you, and Tam and Val wouldn't have made it to shore if you hadn't stepped in. This is your celebration as much as anyone's." She looked at Lalia. "Is Garal around? He knows what Draka likes."

Lalia took it in stride. "Oh, yeah. He's talking to the boys and the Terriallons. You all just get comfortable and wait here. We'll take care of it."

Mak scrutinized Lalia for a second, then grabbed her purse from beside her bed and threw it to Lalia, who caught it without looking.

"Thanks," Mak said. "We appreciate it, but we're paying."

Lalia considered the purse, hefting it. They shared a look, and she said, "All right, sure."

It was pretty clear that there was a lot of pride and mutual understanding going on. I would have expected arguing from both sides, possibly followed by begrudging acceptance, but Mak and Lalia had known each other for years. They simply cut out the pointless back and forth and arrived at the same place.

An hour later we were gathered in the cousins' room. Or rooms, rather. It was the only suite in the inn with a separate bedroom and a sitting room, which was larger than the sisters' room and was where we were gathered.

Only one bed, I noticed, though it was a big one. I decided not to ask; I wasn't sure if I wanted to know.

The table that the humans crowded around on borrowed chairs groaned under a truly decadent spread of breads and meats, jams and fruits and cheeses; the inn was in the most mercantile part of the city, and the cousins knew where to go to get the good stuff and had silver to burn. They had, apparently, opted for fruit juice rather than wine or anything else. I wasn't sure if Mak had sworn off the drink altogether, but not encouraging anyone to get day-drunk when they had a small fortune to take care of was a nice touch.

I sat at one short end of the table. The magic lockbox sat on the floor beside me, and I had my own breakfast arrangements. Garal had, with very kind consideration, arranged a small crate with a variety of fish, as well as some kind of squid and small crabs. If the smell bothered anyone, they didn't mention it, and the things were delicious.

Knocking on the table, Garal silenced the conversation and the sounds of eating. He raised his mug. "Companions, old and new!" he said, looking around and nodding to Ardek. "A drink, if you would, to profitable journeys, safely ended, and to the good fortune of good friends!"

There were cheers all around.

Herald raised her mug and looked at me. "To unlikely friends in unlikely places!"

"To open minds, and open hearts," I said. A little sentimental, perhaps, but I meant it.

"Setting aside your differences in the face of danger," Lalia added.

"To a shitload of gold and silver!" Rib exclaimed, raising her mug high. It was a little against the grain and on the nose, but the cheers she got were as loud as any before.

"To a good story!" Pot shouted. "Tell us the story!"

"Not much to tell, really," Tam said. "Just a lot of long days at sea and on the road, waiting in rooms, negotiation, storms, betrayal, bandits, attempted murder, and pirates."

"Also beautiful landscapes, beautiful art, and beautiful people," Val added.

"Well, yes. Some—a lot, really—of the waiting was spent enjoying everything that Tavvanar has to offer. Within reason, of course. Although . . ." his grin faded, "having heard what you all went through while we were away, I feel somewhat guilty. Compared to that, we were on vacation."

"You couldn't have known," Mak said. "Besides, it wasn't all bad, and it ended well. If anything, I'm glad that you didn't have to go through it with us."

Herald nodded vigorously. "And we would rather not think about all that now. This is a celebration! Tell us about your journey!"

"Right. Well, we set sail on the finest day in living memory . . ."

I wasn't sure how much of Tamor's tale was true, but at least Val didn't contradict him at any point. No matter how much of it had been fabricated or exaggerated, it clearly hadn't been smooth sailing, neither literally nor figuratively.

The trip across the narrow sea to Tavvanar should have taken two days. Instead it had taken four, and everything that possibly could had gone wrong. The food had been bad, causing an outbreak of stomach illness on board. While that went on, a surprise storm had not only stopped their progress halfway across but had torn sails and broken spars, forcing them to spend a day making repairs. While the recovering crew took care of that, one sailor had snuck away from his duties and attempted to burgle the boys' cabin while they enjoyed the fresh air. The would-be thief was only caught because Val had decided just then to go get his paper and charcoal—Tam had apparently looked particularly fetching at the time. A "scuffle" had ensued, which Tam clarified to mean Val beating the sailor to within an inch of his life. Other members of the crew had objected, there had been a standoff, and the situation had only resolved peacefully when another passenger spotted a stolen scarf of hers peeking out of the sailor's tunic.

The man had been thrown in the bilges for the rest of the trip. I wasn't sure what bilges were, but from the reactions of the others, it sounded like a fitting punishment.

The first days in Tavvanar had been considerably better. The boys had apparently just missed some kind of riot, so the streets were calm, if a bit messy. They'd gone to the main temple of the Three, presenting their letter of introduction, and the Three-ers had been shockingly polite and accommodating once the letter had been read. They had been informed well ahead of time that the boys would be arriving, and some high-up had taken the time to find three—of course—possible buyers for the book. They even offered Tam and Val accommodations for their stay, but the men had declined. The cells had been quite Spartan and, more importantly, separate.

Tavvanar was, from the way they told it, a warm, dry city built of gray stone and dressed in reds and blues. And not in the way that Karakan was *mostly* a city of green and yellow; other colors were rare in Tavvanar. They produced their own dyes, it seemed, and were famed for those two colors. The best in the world, everyone agreed. When I protested that the cousins never wore blue or red, I was told that sixteen years of nothing but red and blue was quite enough, thank you very much.

It was also a larger city than Karakan, sprawling along a flat coast and with at least twice the population, though it was hard to be sure just how many people lived in its territories. The kinds of people who might be interested in buying our book didn't spend much time in the city, instead living on the vast estates that divided most of Tavvanar's land between them. City lords, like Rallon, were the exception, concentrating their properties inside the city as opposed to the much more numerous country lords. That, of course, meant that Tam and Val spent a lot of their time abroad, traveling from one potential buyer to another. Tam populated that part of the story with monsters and bandits, mysterious strangers and crafty orphans—a common feature of Karakani stories, apparently. I wasn't sure how much of that I believed, but the man told an entertaining story, and nobody seemed any more interested in calling him out than I was.

The story took a bit of a turn when one of the interested parties that the Three-ers had suggested attempted to murder them in his own home. After a failed attempt to drug them with wine, Tam and Val had barricaded themselves in their room with the guards breaking down the door. As they grimly prepared themselves for a last stand, fortune smiled upon them! A servant girl in the household, a secret spy for a different lord, had grown so enamored with Tamor—Val *did* roll his eyes a little at that point—that she couldn't bear to see them killed, and helped them escape out the window and away from the estate on horseback. The fact that it was her master who ended up buying the book, having heard of it from an acquaintance, surely had nothing to do with it.

At that point Tam mostly wrapped up. They met their rescuer's master, one lord Timerisemmon, got along famously, negotiated a price that was better than any offer so far, and even ended up traveling back to the city in his company. There they were wined and dined and entertained at the lord's expense for several days until the time came to return to Karakan. And, when surprise delays forced them to remain for several days longer, it was seen as divine providence more than anything.

"If only the man had been forty years younger," Tam said, sighing.

"A pity," Val agreed with every sign of sincerity. "But there was some difficulty in keeping up with him as it was."

"Mercies, yes!" Tam laughed. "His lordship really knows how to enjoy a night out! Did I tell you all that we got in a brawl? One that he started? The man is over seventy!"

Rib and Pot had been laughing their hearts out ever since Timerisemmon was mentioned, and Pot finally recovered enough to say, "Timerisemmon! The man's notorious! He's considered a hero and a disgrace to the city! Cousin Mordo's father was close friends with the man! We have to tell him!"

"Semmon!" Rib giggled. "Can't believe you found Semmon! The fucking luck of it!"

"Oh, he did mention that he doesn't get along with most of the upper crust," Tam said. "Military man, and all that. We have a standing invitation if we're ever back. And, ah . . ." He turned to his sisters, scratching the back of his head. "He offered to marry either or both of you. Not sure how serious he was."

"That's . . . kind of him," Mak said, trying to sound serious while fighting a losing battle not to laugh.

Herald didn't hold back. "Write and tell him thank you, but I am spoken for at the moment!" she said, grinning.

Tam smiled back. "Yeah, I told him that I'm not head of the family and that Mak would have to decide."

"Wouldn't worry," Pot said between laughs.

"He's offered to marry half the women in Tavvanar by now," Rib included.

"He's used to rejection! But, Mercies, his lordship Timerisemmon Arpon with two Tekereteki wives? Can you imagine, Rib?"

Rib bent double and howled with laughter, so pure and bright that I found myself laughing, even though I had no idea what the joke even was. "They'd die!" she choked out in a language similar enough to be a sister dialect to Karakani. "They'd die!"

"Who?" I asked, and Rib didn't even bat an eye at my use of what I'd guess to be Tavvanarian.

"The gossips!" she managed after a few seconds. "They'd *die!*"

Being becalmed for several days on the way back turned out to have been the least interesting part of their journey. Having learned from their first trip, one of them remained with their new fortune at all times. They rarely left the cabin.

"Greatly relaxing," Val commented, a peaceful look on his face. From the wicked grin that flashed across Tam's face, though, I wondered how much relaxing they'd actually done.

"Then," Tam said with an air of rounding off, "we convinced the captain to send us ashore in a boat, prepared to die fighting, were arrested by the guard, and here we are!"

"Ending needs work," Ardek said, a little timidly.

"Don't worry," Tam said. "It'll be better tomorrow!" Which got another round of laughter.

It was a lovely meal, all told. Of course someone had to go and end it early by knocking at the door.

Everyone looked at me. We came to a silent agreement, and everyone shuffled around so that I could sneak into the small, separate bedroom, with Herald closing the door on me.

There came another knock, more urgent, and an anxious voice called, "Your lordships? Are you available? There is someone to see you."

I heard the door open, and Pot's voice, sounding more refined than I'd even heard it. "Master Reben. Good day to you. And this is . . . ?"

"Captain Vakkal, with the City Guard, your lordship," said a vaguely familiar voice. Vakkal . . . right! The possibly crooked captain who had stopped Herald, Mak, and Ardek as we left the Night Blossom's house in the high city. There was no way that was good.

"And what is your business with us, Captain?" Pot asked curtly.

"Myself and my men have been tasked with bringing one Miss Makanna and her family, as well as one Mister Valmik, before the council, your lordship," Vakkal replied, his tone polite but firm.

"And what is this in regards to? I should point out that my friends were already harassed by the Guard last night, and the lady justice Sempralia was not at all pleased."

"It is she who has requested their presence, your lordship. And I am afraid that I must insist. The lady justice is waiting as we speak."

There was a short silence after that.

"In that case, Captain," Mak said, "we mustn't waste the lady justice's time. Give us a few minutes to get ready and we'll join you downstairs."

"Thank you, Miss Makanna," Vakkal said, and the door closed.

The door to the bedroom opened almost immediately. "Please, Draka," Mak said. "Stay here. Don't follow us. Guard the treasure. Please." Without waiting for my reply, she turned around. "Rib, Pot, Garal, Lalia, can we count on you to come with us?"

"Try to keep us away," Lalia said, and the others agreed with nods and mutters. "Isn't that the same captain who's being paid off by the Night Blossom?"

"He's one of them," Ardek said. "Maybe. At least he didn't have the guts to risk going against her. Might not be in her purse, but I wouldn't chance it."

"Right," Mak said. "See, Draka? We'll be as safe as we can be. Guard the treasure. That's our future. Please!"

I looked from Mak to the box, and then to Herald who nodded, once and sharply.

"Um, what about me, boss?" Ardek asked. "Do I . . . ?"

"Go with them," I told him. "I want someone who can run back here and let me know if I need to . . . you know. If I'm needed."

He looked more than a little anxious about that, but nodded, like I knew he would.

I had been planning to follow them, of course, but what she said made sense. They'd have four skilled fighters with them, two of whom were actual, real-life aristocrats of some kind. And Ardek, though I wasn't sure what good he'd be in a fight. It was in the middle of the day, so it wasn't like the captain could disappear them, and I'd know in which direction Mak was at all times. On the other hand, with all of us away, there would be no way to know that the treasure was safe, and there was no time to stash it somewhere.

"Fine," I said, to Mak's obvious relief. "Rib, Pot, I don't know if the inn has someone who cleans the rooms regularly, but make it clear that no one is to come in here. I'll be in front of the door, and I will be very annoyed if they keep slamming it into me."

"We'll let Reben know," Rib said.

"Reben? I thought you'd've killed him by now," I said, genuinely confused until my conscience caught up with me. "No. Of course you haven't. Still, why are you trusting this man?"

"It is still his inn," Herald said with a shrug. "And we like it here. So we talked about it. He knows that we will not easily trust him again, so we do not think he will try to betray us. And . . . he did not have much of a choice. He deserves a second chance."

Mak nodded her agreement and said, "Besides, a little forgiveness can go a long way. He's very grateful. And," she added, with a smile that slowly became predatory, "we've been talking to him about buying the place. Together, we can afford it. And owning this inn, no matter what we pay for it, would let us establish a House."

"We could have a name," Tam grinned. "But! If we annoy the lady justice, that might be only a beautiful dream, so . . ."

"Right," Mak said. "Get ready, quickly. Let's not keep her waiting."

I wanted badly to go with them. Even though they insisted they were safe, I didn't trust anyone I didn't know. To be fully honest, I didn't trust anyone I didn't have some measure of control over. Love, respect, or fear, it made little difference.

The dragon in me hated it, but I let them go. If they were the few people that I trusted, then I needed to show that trust. I had to believe that they could keep themselves safe. For all that I sometimes wanted to, I couldn't always be around. They were mine, but they didn't always need me to protect them, and I had to learn to accept that.

I let them go. Then I curled up in front of the door. I rested my head on the red lacquered lockbox filled with my four dear friends' fortunes, and I dreamed of a golden future.

The Humans

When a lady justice of the Karakani ruling council requests your presence, you do not keep her waiting.

The little family dressed in a hurry. Makanna and Herald helped each other into their finest silk wraps, while Tamor and Valmik put on richly dyed wool robes. The quality was nothing remarkable, and they could have afforded better with their newfound riches, but it was the best they had. Even still, the clothes were like new, barely worn, and they had only been able to buy them thanks to their shares of the Old Mallinean silver they'd found together with Draka.

No matter. It was more than enough for people of their standing when going before a councilor. The Tekereteki siblings' choices of bright yellows and greens for their finery was perhaps a little on the nose, but Valmik had insisted that not only would it be a visible declaration of loyalty to their city, but that the chosen shades would complement their dark skin beautifully. And he'd been right, as he so often was when it came to anything aesthetic.

As they each got ready they said a quick goodbye to Draka. The dragon was clearly uncomfortable with the situation, but Makanna and Herald had convinced her that they were in no danger. As they got ready, they gathered in the common room of the inn and, when they were all there, stepped outside. Garal found a street kid and paid him a peacock to go to the Wolves' temporary barracks and report where they were going, with a promise of another when the kid mentioned his name. Neither Garal or Lalia were on duty that day, but it often paid to make sure their fellow mercenaries knew where they were going. Rib and Pot, of course, went where they pleased. Unless Commander Rallon went out himself, they had little in the way of duties, being held back for special assignments. Special assignments such as protecting Rallon's investment in a certain dragon, which included looking after the best interests of that dragon's friends, servants, pets, or whatever else you might want to call them.

Not that either Rib or Pot minded in the least. Where around the Sareyan Sea were they going to find anything more interesting to do than hang around a godsdamn *dragon*?

The small patrol of guards with Captain Vakkal at their head escorted the party down Merchants Street, past the central market, and up Independence Way. They crossed the Forum, climbed the many stairs to the central hill, and entered the Palace, where the council met to decide on matters of high importance and where the justices passed judgment in matters of law. All the way, they were gawked at, talked about or, in more than a few cases, admired. You did not live the kind of life that the little family or the Wolves did without cutting a striking figure, especially those of who were dressed to impress.

Ardek, one time street rat and ganger, did not have quite the same luster as the others. He'd have preferred to stay at the inn, really. He had hoped to never get closer to the Palace than the steps. But the boss had sent him with the others, so there he was, hanging back so that nobody would associate him with them and dull their shine. The guards didn't seem to care whether he followed or not, which suited him just fine.

Inside, Captain Vakkal handed them over to two palace guards. He nodded to Makanna, bade them good day, and left with his patrol. If he had ever recognized them, he hadn't mentioned it.

"That's far enough," one of the guards said, cautioning Rib as she made to follow Makanna and the others. "No uninvited persons beyond the atrium."

"What?" Rib sputtered as she drew herself up. The guard looked entirely unimpressed. "That's—"

"*Lady Terriallon*," Makanna said, emphasizing the title and making the guards look again at Rib. "Thank you, but there is no need to concern yourself. Where could we be safer than here?"

"Yeah, sure," Rib grumbled. "But—"

"We'll be with you soon. And if not, please let our friend know. You know how she worries."

Rib frowned but relented as Pot gently took her arm. "We'll be here," she called after Makanna as they were each led away in opposite directions. "Right here. Not going anywhere!"

The palace guards led the little family through a short hallway lined with columns and brightly clad statues to a set of large, polished wooden doors. One guard stepped up and knocked firmly, and then opened them when a voice inside called out a perfunctory "Enter!" He bowed to the room's occupants, ushered the little family inside, then left, closing the doors behind him.

Behind a low, expansive table, the lady justice Sempralia sat on a wide cushion. She didn't look up, but continued writing, quickly yet carefully, on a scroll which lay rolled out before her. Behind her a man stood, looking in the general direction of the newcomers and so still that he might have been a particularly fine statue. Once Makanna saw him, she didn't want to take her eyes off him; despite his stillness and calm, almost gentle, expression, there was a sense of impending violence about him that made him feel too dangerous to ignore.

"Sit," Sempralia directed them, a flick of her pen indicating a number of cushions arranged across the table from her.

Makanna, as head of the family, took the seat in the center and slightly in front of the others. There should perhaps have been another one similarly placed for Valmik, as he was not formally part of her family, but the lady justice had made no such arrangement, and he sat with Tamor behind Makanna.

For a minute, then two and three and five, there was no sound in the room except the scratching of the pen, and the low hiss of paper as the lady justice rolled up her dry work, unrolled a fresh surface, and slid it across the table. Then, with no warning, she set down her pen and looked up.

"Miss Makanna," Sempralia said, her voice no less rich or firm for her age. "Formerly of Tekeretek, now of Karakan. One of our more unusual citizens. I wish I could say that it is a pleasure to see you, but it is most decidedly not. Last evening I was dragged, practically, from my bed, to expedite a judgment. Normally, I would have dismissed such a demand, but seeing as it came from her young ladyship Terriallon Rebatia of Tavvanar, and was supported by his young lordship Terriallon Poterio, also of Tavvanar, I deemed it politic. Why?"

Makanna was caught off guard by the sudden question. "'Why' what, exactly, my lady justice?" she asked after a short, embarrassed silence.

"Why were you detained, and why were the scions of two Tavvanarian city lords willing to stick their necks out for you? I have heard what the guard captain had to say, now I want to hear your side. And don't try to dissemble or lie. It's tedious. One doesn't become one of the lords' and ladies' justice without being able to see through deception."

"We . . ." Makanna began, but whatever she'd been about to say petered out. She took a breath and began again. "Last night, my brother, Tamor, and his man, my friend Valmik, who are both here with me, returned from Tavvanar after successfully selling an item we'd found in the ruins of an Old Mallinean villa. The Terriallons are friends of ours, and they were waiting with myself, my sister, and some others to welcome Tamor and Valmik home. As they were on their way ashore in a boat, they were intercepted by people we believe belonged to a criminal organization run by a woman known as the Night Blossom. They were saved when the criminals were attacked by a . . . creature—"

"What. Kind. Of. Creature?" Sempralia's words were whip cracks in the silent room.

". . . a dragon, my lady justice."

"Continue."

Makanna swallowed. "The criminals were attacked, and destroyed. Some may have thrown themselves in the water, but there was no one alive on the boat afterward. She . . . the dragon took one of the bodies and flew off. By the time Tamor and Valmik reached the docks, where we waited with some other friends to welcome them home, a guard patrol had arrived and chose to take them into custody, along with myself, as head of the family, I would guess, and my sister. I do not know why they took her. To complete the set, perhaps."

"But you do know why they took your sister," Sempralia stated, her eyes boring into Makanna's. "Such a pointless thing to lie about. Would you care to try again?"

Makanna sighed, and said, "She may have had some harsh words for the guards. They did not appreciate them."

"Better. And the Tavvanarians?"

"The young lady and lord are friends of ours. They felt that we were being treated unfairly, as citizens of Tekereteki origin, and did not want to see us remain in custody."

Sempralia scoffed. "That, at least, is true." Then her eyes locked again on Makanna. "The dragon killed a dozen men and women, but left Tamor, Valmik, and the two crewmen on their launch alone. Why?"

"It . . ." Makanna licked her lips. "They . . ."

"Do not lie," Sempralia said, her cadence clipped, and the man behind her casually took one of his hands from his back and placed it on the pommel of his sword.

"It is all right," Herald whispered from behind Makanna, putting her hand on her sister's shoulder. "Tell her."

Makanna turned around, and Tamor and Valmik both nodded. She looked back at Sempralia, who was waiting patiently, and tried to speak, but the words wouldn't come. "She . . ." she began, but the sentence died in her throat. "I can't," she whispered, lowering her eyes. "I can't betray her."

Sempralia studied Makanna, her gaze heavy with displeasure, but said, "Would anyone else care to try? I will have answers, one way or another." She looked to the three in the back expectantly.

Tamor and Valmik looked at each other, then at Herald, but as Tamor readied himself to speak Herald spoke up first, her voice clear and steady.

"The dragon, Draka, spared Valmik and Tamor because she was there for the specific purpose of aiding them. Because she was awaiting their arrival. Because she cares for us deeply," Herald said, her smile soft. "Because she is our companion in adventure, and a sixth share of the money from that sale was hers by right. Because she is our friend, and we feared they might be attacked, and she will not suffer her friends to come to harm. And because the Night Blossom, whose minions those poor souls on the boat were, harmed us and is her enemy, and ours, and she destroys her enemies. But the two crewmen on the launch were nothing to her. They had not touched anyone important to her. So, they were not only spared, they were simply never in any danger."

The lady justice's eyes widened minutely, but that was the only sign she showed of her surprise and interest. There was a drawn-out silence, marred only by the soft sound of her guard shifting his hand from the pommel of his sword to gripping its hilt, awaiting his lady's command.

"Do you mean to tell me," Sempralia said slowly, "that you are acquainted with this creature? That it is intelligent enough to understand such things as innocence and restraint?"

"I believe that love and friendship and loyalty are more important, and more relevant to our conversation, but, yes. She understands those things, and anything else you might expect from an intelligent individual. Including spite and retribution."

The guard's grip tightened on his sword.

"I had you followed, you know, as you returned to your inn," Sempralia said conversationally, after pausing for several seconds. "I did not see it as just that you should be detained, but I was curious what you might do once released. My investigator reported that something followed you on the rooftops, which concerned him, of course, considering the reports from the harbor. He couldn't quite see what it was, and lost track of it once it reached the roof of Her Grace's Favor, which I understand is the name of the place where you are staying. Do you have any thoughts about that?"

"Draka was worried, of course," Herald said. "There was a real chance that we might be ambushed in the street on our way home. While we could most likely have defended ourselves, Draka does not like to leave our safety to probablies and most likelies."

"You . . . do not lie," Sempralia said. "But you are not telling me everything. Where is it now?"

"*She*," Herald said with emphasis, "is right where she was when we were summoned. At the inn, awaiting our return."

The lady justice clasped her hands in front of herself on the table. "Miss Herald," she said. "With the way you emphasize certain things—loyalty, retribution, awaiting—one might think that you were attempting to subtly threaten me."

There was a dangerous glint in her eye that made Herald pause and consider her words very carefully. The worried glances the others were shooting her did not help bolster her suddenly flagging confidence. This woman had treated them and their parents with great kindness, or at the very least with fairness, but that did not mean they knew her. They knew her by reputation, certainly. It was said that she applied the law fairly and equally. And, it was said that she did not suffer the law to be abused. But that did not necessarily mean that she was beyond pettiness, or anger, or rash decisions.

"I . . . apologize, my lady justice," Herald said, lowering her eyes. "I truly did not mean to imply any such thing. But it is important that I make the situation clear. Draka is not violent by nature—"

There was a quickly smothered snort from Makanna.

"—not *unreasonably* violent, by nature," Herald corrected herself. "She wants only a few things in life. Friends, peace, and treasure. But she loves us, she knows where we are and with whom, and she expects us back, unharmed, within a reasonable time. If that does not happen, I cannot predict her actions, but I know that they will be terrible. Please understand, I only say this because I do not want her to put herself in danger."

"That . . ." Sempralia said slowly, "is the truth. As you see it, at least. Fascinating. You care for this creature, for *her*, don't you?"

"I do. She is my dearest friend. Practically family."

"And the rest of you?"

"It is as Herald says," Valmik said seriously. "Draka is a friend and a companion, and a loyal one."

Tamor nodded. "We are richer, in every sense, for knowing her."

"And you?" Sempralia said, turning her eyes on Makanna, who had remained silent. "Do you consider her a friend?"

Makanna hesitated, then met the lady justice's eyes. "I do not know if friend is an accurate word for what she is to me, my lady justice."

For a long moment, it looked as though Sempralia would demand that Makanna elaborate on that. Their eyes remained locked, but then Sempralia smiled, just barely, and she asked, very carefully, "Do you own this creature?"

Makanna snorted, her mouth twitching. Herald quickly covered her own mouth, Tamor grinned openly, and even Valmik had an amused smile on his face.

"No one could own Draka," Makanna said, shaking her head. "I'd say that I would pity anyone who tried, but so far only the Night Blossom has been so foolish, and she deserves every consequence of that mistake. No, my lady justice. None of us owns Draka."

"The so-called Night Blossom. That one again," Sempralia muttered sourly. "You had a run-in with her, did you?"

"Yes. She had myself and my sister kidnapped and . . . and tortured, my lady justice."

Sempralia's mouth became a tight line. "And why would she do that?"

"Because of our involvement in disrupting her slaving, my lady justice."

"Ah. Your little act of heroism. That was her, was it? Can you prove that? If half of the rumors about her are true, I would very much like to see that woman found, whoever she is. A lifetime of servitude would do her good, I think. But

I need actual, legal cause. She has been accused of much, but that is all I have. Accusations. No investigation has turned up any evidence of wrongdoing on her part. So, can you prove your claims?"

"Prove them?" Makanna lowered her eyes. "No, my lady justice. We can show you where we were held, and we can give testimony. But we cannot prove anything."

"My lady justice," Herald said. "Does this mean that you can tell us who she is?"

"Tell you who she is? No, most certainly not. I will not encourage or aid in vigilantism, and you have made your *friend's* disposition clear enough. Besides that, I simply do not know myself. Now, there *are* several possible suspects, and with a strong enough motivation, I am sure that any of them could be found and brought in. Until I have that motivation, though, in the form of some kind of evidence, or the testimony of several known associates, there is nothing I can do."

"Within the law," Herald added.

"Just so."

There was another long silence as the lady justice studied them. "Does she breathe fire? Is she likely to cause any public harm or destruction?"

"No, and no, my lady justice," Makanna answered quickly.

Something passed over Sempralia's face. A shrewd, calculating look that vanished as fast as it had come. Then she gave a dismissive wave of her arm and said, "Very well. You're free to go."

"We are, my lady justice?" Makanna asked, her eyes widening. "Just like that?"

"Just like that. I have no intention of detaining you without cause. You have befriended a dragon. There is no law against that. Perhaps that is an oversight, but there are no laws regarding dragons at all that I know of in Karakan. Nor is it illegal to defend oneself against bandits or pirates, whether on land or sea, or, as the case may be, in the harbor. If you made a claim of ownership I would have you fined for bringing a dangerous animal into the city without proper precautions, but you make no such claim. But I warn you," she continued, her wrinkled face becoming stern, "neither is it illegal to kill such a dangerous animal, in the city or out of it. This dragon, this Draka, as you call her, has no protection under the law. And I am sure you know that, as a dragon, she will be of special interest to all manner of adventurers, hunters, and glory seekers. If she is harmed, or killed, you have no legal recourse. Attempting to defend her would be unlawful violence, or murder as the case may be. And if she becomes a danger to the public, or a nuisance, she *will* be hunted down. It would be best if she were not seen in the city again. Do I make myself clear?"

"You do, my lady justice," Makanna said, "but, with all respect, we do not control her. We can only ask her to stay out of the city, or at the very least well hidden."

"You do not think that she will do this," Sempralia stated, a small sigh announcing to the room that she had hoped it might be different.

"No, my lady justice," Makanna said. "Not so long as the Night Blossom lives."

"Then, until the odious woman is dealt with, I suggest you keep your distance from your friend, to avoid being implicated in anything she might do. She is not your responsibility, unless you make her so."

"My apologies, but I'm not sure we can do that, my lady justice."

"I thought not. I would also prefer if you did not spread word of her existence unnecessarily. That will certainly happen anyway, but the slower, the better. And I hope you understand that I would be most displeased if you were proven to have exploited your connection to her. Assault, threats, and blackmail are illegal, no matter the means."

"Understood, my lady justice," Makanna said, and then, when Sempralia remained silent, added, "Will there be anything else?"

"No. That will be all."

"In that case . . ." Makanna looked to the others. "With your leave, my lady justice, we'll go. Thank you for your time, and your understanding."

"Remember," Sempralia said. "The dragon is outside of the law. In its eyes, she is an animal. If you wish to protect her, the best thing you can do is make sure that she is not seen in this city. Good day."

"Good day, my lady justice," Herald said as Sempralia's silent guard opened the doors for them, and the others echoed her.

They walked in silence, escorted by a palace guard who had been waiting outside of the lady justice's chambers. When they arrived in the atrium, the relief on Ardek's and the Wolves' faces was palpable. Still, they said nothing until they were well outside, answering no questions until they had walked down the steps to the Forum.

"Did anyone else notice," Tamor asked in a low voice, "how the lady justice didn't actually ask us to try and stop Draka from killing the Night Blossom? Only to try and make sure that she is not *seen*?"

"It was made very clear that Draka is outside of the law, and not our responsibility," Valmik added thoughtfully.

"I did notice that, yes," Herald said, a vicious smile slowly spreading across her face.

About the Author

AvaritiaBona is a proud nerd whose biggest joy in life is to turn tea into words. His stories are about friendship and not being quite right. He lives in Sweden with his wonderful wife, surrounded by supportive friends.

Podium